Auditory Dreams
Volumes 1 & 2

Andy Bracken

A Morning Brake Book

Copyright © 2013-2015 Andy Bracken

ISBN: 9798433392885

First Edition.

AUTHOR NOTES, March 2022:

By request...

Here you go guys and gals - I trust I've improved?

Quiet, Paul Crane!

You'll spot elements that I borrowed or adapted for later books. Tredmouth gets a mention, for example. And there's an early Tommy Histon history, which I later altered. These books led to things. And that's their only real worth to me. Think of them as early acoustic demos.

Overall, though, I don't much care for the stories. The writing is clumsy and in need of edits. It simply isn't what I wish to write, and I had a Literary Agent at the time, who steered me down a path I wasn't keen to tread.

As an example of how the 'game' works, the middle part of the first book (the White Album bit), was seen as backstory, and therefore irrelevant. I was encouraged to remove it. To my mind, doing so would strip away depth and understanding of characters and their motivations. Or, to put that another way, it would remove my favourite bit.

Staggeringly, publishers you will have heard of were pretty keen on these. The only problem being, they were 'too different'. That was the phrase most used. As a result, they couldn't see how to market them.

With hindsight, I think they were right. It's true of all my books. They're different. And most people are afraid of different. I get that. I'm somewhat guilty of it myself. God, I hope I'm still a little open-minded, though.

So, I self-published them in 2015, and about five people bought them. Less than that read them. And I lost most of the people I believed were supportive friends over night! Along with my confidence.

But you nagged me in to it, so I made them available for you, albeit in a very hush-hush way.

I hope they're tolerable. Thank you.

The Gaps Between The Tracks

Part One: The Black

1.

I wasn't always blind.

For the first forty years of my life, I could see. For the first thirty, I could see pretty well. Age played its part, and glasses were worn for a decade.

I don't have to wear glasses now, it's one of the good things about being blind. There are quite a few, believe it or not.

The thought reminds me of the old joke about two guys going to visit a friend in hospital after he lost his ears in a freak accident.

"Don't mention his ears," one says, as they head to the ward, "he's a bit sensitive about it."

"See your eye-sight's improved," the other says, as they arrive at his bedside.

"How do you mean?" asks the man with no ears.

"Well, you're not wearing your glasses..."

The stylus reaches the dead wax at the end of the record, and I listen to the swish as it glides across the smooth wide space and hits the closed-groove buffer that stops it advancing, symbolic of my life.

Absolutely no idea what I'm listening to. A neoclassical album, from Scandinavia, or someplace. Norway, I think.

Bu-bump goes the needle on rotation as I stride over to the turntable via seven measured paces, stopping when the tips of my shoes touch the cabinet. I lay my hand on the edge, the little finger on my right hand acting as an anchor, and raise the arm.

I lift the twelve inch slab off the platter, holding it only by its edges, and flip it over. Standing squarely on to the cabinet, I keep my arms and body as motionless as possible before lowering the record down to the turntable and finding the hole; no adjustment required.

I've done it thousands of times. It's second nature, just behind remembering to breathe.

Nick at the record shop calls me every Friday, which saves me the bother of locating the little bump on the number five on the phone, and working the rest out from there. He lists off all the new releases that week. Not all, just the ones he knows I'll be interested in.

A package usually arrives the following Tuesday or Wednesday. The post lady knows to knock first, and put the parcels in the wooden box if I don't answer. I'm always in, but sometimes I don't hear the door because of the music.

Reversing the earlier process, I use my thumb as a guide to line the needle up as close as I can to the run-in groove. My middle finger lowers the lever, and I wait as it slowly descends. A faint click, as I stay perfectly still while I ensure it remains on the record. No vicious scrape, as the thirty-three and a third revolutions per minute apply a lateral force.

2.

There's a knock on the door timed for the gap between tracks. I hit the volume button on the remote control by my side.

Planting my feet on the wooden floor, I stand up. Four paces later, I feel for the door frame and turn ninety degrees. I had all the doors removed. Couldn't trust the fucking things to stay open.

I walk nine paces and feel again, locating the net curtain. Four inches to the left, or a curved hand width, it connects with the door knob, which I turn. Looking out blankly, I relax when I hear Marc's voice. Or is it Adam's? I can never remember which is which.

"Tony asked me to come and get you. We've received some information. It seems pretty straightforward, but he wants you to take a look. A listen, I mean..."

People do that all the time. It's not their fault, and I don't get offended by it. It's difficult. Our language is peppered with expressions that reference the visual. Things like 'now, look here', 'see you later 'and 'looking forward'.

See what I mean?

"I'll get my coat." And then, "come in, Stereo." That's what I call them, Marc and Adam.

Reversing my steps, I find the record deck and lift the tonearm, retract it and press the power button off. The 'off ' depression has a different feel to 'on'. Something in the slackness of the click. And it projects more.

My shoes are already on. I wear them round the house to save my toes from a bashing every day, soft Brazilian-leather uppers with comfy but durable soles. I like the way they feel. How things feel is vital to me, and how shoes feel is paramount. Sixteen hours a day in them, at least, so I want a bit of comfort.

Besides, if I don't wear my shoes, where would I keep them? Another obstacle to trip over. Best to have them on my feet. Four pairs, I bought, all identical so that I can rotate and let them freshen up a bit. No chance of putting odd ones on by mistake that way. It's the same with socks.

My daughter helps me buy stuff on-line. She knows my credit card details, and I tell her what I need. She's a good kid. Kid? She's nineteen, but she was a kid the last time I could see her. She's doing a degree in Edinburgh. Not a degree in Edinburgh, though I wouldn't be surprised to find out that you can. I mean that's she's doing a degree in medicine. In Edinburgh. I bought the shoes on my own, though. That was a major step forward for me, or so they tell me. A step toward independence.

In their minds, buying shoes implies that I intend going out.

For once they're right.

Stretching, I grab my coat off the hook on the wall where the door would have opened, swing it on, and shrug myself into it. A coarse-haired donkey jacket, but without the leather elbow and shoulder pads. Almost black, I think. Charcoal. Lined with a quilt, with a couple of rips where I walked into stuff and snagged it.

Reaching in the pocket, I locate my sunglasses and put them on. Not for my benefit. It puts other people at ease and sends a message that I'm blind, that there's no sense in looking where I'm not looking.

I pat my pocket to check I have my keys, and throw my fags and lighter in with them. I feel my way through the opening Stereo organised before reaching the step and stopping. No idea where the car is, or which way it's facing. I think I can smell the heat from the engine slightly to my right, and hear the ticking of the motor as it cools. He drove here at a fair speed, I think, for the engine to be smelling and sounding like that. It's only about fifteen miles.

9

Must be important.

"Are you Left or Right?" I ask, as I feel a hand on my elbow. It's one of the reasons I don't have the leather patches on my coat. That, and because I'd look like a bin man.

"Right."

"Hello Marc."

"Hello Lorry," he answers.

Tony effed up with Marc and Adam, but he won't admit it. They're too similar, except Marc is right-handed and Adam left. If you have one, the other one doesn't offer much else. He almost did it right, by going for someone unlike him. That was a smart move.

The fourth member of the team is Sofa. Sophie is on her birth certificate, but we all call her Sofa.

Marc leads me to the car, but has to back me up a bit so he can open the door. He rests his hand on my head as I follow my right leg into the passenger seat. It's how he'd handle a prisoner, except I'm in the front, not the back.

This is the first time I've left the house in at least a week, other than the back garden. I sit in the back garden sometimes when it's not raining, and listen to the birds.

"What you got?" I kick things off.

"999 call. Warning of a bomb."

"When?"

"The call, or the warning?" he responds pedantically.

"Both."

"Both today. The call was logged at ten past twelve."

"How long have you had it?"

"Since half past."

"Okay, so the system worked. Twenty minutes isn't bad."

"Not bad. But two minutes would have been better. Then there's the best part of an hour lost doing nothing since we received it..." he pointedly leaves hanging.

Ignoring him, I ask, "any indication of where or when?"

"None. Just a warning that a bomb is going to be detonated today. That's it."

"And what do you make of it - the call?"

"It's believable. The guy sounds scared, sounds genuine."

"Any accent?"

"Not that noticeable. But we think he might be Serbian."

"Serbian? What, some kind of Milosevic tie?"

"Dunno. There's something on the message that sounds like Serb. And it mentions an airport."

"Which airport?"

"None. Just the word, airport."

"The guy says that?"

"No. It's in the background on the recording."

Marc isn't hanging about. I try to read the car movements, and brace for the bends, but it's hopeless. All I can do is grip the sides of the seat and plant my feet when he hits the brakes.

It's one of the worst things about being blind. I've never been a good passenger and I can't drive any more. That's not true. I can drive, but you wouldn't want me to if you were picking your kids up from school.

"It sounds like he's ringing from an airport," Marc adds.

Feeling a bit sick as we pull to a halt, I scrabble around the arm rest for the down button for the window to get some air, but end up locking the door instead.

"You might want to leave the window closed," Marc says, hitting the sirens, and veering violently to the right. My body slams into the door, and I'm glad I inadvertently locked it.

We have to shout over the roar of the accelerating engine.

"What makes you think he's at an airport?"

"Can't be sure, but the words Serb and Airport are being announced on some kind of PA in the background. A Tannoy, or something. And it just sounds busy. Like people are coming and going. Like an airport."

Tasting bile in my mouth, I keep quiet and swallow it back down. I could never read in the car as a kid.

I suck in deep breaths and attempt to focus, but it's no good.

Reaching around, I try to find something, but the car is spotlessly clean. New. I can smell the newness. Leather seats, and plush carpet under my feet.

Unclipping the seatbelt and taking a gamble, I thrust my head between the seats. I reach into the pocket on the back of the passenger seat and find what must be a map book. I open it up and toss it down in the floor-well, just in time to catch three Weetabix, milk, several cups of tea and what's left of last night's dinner.

"That's unfortunate," Marc calls over his left shoulder, a hint of satisfaction in his voice, not easing up an ounce on the accelerator pedal.

"Sorry about your car..."

"Don't worry about it, it's Tony's."

We both laugh as I spit out the vileness.

"We'll be there in about three minutes," Marc says, "hang on."

Feeling better now I've thrown up, I'm just left with the vulgar taste in my mouth.

"New car?" I ask, clipping my seatbelt back in place.

"No. He's had it, oh, must be three days now."

The car descends a ramp and stops very quickly. I hear the vomit slosh about.

By the time Marc has skipped round the vehicle, I've already got the door open and my feet out, heavily sucking in the air, a cigarette in my hand. Testing the tip with my lip to make sure it's the filter, I hand Marc the disposable lighter. He gets a flame on the fourth try. He's not used to lighters, doesn't smoke.

He helps me up and pushes the door closed as he clicks the alarm set button on the key-fob. Twice, so it beeps.

Taking up position at my elbow, he walks me toward the door.

"No smoking allowed," he tells me, so I stop walking.

"That doesn't apply to blind people."

"I think you'll find that's dogs."

"Dogs can smoke?"

3.

'When Will I See You Again? 'by The Three Degrees greets me as I exit the lift, and swing through the doors Marc accesses with his ID card.

Last time I was here it was 'I Only Have Eyes For You'. The Art Garfunkel version, which was a mistake. They should have gone for The Flamingos.

Bastards.

"Very clever," I mutter in a voice that belies the words.

Someone hits stop on the digital device, and the music ends, along with the chuckling.

"I presume that's your doing, Colin?" I call out blindly as I'm walked across the office.

"Just following Tony's orders," Colin the IT man tells me.

Business time.

Tony Alliss takes my elbow and guides me through to a room.

"I'll be round Saturday, all being well. About seven," he quietly informs me, his mouth by my ear as he steers me to a chair.

"I'll get the strippers booked."

"Female this time, please..."

He comes round just about every week. Usually a Saturday, but sometimes Sunday, depending on work. I hope he comes because he wants to and not because he feels sorry for me.

"Can I get a coffee? Please. Strong."

I need to wash the evil taste of sick out my mouth and throat. I hear Sophie say she'll get it. Sweet girl.

"Hello Sofa, how are you?"

"Not bad Lorry, ta for asking. Yourself?"

"Fine now I've got you looking after me." She's from Lancashire, calls a spade a shovel.

I can hear her pouring coffee from a percolator in the room. The sizzle of a drop hitting the hot-plate tells me all I need to know, in addition to the aroma. I can smell the brew.

Lorry isn't short for Lawrence, or even Laurence. The truth of it is, when I was at school, some wanker noticed my initials were D.A.F., like the Dutch truck manufacturer. So he called me Lorry, and it stuck.

"How many sugars, Lorry?"

"Three, please."

I need the sugar to sweeten my mouth and throat, and it'll give me an energy boost. Replace some of the nutrients I spilled in the back of Tony's new car.

It's probably best not to mention Tony's new car. I notice Marc hasn't.

"What's the time?" I ask, after taking the first sip.

"Twenty past one," Tony tells me.

"Right, an hour and ten since the call came in. Too long. Let's hear the recording."

"Yes, well we've been sat on our arses waiting for you to get here," Adam mumbles, his way of saying hello.

Silence descends as keys click.

Muffled sounds and a scraping noise fill the room. There's interference on the line, something messing with the signal, lucky if there's one pip on the signal indicator bar on the phone, like it's about to drop out, like his hand's over the mouthpiece.

There's a background announcement, over a PA. It's barely audible through the hand over the receiver, 'Serb', or something like it. A voice starts to speak, strained, afraid, as though he's not talking directly into the phone, too busy looking around, checking to see if he's being watched, his head turned to one side. I can't explain why I think that, it's just the way the words form in his mouth. He's crouching down, perhaps, ducking behind something and affecting the signal even more, another layer for it to penetrate. All this over a background hum, the sound of a crowd, but not too close.

"There's a bomb, they've got a bomb, and they're going to use it today. You've got to stop them. I'm sorry, I just didn't think..."

Six seconds of talking, plus a second more split between him starting to speak and pressing the off button. Why did he press the off button? Habit? He could have just left the phone on, and stashed it somewhere. In a bin, for example, and given us something to track.

"Lorry, what are you thinking?" Tony breaks the silence.

"Play it again."

One of the Stereos tuts as I imagine them sharing a look. They think they have this sussed. Serb and airport, that's all they hear. They'd be checking to see which airports offer a direct route to Belgrade and looking for Kosovo independence links here in the UK.

They'd be wasting their time.

The second play confirms all I thought after the first listen.

Draining my coffee, I reach out for a flat surface. Before I can find one, a hand takes it from me. Sophie's hand, I gather, as the waft of her preferred fabric conditioner and moisturising hand-cream carry to me on the air stirred by her movement.

"Right, let's go," I say brightly, bringing my hands together in a clap and rubbing them vigorously.

"Where?" they all ask in unison.

"Waterloo Station and don't spare the horses!"

Tony has to ask. "Why?"

Speaking quickly, as time is of the essence, I enunciate clearly but string the sentences together. "Because the PA in the background is announcing a train, a train that calls at Surbiton and, I presume, Southampton Airport Parkway. Seeing how that could only happen from Waterloo, Clapham Junction or possibly Wimbledon, my money's on Waterloo. Yes, there are other stations on the route, but most of them have only outdoor platforms. Strictly speaking, so do Clapham and Wimbledon, but I think they have enclosed walkways. The low signal on the mobile phone and general boxiness of the call quality tell me that it's being made from indoors, probably below ground level. And besides, if I had a bomb and wanted to detonate it, I reckon I might do that in London itself, rather than the suburbs."

"O-kay," Tony drawls, "and is this a real threat? Can we evaluate this as a real and present threat to UK security...?"

"I'd say seventy percent, yes. The guy doing the calling is certainly scared, but there are a lot of things that can scare people. And there are a lot of reasons why people seek attention. Perhaps he doesn't feel loved by mummy and daddy, or something. Just so you know, he's in his late-teens, early-twenties, of Asian heritage - probably Pakistan or India, possibly Sri-Lankan. But he comes from an area that covers Staffordshire, Shropshire or the south side of Cheshire. He's affecting a London accent, probably to fit in, so he feels like he belongs. That's another thing that worries me. He's impressionable, or why else would he do that? And impressionable kids get their heads turned by people who plot terrorist attacks. Impressionable - able to be impressed. Perhaps he had a fundamental belief system impressed upon him, or perhaps he met someone who really impressed him. Either way, that's not a good situation. So, like I said, seventy percent, and should we head for Waterloo Station now?"

The firm hand on my elbow tells me that we should.

"But this is all completely speculative," Adam says, "he can't know this for sure. How...how can he know all that from a seven second phone call?"

Marc joins in, "it does seem a bit of a risk, Tony, chasing this one lead. What if Lorry's wrong?"

"Lorry? Are you wrong?" Tony barks.

"Not on the Surbiton bit, no."

"Good enough for me."

Tony snaps orders into the radio. He has two settings, one for team communication and one for high level communication. At least a dozen high-ranking people across London get to hear his voice say, "Code Nine. Code Nine. Level seven alert. Elevated amber."

That's as high as it goes without hitting red, and red spells danger. Red means deployment of all the resources at the government's disposal. Tony has that call. This little four agent plus support staff department housed on the second floor of a nondescript building in London has to make the call whether to spend a shit-load of tax payer money on reacting to a threat or not. Seventy percent means, not yet, but they should be primed and ready to jump in.

"Let the head of security at Waterloo know we're on the way. ETA, twelve minutes. Main entrance, along with the Bomb Squad. Twenty uniformed police officers there in half an hour, to help with evacuation, should it become necessary, but keep them low-key till we know more."

I count the stairs, nobody waiting for the lift. Nine, turn ninety degrees left, two long paces, then eight more steps and a one-eighty left wheel. Repeat.

I remember stuff like that. I'm probably Obsessive Compulsive, though I've never been formally diagnosed as I've never asked for a medical opinion. It's never bothered me enough to seek one. There's just something comforting about knowing how many steps there are, or how many windows a room has. Even down to how many objects sit on a table.

It helped me adapt to blindness, for sure, but it's harder to count stuff when you can't see it. Steps are okay, though, I can still count steps.

Tony doesn't stop talking. The radio crackles back as it spits affirmations. One after another the designated Chief Emergency Contacts check in. The Threat Evaluation and Response Advisory, or TERA to use the ironic acronym, sits alongside all other government sections, equally as important, just a lot smaller.

Tony was sent to Washington DC for six months, to learn how not to do it, how to avoid all that budgetary conflict.

"Adam, you go with Marc. Lorry, you're with me. Sofa, you stay and run Funnel from here. Okay?" Tony instructs.

"No," I say, and stop walking. "I'll go with Sofa, you take one of the Stereos, and leave the other here."

"Why?" Marc and Adam ask in unison, ably demonstrating my point.

Tony makes the decision quickly. "Adam, you stay. Marc, with me."

"Suits me fine. Sounds like a wild goose chase, anyway" Adam says, sarcastic but cheerful, before closing the door too firmly.

I'm at the passenger door of Sophie's car by the time I hear Tony groan, "oh, for fuck's sake, Lorry, it's a brand new car...I've only had it three fucking days!"

They take Marc's car.

4.

I've no idea how many steps there are leading up to the main entrance at Waterloo station in south east London. The last time I was here, I could see. I could look up at Victory Arch.

Sophie gives a little upward nudge with her hand for each new one, and I lose count.

There's a group of people, all the voices merging, so I focus on Tony. If it's important, he'll say it.

"Lorry, you said the call was coming from below ground level, right?"

"I'm almost certain, yes."

"Should we start with the tube?" asks a voice I don't know.

"No," I say, "not the tube. You wouldn't hear the train announcements from the tube. Let's just walk around till something rings a bell."

Inside the station a warmth hits my face as we pass the point at which the cold air outside can beat back the warmer air inside.

"Turn left," I instruct. There's no sense in heading towards the International part.

If I recall correctly, there's a tube entrance on the right near this end, so I pause and listen. No, not the right place.

Carrying on, I sense people moving around us, shuffling aside with their wheel-along suitcases, constantly catching fragments of mobile phone calls. Blocking them out as best I can, I summon up the telephone message in my head and attempt to compare it with the noise all around me.

It was definitely made from the far end. It makes sense as that's where all the overground trains to the suburbs leave from.

We bear left across the streams of people, prompting a couple of complaints as I head blindly from the barrier and platform side over to the back of the station, me dragging Sophie as much as she's steering me.

"There's an exit just up there on the left, correct?" I can feel the breeze on my face.

"Yes," Tony snaps back immediately.

"And a small exit over there at the far end?"

"Yes."

Tony answers instantly, precisely, no ambiguity.

"Take me to the area where the escalators head down to the tube and the exits on the lower level."

Tony's huge hand replaces Sofa's on my arm. Someone bounces off him, jolts him just a fraction.

"You okay?" he asks.

"Yep. It was Waterloo, Tony, definitely. This is where he called from."

"Good man. Now, find me the exact spot."

I feel like a sniffer dog.

"Brace yourself," is all I hear before my feet leave the ground, Tony's hands under my armpits lifting me like I'm nothing; all thirteen and a quarter stone of me, or thereabouts, based on the last time I was weighed at the doctor's.

Suddenly I'm planted on the moving metal staircase. Tony has both his hands on my shoulders as he counts down.

"Three, two and one," as I lead with my left foot and shuffle my right to catch up with it. I have to stand still for a second as my legs get used to being back on stable ground. Somebody calls "move" from over my shoulder, and I'm aware that my second's pause has caused a bottle-neck.

But I can't move because there's no hand on my elbow. I start to panic. Where's Tony?

Somebody shoulder-barges past me, mutters, "get out the fucking way."

The jolt propels me forward two steps. I can feel my eyes senselessly moving around. Forty years of being able to see, it's a tough habit to break. Next instinct, my arms come up and splay out in front of me. They offer a barrier of sorts, as i feel a human form push past my hand which rotates me slightly, further disorientating me.

I haven't taken a breath since Tony counted "one". It was an inward breath, instinctive, ready to absorb a potential impact.

I use that breath to call out.

"Tony"

"Here, here, here, Lorry. I'm here."

Two seconds, that was how long I was floating in the dark.

It's the sense of vulnerability that is the most difficult thing to deal with, a physical sense. It's simply easier not to leave the house than to contend with all that, which is why I rarely bother. And even when I do, it's in the company of someone who can protect me, but the feeling of susceptibility is always there, along with the sense of feeling like a burden.

My best guess is that Tony Alliss is six-two in his socks and two-hundred and twenty pounds, fat free. His grandparents came to London from the Caribbean back in the war years, and his dad was born here shortly after.

He's the kind of bloke you'd want on your side in a fight. Or a cricket match.

Having reconnected with my elbow, he guides me away from the crush, driving me over to the left.

"Sorry," he says close to my ear, "someone pushed in front of me."

"No problem," I lie, feeling my heartbeat settle a little and the adrenalin quiet back down. A breath's taken, followed immediately by another deeper one.

"I thought you were paying me back for being sick in your car."

"When I do, it'll be worse than that."

For two seconds I stood alone on the lower level of Waterloo station at the foot of the escalator.

But it felt like two minutes.

Tony was here, just as he's been before, his fuzzy black face the last thing I ever saw on the outside of the inside of my mind.

It was his instincts and experience that stopped me from being killed, his quick thinking that saved my life.

Mind you, he wouldn't have had to, if he hadn't shot me in the head.

5.

The Tannoy kicks in, announcing a train. A service to somewhere, calling at Clapham Junction, Surbiton... Bingo. The Serb in Surbiton is exactly how it was on the call. Tony squeezes my arm, lets me know I did well, that he heard it too.

"Back upstairs," I tell him, certain now that we're in the wrong place, the wrong part of the station. It's too roomy down here where the ceilings are too high, the acoustics all airy and echoing. We need somewhere carpeted, full of heavy items and fabric, full of things that absorb sound and spit it back out in a muffled, understated kind of way. We're looking for a place that takes the vibrations of sound, and softens their edges.

The sound of the crowd is all wrong. We don't want a transient throng, we're after a slower moving beast. We need the area where people wait around, not the area where people head in and out letting traffic noise bleed in.

Tony lifts me on to the up escalator.

"Was there anywhere else leading downstairs? Any other places? Is there a public toilet?" I'm calling out loudly as we ride on the metal steps.

A public toilet isn't right; too bare and too hard, in furniture terms. Public toilets don't have curtains and carpets and soft sofas. At least, the ones I've been to don't.

Marc tries. "Perhaps we should head up to the balcony area. Have an overview of the place."

I ignore him. So does everyone else.

Sophie gets there. "There's a pub."

Tony doesn't count down as we get to the top, he just lifts me up again like I'm nothing. I like the feeling of safety I get from being in his arms.

I don't tell him that. My Emotional Therapist, Dr. David Haversham, tells me I should express my feelings. I expressed to David that I didn't feel comfortable doing that.

Tony walks four paces before he puts me down, carrying me clear of the crowd streaming in to the station behind us. It's always busy at Waterloo, even at two'ish on a Wednesday.

"Where, Sofa?" I call as I float through the air.

"Left. Stay on the back wall. Half way along. See that canopy?"

"Nope, but I'll take your word for it."

Tony picks up the pace. He's driving me like a parent pushes a kid on a bike before he can ride, holding my elbow from the underside in his bearlike hand, lifting slightly, so that I feel stable, letting me know he'll make the adjustment if I teeter, that he'll catch me if I fall.

I hope he doesn't let go of the saddle.

That's why, that's precisely why I told Tony to bring Sophie rather than Marc or Adam. If I was looking for a gymnasium or a vegetarian health food shop, I'd have wanted both of them along.

Ah, but Sophie, she lives down in this neck of the woods - Walton or Weybridge or Wimbledon, somewhere beginning with a W - she would have ridden trains in and out of here hundreds of times.

Marc and Adam wouldn't know a pub, an ominous dark pub at the back of the station down a flight of stairs, down into the unknown, where smoke would gather and fester in a shroud at ceiling height before they brought the ban in.

"Steps," Tony calls.

One, two...I start counting them in my head, running my hand down the bannister it found, one foot, then the other, placing them side by side on each stair, feeling with my toes for the edge, using the balls of my feet to gauge the tipping point and building up a picture in my mind of the exact dimensions and hoping they're even all the way down.

"Fuck this," Tony whispers in my ear, and I feel my feet leave the ground again, weightless and floating. Safe.

As he plants me, I know instantly this is where the call came from. Absolutely no doubt whatsoever.

"This is it."

"Definitely?"

"Oh yes. Tell me what you can see."

"Entrance. Open. No door. Stools to the left. One high table. Small seating area ahead. Ninety degree turn right. Stools along a counter on the right side. Opens up to a bar."

"Too open here. Go to the bar. Imagine you're a shit-scared kid with information you need to make a call on. Maybe you found a reason to nip in here and buy yourself a few seconds - seven seconds - of alone time. Where would you go? Somewhere you can't be seen by anybody coming down those stairs, a place where you're least likely to be overheard. An alcove? A corridor? Something that would box the sound. Anything?"

"Okay, yeah, loads of places. Area to the right is too open, lots of seating in a tight area, people on top of each other, comfy sofas and suchlike. There's a place straight on, further back. It's dark, I can't see what's there. And off to the right of the right...a corridor leading to...a toilet. Ladies and Gents signs pointing the way. That'd be my bet, one of those two. Or maybe he just knelt down at the bar and tied his laces, or something. Shit, this is impossible."

"Relax, we're in the right place, I just wish I could see right now. Okay, okay. Let's have a chat with the barman. Order me a pint and get him on board. Pay cash. It'll be about four, four and a half quid in a place like this with a captive audience. Give him a tenner and tell him to keep the change. He'll be Polish or Romanian, Slovenian, or something. No obligation to help you and be useful. So, money talks."

I'm guided to the bar, bang my ribs on it and wince. The walk-till-your-toes-touch rule doesn't apply on an overhanging bar. I hear the tenner being creased along its length, and imagine Tony holding it out. The guy comes over, asks what he can get for us. He's Eastern European, Romanian is probably correct.

"Pint of bitter, please."

"Which one?" the bartender asks, a bit narked that Tony didn't state his preference and save a step in the process. Good, he's efficient.

"What you got?"

"What you see..." the guy fires back, petulantly. He's ready to move on to the next customer. Time is money.

"Well, he can't fucking see, so tell him," Tony rasps. He's uptight and can do without the bullshit. He wants to pull his ID badge and get things moving, but it isn't the way, not with a guy who doesn't belong here. He'll just clam up. It's the way they are and you can't blame them. Generations of being oppressed, secret police and the like, wrong side of the wall.

I shove my elbow back and connect with Tony's stomach. He's tensed up so it barely makes a dent, but he gets the message.

"Sorry, bad day. A pint of that will do him."

I hear one glass rattle off the top of another. A click as it finds the pump, followed by a sloosh as the first down-pull spits a frothy brew down the side of the glass.

"Yes, me too, bad day is right," the barman relaxes. "And I'm sorry, I did not realise he was blind. Just thought he was looking cool with the shades."

Good, he's amiable and chatty. He tops the pint off. I can picture him as he levels the glass and flicks a few spurts in. No short measure.

His voice is directly in front of me as he informs me, "there you go, sir. Anything else?" he asks, turning his voice to Tony.

Tony must shake his head

"Three-ninety, please."

I speak for the first time. "He'll let you keep the change, if you can spare us a couple of minutes...?"

Sensing the guy reach across, I hear the ten pound note rustle between his fingers.

"Have to be quick," he says, "I'm on my own in here today. Till three."

"Show him your badge, Tony." I leave no gap, as I don't want the guy to process the fact this is official and clam up. "Anything odd happen today, around twelve, twelve fifteen? You were here then, right?"

"Yeah, I've been here since opening time. On my own. Girl no show. Like I said, a bad day." His voice is switching between me and the badge. He settles on me.

"Anything strange? Anything that seemed, I dunno, not quite normal?"

I bring my right hand up, palm towards me, and over the lip of the bar before slowly moving my hand away from me. Very controlled as I use my little fingernail as a guide, feeling it drag over the varnish, skipping across the grain in the wood.

The back of my hand connects with the cold glass, so I bring my fingers round, using the tip of my middle as a guide to trace the form. Standard pint glass, no handle. no weird shape. Twenty fluid ounces and splayed a little at the top third to help with grip.

I bring the glass to my face, keeping it as level as I can, but a dribble spills over and runs down my fingers on the far side, so I make the adjustment and suck a long refreshing draught off the top.

"Like what?" the guy asks. Fair enough question.

"Anything. Please, just think."

"There was the lady who lost her phone."

I'm interested.

"Lost?"

"Yeah. She made a, how you say, right scene? Went and got the transport police. You get that all the time. They have the phones on top of their bags, unfastened. As I said then, it could have fallen out any place."

"Ah, I know. Open invitation to a thief, as well..." I say in a familiar way, like I've known the guy for years.

"It's never their fault, you know? Always looking to blame someone else. And it was only a shitty pay-as-you-go thing."

"Christ, some people, eh? Hey, you notice anyone hanging around at the same time? Maybe just before she realised her phone was missing?"

"Mate..."

He's been here a few years, picked up the local vernacular. Not because he's impressionable, just because the more the customers relate to him, the better the tips and the easier his life. He says 'mate 'but pronounces it 'maite'; can't quite shake the old country.

"...this is a busy station. People hang around all the time."

"I know, I know. But please, this is important. An Asian kid, maybe late-teens, early-twenties. Alone. Nervous. Didn't stay long."

"Probably a dozen people like that in here today. At least. They come in looking to use the toilet. Save them paying to use the public one."

Sophie pipes up from behind my right shoulder. "Need a code, right?"

"For the toilet? Yes. We have to do that, or we'd have a thousand people a day in here using it."

"Can we have the code, please?" Sofa asks gently.

He gives her the four digits. Tony sends them off to check it. One word. "Go." His eyes must do the rest, and tell them they should both check it out; one in the gents, one in the ladies.

Before they can go, I twist round. "You got a mobile phone? Personal, not government issue?"

Marc and Sophie say yes at the same time, not sure who I was talking to.

"Can I borrow it, please?"

Marc offers first. He keeps it close to hand, always checking what he's missing.

"Here," he says, as he presses it against my hand.

"I'll take Sofa's, but thank you anyway."

"Oh, come on, Tony. What is this shit? You got a problem with me, Lorry?"

"Can I go serve some customers now?" the Romanian wants to know.

"Yes, you can. Thank you very much for your time. One final thing, if I may?" I don't wait for permission. "Security cameras. Pointing behind the bar, as usual? Make sure the staff don't steal from the till?"

He laughs an ironic burst. "Yes, that's how it is. For a blind bloke, you see pretty clear."

I smile at him. At least I hope it was at him.

And turn back to Marc.

"Listen very carefully, because we don't have time for this bollocks. You're a technical geek, Marc. No criticism in that, it's just what you are. So, if I take your phone, it'll be the latest all-singing, all-dancing model boasting call clarity, booster signal and fuck knows what else. The guy just told me that the phone we're looking for is a shitty pay-as-you-go thing. Sofa, meantime, took about five seconds longer than you to even locate her mobile. That tells me that she doesn't hold technology in the same high regard as you do. I also know a bit about you both, and know you have a penchant for the latest this, that and the other. And that Sofa would sooner spend a few hundred quid on a case of wine, than a new phone. So, I need a phone that is as close as I can get to the one we're looking for. Odds are that'll be Sophie's and not yours. Okay?"

Marc digests my rapid-fire summary.

"Okay. Sorry."

"But you know what, Marc? On reflection, I'll take both your phones. I don't want you feeling left out. Sofa, is Marc's mobile number programmed in?"

"Yep, under Marc Mobile. As you'd expect."

I hold out my hands. Phones get placed on both my upturned palms.

"Now, stop wasting time, and fuck off and search the toilets," Tony growls. I hear their feet depart.

Tony swears a lot, I think to myself, as my hands go to work on the phones. Some people call him Effing Tony. Mostly people who don't like him.

Marc's is a flip-up model featuring all the latest gubbins, with a screen and dozens of buttons. It must have internet access. Sofa's is comparatively ancient, probably getting on for five years old. An old Nokia, my fingers tell me.

I hand the Nokia to Tony.

"Ring Marc's number," I instruct him.

Clicks and buzzy beeps tell me he's tabbing through the contacts with his thumb. A final definitive depression, and I catch the breeze off his arm as he raises the phone to his ear.

One, and two, and... Two and a half seconds later the phone in my hand springs to life. It vibrates and plays a tune as I imagine it lit up like a Christmas tree. I snap the phone open and kill the tune dead.

"You hear me?" Tony asks.

"Got you. Walk about, and keep talking the whole time. Start with the toilet area."

"What do you want me to say?"

"Anything. Tell me why you go running every morning?"

"Don't start with that."

"How many miles today?"

"About six."

"Ten kilometers, roughly?"

"About that, yes."

"What did that take you, about fifty minutes?"

"Forty-eight. My aim is to get it down to forty-five. But there's a lot of me to shift. Not good...knees..."

"Losing you. Head back towards the bar. And call off the search in the toilets. You hear me okay?"

"Hang on....nearly lost the signal there. Too deep, too many obstacles. Heading for the back corner on the opposite side to the toilets."

"So, what are you doing? Running towards something, or running away from something?"

"Neither, I just fucking run. It makes me feel good, gets me invigorated for the day ahead. Keeps me sharp. Keeps me in shape."

"You in the back corner?"

"Yes."

"Hang on."

The Tannoy comes to life, so I stick a finger in my free ear. It's all wrong. The announcement's too quiet and the television too loud.

"No good, Tony. Head to that area you mentioned at the end of the bar, away from the entrance."

"Will do. Give me ten seconds."

"Running away or running towards? You don't strike me as the kind of bloke who runs away from anything. So what are you looking for out there on the open road? What are you hoping to run into?"

"Perhaps I'm running away from all your analytical shit. There doesn't have to be a reason for everything, Lorry, not in the way you think of it. Sometimes people just do stuff. No intent. No purpose. No great fucking mystery about it all."

"Bollocks, everything happens for a reason. Still, now we know where the guy rang 999 from."

"Here?"

"Yep. Wherever you are now is where he made the call. Hunt for the phone. He'll have left it there somewhere."

I click the snazzy plastic closed and break the connection, imagine it streaming back at the speed of light and dying in Tony's ear. I lay the phone on the bar and relocate my pint using the backs of my fingers. Lifting it to my mouth and tentatively tipping, I wait till the cool beer hits my lips to gauge the level left in the glass and tip accordingly. I feel a tiny stream escape from the corner of my mouth, and use my free hand to wipe it before it can reach the edge of my jaw.

"Got it," I hear Tony announce triumphantly as I imagine him holding it in the air like a trophy.

"Told you she must have dropped it," the Romanian bartender says as he passes me. "Amazed they sent all you lot to locate a shitty pay-as-you-go phone. Must be a quiet day in London, eh?"

"Quiet for now," I tell him. "It might get louder later."

"Another pint?"

"No, thanks. Those security cameras? They point across and along the bar? Or straight down at the tills?"

"Two of them, one each end. They point along. The left one covers the right and the right covers the left, if you see what I mean?"

"I see exactly what you mean."

"Hey, no offence, okay? My grandmother back in Buzau was born blind."

"None taken. Thanks for all your help."

6.

"Get the security footage from the camera above the cash registers, the one on the left as you face the bar. It may just pan across at an angle that will let us see our caller. Where was the phone, by the way?" I impart to Tony as we stand in a huddle at the foot of the steps that lead out of the pub.

"In a plant pot, dropped down the side of a plastic tree."

"What's the time now?"

"Twenty past two. How long you think we have?" Sophie asks me.

"God only knows. Not long enough. The kid on the phone sounded like he was talking about something imminent. But you're getting closer. Now, let's find out who you're looking for, and put a face to the voice. As soon as you have that, check the exit footage from the overhead security and see if you can see where they headed. After that, we have to assume they did their deed inside the station, or got a train or tube. If you spot them leaving, look for a bag. A bag big enough to get a bomb in, however big a bomb might be. Fuck knows, I'm making this up as I go. A rucksack of some description. No bag equals no bomb, and that means they planted it somewhere in here. Three options, guys and gals. They're still here somewhere, and so is the bomb. They planted the bomb somewhere in the station and left. Or they left and took the bomb with them. My gut tells me it's the latter, which means they could be anywhere within a hundred miles by now. Either way, two out of three options says they left, so play the odds. Check footage between ten past twelve and half past. Leave me here, I'll only slow you down, and you don't need me right now for this, it's visual stuff. Stick me back at the bar, our Romanian friend will take care of me, and it'll give me a bit of thinking time. Come and get me when you have something. Okay?"

"Okay. Let's go," Tony affirms.

"Lorry, you got my phone?" Marc asks, a bit more respectful now. Results tend to do that.

"Oh shitting hell. I left it on the bar..."

I spin away - old habits - and smack into a guy heading for a table. I can smell it's a guy, confirmed by the grunt on impact, grunts from both of us. Glasses smashing, liquid splashing, me saying I'm sorry, I'm sorry. The guy swearing, calling me a twat, asking if I'm blind?

Tony, Marc and Sophie step in and tell him to calm down. Money gets handed over, along with pacifying words, enough to replace the drinks, plus a bit extra for the laundry bill.

For a second, just for a second, I forgot I was blind. It's the day, the being out, the being a part of something. It focused my mind so much on other stuff, that I forgot I couldn't see.

I've been trying so hard to visualise the information being fed into me, that my brain is forming clear pictures of scenes for me to analyse. In my mind's eye, I can see, I can see it all.

It usually only happens at night.

Sometimes I'll wake up in the dark convinced I can see. It's just dark because it's the night, that's all that's stopping my eyes from working. It's irrational, but I've been dreaming, seeing things from the past in my dreams. They're as vivid as they ever were, as vibrant and colourful and beautiful as they were on the day they happened.

She. She is as beautiful and vibrant and vivid as she ever was.

And those dreams mess with my head. How can I see them if I can't see? The brain is cruel. It stops me visually perceiving, but constantly plays back those images.

On those nights, I get out of bed and walk to the light switch. I pause for a second or two and hope that this night it will be different, before flicking it on.

But there's nothing; just black.

I refuse to accept the situation, think that perhaps the light bulb has blown, and so head to the hallway and flick on that switch.

Still black, nothing but black.

On more than one occasion, I've checked the trip-switch on the fusebox, or turned on a radio to check there hasn't been a power cut. Only then can I accept it. Only then can I go back to bed to lie awake and stare at the emptiness.

She's never there.

"Lorry? Lorry? You okay? Are you hurt?" Sophie's asking me with concern in her voice.

"No, I'm fine, thank you. Sorry about that. Just sit me at the bar, I'll be out the way there. Did Marc get his phone?"

"Got it, Lorry. No problem."

Sophie's gentle hand finds my elbow, her breath brushing my cheek. It's fresh and minty. It's probably chewing gum. Minty Fresh, they should call it. Perhaps they do.

"There's a stool here." She takes my hand and lays it on the flat surface. I imagine it's her stomach, flat and even, slightly contoured nearest to me where her ribs start. If I go the other way, will my hand slide down the ramp to her pubis? Will I be able to sweep my hands out and find her hip bones?

I miss holding Kate's hip bones, spooned in bed at night.

"Thank you. I'll be great here. Go."

She still has hold of my hand.

"Go. Duty calls. Go, go!"

She goes. Heavy rushing footfalls ascend the steps out of the pub, six or seven people.

"I need to get your security tapes," a man asks. Someone from the station security team, I guess.

"Through there. In the back," the Romanian voice directs. And then, "mind out, broken glass."

The hatch slams open, and a few seconds later I hear bristles on the floor, glass getting swept in to a metal contraption.

It must happen quite often.

We're making headway. That call was made from here on that phone, I'm certain of it. What else am I certain of?

Let's start with the facts. Just the facts.

I clear my mind, wipe the slate clean and set it to a black nothingness on to which I can add images.

A scared kid, but part of a group. He said, 'they've got a bomb'. Not singular, not 'we've'. He's detaching himself. He must have got in to something and that something got bigger than he thought it was ever going to get. This isn't your typical Muslim Holy War stuff, no way. You get in to that, and you know where it's heading, without doubt. In fact, you get in to it because you know where it'll head. That's fundamentalist stuff. This isn't that.

Think.

This is something that escalated beyond anything this kid thought it would ever be. 'A bomb', he said, singular. To the best of his knowledge, they only have one. So, we're probably not looking at any synchronised attack along the lines of July seventh or 9/11 here. It doesn't have the hallmark of Muslim extremism, so dismiss that.

This is something different.

But he's scared, seriously terrified. It's pouring off him in the call. And simply by skulking down here and hiding at the end of the bar, he's telling me something. He came in here and scouted around, picked the phone from the woman, probably as she ordered at the bar, approached from behind her and lifted the mobile. Maybe he headed to the toilets, until he realised there was no signal in the toilet area. Perhaps he used the fact he needed the toilet as his excuse to escape from the rest of them, however many of them there are.

He's a young male of Asian descent. But English, from up north somewhere. But he's down here in London, affecting a cockney patter. Why would he do that?

To fit in, to be accepted. Into a group. Into a neighbourhood, Into a gang. A gang? Possible. Stick to the facts.

'Today'. He said they're going to use it today, so it's imminent. Target? Something happening today that I don't know about. I don't turn on the television. What would be the point? The radio stayed silent this morning as I played vinyl instead. It's what I do, occupy the senses that still work.

'You've got to stop them', he said. 'Them'. Plural. If it was a bomb - singular - and it was strapped to someone, he'd have said, you've got to stop him, stop the guy the bomb is strapped to. So, this is a bomb in a bag. How else would you carry it to London through Waterloo Station? Not a box, it'd be too cumbersome, and not attached to anyone. It has to be in a bag. Tony and the team are looking for a bag.

Good, I got that right.

He said he was sorry. He has remorse before the event has even taken place. He could walk away. Why stay in a situation that terrifies you, and you regret before it happens? Because he's more scared of something else. An impressionable kid, he's scared of how the group will perceive him if he doesn't go along with it. So he doesn't run away, he stays; rides out the fear and sticks with it.

Why?

Why is he in London? One of two probable reasons. He came here on his own to get away from something, probably family, maybe an oppressive family environment. Did they have ideas that he should head back for an arranged marriage or something similar? Or go and get schooled in Islam, or Hinduism, or something? Sikhism? Too much speculation, just assume he might have run away.

Other reason he might be in London; his parents and family moved here and dragged him with them kicking and screaming. They moved to the big city where he knew nobody, left his school and friends behind and tried to start again. It's hard when you're a certain age, hard to fit in when you come from somewhere else via somewhere else. So you ingratiate yourself and adopt the accent, you play along and join in. Till it goes too far, then you get scared. You panic and make a call, tip off the authorities.

All too speculative, but probably not far from the truth.

He just didn't think... That was the last bit before he hung up. Was he disturbed? Did someone come down here looking for him? Or did his nerve go as he bottled it and hung up out of habit, before ditching the phone in the plant pot and heading back before his absence became too lengthy and aroused suspicion?

If he hung up because of habit, then he must have a mobile phone of his own, but he didn't use it. Why not? Because he's smart enough to know phone numbers are logged and can be traced. Or because he was afraid someone might check his phone when the plot was blown and realise that he welched. Previous numbers dialed would show the call.

It seems to me that he's equally terrified in two opposite directions. He's as frightened of the people he's with, as he is getting caught by the authorities.

Detonating a bomb is a serious crime. How bad must the guy be that he's fallen in with?

I said guy, singular. Why did I say that? Gang. Gangs have leaders, right? A head honcho, someone with a strong personality and leadership skills offering something that appeals to an impressionable young man.

He just didn't think... Didn't think they'd go through with it. That's what the rest of the sentence sounded like it was going to be, given the intonation.

"You want another pint now, blind man?"

"Yeah, go on, why not."

"Same again?"

"Please." He must have finished cleaning up the mess.

The bar seems emptier. A lull, I think, between the lunch crowd and the evening trade. A few stragglers in here now, judging by the noise level, two dozen people, maybe. The tourists are off touring, the workers working, apart from a few. A morning meeting, followed by a working lunch before heading back to the station to catch a train. Kill an hour in here, which means it won't be worth going back to the office, and head straight for home.

"I was thinking..."

"What's that?" I respond to the Romanian.

"There was a guy earlier. Asian kid. He was twitchy, you know? Is this the right word?"

"Yeah," I chuckle, "twitchy is right."

"He wanted toilet. I said, no, toilet is for customers only. So he wanted to buy a drink. Lager, I think. A half. He was young. So I asked him for ID, proof of age, you know?"

I say nothing and let him carry on.

"He went to show me, but stopped. Didn't take his ID out of his pocket. Ordered a cola instead. No ID for cola, right?"

"I guess not. But there probably should be."

"He paid. I give him the toilet code. He went. But thirty seconds later, he's back. Not enough time for a piss. Definitely no time for a bigger job. So, he's back, and he takes his cola to the end of the bar, over there where the big black man found the phone. Then I get distracted with customers, you know? Next time I look, he's gone, cola untouched. I think maybe he go toilet after all, but he never come back. After five minutes, I throw cola away."

"Thank you. That's our man."

"Sorry I not think of this earlier. Too many customers, too many wanting toilet without buying drink. You know how it is? Only when I see your mate get the phone over there, I think of the kid."

"It confirms what I thought. Thanks again."

"Your beer is in front of you. Three-ninety, please?"

I pat my pockets. Shit, no money. Having come out in a hurry, I forgot to pick some up from the hidey-hole.

"...you won't believe this, I've come out without my wallet."

"Good job you're blind."

"Why?"

"Because I can't go throwing you out, can I? What would my old grandmother say?"

"I'll make sure you get paid."

Then I add, almost to myself, "I spent it all on shoes. Good shoes. Four pairs, I bought, all the same."

"Like my grandmother. Always the same shoes. No confusion."

"That's right. You mind me asking something?"

41

"Go ahead."

"Your grandmother, was she blind from birth?"

"That's right."

"Does she dream...?"

Before he can answer there's a rumble, as though the earth beneath our feet has a pain. I feel it travel up the legs of the stool and vibrate through my body, much like running over rutted lines at the side of the road in a modern car. A car with good suspension, so that you just feel the tremor, a hint of something.

Enough to warn you.

The glasses and bottles rattle.

The air shifts fractionally.

Followed by silence in the bar, just for a beat.

Two seconds pass while people process the data, two seconds before they start speculating on what might have caused such a phenomenon.

It's far too late to act.

I'm way ahead of them, having been expecting it for the past hour. I smile. It's over now, the pressure's off.

My Romanian friend breaks our own personal two seconds of data processing.

"What was that? An earthquake? Perhaps a train hit the platform?"

"No, that was a bomb," I tell him matter-of-factly.

I slide my hand up to the top of the bar and back it slowly away from my body. My movement is controlled, the opposite of a bomb. No randomness, no sudden explosion of energy. No destruction.

I find the glass and trace it, circumnavigate it and lift it. No spills this time, as steady as a rock as I take a long gulp.

7.

People start leaving the bar as they reason it out. They remember July seventh and the multiple bombs more or less coordinated. Their chatter is about getting out of London, back to the suburbs where it's safe and sound.

Apart from the bombers themselves, I'm possibly the only person in the world who knows there won't be any more explosions today. Well, not from the same source, at least. There's always a chance some other faction may decide to blow something up on the same day, but it's incredibly unlikely.

Here's a thought. It's perfectly feasible, given the speed of light being one billion kilometers per hour, that I could hear an explosion on television before I hear it in real time.

The media can report something to me, potentially, before I can sense it for myself. And that's when I'm sitting within a half mile of it. They'd have to be broadcasting live at the event, of course.

Light travels nine-hundred thousand times faster than sound. Roughly. Let's not get too precise here. The difference doesn't matter that much. I'm not looking to land an exploratory probe on a distant planet.

"No idea why I'm asking you, but I think you're the best person to ask."

It's the Romanian guy interrupting my thoughts.

"I've been asking you plenty of questions, I guess you're entitled to your turn."

"Should I be running out of here?"

"No."

"Because for why?"

His excellent English is slipping. Nerves. His brain is processing too much other data. It's in danger of over-loading, so there's no time or capacity left to translate my replies from English to Romanian, formulate a response in Romanian, and carefully consider the translation back to English.

"Because I can assure you there will be no more bombs today. Because the panic out there will be much more dangerous to your health than staying here. Because that explosion was far enough away to be of no danger to us. And because, if you leave, I'm going to struggle to re-fill my own pint."

"So, I stay?"

"Yes indeed. We both stay. How many customers are left?"

"You and about ten others."

"Pretty soon it'll be just you and me. Nice and quiet - almost cosy. At that point, I strongly suggest you have a drink. You'll need it, because an hour after that, you won't be able to move in here."

"Okay. I'm trusting you, mate. You know this?"

"I know this."

"By the way...?" he adds.

"Yep?"

"You have no money. Who says you get another pint?"

Let's say I'm sitting one point two kilometers away from that explosion. That's about three quarters of a mile, which is not far off reality I guess. Sound travels at twelve hundred kilometers an hour. Thus, I'm sitting a thousandth of an hour away from hearing that explosion in real time. A thousandth of an hour is precisely three point six seconds. It took three point six seconds for that noise to reach me.

When Tony called me earlier, using the two mobiles, the call took two and a half seconds to come through. It was even faster once the connection was established, and that was from old technology. The televisual transmitters and receivers are much more advanced. My best bet is that the pictures and sound could be delivered here, from one point two kilometers away, in about two, maybe even one and a half seconds.

I'd hear the explosion through the television at least a second faster than I could hear it in real time.

Which is why I'm surprised it takes so long for the television channels in the pub to interrupt their programming and go to an emergency special report.

Red strips will be at the bottom of all the screens, just as Tony will have elevated the Threat Level to a ten from a seven. Red; threat is assessed and evaluated as real and happening right now. All the responders move off stand-by and begin rehearsed protocol for a Code Nine, Level Ten situation.

As high as it can go.

This is what I do. It's how I cope. As daft as it sounds for a blind man to admit to this, self-enforced myopia is my adopted tactic for getting through life. By forcing my mind to concentrate on the minutiae of a situation, it prevents me from seeing the bigger picture.

Why do I do that? Because the detail, such as the speed of sound versus the speed of light, shines so brightly at the fore of my mind that it blocks out everything behind it. That way I don't have to think about the real human impact of that bomb, and the fact that Tony and his team might have been killed by it.

The volume gets raised on the television by the bar, my Romanian pal getting informed, getting all the pertinent information. He already has it from me, but that won't be enough, he'll only believe it if he hears it via the media.

But the media won't tell him the truth. They'll hype it up, speculate on all manner of crap as they pull in a load of talking heads, so-called experts on nothing relevant. Things will be hastily discussed, political agendas will be introduced and assumptions will be made from which conclusions will be drawn. And it'll all go out live on the television networks to be absorbed by a hungry public.

Accuracy? Not relevant.

"Now, you are sure we should be sitting here, yes?" he asks me with a bit of levity in his tone. He trusts me to make the call.

"How many customers are left?"

"Two. And you and me."

"How many when that explosion actually happened?"

"Thirty, I guess. Maybe twenty-five."

"Those last two will probably be gone in the next few minutes. So, that's roughly twenty-five people poured out of this pub in five minutes. Multiply that by every pub around here. And then extrapolate that for every office in the area, every shop, plus the thousands of tourists seeing the sights. And then think of the one point one million people who commute into London every day on average, eight-hundred thousand of which use the trains. In short, my man...what is your name anyway?"

"Greg."

"That's the version for the tourists. What's your Romanian name?"

"Grigore."

"Grigore means watchful or vigilant, right? Listen to your name. Stay here. It'll be chaos out there. You're in the safest place."

"Can't argue with you, mate. Hey, how you know all this stuff? How you know the meaning of my name, are you like Rain Man, or something? You know the film?"

"No. I just remember stuff, and I once read a book on name meanings and assumed Grigore would mean the same as Gregory."

"Those two last customers just leave. You want a beer? I'm having one."

"Might as well. Thanks."

"Hey, you know you said about it get busy in here later?" he asks, as he lets my pint settle and flips a top off a bottle of something. Some strong European lager, I imagine. Strong enough to give him a buzz and settle the nerves, but not voluminous enough to fill his bladder as he finishes his shift.

"Yep, in about an hour."

"Why will this happen? Why will it get busy?"

"Human nature. First instinct is to run and find shelter, to get away from the danger. The media will whip up the panic. The businesses won't want to be liable, so they'll send everyone home as they pass the buck to someone else. If their employees get blown up on a train or bus, it won't be their problem. So, stage one will be an attempted mass exodus out of London. But the system can't support it. The roads will be log-jammed, every bridge snarled up. Add to that, there simply aren't enough taxis and buses, even if they could move. And remember, the bus drivers and cab drivers are as keen to run for the hills as everyone else. The police and authorities will slow it all down, as well, as they look for the bombers. So, people will head to the hubs on foot. Stamford Street will be teeming with concerned people all heading to Blackfriars or Waterloo, depending on where they need to get to. They'll avoid the tube, overground will be the way to travel. People feel safer if they can see the sky. The July seventh attacks will play over in their minds - a top blown off a bus, mass casualties down in the depths, tube trains blown apart. A tunnel is a bad place to be on a day like this. Right now, up there, thousands are pouring in to this station, jostling, pushing, shoving, everyone trying to gain an edge as they desperately attempt to get to the front of the queue. But there aren't enough trains, there can't be. So, half an hour to reach the hub, and another half an hour to realise they can't get anywhere. What do they do next?"

"How do you mean?" Grigore asks. I hear him quaff his lager in a greedy gulp, imagine his adam's apple bobbing up and down as he swallows.

"You've been here a while. What do the British do habitually? What do they instinctively reach for in times of trouble?"

"Drink."

"Correct, and the camaraderie that comes with drinking. A realisation will wash over a percentage of the population that if they're going to die, they'll be as well dying surrounded by people, with a drink in their hand. The point is, in about three quarters of an hour from now, this pub will start getting busy, busier than you've ever seen it. And the chances are, your workmates won't be coming to work today, an impossible journey from East London where the housing is cheaper and they can rent a room in a converted house with a shared bathroom and kitchen. And it won't just be lots of people, it'll be hordes wanting to get close to other people. On July seventh, it's precisely what I did, having met my wife in a pub. So they'll drink. They'll drink in a way they normally wouldn't on a Wednesday afternoon. Strangers will be buying drinks for people they've never met before, and will never see again. It's going to be crazy, so have another beer and brace yourself."

He drains his bottle and tosses it into the re-cycling bin where it crash lands and settles. The fridge door squeaks a little as he opens it and gets himself another. It's what I'd do. A hiss as the top comes off. There'll be a curl of carbon gas leaving the top of the bottle as the cold meets the warmth in the bar. The top joins the empty bottles and tinkles down between the gaps.

"Cheers."

I relocate my pint, lift it, hold it out, and hear the chink as he touches it with his bottle.

"Best of health."

The media speculation has already begun. Three mentions of Muslim extremism as well as one of Irish republicans. It's miles away, but it all helps stir up public opinion. Some clown I've never heard of is talking about bomb attacks coming in co-ordinated clusters, that the people of London should expect more. They should get out of town, in his opinion, and if they can't do that, they should stay in their homes and batten down the hatches.

Clueless.

But the truth of it is, on July seventh, I was just like that. I bought in to all of it. Now I can sit here and dispassionately break it all down. I dare say it makes me seem incredibly arrogant.

Dispassionate.

Free from or unaffected by passion. Devoid of personal feeling or bias.

Yes, that's me encapsulated. No passion for life, as any personal feelings died one night a few years back, along with any concerns for my own wellbeing. After all, I remained in this pub, despite knowing the bomb could have been left right here.

There's only Lanie, but she's safely up in Edinburgh. I mustn't forget Lanie, and I don't, but sometimes she isn't where she ought to be in my life order. It's difficult, because when I'm with Lanie, I'm with Kate, and that brings it all back. Besides which, I know a gulf exists between us because I don't want to burden her with the things I witnessed.

The noise from the swell of people above us is starting to penetrate. It won't be long now.

Footsteps clatter down the flight. Sophie breathlessly pants my name.

"Lorry, we have to go. Now. Back to HQ. Meet Tony there."

Grigore has his first customers of the rush. Two guys ordering two pints. It started earlier than I thought it would.

"I owe for a couple of pints, I didn't have any money," I tell Sofa.

She must go to pay, but I hear my Romanian friend tell her it's covered.

"It's not like there's any film in the security camera pointing at that far till at the moment," he says.

"Thank you."

I feel his hand touch mine and flinch at the human contact. He shakes it.

"My grandmother..."

"Yes, blind from birth."

"She dreams. But she only hears the sounds. No pictures."

"Auditory dreams," I say, nodding.

"I don't know this word, but maybe. Like audio, yes?"

"Exactly. She's lucky."

"My grandmother?"

"Yes. Tell her she's lucky. She doesn't know what she's missing."

8.

"One fatality, at least twelve injured. Three seriously, but they should pull through," Sofa details, as we push through the crowd, going against the tide in Waterloo Station.

"Do you know anything about the dead person?"

"Male, twenties, worked in the pub."

"Pub?"

"Ah, yes. The bomb went off in a pub. More of a wine bar place, actually, the Vine Of Plenty. All pine, polished brass and stools at high tables. Not that you'd know that now, but I went in there once. Stayed for one glass, and went somewhere less bright and clinical."

"Anybody claimed responsibility?"

"No, nothing. Adam's monitoring everything from the office, but there's a mountain of knee-jerk information coming in from a panicking public. We have to rely on the emergency services to feed through anything relevant. TERA would need a department of a thousand, maybe two thousand people to sort through it all..." she raps, almost like she's trying to convince herself.

We're by the taxi rank, but I can't hear any distinctive taxi engine rumbles. Nor are there any doors slamming shut or drivers calling 'where to, mate? 'I imagine a long queue snaking round as Sophie calls out "coming through."

"The bomb. Any initial analysis of that?" I ask, to keep my mind working.

"Crude. Homemade but effective. The bomb squad guy used the phrase 'a bark worse than its bite'. The kind you can make with stuff you find in a DIY superstore."

"I heard the bark. How far away is this bar?"

"Half a mile. Maybe a bit more. I was there in less than five minutes on foot, having got there as fast as Tony and Marc could in the car. Some good news, by the way."

Her blunt Lancashire accent and northern ability to see a silver lining make me smile.

"Go on."

"We pulled a lovely snapshot of the lad who made the call, and even though we had to leg it to the bomb scene, the security head here reckons he has some clear footage of four guys leaving via the back downstairs exit. Our phone man is one of them, and they're carrying a sport bag."

"We need that footage at..."

"Already there waiting for us, Lorry lad."

Efficient girl.

"Hey! Piss off!" Sofa shouts, "check the plates, dickhead."

"What's going on?"

"They're about to tow my car."

Sophie twists, holding my elbow with her right hand as she reaches with her left to retrieve something from her right pocket. I hope it's not her gun.

I reckon it must be her ID badge.

"See this, eh? That says Government Agent, Threat Evaluation and Response Advisory, and that's my chuffing mug-shot right there next to it. Clamp my car and I'll clamp you in bloody irons. Understand?"

Ooooh, she's impressive. I could seriously...

My thought ends. I end it. It's been four years. I have no idea what she looks like.

Looks were always important to me.

How Kate looked was vital. Had she not caught my eye as she entered the pub that evening, I wouldn't have watched her. And if I hadn't been watching her, she wouldn't have seen me, and nor would the bloke she was with. The pub was busy, but all I saw was her.

Kate.

Calling out in the aftermath of a bomb blast half a mile away that you're a government agent working for a division most people have never heard of, but is clearly something to do with evaluating threats, probably wasn't the smartest move of Sophie's life.

I can feel the crowd closing in. Hands touch my arms as they clamour for attention, asking questions, the same question asked in a hundred different ways. How can I stay alive? That's all anybody really wants to know. I can fill in the subtext as the bombardment grows.

"Should we stay here?"

"Where should we go?"

"What's the best way of getting out of the city?"

"Will there be more explosions?"

"Is it true the tube has been hit by multiple blasts?"

"Is this another July seventh?"

"Can you take us to the US embassy?"

"We heard it was suicide bombers - who should we look out for?"

"Is it Muslims again?"

"Are they targeting pubs?"

"What the fuck are the police doing about this?"

"Is the geezer in sunglasses a suspect...?"

Wordlessly, Sofa steers me to the door of her car. She opens it, positions me and guides me in with a hand on the top of my head to stop me banging it on the edge of the roof. She slams the door a bit too forcefully.

Five seconds later, I hear her door open. The car lightly shifts on its springs as she swings down on her seat. The door closes. I swallow to clear my ears, popped by the shift in the air. Good seals, indicative of a new car. They have to have new cars for reliability. Not as new as Tony's, though, the edge has worn off the smell of newness.

I should have got the code and used the toilet in the pub. But I hate using public toilets, or any toilets that I don't know. I have to feel around for the urinal or the seat and use my hands to locate and visualise it. I have to check to see if the lid's up and where the flush is. It usually involves me coming in to contact with something unpleasant.

It's another reason why I don't leave the house very often.

"If you feel sick, tell me," Sophie snaps. She's pissed off, and knows she shouldn't have drawn attention to herself.

"I'm fine. I could do with a pee, though."

"Don't piss in my car, Lorry, I mean it."

"I won't." I leave a pause. "As long as we're no more than ten minutes away."

She hits the sirens. The tyres wail in protest as she guns the accelerator. I imagine there's a trail of smoke behind us.

It took twelve minutes to get here, and the traffic will be a lot worse now.

*****

Marc stayed at the scene.

Adam's the Funnel. That's what they call the person who stays at base, the person through who everything pours and gets filtered.

Tony's the Lead. Tony's always the lead when an evaluation hits Red. No matter where he is, or what he's doing, he gets to where he needs to be, and he leads.

Sophie, therefore, is Tony's right hand.

I stand testing the taps to see which one is the hot water.

"You done? We need to move on this. Now."

It's Tony.

"Tell me what you know," I urge him, make the best use of the time.

"Four males, late-teens, early-twenties. Adam has the security footage, and we're ready to run. They have to be our men. Fragments of the hold-all scraped up at the scene look like the bag in the picture, and the young lad who made the call is one of the four. They all look Asian, or perhaps mixed race. Or North African or something. Not Middle-eastern, I don't think. Crude homemade device, made from the kind of stuff anyone can buy in a fucking supermarket. Packed with small nails and set on a timer. Basic but effective. One dead, a barman, Slovakian. Wrong place, wrong time. Poor bastard was just doing his job. We're up to fourteen injured. Most just have shock and superficial wounds, but three are more serious, hospital jobs. One has some nasty internal injuries. She's the only one on the danger list. The others should be fine. They're mostly Germans."

"Germans? Tourists?"

"Football, Lorry. England are due to play Germany at Wembley tonight. Though I have to make the call whether it gets called off or not."

"Why would you call it off?"

"There's been a fucking bomb let off in central London, Lorry. It's chaos out there, with everybody panicking. And the last thing we need is a nice little concentration of ninety thousand people..."

"Relax, they only have one bomb."

"How can you possibly know that?"

"The guy said on the phone, 'a bomb'. Singular."

"One that he knows about!"

"No. One bomb. This isn't what it seems, Tony, I'm sure of that, and I know what the media are saying, and how we tend to think in these circumstances, but something tells me this is the opposite of that..."

Why did I say opposite? What led me to conclude that? The opposite of religious extremism? Where am I going with this? And what is the opposite of religious extremism?

"Paper towels, on your left at neck height," Tony vocally steers me, clocking me twisting left and right with my hands dripping.

Tony's understandably tense. This is what he exists for, today's events. This is what he gets judged on, his mind probably already thinking of the postmortem, working out if there's a better way, if this could have been prevented.

"Ready, Adam?" Tony snaps.

"I've been ready for the past fifteen minutes," he grumbles.

"Run it."

Silence for fourteen seconds as I count them in my head, the amount of time our bombers were on film. One camera, or more than one pieced together, it makes no odds. Grainy black and white staccato pictures, so-many frames per second to extend the capacity of the memory.

"Play it again."

Scrabble slates on a keyboard get depressed in a blur of clicking. Too many clicks coming too rapidly for me to count.

Fourteen seconds of silence.

My mind is black.

The slate is clean.

I need to add the images and visualise it all.

"How many people?" I call out.

"Four."

"The caller. Is he at the back, trailing behind?"

"Yes."

"The leader. Tell me about him."

"Which one's the..." Sophie starts to ask.

"He's the one at the front, or in the middle of the other three. He won't be carrying anything. He has lackeys for that."

"Okay, the big lad. Yeah, cocky stride, a bit of swagger."

"What does he look like?"

"Tall, big build. Bigger than the other three. Jeans, trainers. One of those bomber jackets that make people look even bigger than they are."

"Ethnicity?"

"Hard to tell. Nondescript. My guess would be a product of a mixed marriage. Could be Asian, could be mixed race could be North African."

"Hair?"

"Dunno, his head's shaved."

"Is there anything shared between the four? Any kind of uniform?"

"No. I mean, two have jeans by the looks, and two have those trousers with lots of pockets. It's hard to be specific," Tony adds, "the pictures are too grainy."

"But they look purposeful, like they're on a mission?"

"Hmmm, yeah," Adam chips in, "they look like they're on a mission to Oxford Street to do a bit of shopping."

"One of them has a hat. Baseball cap," Sofa throws in.

"One of the lackeys?"

"Yes. Can't make out the logo, though. Can we get that enhanced?" Tony asks.

Adam answers. "I can try zooming in, but it'll probably just blur. Hang on..."

I hear keys being pressed again.

My daughter set me up with a computer where the screen talks. It tells you whatever's being displayed. Computing for the blind. I should make more of an effort to engage things, but it all seems like too much trouble. I was never a big fan of computers even when I could see.

I can't imagine porn being the same.

"It could be anything," Adam says.

I hear the creak of leather shoes as the three of them lean in to get a closer look, a light scrunch of clothes being creased behind the knees and elbows.

And finally a gentle pop as Tony leans back and releases his hands from the table, breaking the vacuum caused by his slightly sweaty palms.

"What was the first thing that came in to your minds when you saw that hat?" I prompt.

"How do you mean?" Sophie asks.

"The first thing you thought of, before you dismissed it as being too indistinct?"

"A badge."

"Like a football badge?"

"Yes, exactly like a football badge. I can be more specific..."

"Go on."

"It's my nephew, see, back up north, my sister's lad. He's a mad keen Blackburn Rovers fan. The badge just reminded me of that, for a second. I don't know why really..."

A door being opened breaks my train of thought. A voice tells Tony he needs to take a call, urgent, won't take no for an answer.

He leaves the room.

"What are you thinking, Lorry?" Sofa asks, gently.

"Thinking. That's all we ever do in this fucking place." Adam snaps, aggressively.

"I'm thinking that we need to put out mugshots of these four young men to all officers and stewards on duty at the England Germany match at Wembley tonight."

Adam's expression is actually audible to me. A smack as his mouth parts, and a breath of frustration already being drawn in.

His thumb or finger taps on the edge of the keyboard sending little tremors through the table. They end up in my hands.

All of that comes out in his tone. "Right, based on her thinking the blurred thing on a baseball cap in a grainy picture is a football crest. We don't even know that we're looking at the right people, here. These could be innocent guys heading up to Oxford Street for a bit of shopping. They could have been heading to the Millennium fucking Wheel for all we know. So a guy made a call from a pub. So what? Millions of people make calls every minute of every day in London. Some people are never off their phones... This is bullshit."

Tony re-entering the room cuts him off.

"No. I'll tell you what bullshit is. Bullshit is the fact I've just had your daughter on the phone..."

It takes me a beat to work out he's talking to me. I'm the only person in the room with a daughter. I snap my head up.

"Lanie? What? Is she okay?"

"She's fine, Lorry. She rang me to ask why the television news is reporting her dad has been arrested in connection with the explosion in London earlier today. Not that they have your name or anything, but the pictures I've just been looking at are pretty fucking clear. A lot fucking clearer than the footage we have to work with. You look good in them, as well, Sofa..."

"Oh shit, Tony, they were trying to clamp my car, and I..."

"Yeah," he continues, ignoring her, "there's a particularly good one of you escorting the sunglass-obscured suspect, in an armlock, to an unmarked government vehicle, another of you inserting him into the car, and some excellent high definition video footage of you speeding away from Waterloo, tyre screeches and smoke to boot. So now I have to go and sort this crap out, and tell everyone that no arrests have been made. Now that's bullshit!"

"That's what I was just saying," Adam seamlessly continues, "this is all bullshit. We don't know anything. We've wasted..." he pauses to check his watch, his wrist clicks ever so faintly as he rotates it, "...nearly three hours chasing speculation. Okay, so he got lucky on the Surbiton thing, but the rest of it is all completely speculative. We have no concrete..."

"Hang on a second," Sophie leaps in. "If it wasn't for Lorry, we wouldn't be anywhere near this. it was him who..."

"We'd have been where we are now, for fuck's sake," Adam interrupts her, and shouts her down. "The bomb would have exploded and we'd be exactly where..."

"That's bullshit!" she shouts back, getting fired up, rising from her chair, defending me. "At least we know who we're looking for, we have those bloody images."

"Bollocks. We can't even say with any degree of certainty that these are our suspects. How many people come to London every day with bags and make a phone call? When I signed up for this, I didn't realise I'd be left sitting on my arse in an office, having been overlooked in favour of the Blind Prophet here..."

I'm staring at my hands and seeing nothing but black as I feel the chair hit the table and shockwave through those hands before traveling along my arms. and Into my nervous system. A breeze moves my hair, a breeze caused by a large object moving rapidly, from standing start to impact in about one second. Then I hear the dull clap of a hand coming in to contact with human skin. Not a slap or a punch, but a hold.

A croak of a voice tells me Tony has Adam by the throat, and the thud and vibration tells me Adam's shoulders just impacted with the wall behind him.

"Tiresias!" I shout, loud enough that it comes as a bit of a shock even to myself.

"What?" Tony says.

"The Blind Prophet. Tiresias. See, Adam knows that. He knows the name of the Blind Prophet, and Marc would know that, too. But Sofa, and you Tony, you wouldn't know that. And if this case was about literature or Greek mythology or Roman history, Sofa would have been the person left at the office sat on her arse, to paraphrase. But it isn't, it's about something grittier and much less highbrow. That's why I advised you to take Sofa and leave Adam here. No offence, Sophie," I add as an afterthought.

Before continuing, "Tony, to carry on with the analogy, is Zeus. And you don't want to fuck with Zeus. King of the gods, no less. He may have blinded me, depending on which explanation you go with, as punishment for revealing godly secrets."

Adam coughs. That tells me Tony has let go of his throat. You have to be able to breathe to be able to cough. A more relaxed atmosphere takes over the room, something in the way people exhale, more even and smooth.

"See what I'm saying, Adam?" I add, my voice softer. "You and Marc are Castor and Pollux. Which one of you is immortal, I wonder?"

"Who am I, then?" Sophie calls breezily, further lightening the mood.

"Helen Of Troy, of course."

"Well, I love Paris," she throws in. Smart girl.

Adam chuckles. Awkward apologies are passed between him and Tony, him and Sophie.

"Everybody's tense. But we're all we've got, and we need to stick together," Tony says.

"The Colosseum..." I say.

"You're into your classical references today. Care to explain in English?" Tony asks.

"Wembley. It's where you'll find those four bastards who blew up a London pub today. I assume the football match is still going ahead?"

"Unless I make the call otherwise."

"No reason to call it off. There is only one bomb, I'm certain of it. Call the match off, and it'll prove a lot more difficult finding the bombers. Besides which, keeping the match on will keep people assured, and let them know the threat is over without actually saying it."

"How sure are you on all this?" Tony needs a boost.

"As sure as I was about Waterloo Station. Besides, if you find them and arrest them there, you can announce the arrests and the whole business about Sofa bringing me in for questioning goes away. As soon as you have them in cuffs, announce it and stop the panic."

"Let's go," Tony concludes defiantly, before adding, "Adam, with me. Sofa you run Funnel, and keep Lorry company. Oh, and get him to ring his daughter."

I don't complain, as I figure Tony needs to have a quiet word with Adam, and try to work out their differences.

9.

"Hello..." is all I can breezily get out before Lanie begins.

"Dad, what the hell is going on? Why have I just watched you being arrested on national television?"

"It was all a misunderstanding. Tony needed my help, that's all," I say in a placating way, trying to sound nonchalant. I don't want her worrying about me.

"That's all? A misunderstanding? A bomb goes off in London, you're involved in it somehow, and the first I hear of it is on the bloody national news?"

"Lanie, that wasn't supposed to...they got it wrong. You shouldn't pay attention to the news."

"Right, then tell me how else I'm supposed to get any information?"

"Well, if it was anything important, I'd have told you."

"Oh yes, because you're great at opening up and sharing, Dad! What if you were dead, how would you tell me then?"

"Well, Tony would tell you in that circumstance."

"Typical. Absolutely typical. Here's an idea; how about you tell me what you're planning on doing before you do it? That way, I won't be shocked when I see you getting arrested as a terror suspect on the national sodding news!"

To try and calm her down, I decide to say, "ah, it's no different to reality television. Nothing to worry about."

The period of silence tells me it wasn't a good move.

"It's all about you, isn't it, Dad? Just like always. Nobody else in the whole bloody world matters, apart from you. Would you have rung me if I hadn't called Tony?"

I don't answer, because I know the answer's no. Lanie knows it, too.

"No. I'm sick of it, Dad. Sick of all this. When have you ever considered me? In the four years since Mum died, you haven't asked me how I am. Not once. I lost my Mum. I was fifteen! But from the instant it happened, it became all about you. I know you lost your sight. Christ knows I know that, I'm never allowed to forget it." She's about to cry, I can hear it in the static. "But I lost my Mum. She was my best friend, and I can't lose you, as well. That's what terrifies me, Dad. Can't you see that?"

I keep quiet. Something bangs. Her fist on a table, I think.

"Shit, Dad! You're 'The Man'. You have all the answers, you see right through people, but you're completely blind to all the people that are right here in front of you. And yes, I mean that figuratively. Sometimes...no, most of the time, your head's so far up your own arse... You know, Dad, you were blind long before you were blind."

My mind's swimming, my body deflating. It's like Lanie's sticking pins in me, in all the pertinent places.

"Nothing. That's all you have to say? Nothing. Just like always. I know that this Saturday is the anniversary of her death, Dad. How could I not know that? But would you have called me? Has it ever entered your mind that I might need something on that day? You have the perfect excuse, you know that? You can hide behind not being able to see. It must be great, just close your eyes to everything and pretend it isn't there."

Her voice trembles with emotion, and I know that this isn't just about today, that this has been building up inside her for four years.

I feel faint, like I don't know which way is up. For the second time today, I feel sick.

"Lanie..."

"No, Dad, don't even try. There is no explanation. You could have called me. I got you the mobile phone. You could have called me on that. It's what I fucking well got it for! I bet you left it at home, didn't you? I know it's switched off, wherever it is, because I've tried ringing it a dozen bloody times."

She can't keep it going. The shakiness turns to sobs. They take her breath out of her lungs, the wind from her sails.

What have I done?

"I miss my Mum," she whispers, and the hair on my neck becomes charged. "I miss my Mum so much it's like there's this vital piece of me missing...like there isn't enough oxygen in the air."

I can't speak, so I listen to her irregular gurgled breaths, too afraid of falling apart if I say anything.

I've no idea how long we stay connected but disconnected. Four years, perhaps?

"You're strong," I eventually manage, and have to cough the emotion away from my throat, "you're strong like your Mum. I'm weak. And I always have been, Lanie, deep down. And like your Mum, you're selfless. Whereas I'm selfish. But for sixteen years I felt strong, because I had your Mum. I'm sorry, Lanie."

"You have to talk to me, Dad. And you have to let me talk to you. And I don't mean that we have to find solutions to everything. I mean that we just have to talk and listen. We have to be honest. Understand?"

"Yes."

"Let people in, Dad. You have to let people in. Look, I'll ring you later...about half seven. I have to get to class."

"I'd like that."

And she's gone.

"Are you okay, Lorry?" Sophie enquires, swinging through the door.

I don't say anything, just nod.

"Lorry, my love, you're as white as a sheet. Are you sure you're okay?"

"I'm fine," I manage.

"How's Lanie?"

A buzzing from her earpiece saves me from the conversation. It sounds like a wasp trapped in a tin can.

"Shit. You're kidding?"

There's a long pause as she listens. It must be Tony.

"Okay, leave it with me."

"Lorry, that was Tony. Two things. Firstly, they have a positive ID on three of the four suspects coming through Euston Station heading towards the overground train to Wembley. He says, well done, it seems like you were bang on again. The local police are keeping tabs on them."

I nod my understanding. Then, "why only three?"

"That's the other thing. The lad who called us? It seems that he matches the description of a body found about twenty minutes ago. His throat was cut, and he was left to bleed to death on the south bank of the Thames."

"Poor bastard. Any witnesses? Anything to tie it to the gang?"

"No. Broad daylight, in the middle of London, but I guess everyone was too focused on getting home after the explosion."

There's nothing to say, so I keep quiet. It's a peculiar feeling to have listened to his voice leaving a message just a short while ago, and to have replayed those words over and over in my head, to now discover the utterer of them is dead.

Sophie carries on. "Tony and Adam are heading to Wembley to hook up with the local police and stadium security. Marc is nearly at the scene on the Thames to get what he can from the police and medical examiner. Tony asked if you mind staying on? He needs to put this one to bed, Lorry, and he thinks you can help him do that. Those were his words."

At home, that's where I want to be, with my music, waiting for Lanie to call me. But it's for Tony...

"Yeah, that's fine," is all I can think to say.

"Anything you need?"

"Yes, a cup of tea would be smashing. And something to eat, a sandwich, or something. Please."

It's probably a waste of time, but I'm hoping the food will quell the aching in my gut.

She goes to leave. "I'll get someone to pick something up. Any preference on the sandwich?"

"No, anything, thanks. Oh, and when they go..."

"Yep?"

"Can they take me to the door so I can have a cigarette? And then pick me up on the way back?"

"It's bad for you."

"It helps me think. And I need to think." The last bit is said quietly to myself.

"Are you sure you're okay?" she asks again, before leaving the room.

Again, I nod that I am, and keep quiet.

*****

It must be about five, maybe half past four. I've lost all track of time.

This would normally be the beginnings of rush hour with foot traffic gusting by, road traffic snarled up in the arteries that lead away from the heart of the city, all clogged at the points they merge and cross the river.

This is as quiet as I've ever not seen the place.

The distinctive chug of an occasional cab or bus streams through my audible range. Drivers can't believe they're doing thirty at this hour. It's usually quicker to get out and walk. July seventh wasn't like this. On that occasion the transport system shut down, so people were stranded. Today, it kept going, so people evacuated.

I pull out a second cigarette. The first still sits in my lungs, but it isn't enough. A swig of hot tea snuggles in my stomach. It's difficult gauging the distance to the flame. Sometimes I end up lighting it part way down. The end falls off if I do that. Aside from the obvious danger, it has a habit of ruining my clothes.

The tea and nicotine focus my mind. Tony needs my help. Ah, perhaps he doesn't, but he says he does. He makes me feel useful, but Lanie has to be my priority.

She's right, I can't argue with a word she said to me. It was always Kate who took care of that. Sometimes I'd feel like an outsider in my own home, the male sitting at the acute end of a triangle. Strangely, though, I liked things like that.

Yet, for all the upset I've caused her, I feel more alive today than at any time since Kate died. I need this, and perhaps it'll prove to be the catalyst that will free me up, and allow me to move on and get on with my life. And not just my life, but Lanie's life, as well. For the first time in years, I'll actually have things to tell her on the phone later, other than the standard, 'nothing, I just sat in my chair listening to records'.

And because I'll have done things, I'll be more open to asking her what she's been up to, more interested in hearing about her life. The truth is, I haven't wanted to hear about anyone else's life, because all it ever did was remind me of what I was missing.

So I'll help. I'll stay and assist Tony, and do what I can by doing what I do. But I must remember to ring Lanie if it gets past seven o'clock.

Things simply don't stack up. I keep asking myself the same question. Why did they kill the guy?

Because he was crumbling. Fine, but they would only be concerned about that if they were afraid of being turned in, afraid of being caught. And they aren't.

Even the most stupid of villains knows the stats about being on camera in London every ten seconds, or whatever it is. They know they must have been identified already. Yet they're strolling around London like they have the freedom of the city, marching through Euston as bold as brass.

Am I wrong? Could there be another bomb? And could they be looking to use it at Wembley tonight?

Instinct tells me I'm right. Besides, it's bloody difficult to get anything in to a football match in this day and age; there are much softer targets.

The point is, these guys aren't concerned about being caught. If they were, they'd have gone to ground and waited it out. Or, indeed, made more of an effort to conceal themselves in the first place.

Who does that? Jihadists. We're all aware of the way that goes. The posturing for the camera and the public executions and god-fearing messages shown over the internet.

Jihadists do it because they know they're going to die, thus, it's of no consequence. By the time it's viewed, they're in a million pieces and settling down to an evening in with a bunch of virgins.

Again, my gut tells me this isn't Jihad. It has nothing to do with religious extremism, and the description of the perpetrators bears that out.

"Lorry?" Colin the IT guy makes me jump. I didn't hear him approach in his sensible shoes.

"Yes?"

"Sandwiches are here." I hear a rustle of paper and plastic.

Dropping my cigarette butt and failing to locate it with my foot, I allow myself to be led back in.

"Cheese and tomato or ham and tomato?" Sofa wants to know.

"Whichever you prefer least," I tell her.

"Must admit, I'm not too inspired either. Okay, let's do this the other way. Brown or white?"

"Errr, white!"

I listen to the tearing of plastic, and the grate of dried out bread being slid on to a paper plate.

"There's more tea on the table in front of you, and if you hold out your left hand, I'll place the plate on it."

I do as I'm told. She'd make a good Home Help. I don't tell her that.

Judging by the smell of the cheese below my nose, I'd say a Cheddar, quite mature. My tastebuds confirm it. Sophie must hear my stomach grumble in anticipation, but she ignores it.

Her jaw clicks almost imperceptibly every time she takes a bite, a little pop from the hinge. Kate would make the same noise. I attributed it to her having had her wisdom teeth surgically removed, and wonder if Sofa had a similar operation?

Kate always did it, or she did for the sixteen and a half years I knew her. At first, I quite liked the little click. But it grew to annoy me, on nights when I was tired or ill, or just in an inexplicably bad mood. We all have days like that.

Now? Now I'd give anything to hear Kate click her jaw one more time. That's how it goes. The things that once annoyed us are the things we miss the most.

"Sofe, you there?" Tony's voice shatters my thoughts, coming through the speaker because she's eating.

"Yeah, what you got?"

"The lovely coppers up this way just picked up three young men that I very much want to have a little chat with."

"Hey-hey, good news. What next?"

"An armoured van will bring them to Location Zero-Four-Two, and we'll meet you there. Bring Stevie Wonder with you..."

"He's sitting here, on speaker."

"Didn't doubt it. Nice work, Lorry my man! Nice work. Now, get your arse over here and let's put this to bed."

"Can I finish my sandwich and cup of tea first?" I ask, because it's important to me.

"He wants to know if he can..."

"I heard. Eat, drink and be merry. You're nearer the location than us, anyway, so take your time. See you there in - what? - thirty minutes?"

"Sounds good." Sofa's jaw clicks again as she gets ready to take another chunk of sandwich.

Tony stops her. "You heard from Marc on the stabbing? I need the details of that before I get in a room with these bastards."

"No, I'll chase him."

"Okay, thanks. Get back to me."

"Marc, you copy?"

There's a pause. I carry on eating. The bread's too dry so I have to swill it down with tea. It must have sat there all afternoon on account of the mass evacuation, not enough trade to turn the stock over and not enough demand to warrant making more. The staff probably scarpered, anyway.

"Copy, Sofe."

"Tony has the bastards."

"The bombers?"

"Yes."

"Really? Okay, I wasn't expecting to hear that."

"How do you mean?" Sophie asks, a note of non-comprehension in her voice.

"Oh, nothing. It just means Lorry was bloody right, I suppose. We'll never get rid of him now."

I act like I'm deaf.

"What have you got on the body?" Sophie asks a bit too quickly.

"I'm glad you asked. It's our man alright, no question. Doctor on the scene was non-committal, as always, but reckons it might be a professional hit. Throat cut from behind as the victim knelt on the floor. One cut, straight across and through the carotid and the windpipe. A toss up whether he bled to death or the lack of oxygen got him first."

I shudder at the description and stop chewing.

"Weapon?"

"Knife. Flat blade. Very sharp. Like a craft knife or a box-cutter. The killer even had the sense to lever the knife up and down and open the wound up. Less chance of it knitting back together that way."

"Charming."

"Right-handed, by the way, our killer," Marc adds.

"Ask him about the scene," I whisper, "anything to nail it to our suspects?"

She does.

Marc reports, "the tide had come in by the time he was spotted. Something about a seven metre high at about half three in the afternoon? Anyway, it lapped away all the footprints and anything else. Until the Coroner has had a good look, we won't know anything on that, and that'll probably be tomorrow morning now."

He disconnects, and Sofa goes back to eating. A bit less enthusiastically.

Professional hit? None of it adds up. This is as far away from professional as you can get - the Mary, Mungo and Midge of the international terror network - they couldn't pull that off.

I go back to the stodgy stale white bread. I should have taken the brown.

"Oh shitting ruddy nora!" I exclaim, dropping what feels like a slice of tomato on my lap in my excitement.

"What, what, what?" calls Sofa, sounding a bit concerned, "did you burn yourself?"

"No. What?"

"Look, Marc didn't mean anything by what he said about you..."

"No, I don't care about that. I think I know what this is all about!"

I cram the last of the sandwich in my mouth, gulp my tea in with it and swill the lot together to make it palatable. As I stand up, I hear the slice of tomato splat on the floor. Like a red rose, I think. Like the red rose on the Blackburn Rovers badge. Like the red rose synonymous with England.

"Ready when you are!" I announce brightly, and rub my hands in excitement.

Well, that and to get rid of the crumbs.

10.

Another advantage to being blind is that I don't need to be blindfolded or bundled in to the boot of a car with a blanket over my head when being taken to secret locations.

That said, there are enough indicators to tell me we're probably somewhere out near Notting Hill, having come up Park Lane and Bayswater Road.

It makes sense, as it's in the direction of Wembley, nearer us than him, as he said on the radio, and has Wormwood Scrubs just up the road. And the Scrubs is probably just about as secure a prison as will be required for this lot. Nothing less, certainly.

The radio in Sophie's car told me that the threat level is now reduced to Level Five, Amber Low. No direct threat detected, but be vigilant as information received hints at activity.

The truth is, the United Kingdom is almost always on a Level Five Amber Low status. Sometimes it drops to Four, but only when the weather intervenes and stops anyone doing anything. The country grinds to a halt, terrorism included.

Tony and Adam greet us, the former helps me out of the passenger seat as he moans in my ear about his car having been cleaned but still smelling of sick, possibly needing new carpet and how he doesn't have time for this crap.

"Right, what we got?" I ask, mostly because I want to change the subject. But I'm also keen to get on and make sure I'm home for Lanie's call.

"We have the three guys we want in three holding cells inside. Mutism has set in. Not a word from any of them since they were picked up; just a confident silence and a cocky smirk on their faces," Tony reports.

"Have you spoken to them?" Sophie asks.

"Not yet. The police brought them here in three vans. We thought it best to keep them apart and make them sweat a bit on what the others might be telling us. As you'd expect, there were plenty of secure prisoner transfer vans at the football. According to the officers who picked them up, none of them batted an eyelid. One even said, it almost seemed like they expected it," Tony answers.

"Have you seen them?" I ask him.

"Yep. I stuck my head in the cells just to confirm they are who they're supposed to be. That's it. We only got here a few minutes ago."

Tony steers me into a lift where there's an impatient clicking of buttons. My body was braced for an upward journey, but the lift descends. It throws me very slightly off-balance as I shuffle my right foot to steady myself. He must feel the counter movement through my arm.

"You okay?"

"Fine, thanks. Just expected to be going up. When we get there..."

"Yeah?"

"Get the big guy first. The leader. I need you and Adam to question him, one at a time."

"Good cop, bad cop?" Adam asks.

"Similar. Black cop, white cop," I tell him, and smile. "You are black aren't you, Adam?"

He chuckles.

"As white as the driven snow," Tony chimes in. They obviously made up after the earlier altercation.

"What are you thinking, Lorry?" Sophie pipes up.

"You'll see. It's best I keep an element of the impromptu about it, if you don't mind? I don't want anyone being too rehearsed. Can I get rigged up so we can communicate when you're in the room?"

"Already being sorted. Two way mic."

"And I need Sofa to be my eyes. Is that okay?"

"Not a problem. I'm trusting you, Lorry, you get to run this show. Okay?" Tony tells me seriously.

I'm steered to a seat. Plastic is inserted in my ear, hooked up over the top to hold it in place. An arm curves down the back of my lobe and a bar runs to the corner of my mouth. The mic.

"Lorry, you hear me okay?" Tony asks.

"Loud and clear," I say, reaching up and jiggling the earpiece till it sits more comfortably. "Adam? Are you in the loop?"

"Getting both of you. How am I sounding?"

"Less whingy than your boss. Do we have a uniformed officer to be in the room with you two?"

"We do."

"What ethnicity is it?"

"He. It's a he, Lorry. What ethnicity are you?" Tony calls to someone. The it.

"English. Well, my father was Welsh..."

"I don't suppose we can switch him for someone Asian, can we? Indian or Pakistani, ideally. Or anybody of colour?"

"It'll take a while. He's briefed, checked and sworn in. Secrets Act, and all that."

"Ah, fuck it. He'll do. Just tell him to stay still and say nothing."

"He already knows because he's standing three feet away from you."

"Oh, right. Nothing personal..." I say in what I assume to be his general direction.

"It's fine. Don't worry about it."

"...just can't stand the Welsh," I lie. My Nan was from south Wales.

There's more laughter, a nervous outlet. I'm doing it deliberately, easing the tension out of everyone. If my theory's right, a more relaxed attitude will get what we need and force the guy to react to the apparent lack of him being taken seriously, a perceived lack of respect.

"Let's do it," I say, "Tony first, with Dai the Dragon. Act nonchalant, act like you can't really be bothered to be here, okay?"

A door opening and closing signals that it's time to clear my mind and project the images.

"What do you see, Sofe?"

"Cocky guy. Big. Nearly as big as Tony, but twenty-plus years younger. Mixed race, I'd guess. Shaven-headed, a smirk on his face, like someone who knows he's holding the winning hand. But he's not holding anything, because his hands are cuffed behind his back, threaded through the chair. He's slouched in his seat. Just a quick glance up at Tony, then staring straight ahead again."

"If you saw him on a cold dark night in a quiet street, what would you think?"

"I'd think he was up to no good."

"Why?"

"Just how he looks. I don't know. The shaved-head, the tattoo..."

"Tattoo? What tattoo?"

"On his neck, at the back. I can't see without him turning his head."

I hear Tony introduce himself and the Welsh officer, a tired tone in his voice. Good man, he makes it sound like he's been on duty all day and really can't be arsed with all this, makes it sound like someone threw up in his new car, and that he had a falling out with one of his closest work colleagues and ended up grabbing him by the throat.

I hope he's acting.

He's going through the preliminaries, explaining about the conversation being recorded, letting the guy know his rights. There's no response.

"Check the tattoo on the back of his neck. What is it?" I ask in a whisper through the microphone. I don't know why I whispered.

Tony restates the bit about legal representation. His voice has motion, so I assume he's pacing the room so he can see the inscription.

It's met with more silence.

"Do you know why you're here?" he asks him.

He waits for a reply that doesn't come.

"Do you know your own name?"

Nothing.

"Or where you live? How about that one? Do - You - Know - Where - You - Live?"

"Did he react in any way?" I ask Sophie.

"Maybe a slightly broader smirk. That's it."

"Tony, tell him his mate rang us from Waterloo and took all the credit for the bomb. Make it sound like you think the guy who rang us is the leader."

He does as I ask. Sophie sees no reaction again, just a broader smirk. She says, "it's like he's one step ahead of us. He knows we're bullshitting."

"Tony, come out now. Adam, you're in. Same questions, but pretend you're a man who doesn't usually bother to get his hands dirty on the black prisoners. Play up that public schoolboy accent you try to mask, please."

"Ben," Tony says after leaving the room, "the tattoo says Ben."

"Do you think that's his name?" someone asks reasonably. "How's it written?"

"Swirly letters, like a gothic script. And all upper-case."

"Like an acronym?"

"Exactly. Yes, like B.E.N."

I add the detail to my mental picture, and keep layering it up, imagining the stark strip-lights, no external windows, a mirrored one-way pane on one side of which I'm located, Dai the Dragon stood in a corner, hands loosely folded. Adam in his sharp suit and leather brogues, with his obvious Englishness, his inherent superiority.

Adam introduces himself, and uses his middle name so he sounds more grandiose, more English lower aristocracy, a friend of the Princes and the senior Tories. Perfect.

"Sofe, was his initial reaction any different to when Tony entered?"

"Not really. Maybe he looked up for a second longer before going back to the forward stare. He looks like he's about to bark out his Name, Rank and Number."

"Could I have your name, sir?" Adam asks, like a butler might a guest visiting a country house.

Nothing.

"Okay, I'll assume you can't quite recall, and move on. Do you know why you've been brought here this evening?"

Adam's very good, he's even starting to annoy me. The condescension's perfect.

And again, I hope he's acting.

"No? Never mind, we can come back to that a little later on."

I interject in the pause, "Adam, make a snidey comment about him being from overseas."

"It must be difficult for you people, I imagine, coming from overseas and perhaps not being up to speed with the legal process over here."

"Ooooh, now there's a reaction. Anger. Real anger," Sophie tells me urgently.

Fanfare, got the bastard.

"Ask him the other question, Adam, the one about where he's from. Generally, I mean, and do a similar thing."

"Where are you from originally, anyway? Can you remember?"

"Adam, keep going, push him..."

"Help me understand. You blew up innocent people in the name of something...what happened? Another idiot who came here thinking the streets of London were paved with gold? Don't they have Google maps where you come from...?"

"He's getting really wound up," Tony tells me, "his eyes are wild, neck bulging, fists flexing..."

"Keep going, Adam, almost there," I snap out.

Adam scoffs before calmly stating, "they probably don't even have electricity where you're from."

"Fuck you, you piece of shit," the big lad suddenly spits, a London accent very prevalent.

"Adam say exactly what I say, :well, you seem to have picked up the local vernacular very well in the time you've been here.'"

Adam delivers it perfectly. The guy goes ballistic.

I hear the table scrape and crash as it must flip over, an ugly chime as the metal chair swings round and hammers against a wall or the table itself, and the slap of shoes on floor as the prisoner is secured.

"Tony! Get in now," I urgently beat out, "and pick a fight with Adam over the comments. Get Adam out of there."

There's a pause.

"Tony, now! Do it. Act like Adam's your peer. Now you play the good cop role, the good black cop role."

"What the fuck's going on in here...?" he screams as he re-enters the room.

"Be his friend, Tony, and he'll tell you as much as you need to know. And let him know he'll get the credit for his political statement today. Make him feel like the Nationalist hero he wants to be, that you understand why he targeted the German football fans to prove his Englishness. Let him know you understand what it's like being a non-white guy in a white world, and how hard it is to be accepted as an equal. Let him know all of that."

11.

The opposite of religious extremism; that was the thought I had in my head most of this afternoon.

But it's impossible to find an antonym for a word or phrase before you understand the meaning of the 'nym'. So I defined religious extremism. Why does it exist?

Two primary reasons. To fight against a religion or system that threatens it, and to further spread itself over new territories or populaces.

Terror is the tactic of choice for all religious extremist organisations. Because of that, we've become blinkered in how we look at all acts of terror. When Anders Breivik killed seventy-seven people in Norway, I listened to the news breaking on the radio and heard the pundits talking about Muslim Extremists while the bullets were still flying. He was the opposite of that. He wanted to kill the liberal-minded who he saw as responsible for allowing immigrants to enter his country.

This wasn't exactly like that, but it shares commonalities. It's all about acceptance, and feeling disenfranchised from something. Namely, the country in which they all reside, the country of their birth.

A simple trawl of the internet showed B.E.N. to stand for Black English Nationalists, a small site with about four thousand hits. It contains the usual stuff about immigration and European unity being bad. It offers a different slant, though, stating how unfair it is that Eastern Europeans can walk in any time they like and take jobs etcetera, yet, the black immigrants from previous decades had to fight hard to come here and establish themselves. And they had to do that, despite coming from, in the main part, British territories abroad. They were part of the Empire, as English as the tea and two sugars that came here right alongside them from India and Ceylon and the Caribbean.

So what is the opposite of religious extremism? Given the definition, it must therefore be: to fight for a religion or system that they wish to join, or to be absorbed by a territory or populace in some way.

Therein lies what all this has been about. A bomb in a pub, one dead barman. and a dozen or more injured German football fans, three of them seriously. Then there's a young man from Crewe who moved to London with his parents and two sisters three years ago. He had his throat cut on the sand on the south bank of the Thames.

All in the name of acceptance.

Though, to be honest, I'm not buying any of that. Okay, so I'll buy some of it, but there's no way that fool and his two pals spending the night in HM's Custody killed the kid on the sand. No way. And that in spite of the B.E.N. idiot's insistence that he did. Not a hope in hell.

And I doubt the four of them had the nous to assemble a bomb that would actually work, despite what they found on the internet.

They had help, very sophisticated help. Sophisticated enough to ensure things didn't look too sophisticated, and that help has promised them deliverance.

And that worries me.

But I kept quiet in front of the team. Evaluate and advise, that's the role of TERA. The investigation and prosecution? That's for the police and the Crown Prosecution Service. Besides, I need to get home.

"It's not the end, you know..." I start to privately say to Tony as he accompanies me to Sophie's car.

"I know," he cuts me off, his grip tightening on my elbow, "but save that for now. Time to go home for the day. Start again tomorrow."

"But you do know none of this rings true?" I attempt to clarify.

"Yes. I know that. But, to put it in terms you'll be able to easily relate to, sometimes you have to buy the singles before they release the album. If you take my meaning...?"

"Nice work, Lorry," Adam interrupts, and I think he means it.

"Same to you, Adam. The accent was superb. It was the 'you people 'line that first broke him, I think."

I count the laughs, my own not a part of it.

"Look, ah, before you go, Lorry..." Adam awkwardly begins, "I just want to say sorry to all of you for the way I've been today. The truth is, I'm a bit...my mind isn't quite where it should be at the moment. My wife, she's pregnant, and we already lost a couple, miscarriages, so..."

"Oh, Adam, why didn't you say something?" Sophie says gently, "is she okay?"

'Yeah, yeah, fine, and we're past the point that it happened before, so...I didn't want to say anything till then, didn't want to tempt fate, and the doctors are really monitoring everything this time. It's just...well, it's there, in my head all the time, you know?"

"It's not a problem, Adam, apology unnecessary. We got the right result. And congratulations," I say, because I mean it.

"Like you said, we got a result, Lorry, you can cheer up now, you miserable tosser," Tony jibes, as he continues walking me to Sophie's car.

His lowers the volume and asks, confidentially, "Lanie?"

I shrug.

"I spoke with her before you did, remember? She's pissed off, Lorry. You should have told her what you were doing. I'm not here to wipe your arse for you. It's not my job."

I should feel good right now, I know I should. But I don't, so I say nothing.

"She's frightened of losing you, that's all this is. Don't take it so hard. I mean, I'd love for her to lose you..."

I raise my chin.

"...that way I could ask her out."

Bastard.

*****

84

"How do you do it, Lorry?" Sofa asks as she drives me back home.

"What's that, Sofe?"

"How do you piece it all together? How do you do what you did today? I can see you now, deep in thought, processing something."

I blow out a breath. "The honest answer is, I don't know. I guess it's what some people call intuition. Except I don't think intuition exists."

"Women's intuition, and all that?"

"Yeah, that's how it gets dressed up. The truth is, and don't take this the wrong way, women are less aware than men as a general rule. Obviously there are exceptions, but my experience tells me that men are more tuned in to what's going on around them. Women pick up all the details, but more naturally, less systematically. So, for intuition, read unperceived-perception."

"So, people perceive things they don't know they're perceiving?"

"Exactly. Men set out to notice, because we have a desire to solve, whereas women do it more naturally. One night, about five and a half years ago, my wife, Kate, and I had been out to dinner. Kate offered to drive, so I could have a few drinks and relax.

"She was driving back along a route she'd driven hundreds, if not thousands, of times. Near the house was a left turn on to a dual-carriageway. And about fifty yards along, she needed to make a right turn across the carriageway to the road our house is on.

"The trick, always, was to wait for a gap across both lanes so that you had time to get over to the right lane and make the next turn in fifty yards. If you slipped out into the near lane, you'd get boxed in and have a two mile detour to get back. You follow?"

"Yep, I see what you're saying. Go on."

"Kate looked right to see the oncoming traffic, and being late at night on a weekday, it was quiet. So she pulled out. But she pulled into the near lane, not the far one. She did something that she would never have done normally. Something that I'd never have done. We always pull out into the far lane for the turning.

"But as we turned, a car came speeding by at about seventy miles-per-hour. It was going the wrong way down the dual-carriageway, and being unaware it was going the wrong way, it was sticking to its left-hand lane, as though it were on a two-way normal road."

"So, if she'd have pulled out as she normally would, it would have hit you?"

"Without question. And the speed it was going, it would have caused some serious damage. I'm not sure we'd have got out of that alive."

The statement containing Kate and mortality stalls me for a second.

"So why did she break the habit of a lifetime?" Sophie prompts.

"That's the question. We drove the rest of the way home in silence. Kate was shaken up by it, she knew how close we'd just come. She was trembling when I poured her a drink at home. As was I. I remember watching the bubbles being agitated in the glass as I handed it to her.

"After a drink or two, Kate relaxed. She started reasoning out in her head what had happened. Intuition was her first port of call, naturally enough, but then she moved on to an inexplicable sixth sense, all assuming that's not the same thing as intuition. Either way, I don't agree with either of those as concepts.

"Her final docking point was to look to the more supernatural. By her third glass of bubbly, she was fairly sure it was her dead grandmother looking out for her, like some guardian angel. It was her grandmother who shaped her behaviour that night, as she reached out and over-rotated the steering wheel. It must have been, right?

"I didn't have the heart to tell her that it couldn't have been, as her gran never learnt to drive. And I let her carry on thinking that. If it gave her some comfort, and helped her deal with a scary situation, then there was no harm in it."

"But what do you put it down to," she asks, "as I'm pretty certain you don't believe in ghosts?"

"Unperceived-perception. Our brains and instincts operate subconsciously much more efficiently than they do consciously. As soon as we involve consciousness, we start evaluating, and that involves thinking. Thinking stops us acting. It actually serves to stop us perceiving things, as we get wrapped up in what we've already logged, rather than what's going on.

"What do I think happened that night? I believe Kate perceived that car coming. And we can only perceive through the senses we have available to us. Taste wouldn't be a factor. Nor smell. But she may have seen the headlights casting an irregular shadow pattern, forcing them slightly against the natural order, or catching sight of a glint on a road sign. She may have heard it, unknowingly processed the sound of a car engine at seventy miles-per-hour bearing down from the wrong direction. Or she may have felt the vibration, sensed the energy of a car moving at that velocity. More likely, it was a combination of all three sight. Unbeknown to Kate, she picked up all those signals, and her brain processed them and forced her hand.

"Does that make sense?"

"Yes, it does," Sophie tells me quietly, "but I still prefer the ghost of her dead grandmother version. It's more romantic."

"Ha! Me too. Well, that's how I do what I do, to answer your question. I don't allow things such as romance to get in the way. I switch myself on - or tune myself in - to the data available."

"Could you always do this, or is it just since you lost your sight?" she asks, sounding genuinely intrigued.

"I could always do it, but not as well. Being able to see somehow clouded the issue. There were too many other stimuli, I think. It's certainly beneficial to start with nothingness. That way, I only add the pieces I need, and don't get sidetracked. Also, I'm much more aware of my other senses now. The brain has a way of compensating, and the remaining senses become heightened. For instance, if I could see I probably wouldn't have got the Surbiton and Airport connection today. Sounds are more indelibly logged in my brain, and meter and rhyme play a part in that process.

"I'm not sure that answers the question, Sophie, but it's as good as I can get. Throw in that I have an uncanny ear for accents, and that's about it. The accent thing was acquired driving a black cab around London for years. It started as a way of killing the time, playing a bit of a game. I'd try to guess where people were from, and then start a banal conversation to see if I was right or not. In time, in a cab in London, you get to know every accent there is. Even down to the little nuances in the United Kingdom, as well as more generally overseas."

Yet, for all that, I neglected to communicate with my daughter. For all the perceptive this, and unperceived that, I didn't pick up on her pain.

"Here we are," she says, pulling on the handbrake. And then, "I wish you'd come for a drink with us."

"I need...there's stuff I need to do."

"Family stuff?"

"Yes, family stuff. Sorry."

"Hey, don't apologise. Family should always come first."

"Thank you. Thanks for bringing me home."

"We all need a guardian angel," she smiles out loud, as she delivers me at my front door.

"Hey, Sophie," I say, as she walks back to her car.

"Yes, Lorry?"

"For all that crap I just told you, it still took a sandwich to tie it all together."

"A sandwich?"

"Yes, the brown or white bread thing. That was the clincher."

"Good night, Lorry."

I try the door handle before rummaging for my keys. The door swings open. I forgot to lock it again. Lanie would roast me if she knew.

12.

"How was your week, Lorry, anything exciting happen?" Dr. Haversham asks.

"Not really, same old same old," I answer breezily.

"So that wasn't you I saw on the television, being bundled into an unmarked police car on Wednesday?"

He's got me there. I knew he'd rung for a reason. "Oh, that, it was just a misunderstanding."

"Even so. I find myself wondering why you didn't feel you could tell me about it; about being outside, for starters, but also about what must have been an incredibly eventful day?"

Every sentence he utters has a question mark at the end. His voice must be stuck in that raised-at-the-end inflected way.

Annoyingly, though, I quite like the guy. Still, I need a way out of this conversation.

"Ah, the thing is, David, I'm sworn to secrecy. It's a bit like the doctor-patient thing..."

I've got him there. He can't deny that, or he'll be admitting to not adhering to the doctor-patient thing, and where will he be without trust? It'll finish him.

"Hmm, that doctor-patient thing, as you call it, is why I'm the one person you can tell, because I couldn't divulge it, you see?"

Opportunity knocks, as I know I could go all sulky on his asking if I see, and gain the moral high-ground by using my disability to my advantage. But I quite like the guy.

"I do, yes, but there really is very little to tell. I do a bit of consulting now and again, and this was a now and again time. You should be pleased, it got me out the house."

He pauses. He does that. I never know if it's for his benefit or mine. He always makes me feel like it's for my benefit.

Eventually he says, "I am, but why didn't you tell me that when I first asked?"

I know where he's going with this. It's similar to what Lanie was saying on Wednesday, how I don't share things. And I know that I do that because I have to compartmentalise everything so that I can control it.

With that in mind, I tell the good doctor, "it really is sensitive top secret stuff, David. Would you like me to ask the government if it's okay to share it with you?"

This always works, as I begin matching question with question. He'll back off now.

"No, no, not necessary, but I wasn't really interested in the nitty-gritty, just how it all made you feel?"

"It didn't make me feel anything. Should it have?"

"You tell me. I imagine being seemingly arrested on national television on terrorism charges might have invoked some emotional response, particularly for such a violent crime?"

"But I didn't see that, did I?"

"No, you didn't, but did you feel it?"

"Well, have you considered that the bullet took two of my senses that night, David, my ability to see, as well as my ability to feel?" I snap.

"You're angry."

I don't reply. It wasn't a question.

"So, you feel anger? Isn't that an emotion, and aren't you feeling it?" he presses on in his calm voice.

I try to hold back a chuckle, but it pops out of my nose, "touché."

"Indeed. Can we pick this up next week?"

"Do I have a choice?"

"Everybody has choices, Lorry, do you feel like you don't?"

"Next week, then."

"Oh, let's do it at my office."

"But...how...?"

He's already hung up. The slippery little sod. How am I supposed to get to his office? I could ask Tony or Sophie for a lift.

In the three days since Sophie drove me home, I've thought about her a lot.

It was an easy drive to my house, and I could direct her by memory once we got close. She sensed I was a bad passenger, and began announcing the bends and turns. She allowed my body and mind to prepare for the forces.

She probably didn't want me to be sick in her car.

But she cared enough to do all that, and it set my mind to wondering. I wonder what she looks like? In my head I have an image based on nothing but blind assumption, that she has short blonde hair, and quite a boyish physique. Not in an unhealthy way, but one of those girls who are good at sport and can hold their own with the boys. I know she's about five-seven, judged on the angle her voice reaches me, and I don't imagine she wears heels to work. It isn't that kind of a job. Nor is it a job that warrants a lot of make-up. And she doesn't need it. She'll have good skin, kept fresh by exercise and a cheery disposition.

Perhaps a bit of feathering on the blonde hair, curling round in front of her ears and accentuating her high cheek bones. Not a perfect smile, on account of her teeth not being perfectly straight, tilted out of sync by the intrusive wisdom teeth, the removal of which makes her jaw click. But a very endearing smile that transcends to her eyes and comes out in a sparkle. A green sparkle, like an emerald, like a peridot. That's how I imagine her eyes to be.

She won't be flat-chested, but not exactly a buxom wench. And she'll look taller than she is, given her slim hips and long legs in proportion to her body.

Am I even close? I have no idea. And I've built a couple of details from Kate in the mix. I can't fathom being attracted to a woman who didn't look something like Kate. It wouldn't be right if I went for the polar opposite. Disloyal, even.

I don't even know what I look like any more.

All I can base my appearance on is how I looked the last time I could see myself. And seeing how I've been shot in the head since then, spent months in hospital and most vitally, lost my wife, I dare say I might look a bit different.

Rising from my chair, I pace out the steps to the cabinet housing the record deck and amp. I stop when my toes touch the wooden base, and lift the record from the turntable; both sides played.

I stash it back in the shelving unit that runs the length of the wall on my right. Extracting the next LP in sequence, I run my fingers over the strip of plastic at the top left corner, feeling the raised letters with my finger tips to confirm it is what it should be, that I didn't mis-file the last time I played it.

It isn't braille, I haven't learnt braille. I haven't really tried.

Instead, Tony showed up one Saturday as excited as I'd ever seen him. Seven pounds fifty, plus postage, was the only sense I could get out of him.

He'd managed to track down a Dymo machine that added raised letters to tape strips, so he could label my records. I'd been moaning about not being able to find things I wanted to listen to.

In the two and a half years since then, he's sat punching out labels most weeks, usually processing a minimum of thirty-five per week. He's quite fast now, and can get that number done in about an hour and fifteen minutes.

I buy between three and ten new records every week, so we're slowly making an impression. Pardon the pun.

He's up to the letter F now.

Effing Tony.

My fingertip traces over the letters. 'Beatles. Revolver. UK. Mono.'

Correct; the one after Rubber Soul. This is what I do on this day, the day Kate was killed. The day I lost my sight. Four years ago today.

All original Beatles UK studio albums in order are played, until I get to 1968. I don't go beyond 'The White Album'. Nor do I play American issues, as the early ones are all over the place, and 'Magical Mystery Tour 'is omitted as it was a USA only release until 1976.

Nine albums in total. Ten if you consider 'The White Album 'is a double. It takes about four and a half hours to play everything up to and including 'Sgt. Pepper's'. After that I repeat play 'The White Album 'until I have to sleep.

It's what I do on this day.

Am I moving on? Not given this behaviour, clearly. But my thoughts about Sofa are surely a good sign, a sign that I'm finally thinking about a new relationship. Its self-delusory nature aside, I am at least thinking about it.

The Health Service sends me a woman every week. Not like that.

That would be an unforgivable waste of tax-payer money. But rather to clean the place and fetch groceries and other household things I need. Her name's Janet, but we don't converse much beyond the basic pleasantries politeness demands.

My point is, a man came with her a few weeks back, a Home Help Assessment Something. I didn't like him. Instead of being honest about Government cuts, and the need to tighten belts, he lectured me in a very slow meticulous way about having not made any effort to embrace my ailment.

Embrace my ailment! That's what the cock said.

I told him I couldn't embrace my ailment because I couldn't fucking see it. I told him that in the same slow meticulous tone he used on me.

That resulted in him warning me, that if I didn't begin to show signs of moving forward with my disability, they'd have no choice but to review my case. It was, apparently, about time I started helping myself.

An upshot of all of this was my weekly sessions with David the Emotional Therapist.

In fairness, he didn't say disability, they aren't allowed to. Less-abled; that's the phrase they have to use now.

But he did raise a valid point, a question I've been asking myself as much as it's been asked of me by Lanie, David and Tony: Have I accepted my blindness? And not just my blindness, but everything that happened four years ago?

And honestly, no, I don't think I have.

That's why I try to picture Sophie in my mind. That's why I'm thinking about a relationship. But it puzzles me why her looks are still important to me? Why do I care what she looks like when I can't see her? Is it born of a desire to have others be able to see that I'm with someone physically attractive?

'Revolver 'kicks off, so I crank up the volume.

'Taxman'. I try to keep the albums with the A-side facing the front, but it's hard. This time I got lucky, and landed on the first side first.

Prior to this day four years ago, I'd always considered myself lucky, generally speaking. We were lucky to end up living here, for example. It suited us as a family, and it suits me now I'm alone.

We opted for land and privacy over house, location over floor plan. Three bedrooms were enough. One for us, one for Lanie, and the third, a small room just about big enough for a single bed, is now annexed as additional record storage space. The letters T-Z are held there.

Lanie said as much in our long phone chat this week. She said how she loved it here, growing up. Followed by a teasing gripe about not being allowed to have a horse. I don't remember the horse being a big issue, but it clearly was.

She should have had a horse. I wish I'd made that possible.

I turn the volume dial even higher so that I can feel the sound waves from the speakers pulse against my jeans as they shift the air and pass through my body, energising me.

I turn away and count the paces to the opening where a door used to swing open and shut. Kate always loved the openness of this house. She'd like it even more now.

Five long paces get measured out, like a referee setting the distance a wall should retreat from a free-kick. A right turn is followed by three paces before executing a left wheel. I shuffle forward, stopping when my toes hit the skirting beneath the kitchen unit. I shuffle back a touch, reach up and lean back to allow the cupboard door to swing open in front of my head, feeling the draught run her fingers through my hair.

My hair.

Is it grey now or still mostly fair? Salt and pepper.

I fumble through the cupboard's contents, feeling and exploring. Janet doesn't know, and I don't tell her, but I wish she'd put things in the same place all the time. Consistency of placement makes my life so much simpler.

Feeling what I want, I lift down a stack of mis-matched bowls, pick up all but the bottom one and put them back. Okay, step one achieved.

Step two. Find the whisk.

Taking a half pace in reverse, I stoop and open the drawer before rummaging around until I feel the curved metal strands that constitute it. I lift it clear and stand up, walking forward the half pace I relented.

I crack my head on the corner of the cupboard door. A flurry of expletives leave my mouth. A teardrop runs down my cheek, pain and frustration squeezing it out of my eye. I lift my hand to the spot, take the hand away and rub my fingers on my palm. No moisture. No blood, therefore, just a small mound already forming.

I close the fucking cupboard door, and think that I should have all the fucking cupboard doors taken off as well.

Two side strides to the left enable me to reach out and locate the spout over the sink. Tracing it down its long swan neck, I go right and find the tap. Flipping it towards me, I hear the water come out. Cold water. A different sound to the hot, less air in the system, or something.

To the immediate right of the tap, my hand settles on kitchen roll so I tug the loose edge. I feel it unwind before ripping along the perforation. I hold the wad of paper towel under the tap and feel it get heavy in my hand, the water slipping between my fingers. Leaning forward so my head's over the sink, I place the cold compress on the throbbing lump on the side of my forehead.

I turn the tap off after I've splashed water on my face. The pain's still there, but not so sharp. A left turn and I walk on, using small paces now, more shuffles. I've lost my vision of the room. My knee hits the metal bin with a light clang, so I find the foot-lever with my shoe and depress it. The lid comes up and taps the wall, enabling me to drop the paper towel in the bin and close the lid.

Okay, so far so good. Now, where the fuck did Janet put the eggs this time? In or out of the fridge?

I find a dozen in the egg rack in the fridge door, and examine the package with my fingers to ascertain where the bobbles are, the bobbles that stop it opening on one side. Never trust egg packaging.

Setting things up with my hands, I take an egg out and tap it on the edge of the glass bowl, but not firmly enough. Too firm now and it'll shatter and drop shell fragments in the mix, the same result likely if I try and lever it open with my fingers. Instead, I rotate it one hundred and eighty degrees, tap it more firmly on its other side and feel the shell and membrane give way. I open it, and hear the yolk spill out into the bowl as I shake it so the white can follow. The spent shell gets dropped in the sink. Tidy up comes later.

One egg down, seven to go.

This could take a while.

*****

'Sgt. Pepper's 'is two thirds played when the phone rings. Rita, lovely or not, gets quieted before I juggle the receiver in my hand and trace the buttons on the face till I find the receive button. Up two from the five, and left.

"Hello?"

"Lorry, it's Tony."

"Alright?"

"Er, yeah. You?"

"Surprisingly good, as it happens. I'm even trying to cook..."

"Lorry, I can't talk now. Look, I won't be able to make it tonight. I'm sorry."

I don't say anything.

"Things have happened, Lorry. Things I can't talk about. I'm truly sorry. Of all the Saturdays to miss, I know what today is. I know what it means to you."

"It's fine," I tell him. Whether it is or isn't, I tell him it's fine.

"Thank you. Thanks for understanding. Hang on a second..." I hear Tony bark a muffled reply at someone. He must have his hand over the mouthpiece.

"What are you doing?" he asks, when he removes it.

"Nothing much."

"Playing those Beatles LPs again, like every year?"

"Ha! Yes I am. The day wouldn't seem right if I didn't."

"I know, I know that. I can see you now, sat there on your sofa with the stereo blaring away."

Stop. Hang on. Tony knows I never sit on the sofa. I sit in my chair, one of the leather art-deco ones I bought with Kate not long before she died. They're a matching pair. We loved them. They're all chrome and angled. We got them for their aesthetics more than their comfort factor. I sit in the one with the table at its side, a level steady platform for my drink; chairs that wipe clean and the crumbs brush off easily.

And he knows I'll be playing original mono versions. The stereo is an irrelevance.

"Ha! Exactly. You know me too well, Tony." I decide to play along, letting him know I'm on the same page, a page I can't read yet.

"Have you got to 'The White Album 'yet?"

"Next one."

"What's that song? 'Piggies'. I like that one."

He doesn't. He's told me he doesn't like that one. We've had the chat, the one where we try and whittle it down to a single LP, rather than a double, and see if it makes it the best LP ever made.

'Piggies'. What's he trying to tell me? Pigs. Pork. Bacon. Rind. Come on, think.

"Charles Manson was a fan of that one, I think. Is that right?" Tony adds, as my brain processes what he's saying.

He knows that, we've had the discussion plenty of times. We've sat here and dissected the album. He knows it all.

"He was, yes. Used it to justify..."

"Got to run, Lorry. Again, sorry about tonight. You know I enjoy knocking around with my monkey. Good night."

He hangs up. 'Good Night'. The final track on 'The White Album'.

Monkey. Pigs. 'White Album'. Charles Manson.

Sinking in my chair, I shake my head to clear my mind, like one of those children's toys you shake to clear the screen. Something like that, anyway.

I begin building the picture, the reference to Sofa and the Stereos. They're in this, but he couldn't mention them directly. Why couldn't he just say it directly? Because he was worried somebody was listening, someone monitoring his calls and listening in.

Or mine. They could have a tap on my phone.

Monkey. 'Everybody's Got Something To Hide Except Me And My Monkey'. He doesn't know who to trust, but he knows he can trust me. I'm his monkey, I have nothing to hide.

Piggies. What the hell's that all about?

Think. Big piggies are high level people, Tony's bosses. Little piggies are his team. And himself. Tony is one of the little piggies.

No, there were three little pigs, this is about the team.

Tony has a traitor on his team. It must be that. Yes, because the pigs eat the bacon, they eat themselves, like cannibals. His department is being brought down from within.

Why Charles Manson? 'Piggies 'was interpreted by him as an instruction to kill the white establishment in reprisal for the imminent killing of blacks in some apocalyptic race war.

Pigs live in sties. Pig sty. A mess. No. Pens. Pig pens. Pen is slang for penitentiary. Prison.

Think. Think. Think.

The bombers are the race warriors in line with Manson.

Shit, they're dead. The three bombers have been butchered. Someone got to them.

And it all confirms what I thought three nights ago before Sophie brought me home. "It isn't the end, you know..." I started to say to Tony, but he cut me off as the others approached.

A clever, clever man is Tony. People underestimate him, and they do it at their peril.

It was supposed to have been a treat for Tony, a change from the Chinese takeaway or pizza he always calls for on arrival, not to mention a starting point for me embracing my ailment. It's the first proper meal I've attempted to cook from scratch in more than four years.

I locate the bowl of egg mixture, lift it steadily with two hands and carry it over to the sink. Resting it on the edge, I find the tap and turn on the warm water, the tap on the left. I pour the omelette mixture down the drain.

Running the flats of my hands over the cold granite countertop until I locate the bread bin, I raise the hatch and reach in for the plastic bag containing the soft pre-cut wholewheat rolls I asked Janet to pick up for me.

Taking two out, I lay them on one of the plates I had ready. I open them up and dig my hand into the two glass bowls sitting above the plates, one containing cheese I grated, the other holding the bacon bits I cut up and fried till they were crispy.

They were the planned topping for our omelette that now sits in the pipes below my sink.

I drop a handful of each on each roll, close them up and press them down.

Next I head to the sink to wash the grease off my hands before wiping them clean on kitchen roll to rid them of the slimy bacon fat before I handle any vinyl.

I take my cheese and bacon rolls to the table at the side of my chair, deposit them and walk back to the kitchen. It all takes time. I get a four pack of beer from the tall cupboard at the far end and take it through to the barely-living room, and sit it on the floor by the side of the chair.

Back in the kitchen, I turn off the light. I slide my hand up the wall outside and switch off the hall light before walking back through turning off every light in the house.

They were never on for my benefit.

I settle down in my chair for 'Day In The Life'.

Taking a bite of my sandwich, bits of bacon and cheese spill down my jumper, a jumper I put on the wrong way round; a oft repeated mistake since they stopped putting tags on the back of clothing. Added comfort. they claim, as it stops the label agitating the skin and itching. They don't think of blind people when they make improvements.

Soon it'll be 'The White Album'.

Over and over again until I fall asleep.

The phone rings. I wipe my hand on my jumper before lowering the volume. It must be Tony, so I'm keen to answer it.

"Hello?"

"Dad, it's me. Am I interrupting?"

"Hello, Lanie. No you're not, and it wouldn't matter if you were."

She breathes, soft and even, like she's sleeping, like when she was a little girl and I'd sit in her room and watch her sleep, never daring to wake her up.

"Lanie? Are you okay?"

"I'm ready now, Dad."

"Ready for what?"

I'm worried. I don't know what she means by that. There's no immediate reply.

"Lanie, what are you ready for? Tell me, I'm listening."

"I'm ready for you to tell me about Mum. I want to know what happened, I want to know it all. I don't want to be protected any more. I need to understand."

Part Two: The White

13.

It's the way I choose to celebrate my twenty-fifth birthday, alone in a strange place. I look on it as a little adventure.

Parties aren't my thing. People aren't really my thing, if I'm honest. I could handle the party if there were no people there. Just give me the drink, the food and something on which to play music. I'd even dress up.

So I opted out. Maybe I should have told someone. Maybe I should have told my girlfriend, Sarah. But that's the great thing about a surprise party, I'm not supposed to know about it, so can't be held at all responsible for not showing up. It's every other bugger that will face repercussions if they don't attend. I'm in the clear; home and dry.

Well, not home, away from home. The party's at the flat. And not dry. A bit damp. A dreary March day, as it turned out, after a hint of the imminent spring when I walked to the station this morning under a prematurely optimistic blue sky.

March is a good time to be born. Far enough away from Christmas so as not to blur the two together, and the days start to get noticeably longer as spring is in the air, bringing a sense of optimism. Seeing how I went 'full term', I like to think March children are born out of a loving afternoon the previous June. Sun on bodies and relaxed and meaningful, rather than a snatched in-and-out on a freezing night in January with the lights off. An occasion remembered.

Of course, I have no idea about that, and it isn't a question I've ever thought of asking my parents.

Rather, I'm asking myself a lot of questions. It's what people do. More so when they hit a landmark birthday. Twenty-five isn't a birthday they make specific cards for, nor does it signify any great change in life. There is nothing, to the best of my knowledge, permissible today that wasn't yesterday.

The point is, I am now in my twenty-sixth year, and that puts me closer to thirty than twenty. That's how it works. We hit a new decade, or the mid point of a decade in years, and can't help but sit back and evaluate our lives.

If life's good, it takes about ten seconds to go through the process. If it isn't, things can get a bit messy.

Most divorced people I know reached the decision to separate as a new decade approached, or as they nudged closer to the next decade than the one they were in. My own parents split when they were thirty-nine and forty. It isn't something we have any control over, it's just the way it is.

So I go with the flow and let the doubtful thoughts wash over me. I embrace them and allow them to drive me on and shift the balance of things.

Which all probably explains why I'm sitting alone in a pub in London on my twenty-fifth birthday, rather than attending my own party arranged by my girlfriend in my flat, with any friends I have in attendance.

Acquaintances. I don't really do friends.

An advert for a Record Fair caught my eye last week. It wouldn't leave me alone, the date seeming so stark in black and white on the open page. It consumed me. It felt like a calling, pronouncing the date of my birth.

For years I'd wanted to attend one of the big fairs in London with international dealers and stuff you don't see at car boot sales. Stuff I can't afford, but it's nice to look, and I thought I might treat myself. After all, it is my birthday.

A plastic bag isn't adequate protection for records against a sudden March downpour, so when the heavens opened I darted in to the nearest pub to protect the pink Island label purchases I spent too much money on.

Sarah's going to go mental. We've been together for eighteen months. It's starting to feel settled. Like a stomach. Like a couch.

Settle. A wooden bench with a high back, storage space under the seat.

It's starting to feel like that.

Had it not been for the rain, I'd have probably gone to Euston. That was the half-formed plan in mind, to get a train back to Tredmouth. There's a train every half hour, a fast one every hour. I could have been back home by eight, half past maybe. Had I done that, I could have carried on pretending I was happy. I could have carried on doing that for fifteen years or so, and settled on the settle, keeping children's toys in the space beneath the seat as I stretched back against the high wooden frame and waited for something to happen.

A clock behind the bar tells me it's half past seven. But I know the clock will be a few minutes ahead to trick the drinkers into clearing out on time, and let them think they got away with an extra few minutes, an extra half pint.

Sarah wanted me to get a mobile phone. They're all the rage now. My bet is that she's got me one for my birthday, even though I told her I didn't want one, that I can't imagine anything more intrusively appalling.

I even told her that all I'd do is think about how many vinyl records I could have bought with what it cost.

But that's what people invariably do; they buy you the present they'd really like to have. Ah, that makes me sound like a bastard, I know it does, an ungrateful bastard. And I suppose I am, but it's also the point of everything. If she doesn't get that about me, and we're that far apart, do we really have a future?

We could have gone to the record fair together. She could have arranged for us to have a night away down here. We could have been doing this as a couple. Instead, she arranged a surprise party and has almost certainly bought me a mobile phone, both of which, I detest. And when it turns out I missed my own party, she'll justify the purchase by letting me know that if I had a mobile phone, she could have got in touch with me to tell me about the party.

Round and round we go.

This is my kind of pub. A lot nowadays are too shiny and piney, the kinds of places that try to tick all the boxes instead of deciding what they want to be.

Pubs should have secrets hidden in corners, dark shadowy nooks and crannies with random things adorning the walls that you can't quite connect, a reflection of the people who frequent them and the owners who leave their mark. The floor should be very slightly tacky, not highly polished, and the curtains should be dark and velvety, not wood-slatted blinds.

This is that kind of place.

The staff are pleasant enough, but not overly friendly with strangers. And the food smells good, as the evening trade starts to pick up. I watch plates being carried to and from the kitchen, cleaned of their content by hungry punters. Cottage Pie with green peas, big fat bangers with mash and onion gravy. Staple pub fare, no pretentiousness.

It makes me wish I hadn't eaten at a cafe by the record fair; fish and chips and a mug of tea.

Twenty-two people are in here now, as the clock ticks closer to eight o'clock, the time I was told to meet Sarah at the flat. That's twenty-two not including staff. Eleven tables, thirty-two chairs. There are more round the corner in the adjacent room, but I can't see there, so can only count on what I know. There's a large table for six, especially put together, I think, as the latest arrivals take their places at it. The rest are fours and twos, romantic twos for couples, but mainly fours. They must gauge it on something. Experience, perhaps, or the fact their average customer age is mid-thirties to mid-fifties, something which dictates they've been in relationships for a while, and need to dilute evenings out by inviting along another couple.

I pick up my bag and trot up to the bar to order another pint of bitter. I won't leave the bag unattended, it's too precious to me.

However, I did leave Sarah unattended tonight.

Four more people enter behind me. A shape catches my eye, a small shape in height and build, but flesh in the right places, not stick-thin like the models. She has hair I have no idea of what the natural colour is. I assume dark, or why else would she lighten it at the tips? A natural blonde would never add dark undercurrents, would she?

There's a conversation going on about what everybody wants to drink and who's paying. She's not being listened to, as an order gets barked before I can even take my change. A nudge out the way from a guy I ignore, a fifty pound note being thrust forward in the space next to my arm, him being told they can't take fifties, too many fakes, so pulling out a twenty instead.

I take my money, and carry my pint to a different table, one of the romantic twos. No sense in me taking up four spaces. It's a good deed that will probably go unnoticed, but seeing how I didn't do it for plaudits, I don't dwell on it. Instead, I slip the vinyl from my bag, and check for water damage now the plastic has dried out. All good.

The girl I noticed is sitting at the table I left. She waited till the other girl in the foursome sat, and stealthily slid in next to her.

I like her nose, it's perfectly proportioned. My nature makes me want to go up and start measuring her face, but I decide it best not to do that. Instead I calculate it all in my head.

The length from her eyebrows to the bottom part of her nose is exactly equal to the length from the bottom of her nose to the point of her chin. The width of the gap between her eyes is precisely equal to the space between her nose and bottom lip. The width of each of her eyes is equal to the distance from bottom lip to chin point. From where I sit, given the distance to the various parts of her face and the perspective thereof, the width of her mouth is equal to the length of her nose is equal to her ears from tip to lobe end.

Scientifically speaking, I really like her face.

"You want a fucking photograph, mate?"

It takes a second to realise the bloke's talking to me. I must have been staring at his girlfriend. Fiancee. Wife. Whatever she is to him. Barely a girlfriend, I decide. He's trying too hard. The shoes are too polished, and the suit too much. Similarly, the shirt's out of place and too well laundered. And he's just had his hair cut, his neck clean-shaven. I could smell the aftershave at the bar when he pushed me aside. He's over-dressed, and the conversation has been all about him. He was asking questions, but only so he could jump on them. It's all too contrived. hence the fifty when he had a twenty.

She tells him to leave it, that I wasn't staring. But she must know I was, you can sense that type of thing.

At this point I know I should apologise, say that I was miles away, that I didn't mean any offence, that I was just staring into space, thinking about stuff, thinking about the records in the bag I still hold in my left hand. I could even tell them I was reflecting on life, seeing how it's my birthday.

And I know that if I handle it like that, this will all go away. The flash guy might even offer to buy me a drink, attempt to win over the pretty girl via his charitable nature. Then I could continue to sit here and have a couple of jars before heading to the station.

But there's something about this girl, something about how she jumped in to defend me. There was the slightest smile of sympathy. It could just be that she knows the guy she's with has a hell of a temper, and she doesn't want any trouble, doesn't want him getting in to trouble, but something tells me it isn't that. She doesn't know him that well. And there was the slight widening of her eyes and arching of her brows, the almost imperceptible dilating of her pupils, a physical response from looking at me, something over which she has no control, an endorphin rush triggered by an enjoyable thought. Not necessarily a conscious thought; her reproductive instincts would be miles ahead of her.

So, yes, I know the sensible thing to do is to pacify, to look surprised, like I don't really comprehend what he's making reference to, and explain it all away.

But fuck it, it's my birthday. And the four of them are looking at me, waiting to see what I have to say.

"How much is it?"

"What?" the guy asks, looking surprised, narrowing his eyes and twisting his mouth to imply I'm making no sense.

"The photograph. Is there a charge for it? And, if so, how much? After all, don't they sell pictures of all the best sights in London?"

He's angry, mainly because I've batted the ball back to him. Aside from which, I just complimented his date right in front of him. He probably had his reply worked out. Had I tried to apologise it away, he could have played the 'that sorted that out 'card and shown himself to be her protector. Had I become aggressive, given his tone and language, he would have played the 'what's your problem ' card, and won the moral stakes.

By not playing either of the cards he expected, he's left sitting looking at his hands and mobile phone, working out the next move. He plays it. It's a stupid one.

"Fifty quid."

I prop my bag against my chair and pull out the money, before thumbing it out from one hand to the other; two twenties and a ten. I fold it neatly along the length to form a V and hold it out to him in the same manner as he thrust money over the bar, all done to make him feel like a pimp.

"I'd have paid a lot more than that for a picture of...?"

I leave the sentence hanging. Shifting my attention from him to her, I smile and tilt my head back, waiting for her to fill the gap.

"Kate," she says, and flicks a smile at me before he looks round.

"Hello Kate," I say evenly.

People don't give you their name unless they intend for you to use it subsequently.

"I'm Lorry."

She smiles again, before looking away. She uses her hand as a shield as she twists the feather of her short hair that points along her prominent cheekbone. A coy gesture, an alluring pretence of shyness.

Her friend, a toothy blonde, smiles and reaches out for her boyfriend's hand. He takes it. He hasn't made eye-contact with me since this began.

"You're a prick, mate, you know that?" the pimp says eventually. He knows he's lost.

But he has one last play to make.

He drains his glass, places it down on the table decisively and juggles his mobile phone in his hand.

"Right, shall we head to that wine bar up the road?"

"Can do," the other bloke says, and finishes his beer, glad to be leaving an awkward situation. He seems decent, like he doesn't want the grief.

I continue to hold out the fifty quid, as I carry on playing my bluff hand.

His girlfriend, the blonde, starts to rise.

"Kate? You ready?" she asks her.

"I like it here," she replies quietly, "the wine bar's too busy. Too loud."

"Will you be okay?" The non-confrontational guy seems genuinely concerned as he shoots a glance at me.

"I'll be fine. Besides, I've barely touched my wine. I did say not to get me a large one." The last comment is directed at the pimp, a subtle put down for not listening to her request for a small house white, as she lets him know she understands all the reasons he'd want to get her tipsy.

"Are you sure?" the amiable guy double-checks.

Kate nods and smiles. He pecks her on the cheek, tells her to ring him on his mobile if she needs anything. There's enough of a caring affection and facial similarity for me to conclude he's related to her.

The pimp can't let it go. He needs to reassert himself, and human refuge in these situations usually lies in trying to raise oneself up on the shortcomings of others.

"You need to get in the nineteen-nineties, mate," he starts, pointing his mobile at me. "Vinyl died with your haircut, sometime in the eighties when those trainers were made."

He smirks and looks around for approval, but doesn't get any. Kate tightens her lips and focuses on the stem of her wine glass, her fingers resting on the base. Her relative glances at me almost apologetically, and shuffles half a pace nearer the door. His girlfriend carries on smiling. I think it's just what she does. There's no harm in it, it's better than scowling.

Still holding out the fifty pounds, I smile and take him in.

It's what people do. They highlight in others the thing they most dislike about themselves. But they don't do it directly. There's no sense in a fat man pointing out somebody else's fatness. Rather, he'll highlight the skinniness, all in a pathetic attempt to draw peoples attention. The theory being; if they're focused on someone being skinny, they might not notice he's fat.

It's always the same.

"I walked a lot of miles today. The trainers are the most comfortable worn-in footwear I possess. They were put on for a purpose, just as your shoes were. After all, it's difficult to wear lifters in anything but sturdy leather footwear. And the lifters combined with the heel offer you, what...? An extra two inches, I should think. Making you about five-eight in your high-heels, five-six in your socks. You needn't have worried, Kate here only looks about five-one, so probably wouldn't have noticed. As for my haircut, yes, I do tend to let it grow a bit wild and floppy. But at least I can. Better than the alternative of having to shave it down to a number one crop as you do, in a pathetic attempt to hide the fact you're prematurely balding. All done to make it appear like you did that as a fashion statement, rather than because the bald bits were beginning to dominate. And, of course, it has the added bonus of making you look tough, somewhat compensating for the lack of height you feel the need to address. As for vinyl records, I simply prefer the sound and look and feel of them, and don't need to jump on every technological bandwagon that comes along in a desperate attempt to feel current and vital in the world. And if I were sat opposite Kate tonight, I wouldn't have placed my bag of records on the table between us, as you did your phone, and glanced at them every ten seconds. My attention would have been fully on her, as she deserves. So don't blame me for your first - and probably last - date going badly. So, I don't really give a flying fuck what you think of my trainers, my records or my haircut. Similarly, I don't give a flying fuck about your shortness, baldness and the fact nobody rang you and made you feel important tonight. You're completely insignificant to me. But don't let me hold you up, and be sure to have a pleasant evening."

Only now do I withdraw the money and go back to my beer. I keep watching as they walk out the door, play it safe, and make sure the pimp didn't get it in his head to attack.

I hadn't realised all the eyes in the pub were on me. Two dozen people turn away and go back to their conversations, drinks and food. One or two looked like they were about to applaud. I sit perfectly still and let my breathing return to normal, and feel my pulse settle down to a beat every second or so. It takes a few minutes.

A small white square lands on the table in front of me making me flinch. Numbers are neatly written on it. A phone number.

Looking up, I see Kate is watching her hand play with the wine glass stem. The glass is nearly empty. She smiles. Just her lips at first, but she can't contain it, and has to part them to show her teeth.

Flipping the paper over, her face looks up at me, that symmetry, the beauty of her in the passport size photo. Anyone else would look like shit in it.

"Excuse me," I call to her.

She looks over, making a "hmmm?" noise as she tips her head to one side.

"Could I trouble you to watch my bag and save my seat, please? While I go to the bar?"

She shrugs, nods and looks a little sad.

It takes a couple of minutes to get served. I'm glad the guy didn't take the fifty pounds, it's all I have left.

As I spin away, I see Kate has my bag and is glancing through my day's purchases. Anyone else, and I'd be offended, but I can tell by how she handles them that she has respect for the contents.

I place my pint of bitter down before I sit in my seat, and settle the small glass of house white in front of the empty seat opposite me. She's busy sliding the records back in the bag before folding the top over, ready to return them.

She looks directly and completely at me for the first time and holds me with her brown eyes. Undeniable slight dilation of the pupils, even a little flush of red on her neck.

I hold out my hand, palm up, and gesture towards the empty seat opposite and smile.

She makes a play of thinking about it, doesn't want to appear easy. She twists that feather of hair again and purses her lips, before concluding the thought process with an affirmative nod to herself. Kate gets up and walks over. She sits down and shuffles the seat forward before moving the wine to one side. She lays the bag of records down between us on the table and glances at it.

"So," she says, as cool as they come, "the Nirvana 'Simon Simopath 'LP - pink Island label, mono or stereo?"

"Oh, I like you," I tell her, and feel my heart skip two beats in one. A kick in my stomach lets me know I am fully conscious of the fact that I just fell completely in love with a woman for the first time in my life.

"So, you like me, eh? Not enough to buy me a large glass of wine, though, you tight bastard."

And we laugh until our faces hurt.

14.

"So, are you still good for seven?"

"See you there. Get me a glass of wine ready."

"Will do."

"And, Lorry...?".

"Yep?"

"A large glass, please, you tight bastard," she whispers.

It's an old joke between us, a joke going back sixteen and a half years.

Today is our sixteenth wedding anniversary, and I have a plan. I pat my pocket to check the box is in there. It's the eleventh time I've checked. How can I be nervous after sixteen years? Because I still care as much as I did back then, that's why. I'd be more worried if I wasn't.

We've spent every wedding anniversary, as well as my birthday, the anniversary of our first meeting, in the same place. Neither of us like routine, but this is one we immerse ourselves in.

We have an agreement. If there's ever an argument that causes us to be apart, we meet in our pub. If we ever find ourselves out of contact for whatever reason, we meet in our pub. When the July seventh attacks happened, we met in our pub. Kate walked there from work, I drove as far as I could, and ran the rest of the way. When my Dad died, we met in our pub. Same thing when Kate lost her mum.

Suzie owns the place. She's been there for about ten of the sixteen years, but instructions were passed on from the previous owner.

It's our pub.

*****

"What are you counting?" Kate asks, as she swings through the door.

The sun's just setting, though it was blocked by buildings an hour or two ago. It tells me that she's right on time. One minute past seven was the sunset time for this day.

I hold her and kiss her before I answer, let the scene play out as Suzie and the staff all hug her. They make some comment about another anniversary, ask her how she's put up with me for...how many years is it now?

She tells them I'm not so bad and ruffles my hair, like I'm a kid. Sixteen years, she reports. But she says it in a way that tells of her pride.

"Pictures," I tell her.

"What?"

"I was counting how many pictures are on the walls"

"How many?"

"Fourteen, in this area. Fourteen! There used to be over twenty. Suzie must have taken some down."

"And remind me why it's important to know that...?" she says in a teasing way and twists the bit of hair by her cheek between her fingers. She's always done that when she's teasing me.

"You never know, it could be."

"How? How could it ever be important to anything?"

"I don't know, I just like counting things."

She chinks her glass against mine and takes a sip from her large glass of wine. Large. She smiles over the rim at me, silently acknowledging the in-joke playing out to the punchline.

Suzie starts 'The White Album 'on the CD jukebox. The same thing every year. Kate grins. It's our favourite album.

"How was your day, Dear?" I ask her as she settles in her seat.

"A bit shit, actually, Lorry."

"Oh dear, Dear. I'm all ears."

"Well, I don't really want to talk about work all evening, but...you know I told you about cut-backs, printed publications struggling etcetera?"

"Yes, I remember."

"It was announced today that redundancies are necessary. And, of course, I've got to manage that."

The last round really upset her. It's cruel that the thing that makes her such a good boss is her caring nature, but that same generosity of spirit makes certain elements of her work so difficult.

With that in mind, I tell her, "I'm sorry, Kate."

"And guess who was first in my office after the announcement?"

"Wild stab in the dark, but it wouldn't happen to be that John bloke, would it?"

She nods her head, and quaffs more of her wine, the tension evident in the size and frequency of her gulps.

"That man makes my skin crawl. Do you know what he said to me?" The question being rhetorical, she ploughs on, "your hair looks nice. Do you know why he does that, Lorry?"

"Because he fancies you?"

"Nope. I mean, whether he does or doesn't is an irrelevance. He'd sleep with me anyway, just to get on. Christ, he'd sleep with the bloody photocopier if it helped his career. He does it to butter me up, to wheedle his way in, even after everything he's done."

"He's just a sycophant, a brown-nose."

"You're lucky driving a cab, you know that?"

"I like it."

"There are no politics. You go to work, do what you do, come home, and that's the end of it."

"Yes, but there are no promotions to be had. It's not like I can become a Senior Cabbie, or a Taxi Driving Director. The only way any of us can earn more is to work more hours. It's as simple as that."

"God, what I'd give for that. It's the politics that drain me, Lorry. For years I've had to watch my back, fend off John trying to undermine me, sniping behind my back, having to worry about taking a holiday because of what he might do while I'm not there. He's even tried to sabotage projects, just to make me look bad, just so he can ride in and put it right."

Patting my pocket, I check the gift is safely tucked away. I want to move this on, and not have her get upset about work all night. There are more important things in life.

Kate's always known me better than I know myself, and she reads my mind.

"I'm sorry," she says, taking my hand, "I do prattle on about work, don't I?"

"Ha. Yes, but it's a large chunk of your life. I get it."

"It's that bloody compliment that gets me, Lorry. As soon as the shit hits the fan, he can flip and want to become my best friend. It tells me all I need to know, that I've been right not to promote him, because he has no integrity. I mean, I wouldn't want him on my side in a fight."

I have no idea how Kate puts up with it all. So much of our life is taken up by talking about and dealing with crap like this. It's endless.

"Do you want me to kick his head in?" I offer, half seriously.

"Oooh, would you? Can I watch? I hate the way he uses me. That's the bit I can't get over, how he can try to erode my position, right up to the point there's a threat, and then flip over and run to me for shelter."

"So, you're the equivalent of a toilet with no external windows?"

"Wow. A toilet with no windows! You know how to flatter a girl."

Kate laughs and watches me with her whole face smiling. It makes me self-conscious.

"Your hair does look nice, by the way," I tell her, to shift the focus back her way. "As does the dress and everything else about you."

She's wearing a white dress under her black coat, the coat now on the chair by her side. We both know she wore the white dress purposefully. I adore her in white. Her dark hair and natural tan shine in white. It's new. She must have bought it specially and kept it at work.

"Thank you. Your jeans look nice, as well."

"Clean on this morning."

There's a pause. Something more's on her mind.

"Anyway," she says eventually, " as I said, I don't want to talk about work all night, but I'm thinking of taking a redundancy package..."

Sipping my beer, I weigh up what she just said. My thoughts are selfish, concerned only with how that would impinge on my life and routine.

She picks up on my pause, causing her to fill the gap and try selling it to me. Ever the professional.

"It's a really good deal, Lorry. And Lanie is fifteen now. We don't have to worry about her. She'll go to university, I expect, but that's factored in. We have no mortgage, we don't plan on moving again, we don't plan on having any more kids. You have the money from your Dad's estate, my pension's secure, and with the savings..."

"It's fine by me."

The White Album 'moves on to what would be side three if it were on vinyl. 'Birthday'. Except it isn't.

"But am I mad to give it all up? I suppose I'm trying to convince myself, really. I'm just so sick and tired of it all. My whole working life is spent fighting battles. All of the creative side, all of the fun bits have all gone, replaced by technology and over-ambition. But would I drive you mad, being at home all the time?"

"No. I'd love for you to be at home all the time. We could have sex every morning. And you could make me tea in bed. It'll be fantastic."

"The tea or the sex?" she asks, taking my hand again.

"Both. Just not at the same time."

"You know why I love you?" she asks, back to twisting her hair.

"Is it the sex?"

"Errrrm, yes, that too." A little flush rises on her neck. She can't see it, but she otherwise senses it as she brings her hand to the spot and smoothes the lusty notion away till later.

"Then is it because of my cheeky smile and winning personality?"

"You don't have a winning personality. Only with me. You avoid everyone else like the plague."

"Oh yeah. Okay, no idea. Why do you love me?"

"Because I have no doubts. No doubts at all, that I can give up work and spend every minute of every day, for all the years we have left, with you."

And I know, I know deep down that I'm the luckiest man in the world.

15.

Effing Tony, they call him. He's relaxed a little since the sun set. It's easier in the dark, less chance of being made by the targets.

He shifts his muscly bulk to ease the discomfort on his backside, and starts forming a new pressure point. He does the adjustment carefully as he doesn't want to rock the van and give the game away.

"Give me a status report," he breathes into his radio.

"Same as it was three minutes ago," a weary voice mumbles.

"A lot can happen in three minutes. Nuclear weapons can be launched. A life-changing song can be heard. You could fall off a bridge. Give me a fucking status report."

"Three men in the living area, talking in Arabic. Mostly about how much they hate Israel and its allies. The usual stuff. No sign of anyone coming and going. No sign that anyone's going anywhere. And no sign that they're expecting company. Not unlike us."

"Hmmm. Stay alert. The intel hinted at something happening tonight. I want to know if someone farts, okay?"

"Yes, Boss."

Tony's nervous. The nerves are good, they keep him focused. The day he isn't nervous is the day he should pack it all in.

It's over a year since anything bad happened. Back then they didn't listen to him, they didn't take the evaluation seriously. In the meantime there have been a lot of raids, pre-emptive strikes, some of them worthwhile, most of them not. False alarms are inevitable when you're dealing with that much information.

But this one's different. Three known bad boys who went off the radar fourteen months back, until two days ago when a vigilant Eurostar employee smelt a rat. He couldn't fathom why three guys he'd seen chatting on the platform sat in seats on three different parts of the train. It wasn't full.

The evaluation was done, a real threat to be pursued. This is the final stage of that investigation.

"Here we go," the radio spits, "a man approaching the door carrying a bag,"

"I see him," Tony drawls, "anyone recognise him from the known associates reports?"

The question draws a negative response.

*****

"You first," Kate says, and smiles at the wrapped packages on the table.

Hers to me is neatly done, equal triangular points on either edge, showing that she painstakingly centered the gift and trimmed the edges square and sealed it all up with invisible tape, before feeding two strips of gold ribbon over and across, all symmetrically aligned so the square in the top corner is proportionately pleasing on the eye. A bow marks the point where all four ribbon lines cross.

Mine to her is haphazard, unequal on the sides, and a bit concertinaed where the paper slipped before I applied the tape. A little white shows through where I tried to remove the tape, but realised it would tear the paper away, so left it how it was. It does have a bow on top, however, but it keeps falling off because I used a rolled piece of tape to affix it, and my fingers took the stickiness and left an oily residue.

It seems almost a shame to ruin the beauty, but I lever the ribbon off and tear at the silver and gold paper.

"I wonder what it could be...?" I tease, fairly confident that the object inside the paper in my hand is a book.

Kate smiles demurely, more on one side of her mouth than the other.

"It's not your actual present," she says as I slip it free of its envelopment, "you'll have to wait till we get home for that. But it's a clue as to what that might be."

An early edition copy of Graham Greene's 'Brighton Rock' looks up at me. "A dirty weekend in Brighton?"

"No, try again."

"A stick of rock?"

"Noooo!"

"A flick-knife? A day at the races? Look, I don't know."

"Well, you'll just have to wait, then."

I breathe out a frustrated half-breath.

"Open yours," I urge her.

"Aw," she coos, almost to herself, "you wrapped it so carefully."

"I tried." She notices and appreciates the effort.

Watching her face as she opens the box, I'll know if she's really pleased or not, whether she genuinely loves it or not.

Her hand goes to her mouth and catches the little cry that wanted to come out. A piece of it escapes through her fingers. Her lips clamp shut as her hand goes back to the box and touches the necklace inside. I watch her as she blinks away the tears. Her lips tighten to hold it all in.

"Do you like it?" I ask, but I already know she does.

"Lorry...it's beautiful," she finally says.

I nod. It is. I'm not one for jewellery, but even I have to concede it is a beautiful thing.

"It's white gold," I say, leaning forward and pointing, "and those are diamonds, and those green things are peridots. And peridot is your birthstone. Not to mention the Modern Anniversary gift for sixteen years, not that I buy into all that crap, as it seems to me it's just a way of getting people to spend money on stuff, a bit like the greeting cards they invent for every bloody occasion nowadays, and the national days they invent so that we all feel obliged to..."

"Lorry, stop talking now."

Kate calls Suzie over and asks her to fasten it for her. She knows my clumsy fingers will never manage the delicate clasp mechanism. Besides, she wants my opinion once it's on. Her turn to read my face and reaction.

*****

"Two leaving, two staying. What do you want to do, Boss?"

Four targets splitting in to two twos gives him a problem. He has six bodies on the surveillance team. Three from TERA, including himself, the fourth running Funnel back at HQ, and three seconded in from the Met. It was all they'd let him have, despite his pleas for more. He'd have needed to raise the threat alert level to get more, and he was loathe to play that card. He didn't want to be the boy who cried wolf.

Six should have been enough to follow three men, but four gives him a few concerns.

"Okay. Is the guy who recently arrived one of them?"

"Yes."

"Does he still have the bag?"

"Yes."

"Leave the surveillance man, and you two take them. Trail and observe. Chris will hook up with you. The first sniff of anything untoward and you strike. Pick them up and bring them in. Leave them to stew. We'll stay here and watch the other two. Copy?"

"Copy, Boss. We're on it."

"And keep me posted of everything. Even the slightest little thing, okay?"

"You got it. Out."

Tony nods at Chris, enough to despatch him on his errand. Chris is one of his sort, ex-Special Branch, and a good man to have around.

The unknown recent arrival bothers Tony. Who is he, and what is he? Is he the senior man? Is he the boss? If so, Tony would want to be there, not here.

"Entering the Tube," the earpiece hisses.

Tony builds the picture in his mind. Three men trailing two suspects entering the underground. Even if they split, they can take one each, and the Met man can accompany one of them, the one with the bag.

He relays the instruction.

Most surveillance comes to nothing. Ninety-nine percent of it is a waste of time, but you do it for the one percent that makes it worthwhile. Play the odds, and the chances are, this will be an arse-numbing night in a cold van, one of hundreds he's spent fruitlessly.

One percent. He thinks it through. Do this for a year, every night, and maybe it'll pay off four nights in total.

Besides, the Intel wasn't clear, and didn't hint at anything definite. Just a date that kept being referenced via the phone and email communication. But these people are well prepared, they know the drill. They assume they're being monitored, even when they think they're off the radar.

It's all a game.

Tony gets ahead of himself. If the two remaining men leave... They probably won't, but if they do, he'll take them with the Met man and leave the surveillance guy here just in case. You never know, this could all be a ruse, a way of getting rid of the watchers, leaving the flat empty for someone else to collect something from, something they brought into the country, perhaps.

16.

Kate drops her chin every few minutes to catch sight of her new necklace. The green suits her. I can't really say why. Her dark brown hair and skin colour seem to naturally gel with it. Green and brown, like nature, like earth and trees, like mint and chocolate. Some things just sit right together.

"Do you know, gold, when termed such in jewellery, is actually an alloy?" I ask her as we both sit back and let the dinner digest.

Good proper pub grub. Nothing fancy, just the basics done well.

"Erm, no. Not something I've ever researched, to be honest."

"Hmmm. Well it is. The gold content of gold is only about seventy-five percent. It's then alloyed with another metal to give it the nice colour and harden it up. White gold is alloyed with nickel or palladium. Mostly palladium in Europe as nickel can be nasty. See, gold on its own is too soft, it would dent and scratch too easily. Incidentally, palladium is also the stuff they put in the catalytic converter in your car exhaust system. There's a lucrative crime business to be had out of nicking catalytic converters. Lots of precious metals."

"How do you know all this?"

"Dunno."

"And what use is it, knowing all this? I mean, and I'm not being funny, but you're never going to do anything with the knowledge. It's the same as the counting the pictures thing. What's it all for?"

"I just feel more comfortable knowing it. When I buy you a necklace, for example, I want to know how it's made. Don't even get me started on peridot and its occurrence in pallasite meteorites..."

"Ooooh! Is my necklace from outer-space?"

"Well, no, it's from Bond Street."

"Oh, what a shame. The peridots, then, are they from outer-space?"

"Erm, no. Egypt, I think. Are you taking the piss?"

"Yeah!"

She's had a bit too much to drink. A nice amount over the limit. The right amount so that she feels relaxed and sexy. Enough to make her switch off from work, and retirement, and just be.

Kate's always been happy in her own skin. She's confident and strong, and by association, she makes me like that.

The truth is, though, I arm myself with knowledge because I'm not. I hate not knowing things. A chip on my shoulder? Yes, I think so. I have no qualifications, no vocation. I'm just me, a licensed London cabbie.

Kate makes me much more than that.

"Tell me about the day Lanie was born," Kate asks, twirling her wine glass stem between the thumb and index finger of her left hand.

"Ah, you know it all as well as I do."

"I was out of it on pain killers. Please, tell me again," she implores, and gives me the wide-eyed pleading face she knows I can't resist.

*****

Two concurrent messages collide in Tony's ear, one telling him that the two guys with the bag split when they left the Tube, the other informing him that the two men left in the flat are getting ready to leave.

"Bollocks," he growls, "are they on to us? Are they fucking playing us?"

He has to think quickly, and he has to get it right.

"Chris, you take the guy without the bag. Smithy and Met Man take Bag Man. Copy?"

"Copy, Boss."

"You alright on your own, Chris?"

"Yeah, no problem. How you want to play this, Tony?"

"I dunno. If we pick him up now, we have nothing except what might be in that bag, and we potentially tip off all the players. They'll just shut it down. We know the form. First sniff of us, and they disappear. Okay, let's play this out for another twenty minutes, tops. Mark the time, gentlemen. Nine-thirty on the nose. We're going mobile this end, just our Watcher staying at the flat. Stay in touch."

Tony's out the van before the men switch off the light and leave the flat in darkness. His black form disappears in the shadows. Mustn't smile, he thinks to himself, a parody of a line once uttered to him by an instructor he had when he first undertook surveillance training, they'll see the teeth. It wasn't even meant in a racist sense, but it smarted a bit.

He's just thinking through the scenario of what to do if his two marks decide to split, when that's precisely what they do. Each turns a separate way at the end of the road where it forms a T-junction.

"They must have made us. Divide and conquer," he rasps, frustrated at himself for not pushing for more resources on the job, for not upping the threat level.

His mind's racing.

"Confirm - no calls incoming, and no calls outgoing from your end Chris, Smithy?"

"No calls, but they could have sent a text. Or played a system. Leave the flat, see who follows, head back after fifteen minutes if all clear, stay away if followed. It gets the message across."

"Yeah, I hear you. They know we're here, I'm sure of it. We're splitting this end, taking one man each."

A nod and a point of a finger tell the Met man to go right. Tony heads left at the junction and trails his man.

It's a quiet partly cloudy Monday evening in September. A few people walk the streets, the late workers, the dog walkers and people heading to and from the pubs and restaurants. Busier would be better, confuse the issue a bit and make it unclear how many people Tony has at his disposal.

"We've got a problem..." the man on Watch reports into five sets of ears as they follow four suspects around different parts of London.

It's like a spider's web, stretch it too much and a strand will break. That happens, and the integrity of the whole structure is ruined.

"Talk to me," Tony breathes, no doubt now that he's being played.

"There was another body in the corridor as they left the building. They switched, Tony. I'm sorry, I missed it. Shit."

"Okay, relax, it can't be helped. What do you know?"

"As they were leaving, someone emerged from another flat, went to the postbox area, then walked back. As they crossed in the corridor, two people switched, turned one-eighty, and assumed one another's positions in the crowd."

"Three's a crowd, eh?"

"Yes, I'm afraid so, Tony, I'm sorry. It was so quick, I missed it. Had to re-run the imaging tape in slow-mo to spot it. It was slickly done."

"As you say, it's done, can't turn back the clock. Where's the switcher now? Do you know?"

"Left the building ninety seconds ago. I'll lose him if I don't go now. What do you want me to do?"

"Where's he heading?"

"He turned right out the building...hang on...a right at the end of the road."

"So he's walking parallel to me, and behind by a few hundred yards?"

"Yes, assuming he doesn't take a detour."

"Right, fuck this. Stay at the flat. I'll take him. Pick the rest of them up now, fellas. Now. Go, go, go!"

*****

"She smelt like an uncooked chicken, I remember that," I continue telling Kate, as she relaxes in her comfy solid wood chair, with smooth worn arms she can drape herself over.

"The midwife gave her to me to hold while they checked you out and stitched you up. You know, I never told you, but I was scared up to that moment, scared of becoming a dad. I suppose I'd never really been responsible for anything important up to that point in my life. Suddenly, I was - for want of a better phrase - left holding the baby. It was the first, and probably only time in my life I've been truly terrified."

"Why didn't you tell me that?"

"I don't know. You had enough to worry about. You were the one having to carry the load and give birth. But I remember going to the childbirth classes and seriously doubting my ability to do it all. But as soon as I held her, I knew I'd be alright. And I knew if you could go through your part of it, mine was a breeze."

"You memorised all the books, I remember that."

"Yes. I still remember my Braxton Hicks, mucus plugs and episiotomies."

"Lanie hates you for that."

"What?"

"That you didn't give her your memory. She got mine."

"Ah, she'll forget about it when she's older..."

Kate giggles.

"You sat in the delivery room memorising a book on baby names and their meanings. To take my mind off the contractions, you'd call out names and ask me what I thought of them?"

"Yes, but we couldn't decide..."

"Couldn't agree, you mean."

"Okay, we couldn't agree, and it was hard because we didn't know what we were having."

"I told you she was a girl. I always said she was."

"You did. And I told you that your woman's intuition was a load of bollocks!"

"And you were wrong."

"To be fair, it was fifty-fifty."

"Admit it. I was right, you were wrong."

"You were right, I was noncommittal."

"That's as good as I'm going to get. So, you'd done those compilation tapes to play during labour..."

"Indeed. And you took so bloody long about the whole business, we ran out and had to play half of them again."

"Er, not me, thank you. It was Lanie taking her time. A bit like you in the mornings."

My turn to chuckle.

"She had jaundice, so she was a bit yellow, So there I am, holding this little bundle of corn-fed raw chicken, when the song playing penetrated my conscience."

"It was strange, wasn't it? We both heard it, in spite of everything."

"'Into White 'by Cat Stevens."

"We said it together, Delanie, and that was her name. I don't think we even discussed it. We both knew."

"We always said we wanted a name with scope," I recall.

"So we did. Like Katherine and Daniel. Kate and Danny."

"Except I'm Lorry. Does she like her name?"

"You should ask her some time, Lorry. You should ask her all those kinds of things."

"Ah, you know me. Besides, she's fifteen, it's a funny age..."

"She talks to me. And me to her."

"Yes, but it's different. You're a woman. You have..."

I can't think of what I'm trying to say.

"I don't understand you, Lorry. You sit here and charm me. You're the only person in the world I can say anything to, yet you can't engage other people. No, that's not true. You can. If you try, you're very good at it. You're funny, clever...fascinating, even. But you don't bother. I don't understand. We wouldn't see anyone if I didn't set it all up and make you go."

"I'm happy with you and Lanie. That's enough for me. Anyway, I engage with people all the time when I'm taxi-driving."

"Snapshots of conversation with people you know you'll almost certainly never see again!"

"Well, yes. That's the way I like it. As I said, you and Lanie are enough for me."

"And the music..."

"Yes, okay, and the music. Funny you say that, but I do get a lot out of my relationship with music, I suppose."

"But is it enough, Lorry?"

"How do you mean?"

"Well, say something happened to me. Would it be enough?"

17.

Tony snaps a handcuff round the wrist of the man he was following, spins him so his back connects heavily with a lamppost, clips the other cuff on his wrist with the lamppost between his arms, and pats him down. No weapons, just a phone. He takes it and slips it in his pocket.

The whole process takes less than ten seconds.

"Now, be a good boy and stay here," he tells the man, before spinning away and calling for the police to pick him up.

He's running hard. Tony runs a few miles every morning, sometimes more in the evening, work allowing. At night, in bed, on the rare occasion he sleeps well enough and long enough to register dreams, he dreams he's running.

Until his legs become like concrete; he can't run then, as it slowly sets. He can't get there when that happens, and he wakes up in a sweat, the sheets all kicked off.

"Tell me who I'm looking for?" he huffs out as his legs pound the pavement.

He takes a loop, hopes his timing is right and that he can drop on the road in front of the suspect on the road running parallel. He'll be busy looking to see if anyone's behind him.

The description comes through, the basics, the stuff he already knew. Middle-eastern appearance, dark hair, patchy beard, dark trousers and navy jacket.

"Narrow it down," he snaps.

He snatches a recently discarded newspaper from a bench as he passes. Not to stand and read, that's way too amateurish. Instead, he rolls it up, carries it in his hand, just like all the other commuters, as though he's carting it along to sit and read on the train on the way home.

He checks himself in a passing window reflection, suit jacket and trousers, shoes that need a polish and a shirt with no tie. He rubs his eyes hard, agitating them with some of the newspaper print. He looks like he's spent the day in an office, staring at a computer screen, maybe grabbed a swift couple after work.

"White shoes. Trainers, I think. White like fucking snow, Tony, you can't miss him."

"Roger. Going dark this end. Check in with you in a while. Over."

Tony reaches the main road running parallel. He politely stops to let a couple walk by, smiles and accepts the thanks, uses the second to flick his eyes along the road, looking at the feet picked out in the light from the shop and restaurant windows. He sees what he's looking for, and seamlessly slots into the flow of people, but deliberately allows himself to get caught behind a lady with a slow gait. Not obviously stalling, just unlucky in the lane he chose.

All completely natural.

He stuffs the paper in his left side hip jacket pocket, done to mask the fact he has a nine millimetre in a holster sitting on the left side of his ribs.

Skewing his eyes without turning his head, he looks down at the shoes of the people immediately behind him. He stops at an intersection and waits for the green man to flash, or for a break in the traffic. A regular commuter never waits for the signal if he doesn't have to.

He shrugs his shoulders like he's shaking off the day, and casts his eyes and head down. The white trainers are there, through his own legs, slightly to his left.

Continuing to look down as though he's not paying attention, he only looks up when the people start to move. He loses half a second and purposefully aims towards a couple walking the opposite way arm in arm, having to give them a wide berth, losing another couple of strides. He swings back across to his left and falls in step behind the white trainers.

Tony weighs up the man wearing them. Average height and build, five ten, eleven stone at the most. He notes a purpose in that stride.

They both enter the Tube station. This is where the planning comes in. It's also where the planning goes out the window.

He has a rule; always carry the special all access equivalent of an Oyster Card. It allows him on any train, tube or bus any time. A commuter would have a card, or a season ticket, or a travel card or just a return. He wouldn't piss about getting a ticket.

Unfortunately, his mark has to do exactly that. He wheels away right and starts reading the machine, working out how to get a ticket to where he's going.

Tony has a problem. There are two Tube lines in this station, each heading in two directions. Four options, north, south, east or west. He's east of centre now. The smart money would be on west, but it's impossible to know.

A stall will give him away unless he can think of a legitimate reason for it. Even a natural reason for a delay will draw attention to him as he'll be the only person standing still on the wrong side of the barrier. A static object of his size in a moving beast is bound to draw the eye.

All black people look the same, he thinks. It's a bias in some people...a lot of people. He'll play the race card.

He scans the on-comers looking for an in, and spots her walking alone. She looks tired after a long day on her feet, sensible shoes worn for the commute. He knows the blue and white uniform and the crest on the pocket of her coat. Her name badge is obscured, but he can blag that one.

A well known airline, she must be heading in from Stansted. Why else would she be here, heading in from the east? That's why she's on that side of the walkway, no way she came in from the west and crossed all the way over.

He cuts steadily across without causing disruption to the flow and waits till she's two strides away before pretending to recognise her.

"Hey, how you doing?" A big smile and a pause of expectation on his visage, as he raises his eyebrows and makes himself look earnest.

She looks blankly at him and tilts her head, trying to summon him up in her memory. All black men look the same, but she can't admit that prejudice to herself and certainly not to him. She doesn't want to be rude, so has to hedge her bets and play along. She takes a couple of crab steps as her brain tries to work out what to do. Maybe it was a drunken night, or perhaps he's a friend of a friend?

"Oh, erm, hello?" She says it like a question.

"You just in from Stansted?"

"Yeah, yeah."

She stops walking. It's not so busy that the crowd carries her along, there's room for them to stand and communicate. He waited till she was close so that she'd have walked slightly past him by the time she stopped. It results in him facing the way he's just come, looking back to where the guy in white trainers will approach from.

"You don't remember me, do you?" he says, still smiling. She's attractive. A bit heavy, but pretty enough. Nice tits, judging by the mounds under her coat. Good enough legs to carry the skirts they make them wear.

She blinks away the doubt. "I think so, yes. Can't think where from, though..."

"Oh, I'm disappointed. Am I that forgettable?"

"No, not at all. It's just...I have to deal with a lot of people. At work, I mean."

Tony spots the target at the barrier working out how to insert his ticket. Another fifteen seconds should do it.

"Who's the manager out at Stansted now? It used to be...ah, I can't remember the name..."

He keeps it gender neutral and leaves a lot of space. Most people are more than happy to talk about their own situations, work or personal. You just show them a chink of an opening.

"Oh, are you thinking of Tracey? She left about three months ago. We have Drew now. Gay guy?"

"No, I don't know Drew. Yeah, Tracey, I'm sure that was it. Why did she leave, I thought she'd been there for ever?"

"Her husband. He got a job abroad somewhere. Look, I'm sorry, but I can't quite place you. Do you work for the airline?"

Almost time to go, she's starting to get curious. Fifteen to thirty seconds is all you can ever safely buy on these kinds of manufactured encounters. That's how long it takes the human brain to process it all and work out that the information being put out is far in excess of the data being volunteered. That's how long it takes the average person to smell a rat.

"A bit of consulting. My name's Tony. Hey, I should probably get moving and let you get home."

They both start edging away from one another. She nods and smiles, relieved to be getting out of the awkwardness of the situation, her mind half wondering now if she's being manipulated, but still half trying to recall when she might have met him before. He looks amiable enough, with a big smile on his big face.

The white trainers are five paces away, three seconds before Tony can step in to his slipstream. One more card to play and make sure his mark knows this is a natural conversation. He speaks loudly as he moves away from the girl and flutters a hand of farewell at her.

"Hey, listen, great seeing you again. If you see Tracey, tell her 'congratulations'."

"Will do, Tony, no problem. Take care." She says it brightly, allowing her relief at leaving a slightly difficult encounter to come out naturally.

"You too."

He wheels away with perfect timing and follows the guy down the escalator to the westbound line. It was the most likely, but too risky to call.

A breeze being squeezed from the tunnel announces the train. Tony loves that breeze. He always has, since back when he was a kid with his uncle, heading up to Leyton Orient, or Fulham, or even Brentford on a Saturday afternoon. The lesser clubs, the ones in the lower divisions, whichever was at home. The breeze smells of London. He's been on other underground transportation systems, Washington DC, New York, Tokyo, Moscow, Paris, Berlin, and more. None of them smell quite like London.

There are plenty of seats at this time of night. The white trainers turn left and find one against the perspex partition.

Tony sits down opposite his mark and looks at him directly for a second, just as he would if he were traveling home from the football with his uncle. You naturally glance around to see who you're sitting near or next to and avoid the nutter who might start mumbling. Or the homeless person who will smell. Or the thief who will pick your pocket. Or the drunk guy who might pick a fight or throw up on your shoes. Or the young child who might scream and cry for the duration when his ears pop in the tunnel. Just a quick flick of the wired tired eyes, taking in all the people around him, the most natural thing in the world.

The guy seems calm. No indication that he's had any communication from the others as he pulls a phone from his pocket and checks it. No signal down here, so he puts it back where he took it from.

Tony notices the way his coat hangs on one side, something heavier than a phone in the other pocket. He took the mobile from his right pocket with his right hand, but shuffled it to his left to press the buttons with his thumb. He's left-handed, so whatever is in his more accessible left pocket is heavier and more important to have to hand than a mobile phone. He also instinctively sat with his left side to the perspex. That's the side he wants to protect. It must be a gun.

Tony's dad taught him the opposite. He can hear him saying it. 'Always keep your sword arm free, Boy'.

The threat's imminent, Tony can sense it. The calmness is a giveaway. This man is more than ready to sacrifice his life for a cause. He's seen it before. The ones who get excited and jump around, they're the ones who will either bottle it or miss the target. It's the calmness that always worries him.

Tony tips his head back, closes his eyes almost completely and sees the guy in white trainers looking up at the Tube route on the strip above his head. He watches his eyes bounce along the station names and sees his lips almost invisibly count out the number of stops. Five more.

Westminster.

No great surprise that he's going to Westminster at ten o'clock on a Monday night in September with a gun in his pocket, having gone to great lengths to lose the people he assumed would be watching him.

Chances are he isn't about to cross the river and have a look at the Millennium Wheel.

Before Tony was asked to form what became TERA, he was at the disposal of Special Branch. He was a security specialist who looked after Royalty on trips around the UK and abroad. He looked after Prime Ministers and visiting Presidents, Foreign Secretaries and Heads of State.

He still gets an itinerary every morning, showing where the likely targets will be at any given time - for his eyes only, top secret - so he knows that the Middle East talks are going on in London, and that a succession of foreign dignitaries will be giving statements from Downing Street at ten fifteen.

Beamed around the world, live via satellite television.

*****

"We should get going in a minute," Kate says.

"Ah, relax. Lanie's at a friend's house for the night. No rush. One for the road?"

We're the only customers left in the pub, just Suzie and Lena the waitress for company, but they know we're best left alone.

"Any fear of some service?" I call out as I walk towards the bar, empty glasses in hand. I glance up at the clock, seven minutes to ten.

"Oooh, a late one for you two tonight."

"What are you saying, Suze, now we're over forty we should be in bed by nine-thirty?"

"Yes, darling, but not for sleepin'! It is your wedding anniversary, after all," she retorts, winking at Kate as she does so, prompting more giggles.

"Well," Kate says flatly at Suzie, "I did say I might not be in till late tomorrow, so he'd better not disappoint me."

Appoint.

To provide with what is necessary.

Ergo, to disappoint might mean to provide with what isn't necessary, or not provide what is.

Yet appoint and disappoint aren't generally used as antonyms for one another. Nobody thinks of a disappointment as the opposite of an appointment.

Language often gets altered in the passage of time. I wonder if that's what happened?

Relationships between things take different courses, new identities become established. Things grow apart, but Kate and me, we're doing okay, better than okay.

"Penny for em?" Suzie snaps me out of it as she places the drinks on the bar in front of me.

"Very cheap, I'll take 'em," I snap back with a grin.

"Oooh, he's good, Kate en'e?"

"He's very quick!" Kate says proudly.

"Hope he's not that quick in the bedroom...!"

They all laugh at me, lost for words for once.

"Can you get tomorrow off?" I ask her when I get back to the table.

"I'm a Board Level Sales and Marketing Director on two-hundred grand a year with a maxed-out pension. I can pretty much do what I want."

"Let's drive out in the country tomorrow and hike a hill somewhere. Get some fresh air in our lungs. Soak in the scenery. Immerse ourselves in nature. See what retirement looks like. We could go to Sussex, walk the cliffs, head to Brighton afterwards."

"Okay, that sounds like a plan," and she toasts the idea with her glass of wine. Large.

"Fancy a bit of nature do you?" she asks coyly after a pause for a sip.

"Yes. As it happens, yes I do."

"Good, because I'm au naturel tonight," she whispers, and checks behind the bar. Seeing it's empty for a minute, she makes sure the curtains are drawn on the windows, the heavy dark drapes that look like they've been here since the War. Blackout leftovers.

She takes my hand and guides it beneath the dark wooden table, into the shadows where she parts her thighs.

18.

Tony rises as soon as the tube train starts to slow down. He's up on his feet and standing at the door to the side of the white trainers before they even realise it's time to move.

He could be wrong, and may have misread the stops the guy counted. But he isn't. The guy twists his head to read the station sign and raises himself up. Now it's almost as though the roles are reversed. Tony is the one being followed.

Which is just how he wanted it. The guy has no clue he's being tracked. In the reflection in the window, Tony sees him scouring the carriage, seeing if anyone's rising to pick up his tail. He's well beyond the point of even considering Tony as his shadow.

Then it gets even better, he actually asks Tony a question.

In a thick middle-eastern drawl, his English being very good, he asks, "excuse me. Which way is Big Ben, please?"

"Ha! You can't miss it, mate. You'll see it as soon as you leave the station. And the Houses of Parliament."

The guy break eye contact as he says "thank you," and goes back to waiting for the automatic doors to open.

"I'm going that way, follow me," he calls over his shoulder, and strides off without waiting for affirmation, fast, to keep the guy on his toes and make him a little disorientated.

As they emerge he spins his body and carries on walking backwards, points at the clock and doesn't say a word.

Tony watches as the white trainers follow the instructions he's committed to memory. He gets his bearings as he spots the bridge and tracks it away from the river, to Big Ben, the Houses of Parliament, Westminster Abbey, Parliament Square. He's taking it all in, matching it up to the images he saw on the internet, or via a series of photographs or video footage shot by someone posing as a tourist.

Tony trails him up the other side of the broadness of Whitehall, and stands in a doorway, keeping the white trainers in view. He takes his handgun from the shoulder holster and checks it; full clip, one in the chamber. He slides the safety off.

He observes as the guy takes the phone from his right pocket and, as before, shuffles it to his left hand. He thumbs through the messages and missed call log before holding it up to check the signal, weighing up why he has no messages and what the possible reasons could be. He stops walking and looks around, a three-sixty scan, still with the phone in his grip.

Something sets his mind at rest. Tony sees the definitive nod of a mind decided.

He's clear.

Clear to do what he set out to do.

The thought of the act forces him to touch the heavy metal pistol in his pocket.

Big Ben strikes the hour of ten o'clock. It distracts him, or, rather, brings him back to reality and focuses him. He flips the phone from hand to hand, drops it in a bin and walks on.

Is the fact he's here now and almost certainly armed enough to make the arrest, enough to make a terror charge stick? He can't let this play out much longer, he has to consider the safety of the public. It's a fine line between that, and some clever solicitor getting him off on a possession of illegal weapon charge. He has to have enough to show intent. And if the flat's clean, and nobody coughs up information... The game has to play out almost to the end.

Tony stands opposite the black iron gates at Downing Street, looking across. He can see the lights from the television crews, pick out the logos of the international media gathered, the crowd of hacks milling around, their shoulders hunched. Cameramen are checking their equipment. Areas are set up a few yards farther back for the summaries and analytic discussion that will follow the statements, all timed to coincide with the second half of the ten o'clock news, just before they do the sport and weather.

For the first time in nearly half an hour, Tony switches his radio on.

"Evening gents. Guess you got them all, then?"

"Where the fuck have you been?"

"Sorry. Had to go dark for a while."

"You're dark enough..."

"Yeah, yeah, yeah. Right, do we have everyone in custody?"

"All four sitting in cells, Boss."

"Any intel from the bastards?"

"No. Not saying a word."

"Anything in the bag?"

"A blanket. Obvious decoy."

"Number five is right here in front of me. I used my cuffs on the other guy, so I'm going to have to use my imagination on this one."

"What do you need, Tony?"

"Get a van, unmarked, over to Downing Street. Give me an ETA on that?"

"We can get one there in...four minutes."

"Do it."

Tony checks left and right as he rocks on the balls of his feet stretching out his hamstrings. He uses the outside broadcast vans as cover. His man is stood back, blending in with the small band of tourists straining to see through the gates, desperate to spot, in real life, someone they've seen on the television.

*****

Kate wants to walk down to the river when we've finished.

"Get some air and build up an appetite," she says saucily.

"Hey, you know, I've been thinking," I change the subject.

"Go on."

"This horse Lanie wants?"

Kate listens, a playful smile on her lips.

"She's been riding for a few years now. It's not a fad, is it? I've decided she can have one."

"You've decided? Wow, very authoritative. I do love it when you get all masterful on me!"

"I'm serious, Kate. She should have what she wants, that's all I'm saying. Life's too short."

"Good. I'm glad to hear it."

"We're agreed then?"

"It seems we are."

"Perhaps for her birthday in April."

"I think we should do it before then," Kate tells me.

"Really?"

"Yes. I mean, as you said, life's too short, isn't it? And, anyway, I've already put a deposit on a horse and agreed to

147

rent the small field at the side of the house from the man who owns it..."

"Right. Erm...fair enough. Just nip to the loo before we go."

"Yes, trot on. Giddy-up!"

*****

Tony's counting the seconds. Three minutes on the van arriving. He slows his heartbeat down to a beat a second, controlling it through deep inhalations through his nose. He clears his mind and starts walking across the road when he gets to one-hundred and twenty.

A minute till the transport arrives. Timing is everything, particularly as he has no cuffs. Perhaps he can get one of the security detail at the gates to Downing Street to chip in. Probably not. They won't leave the post, not on a night like this. No problem, he can restrain him for as long as it takes.

He plays it out in his head. Approach him from behind, but slightly to the right. He'll instinctively be more guarded on his left side. It's where he has the gun. And he's left-handed, it's his dominant side, the side he'll check first if he scans up and down the street. That knowledge could buy Tony half a second.

He'll then step across the back of him, armlock his left arm, twist it and push forward, taking him face down on the pavement parallel with the gutter. He can do all that one handed, leaving his left hand free to take the gun.

Three things to consider. An accomplice. Almost no chance of that. The white trainers never looked for one, and Tony kept his eyes peeled. There's nobody fitting the bill.

Then there's the fact he may have more than one weapon. As soon as he has him face down and the left pocket contents are secured, he'll check him over.

Thirdly, and the biggest danger, are the security guys on the gate. In addition, it's normal on a night like this to have a couple of Blenders in the crowd. They dress and act like tourists, cameras at the ready as they mingle with the masses to see what they can pick up. Tony's set up ops like this a thousand times, he knows the drill. The point is, if they misinterpret the situation, he could well find himself shot. Or at the very least hit with a stun gun, and he can't afford for his prisoner to escape.

He retrieves his ID card from his inside pocket and slips it in his left trouser pocket. As soon as the gun's secured, he'll pull it out for anyone who needs to see it.

Tony Alliss makes his move. He feels his heart rate suddenly spike in direct equal opposite measure to the adrenalin secreting into his system, a secretion that he channels.

Both men see it at the same time, the monitor on the outside broadcast vehicle, the live streaming of the ten o'clock news on some channel or other.

The picture couldn't be clearer, a man handcuffed to a lamppost in a street in London, an unmarked van pulling up and taking him away.

The white trainers swivel left then right. He looks straight at Tony. Instant recognition, a widening of the eyes. The half a second isn't enough, Tony can't get there. His six-feet two-inch two-hundred and twenty pound frame is a lot to get moving, inertia to be overcome.

That acceleration buys him four yards, even from a standing start. Tony was certain he'd take off left, it all stacked that way. Predominantly left-handed, slightly to that side of the gate and it was the way he came, the route he was familiar with. Had he read it, he may have been able to adjust and rugby tackle the guy, but he didn't. It made no sense.

Then the white trainers get lucky. He arcs right and sprints across the road in front of the very van that was arriving to pick him up. It slides to a halt in front of Tony and blocks his path. He has to navigate round the front of it. Another few yards get opened up.

It all happens too quickly for the two Met men in the van to act. Tony, still running, pulls his ID and gun in one fluid motion, the gun drawn from across his body by his right hand, the ID slipped from his pocket by his left. He holds the badge so the Met men can see it and levels the gun at eye height and looks for a shot. A leg shot would be ideal, but he's scuppered by the people milling around.

He takes off after the white trainers up towards Horse Guards Avenue, losing ground with every stride. They hang a right, down towards the river.

A shot is fired back over the shoulder. Not a threat, but enough to make Tony stick to the sides, enough to cost him half a pace and remind him that this is a dangerous situation, that there are innocent people on the streets.

Tony runs every day, sometimes twice a day. At night, in bed when he can't sleep, he dreams of running. But it always turns into something. His legs get heavier and heavier until he can't run any more. And he knows that if he comes to a standstill, he'll die.

So he forces his leaden legs on, dragging them along the ground, pulling them with his hands, willing his legs forward with his mind. A millimetre at a time, it doesn't matter, as long as he keeps moving forward. Just that fractional movement in the right direction is enough to sustain him.

19.

He knows he'll catch him eventually, as his feet slap the pavement along the north bank of the Thames.

That knowledge buys him time to report in on his radio. Between exhalations, in staccato form, he reports his position and calls for armed back-up.

The white trainers must know he's catching slightly, perhaps from a quick glance back, or maybe from the footfalls he can hear.

Tony Alliss can read his mind as he watches instinct kick in. He has to change the force and mix it up a bit, which is why he hangs a left away from the river and heads uphill. It wasn't a conscious choice, his subconscious telling him that a heavier item will be hindered by an incline, that a lighter object will ascend more rapidly.

Besides, a long straight course might encourage a bullet; better to keep a bend or turn between them. Bends and turns also suit him for the same reasons, he should be more nimble. Sideward force will affect the larger heavier object more, and either make it run a longer distance or make it slow down.

Three right turns after the initial left and he's heading back the way he came, through a small street that links two bigger streets.

It's a mistake, as it allowed the van to cut off his escape at one end. It nearly overran the turning, but spotted him and reversed up and sealed his exit.

With no other option, the white trainers step through the door of a small quiet pub tucked away on a nondescript side street in the old City of Westminster.

Tony catches sight of one of those white shoes just before it disappears.

He draws his gun and puts his shoulders to the brickwork, sliding along the buildings, ducking down to clear the windows.

He flinches at each of the three shots that bark out.

*****

"You ready?" I ask Kate as I re-enter the bar.

She drains her wine glass and tells me she is with a nod. She stands and reaches a hand out towards her coat.

I hear the door of the pub hit the wall. Instinctively I glance at the clock. Not even a quarter past ten, plenty of time till last orders, though Suzie will probably call time on the place as soon as we leave. There's no sense in keeping the lights on for no customers.

The bang is huge, the loudest one I've ever heard. I feel my whole body recoil at it and can feel my pulse in my temples, blood instantly spiked in my whole body.

Pure instinct, but I know it's a gun shot.

As soon as I've thought that, there's another one. And another.

All in the space of about a second.

Kate has made the same leap. Her eyes are wide and her jaw set. The colour has drained from her face. I imagine I look the same.

Processing the data, I try to isolate the sounds in the mix. The door hit the wall with force as somebody entered. They entered in a hurry. Why would somebody enter in a hurry? Because they're trying to escape from something.

I heard Suzie. She said, "sorry, we're closing, darl...".

She never finished the sentence, because the first shot cut her off.

Suzie has been shot. By a man. A lone man.

Suzie always calls men darling,, it's what she does. She'll call Kate darling, but only because she knows her so well. It's normally reserved for men.

And if it were more than one person, she might have said 'my darlings 'or 'gents 'or 'folks'. She would have used the plural term. She didn't. She used darling. One man.

And the door only opened once. It hit the wall and bounced shut again. I remember hearing the wood wedge on the frame after the clout against the wall. One man. Definitely.

A robbery? Not likely. There would be no need to enter the way he did. That smacks of fleeing something or somebody. And why would a robber start shooting on entry? A thief would want information, and he probably wouldn't feel threatened by two women. He might shoot one of them, but not both.

And he did shoot both, because I heard the scream. It was Lena. Half a scream, in the half a second between shots. I heard the two bodies hit whatever was behind them. I heard things breaking fractionally before I heard the bodies hit the floor.

Bodies? Are they both dead, Suzie and Lena? If not dead, then close to death, because they stopped making a sound when they were shot.

So the man knows how to shoot people. He may have got lucky, but chances are that he's had training.

And who is he running away from, and is the chaser even more dangerous than the chased? I have no idea.

His feet made no sound on the stoned floor leading in to the old no smoking section. Kate's heels would click sexily on it. Mine would clump down, wearing away the outside of the heels, the soles shuffling slightly and grating away on the rough stone.

The guy must be wearing trainers. But as that door hit the wall, I heard footsteps slapping the pavement outside before sliding to a halt. Proper shoes, like the shoes I wear. Leather, with soles that grate and heels that clump.

Whoever is chasing him isn't a punk kid in trainers. He wears proper shoes but wasn't far behind the guy. A fit man. A fit man who had the sense not to burst in and start shooting. A fit smart man who feels the need to protect what may lie within. A fit smart man whose primary concern is the safety of the public, but is prepared to give chase to an armed man in the dark through London.

A policeman, or similar, that's my guess.

So the man in trainers is a criminal, but isn't here to rob the place. The police are on top of him, and he's probably just killed two people in cold blood. He has nothing to lose.

Kate spins her head and looks directly at me. I bring my finger up to my lips. Silence.

Perhaps we'll get lucky. He'll run out the back of the pub and not make the right turn into the bar. He must have heard Suzie start to say they were closing, and that might suggest to him that there are no customers left.

Using my hands, palms down, splayed fingers pointing up at forty-five degrees, I motion Kate to stay perfectly still.

She's breathing hard, the two adrenal glands sitting above her kidneys have secreted adrenalin into her body, hence the pale complexion and accelerated heart and lung function. Her digestive system may well have ceased functioning, and her blood vessels are priming and fueling her muscles for a fight or flight action.

It's the exact same reaction as me. I feel mine, I see hers. Thinking.

If we move, he'll probably see us through the mottled glass on the door between the two bar areas. Even sinking down out of view could draw his eye. It's best to stay perfectly still. If we get the chance, and I see him move past the door, we can try to creep behind the bar, at least have a barrier between us and the nozzle of his gun. And if I can then find somewhere to hide Kate, I will. She's small enough to fit in a cupboard.

I cast my eyes around the room, looking for anything I can use as a weapon. There's a set of iron hearth ware in front of the unlit fire. I clock the spiked stoker. If I can get to it and position myself near the door, I may have a chance.

Failing that, bottles are my best bet. But they're all far off behind the bar. To get to them I either need to vault the bar or lift the hatch and open the half-door.

He'll see the movement.

I force a smile at Kate, as I try to be reassuring, and move my hand very slowly, the movement obscured by my form. I make the same hand indications as before. Stay perfectly still. Keep perfectly quiet.

And hope this will go away.

20.

Tony remembers his sister skipping along in her best dress. It was red and white. White mainly, with red hearts on it, and the sun was so hot that day, as she skipped through the streets of the old neighbourhood, running her hand through the bunting, the red, white and blue flags that connected all of London in honour of the Queen's Silver Jubilee in June 1977. His sister was excitedly smiling so broadly in her new dress.

Tony smiles back at his little sister as, crouching down, he tenses his not inconsiderable bulk, carefully leans a shoulder against the lower part of the wooden door, and looks at the reddish streetlight playing with the dull grey metal of his gun.

The music washes over him faintly through the barrier that the door offers. The Beatles, he thinks to himself. 'Ob-La-Di, Ob-La-Da'. His dad always liked this song. His sister would dance to it, the reggae influence, Desmond Dekker. His grin broadens as he shows his teeth.

He sucks in a huge breath through his nose.

And holds it...

*****

A tiny nod by Kate draws my attention back to the door. He's coming.

We all think we have a plan, what we'd do if someone came into our house at night, or what we'd do if a street mugger pulled a knife, and some of us might actually adhere to it, rightly or wrongly, but most of us wouldn't. The majority of us would play along.

A survival instinct kicks in that makes us act in a way that best suits our physical and intellectual limitations and strengths. We instinctively play the card that gives us the best chance of survival, given the hand we have to play with.

A fire stoker against a gun? No chance. And Kate could get hit in the melee. Besides, I know there's a man outside the pub who is on our side. I'm certain of it, and he'll be trained, he'll know what to do.

So I need to buy time for that particular player to show his hand.

The door opens. Kate makes a noise at the back of her nose, carried on a breath. She's breathing. I'm not. A gun appears first, then a white training shoe, followed by a dark trousered leg and arms covered by a dark blue jacket.

"You'll need hostages," I say calmly, "if you plan on getting out of this, I mean. You'll need some bargaining chips..."

A Middle Eastern looking man enters the bar. The gun and his hands cover most of his face, held at arms-length at eye height. His left hand fingers the trigger as his right adds support.

He sweeps the room as he lets the door close behind him with a thud of wood wedging on wood. His eyes flick over the windows and take in the heavy dark curtains. There's no way someone on the outside can see through them. I can see his mind arriving at the conclusion. There are two points of entry; the door he came through, and a door leading out behind the bar.

He motions for me to back away, jiggles the gun barrel, pushing me over towards Kate. I keep my body between her and the gun and walk backwards over to her, desperately trying to keep my face calm and relaxed.

The fact he hasn't shot us has to be a good thing. Suzie and Lena didn't stand a chance, a panic reaction on his part on entering the pub as he found himself unable to differentiate between the threat pursuing him and the two people he encountered. But now his system has slowed down enough so that he can think along reasonable lines.

Reasonable. Agreeable to reason or sound judgement. Capable of rational behaviour or decision.

"This is Kate. I'm Lorry," I say, introducing something personal to make sure he knows we're human, and less likely to kill us, therefore.

Flicking his eyes between the bar and us, he works out how to gain access. He sidesteps over and lifts the hatch before nudging the half-door with his toes. He steps behind the dark mahogany structure.

He takes the gun off us and swings it into the back room. No sooner have I spotted the opportunity, than it's taken away. Perhaps, in that moment, when the gun was pointed away from us, we could have made a lunge for the door.

It's too late. The gun's back on us. He reaches in and takes the key from the lock on the other side. He closes the door and locks it, before tossing the key on the floor behind the bar and walking back through.

He speaks for the first time.

"What makes you think I want to get out of this?"

A thick Arabic drawl, but otherwise excellent English, probably educated in an English school abroad. It's too precise to be done here. He'd have picked up inflections and colloquialisms. Yemeni would be my guess. You pick up the accents driving a cab.

"You're sweating and breathing hard," I say, with as much confidence as I can muster.

"So...?"

"So you ran. And you didn't run towards this. So you ran away from something. If you didn't plan on surviving you wouldn't have done that."

"Very good. But perhaps I just want to kill as many infidels as I can before I offer myself for Allah?" He says this almost mockingly, like he's testing me.

"Then you'd have shot us and moved on. Or just moved on. There's a back exit on the pub, but you didn't take it. You sought a shelter. Shelter. Refuge. Protection. Definition of protection is preservation from injury or harm. The only thing I can think that you want to preserve is your own life."

"You are a clever man, I see. Yes, perhaps I need to survive. Perhaps Allah still has use for this body before I em welcomed to him."

"Then, as I said, you need hostages."

"You are correct..."

He's about five nine, maybe five ten in his trainers. Not big built, but has that wiry toughness some people have. He's fit, I can perceive that, his breathing is almost back to normal. Recovery time from exertion is excellent. His hands on the gun are as steady as a rock. His clear-eyed freshness and skin tell of a good diet, if not a substantial one, lots of fruit and rice. Water is his staple drink. I can almost see him on a training camp in the desert.

Kate's breathing settles a little behind me. She has very mild asthma, stress can spike it. It's why we don't have any pets.

"You okay?" I say to her softly over my shoulder.

She nods, but I can see she isn't. She can't control the rush of adrenalin yet, it's still coursing through her body. She's starting to move from dazed to agitated. I can see her hands clenching and unclenching to soft fists by her sides, trying to get a grip.

"Correct to a degree," he says after reflection.

And I know what's coming.

*****

Tony was on the brink but the noises stopped him. The increase in volume of the music, indicative of a door opening. And then the sound of a voice, an English accent and not the voice of the white trainers. He heard the word 'hostages 'before the door closed and muffled the noise. Just the faint rhythm and lyrics of 'Ob-La-Di, Ob-La-Da ' winding down remain.

He speaks into his radio, hushed but distinct. "Three shots fired. But we have hostages inside. Plural, copy?"

"Copy Tony. We're two minutes away. Armed response unit coming in. Two Met officers on scene are working their way through to the back of the building. Can you hold the front? Over."

"Roger that. I'm going in to take a look."

"Tony, wait for..."

He silences the radio and slips the clip out of his gun. He removes all but two bullets. It's a precaution, should the gun fall into the hands of the white trainers, he wants to minimise the potential impact. He drops the bullets into his jacket pocket and twists his shoulders so the jacket falls away. He pulls his arms free and screws the jacket into a ball and tosses it into the gutter.

A black dog is simply suddenly there. It came from nowhere, strolling up to him. It sniffs his jacket before skipping up the kerb. It comes right up to him, tail wagging but down, happy but cautious.

"Hello girl," he says, not sure why he thinks it's a girl.

He scratches behind her ear with his free hand. The dog cocks her head over. No collar but not homeless, Tony believes, too neat for a street dog, but not well loved either.

"You'd better go, it's about to get noisy here," he tells the dog gently before pulling his hand back. The dog licks it and looks right at him before turning and walking away.

The tensed muscles in his arms stretch the cotton of his shirt. He was born big and naturally muscular. Aside from the running, he doesn't do anything to maintain it. Perhaps, as he gets older, he'll need to change that, or turn flabby.

If.

If he gets older.

Slapping the clip back in the gun, he engages the mechanism and fires a bullet into the chamber. Two shots, one to kill, the other for insurance should he miss. But Tony never misses.

Except once, one time in his life did he miss. The most vital time.

He peers up through the lowest glass panel in the pub door. It's slightly brighter within than without. He sees the two bodies on the floor, female and not moving.

There's a door leading off to the right, another at the rear probably leading to the kitchen. It's in darkness, the kitchen staff sent home early on a quiet Monday night.

It's unlikely that the music's emanating from the dark kitchen, so he deduces that it must be from the door on the right.

He pushes open the front door with the palm of his left hand. It squeaks a little. He steps in with his gun leading the way.

*****

A door squeak interrupts his train of thought. I breathe again. He was just about to work out that he only needs one hostage, that having two bodies in the room with him is a chance to be over-powered or distracted.

"Move," he hisses, the gun pointing where to.

He needs to move himself away from the door. The glass panel, though mottled, is the only view in, and he needs to keep the two doors and window in view. They're the only three weaknesses in the structure and he needs to cover them.

He arcs round to the wall with the fireplace in it and puts his back to it.

Reaching behind me, I find Kate's waist with my left hand, and use it to steer her to our right keeping my body between her and the gun.

I can feel her warmth and her trembles. Her left hand finds mine, skin on skin as it grips tightly.

We're still alive, I say to myself. Warmth, movement and the strength to grip are all vital signs of life, along with her laboured breaths. We just need to hold on, I think, and will my thoughts to Kate.

"Yes," the wiry man says, as much to himself as us, "perhaps a hostage will be advantageous."

A hostage. Singular.

Time to act. If he's going to have just one hostage, I decide it will be Kate.

We can only ever truly feel one emotion at any given time. There is no such thing, in literal terms, as bittersweet. Instead, at times it's bitter, and at others sweet. I decide to take one emotion, fear, and turn it into anger. Anger and fear are, after all, closely related, one always follows the other.

Pulling my hand away from Kate's warm grasp, I scream at him.

"Come on then, you rag-head bastard!" The words leave my mouth in a cloud of spittle spray, as I feel the blood flood to my head.

He flinches at the ferocity of it, the tables somewhat turned, the aggressor roles momentarily switched. The terror is now coming from me.

"Religion? That's what this is about? Your religion is blinding you. Listen to me, things are different here, a woman will offer you better protection. They're much less likely to shoot you if you have a woman hostage..."

I advance slowly towards him as I speak, moving slightly to my right as I do so, edging towards the bar and drawing the line of fire away from Kate.

Kate speaks for the first time, "Lorry..." is all she says. Her emotion is still fear, but now it's fear for me rather than for herself. It's a good thing. She can perceive that I'm now the one in danger, even more so than her.

The gunman, likewise, moves somewhat from fear and more towards anger. I can see the flush in his skin. Now there is a little tremor in the hands holding the gun.

"Pull the fucking trigger," I urge him, simultaneously hoping the door will open and help will arrive. Kate is my only concern now. We have a daughter, she needs her mum.

I'm on top of him, but he still doesn't shoot. A yard, a stride away from the end of the barrel, but I'm looking in his eyes an arm's length farther back.

Bizarrely, his eyes are the exact same colour as Kate's. It disarms me for a second and stops me walking forward. He senses the hesitation.

"That is why you should die. You are godless, and thus serve no purpose." His voice is as loud as mine.

"So kill me. Shoot me right now. Do god's work for him. See where it takes you. There's nothing after this, so there's nowhere for me to go. And I wonder at what point that will dawn on you? Probably never. It'll be too fucking late."

"No," he says, calmer now. "God has told me what to do. He told me through you. God is everywhere, you see. You talked about shelter and protection, you have stood in front of her to shelter and protect her. That is your role here. She is too small to offer shelter and protection. But you...god put you here for me."

And I know he's right, that there's nothing more I can say to him. So I half turn my head to look at Kate.

Is it disappointment I see in her expression? Me, the fast-talking, quick-witted master of verbal assassination, and I got it wrong. All those times that I got it right when it never really mattered, but the one time it does...

I may as well pull the trigger myself.

Kate speaks. "Lorry, tell Lanie I love her."

So I play the only card left in my hand. I lunge.

But I can't get there

And a shot barks so loudly that time stops and I seem to float in the air motionlessly.

Before the impact.

21.

Tony peers through the thick mottled window but sees nothing but blurs.

He can make out forms, but only when one moves does it become human. And he clearly hears the voice, the same English voice he heard say 'hostages 'is now screaming about religion. What the fuck is he doing, Tony asks himself, is he trying to get himself shot? Before he finishes asking himself the question, he's answered it. That's exactly what he's trying to do.

All done to a soundtrack of 'Wild Honey Pie'.

Tony knows the album now. If it is the album in order, then the 'Bungalow Bill 'song should be next. He remembers his dad having the vinyl record. It was the only Beatles LP his dad owned, as far as he can recall, and he taped it for the car. One summer was spent listening to this Beatles album. It's ingrained in him, etched indelibly. But he couldn't tell you the names of the tracks, his dad never bothered to fill in the track details on the cassette insert.

But he knows all the words.

He hears the white trainers screaming back at the English voice, and there's a woman's voice in there, too, saying a name. Lorry, was it? Followed by more arguing between the men, as the blurred shape moves forward. And then a calmer statement from the white trainers, an almost soothing quality to his tone.

Tony pieces it all together, just as the short song ends.

"Lorry, tell Lanie I love her," he hears the woman say.

The shot instinctively forces him half a step from the door. He waits a heartbeat to see if any more are coming, and hears the clatter from what he assumes is another corpse hitting the floor.

He steps into the room, looking down the shaft of his gun.

He sees the white of her dress.

Swinging right, his eyes settle on two men on the floor, one in white trainers holding a gun, the other staring blankly at the white dress, the gun pressing firmly into the side of his head. The English voice lies on top of the white trainers, shielding him from Tony, an arm locked round his neck to stop him rolling away.

A patch of red spreads over the white. Like a heart, thinks Tony, just like a heart. Like his little sister's best dress.

*****

I wish for death for myself. I would give my life right now for Kate's.

And that's why there is no god. Or, if there is, it isn't a god I want to know. Kate isn't like me, she refused to accept that line and said that nobody could prove there wasn't a god, so she'd await more information before reaching a decision.

For the first time in my life, I desperately want to be wrong. I want there to be somewhere for Kate to go, a place where I can see her again. I wish I had that faith.

Because I know she's dead. Her eyes tell me she's gone. They see nothing.

Whereas all I see is her, along with an eternal life without her as fear washes over me, a similar fear to that I felt when Kate was pregnant with Lanie, an overwhelming sense of some momentous change taking place, but without the hope that it'll all be okay in the end. I'm numb, both physically and mentally, and all I want is to be with Kate, for another shot to blast out and end this.

Oh, but Lanie...what about Lanie? How can I even begin to tell her about this horror?

Everything rushes in at me, the whole room feels like it's pressing down and merging as it swirls, the enormity of what just unfolded sending me into shock. I have to focus on something specific, or I know I'm going to pass out.

Perhaps passing out wouldn't be such a bad idea? I could just close my eyes to all of this and hopefully never wake up...

Lanie. The thought of Lanie snatches me back.

The overriding emotion I feel is grief, a selfish grief for the life I'll now have to live without Kate, and a dreadful grief on Lanie's behalf. I need to replace one emotion with another, that's how this works.

Anger and rage are what I need to summon up in this moment, and to get there I need to look, I need to think about what just happened, not what will happen at the end of this.

The shot hit Kate close to her heart, if not directly on it. I imagine the bullet shattered her sternum and ribs en route, sending splinters of bone into her lungs before her tender heart exploded and bits of everything exited the back of her body.

All the bits of her were thrust back by the force. Her petite entirety hit the wall, indicating the bullet hit bone and met resistance. Death was instant.

She slid down, her tiny feet - feet so small, that they made it so hard for her to buy shoes - scooted forward, and her eight stone of mass followed, driven by gravitational pull to the lowest point, her muscles no longer operational and no longer capable of working with her bone-structure to hold her upright, no longer able to counteract gravity.

As she slid down, her new white dress shifted upwards as it snagged.

Here she lies, an ever-widening red stain spreads on her dress, the new necklace sparkling around her neck, bits of her on the wall behind where pictures hung until recently.

But the worst? The worst thing is her nakedness, her exposed vulva, one leg slightly bent, opening her up.

There is no dignity. I hate these two men looking at my wife.

And as my ears clear themselves of the ringing the shot induced, that's when I dig my feet in and summon up all the rage and anger I now feel, as I arch my back and thrust my head backwards trying to make contact with the man holding me, the man who killed Kate and took my life at the same time as he ruined a fifteen year-old girl's life with one pull on a trigger, all for reasons I know I will never understand.

I ram my head back towards him, screaming, shocked but comforted by my own violence. "Fucking hell. Fucking hell. Fuck in hell. Fuck in hell. Hell. Hell. Hell." Every wailed syllable is accompanied by a ramming of my skull towards him as he lies beneath me.

But he has me in a tight grip.

"Hey-up. You a'right?" the large black man who just entered the room says loudly. He has a gravelly voice, the kind you could grate cheese on. And his face, big and broad, is a mess of contradictions.

His eyes are terrifying, they could bore holes in things. But his mouth is soft and relaxed, at odds with his teeth that are clenched in his set jaw beneath the soft lipped look and the easy deep gravel.

"Relax, he's only got one bullet left," he says calmly, before explaining to me, "that's a Taurus Model 82 38 caliber revolver. Made in Brazil and, most likely, smuggled into the UK to sell on the black market. A few of them have turned up recently. The thing is, it only has six bullets in the revolving chamber, and he's already fired five. I didn't see him re-load, did you?"

His eyes are locked unwaveringly on mine. I suppose I must be completely obscuring the guy beneath me, but I get the feeling he doesn't want me to look at Kate.

He holds me in his magnetic gaze. I'm so focused on his face that the gun he holds becomes almost periphery.

He walks across the room towards Kate. He must sense my anxiety, the way my body tenses and the man holding me has to tighten his hold as he feels me kick.

Bending down, he pulls Kate's dress straight and covers her up. He gives her some dignity.

The man beneath me utters, "infidel whore."

"Lorry, right?" the black man asks before I can react.

"Yes," I say.

"I'm Tony. I'm sorry about...is she your wife?" He asks it in hushed reverential tones.

"Yes," I say again.

"What's her name?"

"Kate. Her name's Kate." I'm aware we're talking about her in the present tense. Her name is still Kate. She is still my wife.

"I'm sorry about Kate. Any kids?"

"A daughter."

"I want you to think of your daughter right now. She's going to need her dad. You a'right?"

He says it oddly, almost like he's slurring the question 'are you alright? 'I wonder, in the surreal moment of it all, if he might be a bit drunk.

"Hey-up? I said, you a'right?"

Hey-up? It's a northern expression. This guy is an out and out Londoner. A thick southwest London accent. he wouldn't say 'hey-up'. And that slurred question? He just did it again, that's three times. Every other word he says is clearly pronounced.

Can he be as clever as I think he might be?

He doesn't look that clever, but then what does clever look like? Am I being blinded by a racist stereotype; large black men who carry a gun can't be very bright?

Let's assume he is that clever.

"Yes, I'm a'right?" A pause. "Hey-up, how do you know he won't use that last bullet on me?"

An almost imperceptible nod lets me know I understand him, nodded with his eyeballs only. A little dip up and down, like he might have been acknowledging my question.

"Because of what I'll do to him if he uses his last bullet on anyone but me."

Tony says it in a way that is matter-of-fact, and leaves absolutely no doubt that he means it.

"Love this song," he suddenly says brightly.

I can't work out if this guy's a genius or a bit tapped.

He starts dancing. His gun never leaves us, doesn't even waver as he dances on the carpet, dances round his gun as he adds some singing.

"Ah, my old man used to play this album in the car all the time. This was my favourite track."

Tony carries on dancing on the spot. In spite of everything, I have to smile. As much as I don't want to, I can't help it. I even give a short snap of a chuckle, as much in disbelief at the spectacle as anything. It's like your dad at a wedding, his knees bending and twisting, his shoulders rolling.

But the gun never leaving its mark.

My head starts to throb at the pressure from the gun at my temple. Perhaps I could roll over, drag him with me, and expose him to Tony for a shot. No, as mad as he looks, I trust Tony on this. I'll play along.

For the first time, the man beneath me tries to address Tony.

"If you want him to live, I will need you to leave here and get me a car outside the door."

He totally ignores him. Dancing and smiling, I'm utterly transfixed. The man beneath my body has no idea at all what's going on, he's stunned into complete inaction by the whole farce.

There's always the possibility I could be wrong. But so what? Perhaps I shouldn't do what he wants, but let him think I'm going to.

He must read my mind. Perhaps he sees in my eyes my flagging resolve.

"What's your daughter's name, Lorry mate?"

"Lanie. Delanie."

"Nice name. Does she look like Kate or you?"

"More like her mum. Dark and petite..." I trail off and picture Lanie in my mind. She's at a friend's house, she's safe. How can she be safe after this, how will she ever be safe?

"She needs her dad, Lorry. You hear me?"

"Yes," I say. "I know."

He carries on dancing, twisting his bulk from one side to the other, moving his head in time with the music, but never taking his eyes off the prize.

The track winds down, the chorus on repeat. A trombone plays the ditty, except it's not a trombone, it's a Mellotron on a trombone setting. Nothing is as it seems. Next comes applause, applause which Tony adds to as he taps his free hand against the hand holding the gun rigidly still.

He dances and laughs as he claps.

And I know it's imminent, but I can't quite remember at what point it comes.

Because there is no gap between the tracks.

And it doesn't come in a logical place, it's almost random. It sounds different every time you listen to it, impossible to pin down.

And I'm listening so intently that I hear the few little plonks on a piano that I've never noticed before. They're way down in the mix.

Waiting.

Dancing.

Is it George who shouts it? Or is it John?

Being northern lads, whoever it was doesn't pronounce the 'H', so it comes over as 'Ay-up!'

Two syllables, and I go before the first one is complete.

I jerk my head and then body suddenly and violently to my right.

Just as Tony had slurred.

Two shots ring out, so close together that they merge into one.

They're finished before the '-Up 'syllable can even be called, just the resonation bouncing around the room as 'While My Guitar Gently Weeps 'begins.

The pain stabs me.

So hot.

In the back of my head.

And everything goes black.

Part Three: The Grey Area

22.

Kate was the black to my white, the dark to my light. Not in a sinister way.

We could look at the same page in a book and I'd see all the stuff between the lines, the white area, the hidden subtext and meanings. Kate would see the words for exactly what they were.

Without Kate I am just a blank page. The narrative that was my life stopped suddenly in the middle of a tale. Stark white empty sheets follow. It's not that the words aren't there, just that I can't see them without the contrast.

But today, for the first time in four years, I'm starting to see the plot again. Because of Lanie? Yes, her and Tony, and the TERA involvement. Credit where it's due, as well, even David the Emotional Therapist has given me a bit of impetus.

Today is the first day of my fifth year without her. I didn't even get to say goodbye. The funeral had to take place without me in attendance. Four months in hospital saw to that, the first few weeks in a medically induced coma.

The past four years in a self-induced coma.

It's twenty-four hours since I heard from Tony. It's a Sunday night, except the days are irrelevant. It could be any night. They become such when they're all the same. Nearly all the same.

Tony offers me a change. I'll never tell him, but I missed him last night. Lanie says I should tell people those kinds of things, but I can't.

He visited me every day he could in hospital. He's sat with me, sorting records and typing out Dymo labels just about every week since I came home. And he's involved me in the TERA work, all of which has given me some purpose in life, and given me a reason to carry on and get up every day.

Rising from my leather art-deco chair, I measure my steps to the cabinet housing the music system.

There must be a path worn between my chair and the turntable. It is, without question, the most well trod path in the house.

I follow the routine, and cue up the other side of the LP. Absolutely no idea what I'm listening to, but it fills my world. It's something from the thousands of LPs Tony hasn't labeled up yet, a record I bought at some point in the past few years and I never got around to playing.

The metal prong at the centre of the deck on the turntable struggles to penetrate the hole at the mid-point of the vinyl record. It takes a little pressure once I've ensured it's lined up correctly.

In a similar way, the bullet that penetrated my grey matter before lodging in my occipital lobe, nudging up to my primary visual cortex, only partially entered me. I'm no brain surgeon, but this is an area at the back of the head. The impact had an impact, but the heat did most of the damage, so I believe.

That's the bit I never knew about bullets, they get hot. Knowing what I now know, it's logical. The initial charge is based on heat, and the friction as the bullet spins through the barrel adds to it. Considerably. Then there's the friction from the air as it travels, as demonstrated by space shuttles and their heat shields. As it loses velocity and impacts on things, energy is dissipated, and heat is lost as a consequence, but the doctors estimate that the bullet was three hundred degrees C when it came to rest, or five hundred and seventy in Fahrenheit. That's an awful lot of Kelvins. Essentially, nothing lives at that temperature.

It was the second bullet Tony fired that got me. Having followed the path of the first, it nicked a bit of bone as it exited the already dead gunman's skull, which deflected it slightly away from me. It encountered one of the iron hearth ware implements, which forced it to hit the stone fireplace floor and ricochet back up and enter the back of my head.

My only recollection of anything is hearing, ironically enough, 'Happiness Is A Warm Gun 'playing along as Tony hooked a finger inside me and dislodged the bullet. He saved my life, such as it is.

In short, that stray projectile irreversibly cauterised bits of my brain, most notably the bits to do with visual processing.

There are so many things I wish I could see, but there are so many things that, even if I could, I can never understand.

Kate would use tickets as bookmarks. On a plane she'd slip in the bit of the boarding pass they let you keep. On a train it was the orange ticket, or she'd use a cinema or concert ticket that she had about her person.

She said she did it for a number of reasons. It meant she knew where the ticket was if required. It served the obvious purpose of marking her page without having to fold the corner down. It cost nothing and it meant less litter. But mostly she did it to preserve the memory.

If she picked up a book at random from the shelf, she'd more often than not find an old ticket inside. There were books from before we met, that she brought with her when we got together, and they had tickets and other paraphernalia in them. If I ever borrowed a book she'd read, I'd find the hidden marker.

Sometimes of an evening, we'd play a game. Lanie would pick a book at random and hand her the ticket, a train caught from Euston to Chester on May twelfth, 1988. She couldn't tell Lanie and me anything about the book, but could recount the day thirty years before in vivid detail. A trip to the horse races one Spring Thursday, a jolly from a printing firm up north. Her being a client, albeit a sprog of not much importance at that stage, she and two dozen or so of her peers and seniors in the magazine publishing world had assembled for champagne, posh nibbles and business talk.

The sun shone and she won on the horses. About fifty pounds, if she remembered correctly. Back when fifty pounds was a lot of money, she joked, and she picked her horses simply by them having nice names.

Lanie asked her if she was with Dad then? "No," she said, "it was five years before I met your Dad. I was only twenty-one." "Did you have any romance at the gee-gees?" Lanie persisted. She was thirteen or so at the time, and just starting to really notice boys. And horses, she was obsessed with horses.

Kate shook her head, but we both knew it was a fib. An acceptable lie such as 'nits only live in clean hair', something said to spare the feelings of someone else.

The point is, there are tickets in many of the books in the house, but I can't see them. And even if I could, if they weren't from a time I was in her life, I might not know the tale associated with them, and those tales are now lost.

For some reason, that fact breaks my heart all over again every time I think of it.

If I could have that time all over again with Kate, I'd make her tell me every single story relating to each ticket in those books. I wouldn't get upset at the stories that involved other men. I'd ask her to tell me it all, warts and all.

I open a can of beer having rotated it and located the ring-pull. Blindness involves a lot of rotating stuff. It must be about eight in the evening. I should think about eating something.

In a while.

A shiver ripples me like a ghost passing through me. A breeze, slight, but enough, sufficient to lick the hairs on my neck, just a short burst bringing the accompanying few degree drop in temperature.

The back door wasn't open for long.

"Hello Tony," I say calmly and quietly, just audible over the music.

"How...? I used to be good at this. Before I met you, I could move undetected. And how did you know it was me?"

"Well, I felt the breeze and drop in temperature when you came in through the back door. It was just a shift in the air, but it was enough. If it was anyone else sneaking in here, their unfamiliarity would have hindered them and slowed them down, especially given the dodgy mechanism on the slide door. You've been here so often, you know how the latch works, and how to negotiate the obstacles in the dark. I assume the lights are still off? And you're the only person on this planet who could have got to me as quickly as you did. You made the trip as fast as I could, and I live here and I live in the dark. Add in the fact you knew exactly where I'd be, even though you couldn't see me over the high winged back of the chair, and it almost certainly had to be you."

"Fuck me," Tony says with utter exasperation.

"Do you mind if I don't?"

"Leave that on, please," Tony snaps as my hand reaches for the volume on the remote.

"Interesting. So, you sneak in, and now we need noise to mask our conversation. If I tie that in to the cryptic call from last night, might I assume you have a bit of a problem?"

"Yep. Sit tight, I need to sweep this place for bugs."

Five minutes later, he's back. "All clear."

He takes the beer I offer him.

"What are you listening to?" he asks me.

"Absolutely no idea. It's from the section you haven't labeled yet."

"Mind if I switch a light on?"

"No, doesn't make a blind bit of difference to me."

There's a click from the lamp.

"Jesus," he suddenly exclaims, "what happened to your head?"

"Where?"

"There."

"Well, don't fucking prod it. Christ."

"Does it hurt?"

"It does now!"

I know he's talking through a grin.

"How'd you do that?"

"A tree."

"There's a tree growing out your head?"

"What? No, Tony, I walked into a tree."

"What did you do that for?"

"Well, I didn't fucking do it deliberately."

"Where?"

"In the garden."

He pauses to take stock.

"In the back garden?"

"In the only garden I've got, yes."

"So, to be clear. You walked into the only tree in your garden, a tree that's been there since you moved in?"

"Yes. I didn't walk into the trunk or anything stupid. It was a branch, I lost my bearings."

"What were you doing out there?"

I don't want to have this conversation, so mumble an incoherent response.

"What? You were purchasing a ticket...?"

"I was practicing my cricket," I snap, giving in.

I put on my best pissed off expression as he bursts out laughing. Here we go, this is why I didn't want to tell him, this is why I don't tell people about my life.

"How?" he manages to ask between heaving breaths.

"How what?"

"How's that? How can you play cricket?"

"I wasn't actually playing a Test Match or anything. I was just getting used to the ball by bouncing it off the wall. The ball's bigger. And it has ball-bearings in it so it makes a noise."

"Really? Let's have a look."

"Not now, Tony. Just drink your beer."

"Ah, come on. Where is it?"

"I don't know."

"Why don't you know? You know where everything else is."

"I lost it, alright? I lost it. That's how I banged my head on the tree, trying to find the fucking ball. It only makes a noise when it's moving."

This is hopeless. I try to embrace my ailment, and I end up making myself a laughing stock.

"Hold out your hands," Tony tells me.

"I don't want to, you'll just hurt me again."

"I won't, I promise. Go on, trust me."

Reluctantly, I splay my arms in front of me. He lays something across my palms. I feel it, and try to work it out.

"A cricket bat?"

"Yeah. Lanie told me. Play the sweep shot. Give you a better chance of making contact."

"Lanie told you?"

"Yes, we had a quick chat the other night."

"Why were you talking to my daughter on the phone?"

"It was just a...she was worried, okay? About you. After what she said to you on Wednesday."

"She told you what she said on Wednesday?"

"She gave me the gist of it, yes."

"She wants me to go up and visit."

"I know. We'll see what we can do about that. Now what's this other lump on your head? You growing horns?"

"Ouch! Shit, Tony, stop prodding my head. Is this payback for being sick in your car?"

"Yep. Now, how'd you do that one?"

I flap my hands in front of my head before he can prod me again.

"Kitchen cupboard. I'm thinking of taking all those doors off, as well."

"They won't be cupboards then."

"What? What will they be?"

He thinks about it as he settles in the other chair. "Shelves."

He's got the devil in him tonight.

"Thing I don't get," he starts, "why cricket? You've never even mentioned cricket in the four years I've known you."

"I'm sure I have."

"No, you've mentioned Buddy Holly & The Crickets, but not cricket."

"I used to play."

"When?"

"A few years ago, admittedly."

"How many years ago?"

Strewth, he's grilling me like I'm a sausage.

"Quite a few. But it's like riding a bike..."

"Don't tell me you're taking up cycling, as well?"

"It was one of the options."

"Options?"

"Social Services. Cycling, canoeing, archery... I went for cricket."

"Because you used to play?"

"Yes."

"When was this?"

It's unstoppable. I may as well just tell him and get it over with.

"At school."

"So, thirty years ago?"

"Bit more. Okay, I give in. I played for about a year after that Ashes Series with Botham and Willis. 1981, I think it was."

"So you were twelve or thirteen?"

"Yes, Tony, I was about that age."

"Were you any good?"

"Not really, no."

"I think it's a good idea."

I think he's being serious.

"Right, well, thanks for the bat, then."

"Can I stay here tonight? Not really safe for me to go home," he asks. And then, "hey, mind if I have a shower? I've not had a chance since Friday."

"Sure, you know where everything is. Incidentally, that's the other reason I knew it was you earlier on..."

"How do you mean?"

"The smell, Tony. I could smell it was you."

Off he goes, sniffing himself.

23.

"So, you need a bed for the night, and you hadn't showered since Friday morning, after your run, no doubt. Care to tell me what's going on, Tony?"

"I'd love to, except I'm not sure myself. But I'll tell you what I know. The reason I couldn't make our date last night..."

"Don't call it a date, please."

"The reason I didn't show up as arranged last night was because I was called to a meeting that went on for hours, full of the top brass. The Home Secretary was there, Lorry. Half of it was the obvious postmortem on why a bomb blew up in London on my watch on Wednesday. The thing is, nobody seemed interested in why one of those bombers was killed in the middle of London, nor how the others were killed in prison."

"Not interested?"

"No. They didn't seem to care. It became a witch hunt for me instead."

"Perhaps they weren't interested because they already knew the answers?" I suggest.

"That's pretty much where I arrived at. You worked it out, Lorry. You smelt a rat, and effectively said as much to me on Wednesday evening before Sophie dropped you home. Look, there's no way those bombers could pull this off. Not a chance. I've been doing this for a long time, and you get to know the type. It's possible they might have cobbled together a functioning bomb, but they didn't kill that kid on the bank of the Thames despite their claims to the contrary. That was a professional hit. The killer even levered the blade up and down to open up the wound. My guess is, the killer knew the tide times, and planned it around them. Think about the inconsistency in that.

Someone who can kill like that would know how to make a better bomb than the one they had. Agreed?"

"I wouldn't know about that, to be fair. What struck me was their cockiness. From the way it was described to me, they acted like they were untouchable, like they were somehow protected."

"Exactly. And they were got at in prison, Lorry. That's actually a pretty difficult thing to pull off. It takes a lot of influence and know-how. It feels like the whole thing was orchestrated from the beginning, like it was all a game. And the things they were going after me for last night..."

"Going after you for?"

"Ah, stuff. Daft things from my past, irrelevant things that I thought were long gone."

"Such as?"

"Oh, I got picked up but not charged with anything at Notting Hill Carnival in the early-eighties. It was something and nothing, mistaken identity. Suddenly this is being brought up in the meeting, with the Home Secretary sitting there. And that Miller, the snidey bastard..."

"Miller?"

"Ex-Military Intel. He's now the Home Secretary's liaison to MI5 and MI6. A man who thinks my set up is all wrong and that we should be big like the USA, and he's made no secret of the fact. You ever meet him, Lorry, watch yourself. That's my advice."

"Bit tricky, but I take your point. So, what? You think this is all an elaborate power-play?"

"Yes. Yes, I do. Even you, Mister Avoid The News, must have heard about all the public spending cuts over recent years?" I nod. He must have seen it, as he continues. "Budgets have been cut across the board. Except mine.

Mine gets frozen. Not much could be trimmed off it anyway."

"Envy?" I venture.

"Nah, not envy. This isn't out of spite, as spiteful as Miller might be. This is about taking control, instigating Miller's philosophy of a huge National Security set up, and through that grabbing the lion's share of the ever-shrinking budget. They don't care where it comes from, as long as they survive and, ideally, prosper. Only so much money in the pot, Lorry, same as any other business. You make one thing bigger, and something else has to become smaller to compensate. How will that go? Troops going in to battle without adequate body-armour? Police running around in old cars that can't keep up with the villains? Cancelled contracts on weaponry? Pick one, pick them all."

"And you think someone on your team is batting for the wrong side?"

"Cricket reference - very good. Yes, I'm certain of it. The stuff they knew, Lorry, it could only have come from my team."

"Such as?"

"Which prison those bombers were in, for starters. I kept it off the radar, used it as a trap. Only four people knew who they were and where they were taken. You and me. Adam and Sophie. I didn't even tell Marc. So, it seems, he's not my mole."

"But Sophie probably told Marc."

"Why would she do that?"

"Because I think they're seeing one another, Tony."

"How do you mean?"

"You know, seeing one another."

"Dating?"

"Yes."

"No. I'd have spotted something. What makes you think that?"

"Got any money?" I ask him.

"I'm not betting with you..."

"Relax. I just thought we might order a pizza. Dial the number, and let me do the talking. Usual?"

"Yes," he answers, fetching the phone, calling out, "and then you'll tell me all about Marc and Sophie?"

"I will."

"Incidentally, do you ever have any bloody money?"

"Well, I would have, if you ever agreed to bet with me."

*****

"What the hell happened in there?" Tony asks, returning from the kitchen with salt and pepper and some plates, a delivery pizza sat on the table.

"How do you mean?"

"The kitchen. It looks like a war zone."

"I made an omelette last night, if that's what you mean."

"Were the eggs still in the chickens?"

"It's not that bad," I say, but not terribly convincingly. Perhaps there was a bit more blood than I thought, after I cut my finger chopping the bacon.

He hands me a plate with a slice of pizza and a few garlic dough balls on it.

"Right, explain about Marc and Sophie," he encourages.

"Ever watch Name That Tune on the telly when you were a kid?"

"Not really, but I remember it. Des O'Connor, wasn't it?"

"Close, Tom O'Connor. Well, this is a bit like that. When you rang me in the pub at Waterloo on Wednesday, I had Marc's phone, and you had Sofa's. I heard a couple of seconds of a tune before I answered. It was set as the ringtone, and it was bugging me what it was."

"What what was?"

"The tune."

"And what was it?"

"The Wannadies, 'You And Me Song'."

"So what?"

"Think about it, Tony.'You And Me Song'. Marc's a geek. He'll have a different ring tone for all his contacts, and that's the one he has for Sophie."

"That's it? You're basing your assumption on that? He might just like the song."

"Nah, it's more than that."

"Well, he might fancy her, but it doesn't mean anything's going on."

"It's a song about an existing relationship, and wanting it to continue. I'll stake my reputation..."

"What reputation?"

"...my record collection, then, that there's something going on."

"Right," he says, not even bothering to hide the note of scepticism, "Even if it's true, how does it help?"

"We've established a relationship. Now, one could be using that to manipulate the other, or they could be in this together. Or, indeed, your mole could be Adam, and this is an irrelevance. Whichever way, we know something, and the fact we know it means somebody cares about somebody else. And that's worth knowing, Tony. It also means that you can't eliminate Marc as your mole, because it's likely, assuming I'm right, that Sophie might have told him."

"I just can't see Marc and Sophie together, that's the problem here."

"What makes you say that?"

"They're too different. As you said, Marc's a geek. He's clean cut and smooth. Nice guy, but... And Sophie's - what's the phrase? - a rough diamond. You highlighted the differences in them last week in that pub in Waterloo. He's wine bar and health food, she's a few sherbets down the local and a kebab on the way home. I don't get it."

Tony's right, it doesn't stack up. So perhaps one is using the other. I let it go, and ask more generally, "so what do you want to do about this?"

"Find out what's really going on."

"Confront it? Head-on?"

"Yes. I need a few hours here to re-charge my batteries and clear my head."

I'm thinking, wondering how to handle this.

"Tony, why do you run every day?"

"Not now, Lorry. It's not the time for that."

I ignore him.

"I know you run towards something. You've never run away from anything in your life."

He doesn't say a word.

"Me? I'm not like you. I shy away from things - everything - unless I'm backed into a corner, I just want the world to leave me alone. That's the difference between you and me."

"What are you saying?"

"I'm saying that we should both ignore our tendencies, and that you might be better off simply not running."

"Do nothing?"

"Let them come to us, whoever they are. That way you'll be sure who you're dealing with, and you'll probably discover what their plan is. You're running blind, otherwise."

He thinks about it. "Is your old car still in the garage?"

"No, Lanie has it. I gave it to her. It wasn't much use to me."

"Hmmm, I didn't bring mine. Too conspicuous to anyone looking for me, and too easy to track with the navigation and chip. Besides which, I'm not ever letting you in it again."

"There's the cab."

"Your old black cab?"

"Yep," I say through a bite of pizza.

"Where is it?"

"In the garage. It could probably do with some air in the tyres, but I know it turned-over and started a few weeks back. I didn't want it seizing up."

"Perfect. I'll go check it out later. I just feel more comfortable knowing we have an out if we need it. I'm not even armed," he muses. "They made me hand in my gun, warrant card and comms. Pending an enquiry, I've been advised to take a few days off. This could be a dangerous game to play, Lorry, sitting here and waiting. Are you sure you're up for this?"

"Trust me, it's no more dangerous than driving that taxi. It hasn't been on the road in four years. So, how do we draw them to us? How do we let them know where you are?"

"Ah, I wouldn't worry about that. It isn't like there's anywhere else they can look once they've worked out I'm not at home."

It's a shock to hear him say that. I always thought Tony had a whole life I didn't know about. A life he kept from me, not wanting to rub my nose in the fact I rarely left the house, rarely saw a soul.

"At least we're not completely defenceless," I say brightly, picking up the cricket bat leaning against the chair.

24.

"What time is it?" I feel the need to ask.

"Just after half six."

"In the morning?"

"That's right."

"No, it's very wrong."

"I brought you some tea. Lorry? I made tea. Wake up. Here, I'll put it on the bedside table."

"Use the mat, or it'll leave a ring."

I fumble around, feathery movements with my fingers, light, so they can't upset anything. Finding the cup with the back of my hand, despite the hour I can at least appreciate the handle being placed in the logical location for my right hand to locate it. Bringing it to my mouth, I slurp. It's a bit too hot and too full, but I don't tell Tony that. It's nice to have a cup of tea in bed. Kate would bring me tea in bed most mornings.

I never told her how much I appreciated it. There are a million things like that. Such as the way she'd always flatten the sheets and straighten the duvet while I was brushing my teeth.

"How long have you been up?" I ask Tony, to switch my train of thought.

"A couple of hours."

"What have you been doing?"

"Well, let's see. I cleared the egg shells and the kitchen roll blocking the drain and the dishwasher's loaded and on. The surfaces are wiped, old bits of bacon and grated cheese thrown away, the stinking bin bag is in the outside bin, along with the empty pizza box. Beer cans are rinsed and in the re-cycling and the black cab is checked over. I've put air in the tyres, topped off the oil, and parked it in a lay-by up the road, obscured by the bushes that need cutting back."

"You're obviously a morning person."

"Oh, and the cricket ball has been located," he adds.

"I was thinking last night before I shut my eyes," I say, to move things on from my tardiness.

"What's that?"

"The traitor in your midst..."

"Yep."

"Who's your money on?"

"Honestly, I don't know. I thought I'd picked carefully, thought I could trust them all."

"Think of it the other way. If you were to be fired tomorrow..."

"A distinct possibility, as it happens."

"...who would you recommend as your successor?"

He only takes a couple of seconds. "Sophie."

"Why?"

"She thinks differently. A bit more like me, I suppose. And of the three, I always thought she 'got it 'more, the small versus large set-up, I mean, and the function of TERA. I don't know, I believe she's the most loyal."

"And loyalty's important?"

"Absolutely."

"The other two, Marc and Adam. Disloyal?"

"No, I never thought of them like that. But perhaps not as true to the cause as Sofe, for want of a better phrase."

"Do you think The Stereos are aware of your favouritism?"

"Not sure I'd call it that, but no, they aren't. If anything, I gave Sophie a harder time because of that. After all, she's the youngest. But she thinks outside the box, she doesn't take shit from people, but can play the game when she has to."

"Youngest?"

"Yeah, Marc's a year older. A bit more, I think. And Adam's got about five or six years on Marc. Thirty-eight last birthday, I believe."

"So of Adam and Marc, who's the most likely traitor?"

"Honestly, Lorry, I've thought about it almost non-stop for the past few days. I don't know. They both blew up on Wednesday - Marc in the pub, and Adam in the office - but Marc's a thinker, and he likes to see things laid out before he buys into them, and your methods are a bit unorthodox, a bit off the cuff. Adam, meantime, was pissed off at being left out. He's an action man who likes to be directly involved. You saw how he changed once we got in the room with the bomber. He came to life and played his part brilliantly."

"Yes, but have you considered that he was happy to play the part once he knew the lad who called in was safely disposed of?"

"No, I hadn't, to be honest."

"So, Marc's the most likely, then? After all, he wasn't supposed to be aware of where the bombers were being held, so he was free to spill the beans."

"No. Deep-down, I can't see it being any of them. Perhaps there's something we're missing, some other factor we can't see in all of this. Look, if Marc's loved-up with Sophie, why would either of them want to ruin that? And Adam's about to become a dad..."

"But that can change a man. It changed me."

"For the better?"

"I think so."

"Christ, how bad were you before?"

I ignore him.

"But you know when Marc lost his rag in the pub over the phones?" I continue.

"Yep."

"He still deferred to you. He said something like, 'come on, Tony'. I can't recall Adam doing that in the meeting room later that day, he was almost trying to undermine you."

"What are you trying to say?"

"Dunno. I was just thinking, that's all."

He's defensive, and reluctant to believe any of his team could have done this to him. It's understandable, so I don't push it.

"I do have a nagging memory of Adam not arguing when I listened to your advice last Wednesday, and took Sofa to Waterloo in his place," he muses. "I was ready for an argument there and then, braced to head it off, the action man being cut from the action. It was almost like he was happy to be left behind running Funnel, perhaps because he could better monitor everything..."

"But the frustration came out later, back in the office," I counter-argue.

"Come on Wee Willie Winkie, up and at 'em! I need that computer Lanie got you," he chimes, as his voice leaves the bedroom.

*****

"I don't want to tell you," I tell Tony, because I don't.

"Well, how can I log in if you won't tell me the password?"

"Lanie said not to tell anyone the password."

"Yes, but not me...I'm not here to steal your identity, Lorry. This is pathetic!"

"Look, it's just...I miss Kate."

There's a silence. I know he's looking at me in that pitying way.

"I know you do, Lorry, I know that, and we should probably..."

"No, no. That's the password, all one word, 'IMISSKATE'."

I hear him tap it in, followed by a more definitive Return.

"We probably should talk about that, you know," he says after a few seconds.

"My Emotional Therapist thinks so."

"We should definitely, you know..."

"You want some more tea?"

"Love some, thanks. By the time you've made that, I'll have everything up and running, all assuming they haven't rumbled me."

Tony made tea in the pot, so I'm back after a couple of minutes.

"How's it going?" I inquire.

"All good. So, back end of last week, when I smelt a rat after the bombing, I managed to set up some surveillance in the office one night. I've got three cameras with built in microphones hidden away, each activated remotely, and able to stream to a secure website that I'm looking at now. Only one camera can stream at a time, so it involves a bit of flicking around, but..."

"Is that even possible?"

"Yes, I'm looking at it now."

"How does it work?"

"I haven't got a clue. IT Colin just gives me what I need, and tells me what to do. At least I know I can trust him, by the way, as they're all still operational. He could have blocked the signal any time he wanted."

I'm struck by how easily intrusive technology is, and how the world seems to have moved on since I could last visually embrace it. No wonder Tony checked for bugs on arrival last night. We all judge based on what we know.

"Where have you got the cameras? One in the toilets?"

"Why would I put one in the toilets?"

"Well, from what I recall of television dramas, all the gritty stuff gets discussed in the toilets."

"Er, no," he says, sounding a bit confused, "one in the main meeting room, one in my office, and one in the general open-plan area."

"Fair enough, if you think that covers it."

"Here we go," he begins narrating, "a nice cosy seven o'clock meeting."

"Who's there?"

"Everyone on the TERA team, all summoned in early."

Tony raises the volume.

Someone enters the room, I gather by the sudden hush and firm closing of a door. He introduces himself as Miller. That's it, just Miller.

"Ah, Miller. I knew you'd be there, you slimy turd," Tony mutters, "in the designer suit you can't quite carry off."

"This place is now on lock-down. Nobody is to leave this building without my permission, nobody incoming, and no personal internet or phone use. Understand?" Miller curtly asks, and takes silence as affirmation.

"For those of you that don't know me," he barks from his Scottish throat, "I've been gainfully employed by Her Majesty's Government for over thirty years, and I've got a reputation for being hard but fair. Do your job as I order it, and you'll no go far wrong. Anybody got a problem with that?" He drops his Ts and pronounces it "wi 'tha'"

Nobody says anything.

"Where's Tony?" Marc asks, after a long pause.

"He almost raised his hand before speaking," Tony adds.

"That's the bloody question, isn't it?" Miller doesn't add anything, and the drawn out silence becomes awkward even from my living room.

Sophie must go to pour some coffee from the percolator in the corner of the room, as Marc calls out, "oh yes, go on Sofe, and stick me half a spoon of sugar in, please?"

"Me, too," Adam follows the lead, "but no sugar, thanks."

The cups clank together as she lines them up, calling out to the administrative staff, asking if they'd like a coffee. A good girl, a caring girl who never treats the non-operatives like scum. One of them offers to lend a hand, a middle-aged-but-acts-older lady called Maggie.

Maggie can't help herself, though, and has to ask him, "would you like a cup, sir?"

"Miller! My name's bloody Miller. Not sir. Coffee? That's the priority here, is it?"

"It's the priority for me, yes," Sophie says, sounding narked, "I've been on call all night, and if you want me awake today, I need a cup of coffee."

"That Lassie..." Miller says, a bit more nasal now, but still shouting - it's hard to imagine him speaking without shouting, "see that wee Lassie? She's got more bollocks than the lot of you put together."

He reverts back to silence.

"What's he doing?" I ask Tony.

"Just standing there with his arms folded staring around the room at people," Tony tells me.

"So, where is Tony?" Marc asks again.

More of the same as I imagine Miller looking from face to face waiting. Sophie and Maggie hand the coffees out, as people mumble their thanks.

"Ach, come on? Where's Tony Alliss? That's the bloody question. Mister Alliss is taking a wee bit of time away from duty pending investigations into his recent, and past, conduct. And those investigations are going to be performed by me, with this department's help, seeing how I'm now the interim Head of TERA. And you will help, or you'll be considered an accomplice and detained at my pleasure. Understand?"

"Not really, no. What's he done?" Colin the IT guy asks.

"What he's done, is to get himself considered a possible threat to national security. Hence why it's a TERA case. Our job, boys and girls, is to evaluate the level of threat Alliss poses, and advise on how he should be pursued. That's what you do, isn't it?"

Nobody answers.

"And how do we best achieve those objectives?" Miller continues.

"By finding Tony," Sophie calls from what sounds like far away.

"She didn't even bother to turn round, kept her back to people as she said it, busying herself with the sugar sachets and empty plastic milk pots, tidying up," Tony tells me, "she's not even bothering to hide her contempt for all this," he adds gleefully.

"So? Get on with the bloody job in hand! I want him found, and I want him found now. Any information, give it to me, and me alone. We don't know what friends Alliss might have on the inside. Anybody not understand that?"

"Tell me what's going on, Tony, describe Miller to me, please?" I implore, feeling the need to picture this man, get a sense of what we're dealing with.

"The team are all stood looking at Miller, all except Sofe who is doing everything not to. Ah, where do I start with

Miller? His face is at odds with his demeanour and mannerisms, all smooth and wrinkle-free. His voice is the polar opposite of that face, gruff and gnarled in every way, but his face shines. Porcelain is too obvious a comparison, but you could see through it, if you held it up to the light or held it close to a flame. It's like a polished shell. Like cheap toilet paper."

"You," Miller interrupts, "I want a list of known associates. You. I want to know what he does. I want to know at what time of the day he takes a shite. And you, when you've finished your coffee, of course, you get back to me with a few suggestions on what he's likely to do now. The rest of you, pick one. Pick one of these three, and give them everything they need. Go. I want reports in thirty minutes."

The room begins to clear, but Miller stops someone as they go to leave.

"Sophie, right?" he asks her.

"You already know that." I can hear the disdain in her voice, the distaste for him is in her mouth.

"Aye, that I do. I'll have that coffee now, Lassie. No sugar, no milk. Black, like the bastard I'm hunting. And when you've done that, go out there and tell that IT boy to check the B.E.N. site. I want to know who's been looking at that recently."

25.

Half an hour later, Tony and I are back at the computer.

"You. Speak." Miller snaps.

Adam's voice fills my ears. "List of known associates. It isn't very long. This is his dad, but they have no contact and haven't done for years. There's an uncle he stays in touch with via the odd phone call, that's this one here. Christmasses and birthdays, by the looks. He's his deceased mother's brother. He has two cousins, some second-nieces and nephews - names are here - but there's no evidence that he has anything to do with them. That's it, all the living family that we can find.

"Working from his phone logs - mobile, home and office - and his email account, he doesn't have very much to do with anybody. Outside of work, that is. Look, Miller, I've worked with the guy for three years, and that's all he does, work. If I have a problem with Tony, it's that he expects everybody else to work as much as he does. And the rest of us have a life. I don't buy any of this, I really don't. He's not married, doesn't have a girlfriend, no unusual cash withdrawals. He has quite a stash in his savings, but it's pretty clear to see he has that because he never spends his salary. No large influxes of money, no break or blip in spending pattern in the past five years. No holidays abroad, just work related trips. In fact, no holidays, abroad or otherwise for as long as we have records. No known criminal associates, other than the ones he's put away, and no criminal record. It pretty much continues like that."

Strewth, even my life is more interesting than Tony's. At least I've known a few petty criminals from my days of taxi driving.

"Who's this? Daniel Andrew Francis? He rang his number more than any other," Miller asks, obviously looking over the report himself, and attempting to act as though he's just come across my name for the first time. He's a bad actor.

"Oh, that's only Lorry. A bloke he shot four years ago. By accident, I should add. He's the only person you could term as Tony's friend."

"Right, and you didn't feel the need to highlight that? We'll come back to that. You. Speak."

Marc's turn. "Not much to add to Adam's report. Geographical analysis shows his spending and cash withdrawals all happen around his work and home. A few on-line purchases, but nothing worrying. No sexual perversions indicated by his internet access, here or at home. His car service records show no mileage peaks that can't be explained by work. He seems to sleep about four hours a night, at the most. He gets up and jogs every morning at five-thirty. He works twelve to fifteen hours a day, pretty much every day. He often jogs in the evening at about ten. He lives on chinese and pizza, along with fruit. He eats a lot of fruit and cereals, according to his purchases at the supermarket, that is. He takes regular drug tests through work, always clean. He drinks the odd beer or glass of wine, but never in excess. He doesn't smoke or gamble. Oh, and he generally disappears from his desk for five minutes at ten every morning..."

"Oh, aye? And what's that all about?"

"Well, I assume that's the time of the day when he takes a shite, sir."

"Are you trying to be funny, Laddie, are you? You wee prick. Are you in bed with this man, are you Marc? That's your name, Marc, right? No married, are you, eh? How come? Prefer big black men, do you?"

"Guess I just haven't met the right woman," Marc calmly replies, not rising to the bait.

"What's Miller look like now?" I ask Tony urgently.

"His face is redder than his lips, the man for who 'incandescent with rage 'could have been coined. He's like a photo negative of himself. The few wispy hairs left on his head are standing up with the anger fueled static. Oooh, Marc glanced at Sophie there, but she didn't even notice."

"What's she doing?"

"Staring down at her shoes, or the creases in her trousers, or something. She's waiting for her turn."

Miller's angry snarl pops from the tinny computer speakers, "what else? Patterns, Laddie, look for patterns?"

"Saturday nights. There's a pattern that shows he is sometimes unavailable on Saturday nights. But that's true of all of us," Marc reluctantly answers.

"Any indicators telling us where he is on Saturday nights?"

"Well, yes, the odd food delivery order put on his credit card. And there's a slight pattern of mobile phone call activity taking place on the Saturdays we know he was needed here."

"And?"

"I think you already know the answer, but it's Lorry again."

"Right. And yes, I did already suspect that to be the case. But it needs proving. It needs, what do you do again? Evaluating. The threat needs evaluating.

"So, we have a wee pattern emerging. Daniel Andrew Francis is that pattern. I like patterns, they remind me of tartan. They tell you things. In addition, if you continue the pattern, they lead you to things."

Silence descends again.

"It's like he's fishing," Tony tells me, "fishing for salmon, flicking out a fly on a line and waiting for someone to bite."

"And you didn't find anything else on his internet access?" he says eventually, when the silence fails to attract a nibble.

"Again, I think you know we did," Marc speaks up.

"Then why are you holding it back, you shifty little shite! I am smarter than you. I am more experienced than you. I have a better nose than you. I smell a rat from a hundred yards. What did you find?"

"Tony had accessed the B.E.N. site several times, the last being a day before the bombing. He'd deleted the history from his computer, but Sophie suggested checking it from the other end. We went to the hosting people, and even though the site has now been taken down, they gave us a list of unique IP addresses. It had been accessed seven times in two days from Tony's personal laptop. But he could have suspected, and begun digging, or someone else could have accessed it when he was out, or..."

"Really? Very interesting. So, a black man is accessing a Black English Nationalist site a full day before they explode a bomb in central London? An organisation he claims to have never heard of prior to that day? Rats, Laddies and Lassies, I can smell the bastards. And have you ever investigated this Daniel Francis character? Has any kind of background check ever been performed? Tell you what, get me his signed Secrecy Act papers? He's been working with you, correct? So he must have signed the papers."

"I'll go and dig them out," Adam offers.

"Don't waste your fucking time, Boy! And don't even think about wasting mine, because that is far too precious! He never signed the fucking papers, and well you all know it. What kind of a set-up is being run here?"

Adam's had enough. "Miller, I won't do this."

"How d'ya mean, Boy?"

"I simply refuse to do this."

"You're quitting? You're a quitter? A no-good whinging little shitter?"

"No. You want me gone, you have to suspend me. I know my rights."

"Out. You are suspended pending investigation. Immediate effect. Surrender your weapon and ID to me now, along with your communications piece and any Government issue phone and computer. Put them on the table. You can't say you weren't warned. Do the job as I order it, was all I asked. Now, leave!"

Adam slams the requested items on the meeting room table.

A door opens and bangs into a wall, but never closes.

Miller shouts after him, but it's intended for everyone. "It never occurred to you, did it? None of you. Tony Alliss shot a man in the head. Alright, by accident we're told, but what about the guilt? Guilt can eat a man up. But it's worse than that. This Francis guy - his wife was shot and killed in front of him, by a man Alliss let slip. Double guilt. A double debt owed. Patterns! You should always look for patterns. For four years, these two men have been practically living in cohabitation!"

"It seems like Adam isn't my rogue," Tony mutters.

"Can you flip across to the main area, watch Adam leave, see if he does anything or takes anything with him?" I hiss urgently.

"Ah, got him! Striding across the room, not even going to his desk, into the lift, hitting the down button. A smile, I see a smile on his face, looks like relief. Good man, Adam. Thank you."

The computer audio kicks in again.

"You. Speak." Miller snaps.

Sofa takes over, her voice devoid of its normal cheery Northern inflections. "Tony's service weapon was turned in on Saturday, I believe..."

"Incorrect. He was supposed to bring that in today, but hasn't shown up."

"That's bollocks," Tony spits, "Miller's security staff took it from me before I entered the room with him and the Home Secretary on Saturday. I didn't need to hand it in to them, because they'd already taken it. Lying little shit."

Sophie carries on. "He may have an unregistered private weapon, but as far as we know, he's unarmed..."

"We know no such thing. The man is a weapons specialist, top of his year back in his Special Branch days. He'll be armed, you can be sure of that, and we'll treat him accordingly."

"I wish I was," Tony muses.

"...and his ID and official communications devices, including Tablet and laptop, were handed in on request on Saturday night. But you know that, because you were there. He was supposed to be here first thing this morning to clear any personal effects and brief the team. He's off duty, as you know, and he doesn't have much of a life outside of work, as already demonstrated. He has a personal mobile, but it's been inactive since Saturday night. He made one call on Saturday during a break in his hearing, and that was to Lorr...Daniel Francis. Probably explaining why he couldn't make their Saturday date...I mean get-together. I've also checked the phone call log from Lorry's home and mobile phones. Three calls of note. The aforementioned call from Tony, one ordering a pizza last night, and one from his daughter on Saturday early-evening. That's it in the past forty-eight hours from his home phone. It seems he's never actually used his mobile."

"What's this call here?" Miller snarls, a thud resounding as he must stab the print-out with his finger.

"It's nothing, just Lorry's Emotional Therapist..."

"A therapist! A fucking therapist? Therapists are for people who have something wrong with their heads, you do realise that, Lassie, aye? Christ above, what a basket case. Does he normally order a pizza on a Sunday?" Miller wants to know.

"No, the takeaways are usually on a Saturday."

"When Alliss is there, right?"

"Right," Sophie concedes.

"So, I think we can safely assume Alliss was at this Francis character's last night. What else?"

There's a rustle of paper, Sofa quietly thanking Maggie for something.

"Ah," she struggles, "we've just learnt that, erm, Saturday, when Lorry's daughter called him..."

"Aye?"

"It was the anniversary of his wife being killed and him being shot."

"Interesting. So, this bitter man with a grudge has all this going on in the same week a bomb goes off in London, and Alliss is there every step of the way. Now, that is what I call a pattern."

"Does this Daniel Francis have a car, that we know of?"

"He's blind, so it's unlikely."

"Check it anyway. Go."

Tony fills in, as I hear shuffling feet. "Everyone's filing out, just Miller left in the room. He's got a grin on his face like you wouldn't believe. I've never seen the bloke smile before. He's trying to shaft me seven ways from Sunday. Hold up, he's on the move."

Marc calls out, picked up by one microphone or another, "no car registered in Lorry's name. He had a taxi and a Honda four years ago. His daughter now has the Honda, no record of the taxi, but seeing how it's not been taxed, insured or serviced in that time, I assume it's either seized up in the garage, or scrapped or something."

Miller grunts his understanding in place of the customary thank you.

*****

All that stuff I heard about Tony has somewhat taken me aback. I knew he worked a lot, but I thought he did other things outside of that. Yet, having listened to the reports, I'm lucky by comparison. I have Lanie, for starters, and I had Kate. Tony has nobody, and seemingly never has. He's worse than me.

Excepting his diet. He definitely eats better than I do.

"Sophie just left the building," Tony calls through to me as I sit in my chair.

"Any idea where she's heading?"

"None, but she had to get permission from Miller, so I'm assuming she told him some tale or other."

"Why couldn't you hear it?"

"It was done in the corridor, too far away from a mic, and it was done in what looked like whispers," Tony outlines

"What, in the corridor just by the toilets?" I ask pointedly.

The radio's on. Eight o'clock, it tells me, as Tony insisted on checking on the news and traffic. A wash and a teeth brushing leave me feeling almost human.

I'm not a morning person, unlike Alliss. When I'm Prime Minister, I'll ban conversation before midday or the consumption of the second cup of tea, whichever comes sooner.

We're killing time, waiting for something to happen. It doesn't suit Tony. He's pacing around, his voice moving through the kitchen and hall.

"Here we go," Tony calls, "Miller's leaving the office, says he'll be back in an hour. No explanation given, and instructions left to contact him if they have any news on me. Marc's watching him go, through the blinds, ensuring he leaves the building."

I measure my way through to the kitchen and lean my back against the countertop.

A busy chatter starts up as soon as Miller's safely out of the way, nothing discernible as everybody in the office begins speculating.

"Right, listen...please, let's have some hush. Fucking quiet!" Marc has to shout, against his nature as he immediately apologises.

Silence descends.

"Maggie, please will you watch the window in case he returns? Thank you."

I hear Marc take a deep breath.

"Right, does anybody know anything about what's going on?"

"It's obvious, isn't it? They're trying to discredit Tony, stain him with a couple of scandals, prove that TERA doesn't work, and absorb it all into MI," IT Colin calls out, as concise as always.

"Okay, I agree, and those scandals are?"

"Tony's links with the black nationalists, and his relationship with Lorry," Maggie adds from her look-out post.

"Right. Let's start with the links to B.E.N.; they've doctored the history at the website end, or someone's accessed or hacked it without his knowledge. Look, let's assume Tony's innocent, because I believe he is. What that means is, either Tony accessed that site for research purposes which he failed to mention, or somebody accessed it with all this in mind. The only people who could have done that are in this office on a daily basis, or in a sister-department of Military Intel. I know it's not me, and I'm pretty sure it's not Adam, or he'd be here. So that leaves one of the rest of you, including Sophie.

"To be honest, I don't know what's going on with Sophie, but I know she's having some personal problems, some family issues. And she's just, I don't know, not right at the moment, so let's keep her out of this until... I know her as well as I know anybody, and whilst I trust her, she looks about ready to break, so let's keep her out of everything we do. Okay?"

Nobody utters an objection.

"Alright, so let's focus on the bit we don't know. How is Miller looking to work the Tony and Lorry scandal? He mentioned the unhealthy state of their friendship...used the words cohabiting, like a couple, like it's sexual. How would you achieve that? They'd need to be found in a compromising position, caught in the act, as it were. Or there'd need to be irrefutable evidence proving it. Such as...? Come on people. Help! Think! This is what we do. Anyone?"

"Whichever way, caught in the act or photographic evidence, the thing would need to be staged. That would take a location, time, planning, coordinating..." somebody calls out.

"I agree. Let's work on that. We need to work smart, ladies and gents. Colin, can you clear up this business with Tony and the B.E.N. site, please? Either prove he didn't access that site, or prove that he did, and find me a good reason why?"

"Love to," he reports.

"Good old Colin," Tony says.

"Oh, and Colin," Marc adds, "are you still in contact with Gillian Grey?"

"Absolutely not," he says, in a voice that says he absolutely is.

"Then you must be overdue calling to see how Gillian is...?" Marc suggests.

"Long overdue a catch-up," Colin confirms, the glee apparent in his voice.

"Maggie, how do you feel about investigating the investigator? Miller, I mean."

"Can't think of anything I'd sooner do than dig up some dirt on that man," Maggie beams back at Marc.

"Thank you. Get me everything you can on Miller, and find out where he was last Wednesday when that bomb went off in London. I want to know every call he made and every person he had contact with.

"Robert, I need you to get in touch with Adam. I don't care how. We need him in on this, particularly as he can move freely outside of here. When you do, arrange a meeting. Him and I, somewhere private. As soon as possible, please? Actually, tell him I'll see him in the place we went last week. He'll know what I mean. Don't be any more specific, just in case somebody's listening in. Oh, and when that's done, see if you can find Tony's service weapon for me, please? I don't like the idea of that being anywhere but in a safe place of my choosing."

"That's the way, Marc, use their skills," Tony adds. I know Robert and Maggie are analysts, detail people, poring over endless reports.

"Jaisal, can you and Kev start messing with their heads, please? I want their access cards scrambled. I want their computers dropping off-line. I want their phones to start acting up, their radios to cut out. Anything you can think of to mess with their day. Okay? I want them to not be sure who's doing what to them. I want them scared. Scared people make mistakes."

"When you say, they...?" Jaisal inquires, tentatively.

"Miller and Sophie," he informs him flatly.

"Scared people also act rashly..." Kevin adds concernedly.

"No time to waste, then," Marc concludes, before adding, "no electronic communication, people, please. We do this in the dark."

"Marc's not my traitor, then, and seeing how Adam's out the picture, it has to be Sophie," Tony summarises.

"Has Sofa ever tried to get close to you?" I ask, because it needs to be asked.

"How do you mean? Seduction?"

"Yes, that, or just overly-keen to be friends."

"No. She's not my type, anyway."

"If she wanted to use her sex to get something, why would she go for Marc? She'd go for you. You're the man with all the power, the man with the knowledge. If she's driven by ambition, she'd aim for the highest branch."

"Maybe, but you're looking at it wrong. This is about getting rid of me and the whole section. How would a relationship help with that?"

"Pillow talk - reveal some secrets?"

"I haven't got any, there's nothing that isn't known. Nothing they didn't bring up on Saturday night, albeit twisted to suit their agenda."

"Apply the same logic, then. What's to be gained by her having a relationship with Marc? Or, indeed, the other way round? What's in it for either one of them?"

"Other than gaining an ally, potentially? Nothing that I can think of."

"Would one have knowledge, generally, that the other couldn't gain access to?"

"No."

"The more I think about it, the more I think it's a genuine affair based on fondness, or something. Love, even."

"I don't know, Lorry, but I know I'm missing something. It's like I'm too close. I can't see the wood for the trees. Anyway," he concludes, "it's only your theory that there is a relationship. Based on what? A snippet of a song saved as a ringtone?"

That line of enquiry closed, I move off on a tangent.

"Family."

"What about it?"

"Something Sophie said when she dropped me off the other night, and Marc just reinforced. Something along the lines of family always coming first. I don't know what made me think of it, the way you described the department, I think. It made you sound like the dad, and the three operatives are your kids."

"I do think of it a bit like that."

"What do you know about their personal lives? Siblings, parents etcetera?"

"What's in their files. Plus bits I've picked up from conversations over the years. It's private, Lorry, between me and them."

"Understood. But can you give me a snapshot, it might reveal something?"

He takes a few seconds, weighing up what he can tell me.

"Marc definitely has a sister. Older, I think. There are pictures of his niece and nephew on his desk. Parents alive, living near Tunbridge Wells. The family's Irish originally, though. They're all very well-to-do, but self-made. His dad owned a business, sold up and retired a couple of years back. I remember asking Marc, over a drink, why he never went into business with his old man? He said it didn't appeal to him. Quarry work, I believe. Mining.

"Adam comes from a long line of military men. He's very proud of his ancestors, stretching back to Napoleonic wars, he even traced his family name back to Norman conquest times. They seem to have always been down in the Sussex area. His family owns a fair chunk of land down there. He has a brother, younger, in the military. Tanks, I believe. He was, anyway. And his dad was in the Falklands. Divorced parents, but they still get together at Christmas and suchlike. As amicable as a divorce can be. Married, and as I said earlier, first kid on the way. Hopefully.

"Sophie is from north of Manchester. Blackpool, Bolton, Blackburn. Somewhere beginning with a B. Let me think...two older sisters and a younger brother. The brother came along later, which was a bit of a shock. To Sophie, at least. Her mum and dad still work full-time. She says it's because they'd sooner work than be with one another. One of those working class northern families who are actually middle class, but haven't worked it out, or aren't prepared to admit it. Her brother had some trouble a few years back. Depression, and got addicted to the meds, I think. But he got straightened out before he got in too deep.

"They're all pretty normal, really," Tony concludes, before adding in a mutter, "more normal than you or me, anyway."

26.

"Can I trust Sophie?" Tony calls out to me.

"I think you can. I know this: when it comes to the crunch, Sofa will do the right thing." I say that, but immediately wonder if my recent personal feelings for her aren't blinding me.

"You haven't been wrong on much this past week. Anyway, I think we're about to find out."

"She's here?"

"Yep. Stay in the back there, Lorry, and let me deal with this for a minute."

He thinks I'm stupid, I heard him take the knife out the block on the kitchen counter.

There's no knock or bell ring, so he opened the door before Sophie could reach it, and I know the door's open because I can feel the draught, a through draught where Tony must have opened a window at the rear of the house earlier. The place is a bit stale, the fresh air overdue.

A hand clamps my mouth and I feel cold metal press at the back of my head.

"Do not even think about moving, Laddie," Miller's growl says, right by my ear.

"You alright, Lorry?" Tony shouts, "is that that slippery bastard Miller's voice I just heard?"

I make a noise through Miller's fingers, a kind of hmmph.

He timed it well, using the front door opening to hide the fact he entered through the back. They co-ordinated it perfectly. I may have picked it up from the tug of that through draught, but I doubt I could have done anything.

Beyond shouting a warning to Tony, perhaps.

"I need to pat you down," Sophie says from the hallway, and I know she probably has a gun leveled at Tony's head.

I also know that he'll put my safety first and play along.

"I know what you're capable of, Alliss, so you ought to know I will pull this trigger if you even look like you're going to breathe in my direction," grates the too Scottish accent.

"Hello Sofa," I call out as Miller lets go of my mouth.

She doesn't answer.

"Sorry, Tony, it seems I got this one wrong," I add, and again receive no reply.

Metal clicks, the unmistakable sound of ratcheted handcuffs being snapped into place and secured, followed by a clanging tug on the metal to check they're properly locked. It's something that actually does sound in real life like it does on the television. They're on Tony's wrists, I'm guessing, certainly not on mine. The gun is removed from my head, things a bit more relaxed now Tony's restrained, I figure.

I decide to take advantage of my freedom, so feel my way to my chair and pace out nine strides, stopping when my feet hit the cabinet. Muscle memory kicks in. Anchoring my little finger on the turntable base, I use my thumb as a guide and swing the arm over. It has to be right first time, no chance to adjust if it spits off the surface once the lateral force of thirty-three and a third revolutions a minute kick in.

"What's he think he's doing?" the overly-Scottish snarl says. He must be talking about me.

Tony answers. "It's what he does. It's about all he's done in the four years since his wife died."

Mister Scotland Personified must look at Sophie for confirmation. Her voice sounds like it's coming from inside a hole. "Yeah, we even have to wait for a gap in the tracks when we knock the door, or he won't answer."

He must be okay with this, as I finish my round trip and sit in my chair, the chair I always sit in and listen to music.

The leather makes it easier to brush off crumbs and ash, easier to wipe up the spills.

My right hand locates the remote control on the small table by my side. I press a combination of buttons. The music starts, a compilation of late-sixties, early-seventies folk tunes.

Tony's led to the other chair, away to my left. His bulk squeezes air from the leather cushions as he lands on it heavily, unable to control his motion, I gather, with his arms cuffed behind his back.

I recognise the sound of tape ripping, parcel tape, Royal Mail approved, thick and very sticky. There are a few rolls of it in the back room.

Sophie asks for McScotland's cuffs. For me.

He tells her he doesn't have any, that tape will do, and adds, "a blind man probably won't be much of a flight risk, anyway."

Using the exchange as cover, I discreetly move my arm and drop something down the side of my chair before tucking it down with my hand.

"What are you hoping to achieve by this, Miller?" Tony says as I do that, further drawing the attention away from me.

"Hoping? I never hope, Laddie. I do."

"So, you're looking to absorb TERA into Military Intelligence, I get that."

Silence.

"Talk to me, Miller. Who knows, we may even want the same thing?"

Miller ignores him. I know the sort, I had a boss like him once. He thought the silence made him seem strong and dominant, and hoped it would draw things out of others.

People feel the need to fill a gap. It's what Dr. Haversham does.

The tape continues to rip. They must have found the rolls in the box, the ones I had from when I used to sell a few records. But I suppose they could have brought their own.

"How long have you been in Military Intelligence?" I ask loudly. I know his sort, he'll want to brag, to tell us all about his loyalty and impeccable length of service. It was part of his introduction to the TERA team earlier. It's why he calls Tony 'Laddie'. He wants him to know that he's the senior man with the history.

"Thirty-three years, Boy. No, I lie, make that thirty-four."

"Really?"

"Aye, why?"

"Always in London?" I ask, as Sophie pats me down and checks my pockets. It's quite erotic.

"Of course. I've never been farmed out to some satellite operation, Boy, I've always been at the hub."

"Wow, that's impressive. So, how old are you now then?"

The tape carries on ripping, but now it's for me. Sofa's minty fresh breath hits me, warm on the side of my face. She whispers that she's sorry as she takes my cigarettes and lighter from my hand. I whimper a protestation.

"I'll be fifty-eight in June..."

"Can I have one before you take them?" I ask her imploringly. "I figure it might be a while before I get another chance."

Her head swivels away from me, and Miller must nod his assent. I hear the slight grind as the top flips back on its hinge and rubs against the foil. And I hear her jaw click ever so slightly as she opens her mouth and inserts the tip.

The lighter fizzles and spits, and I smell the tobacco. Holding up my hand, she slips it between my fingers. She continues to tape up my legs, binding them tightly to the chair legs.

"Fifty-eight, you say? Later this year?"

"Aye. What of it?"

"It makes you an inadequate tosser, in my book."

I can sense his anger, something about the tightness of his breathing. Before he can respond, I plough on.

"I've met people, born and raised in England, and they go and live in America. Three or four years later, they come back, and they have this slight American accent. They're impressionable, you see, they want to fit in, and the best way to fit in is to not stand out. And the best way not to stand out, is to sound and look like the local populace. So they come back to England in the middle of winter, wearing shorts, flip-flops and a baseball cap, having adopted a nasal quality to their voices.

"But you? You're the opposite. You've hung on to your Scottish accent with desperation. In fact, you've done more than that. My guess is that you're actually from the borders, possibly even the English side. Berwick, or thereabouts. I'll give you the benefit, and say that you originated from some small village just on the north side of the border. A low-lander, at any rate, probably from a wealthy land-owning family. Your ancestors would have sided with the English, done deals for that land and pledged support for the crown. Wee Jock Miller the Elder palling up to Edward Longshanks and taking one up the arse in the name of personal gain. And you spent your formative years re-inventing history in your head, telling anyone who'd listen how Scottish you really are. I bet you drink Scotch, even though you don't really like it. And, despite living at least thirty-four years in London, you've become even more Scottish, as you desperately try to inflect a Glaswegian growl. Where'd you hear that, on the telly? You know, I'd even put a fair chunk of cash on you having some tartan about your person right now, because you're so desperate to portray yourself as something you're in fact not."

Miller's keeping quiet, attending to Tony as Sophie tapes me up. I push on.

"And why, I'm asking myself? Why would you do that? If others too readily adopt an accent because they're impressionable and desperate to be accepted, then you do it because you're the opposite of impressionable. So you are unable to be impressed upon.

"And if that's the case, then it's because you want to be the one doing the impressing. You want to control and dominate others. And why do you have such a desire? Because you're an inadequate tosser, as I said. Deep down, you know what an inadequate you are, an ineffectual little man who was bullied at school. You were always excluded, so now you preempt that lack of inclusion by excluding yourself.

"Or at home, perhaps you had a bully of a father. Is that why you call people Laddie and Boy? Derogatory terms that deny the maturity of those around you. Perhaps you even wish they were boys and laddies, and why would you wish that? Hmmm, because you find them more attractive in those terms. Were you abused as a child, Miller? Who was it? Your dad? A teacher at school? An uncle or other family member?"

Silence.

"That accent is a defence mechanism, a shield for an inadequate little prick. Come on, where's the tartan? My money's on the underpants. That's the bit you're trying to big up, after all..."

A solid object crashes in to my head. The butt of his gun, perhaps? But then I remember the cricket bat, as the impact screeches in my ears, a throb at my temple, a metallic taste in my mouth as I bit my tongue mid-word.

"Empowerment," I manage, spitting out the blood, "objective achieved. A big man now, having blindsided a blind man. Congratulations. Come on, tell me, where's the fucking tartan?"

He's standing over me, the tape now up to my neck, just my smoking hand and head are free. His breathing is shallow and laboured. His spittle hit me when he struck. I smelt his stale odour, the stale Scotch.

"I'm going to look forward to coming back here this afternoon," he snarls at me cryptically. I've got him where I want him, revealing information. He can't keep the silence now, he's too angry. It has to have a release, and he can't hit me again. If he does, he'll know I know he's a coward. And he'll know Sophie knows it.

I switch his own tactic back on him and employ silence, smiling up at where I imagine his face is. Not too high, he'll be a short man, they always are.

"Much as I'd love to put a bullet in your head right now, we'll be back later to check up on you," he says, not quite so Scottish now, "and by the morning, it'll all be signed off. No way back for you, Alliss," he calls over his shoulder. "We'll have what we want, and you'll be on the front page of the papers with your trousers, quite literally, around your ankles. Not that you'll see any of it," he snarls quietly at me.

A hood is pulled over my head. It makes no difference to me. It feels like a pillow case and smells of the conditioner the home-help uses. The cigarette is taken from between my fingers and dropped on the floor. A twist of a foot kills it.

The tape rips and my right hand is taped to my body. More tape tears, and I feel it applied tightly to my head and neck, just my nose to be left free for breathing, as any further words of mine are contained.

*****

The record ended a while ago. Bu-bump, bu-bump, it sounds as it continues to ride the pointless rotations and butters against the middle raised barrier at the hub.

But the music plays on. 'Hang On To A Dream 'by Tim Hardin. It's a beautiful track.

A trained eye would have spotted it, even a trained ear, the slight grind of the stylus as it traversed the platter, and the digital busyness of sound and lack of warmth that are contained on a compact disc.

Tony might have spotted it. I'd ask him, but we're both mummified in opposing chairs.

It was the nine not seven steps that were my indicator. Two extra paces took me past the usual turntable.

Relaxing my right hand, I buy a few millimetres of wiggle room. I flexed my fist as they bound it. It isn't as well secured as the rest of me, having been left till last as I smoked the cigarette.

Unlike Tony, who, I imagine, has his hands cuffed behind him, mine are taped to my sides. I begin sawing at the tape with my nail. Nails that are too long because I can't see to cut them.

Five more tracks play on the CD, allowing me to gauge I've been sawing with my nail for about fifteen minutes.

Four more come and go. I can hear Tony wheezing in the gaps between the tracks, his breath impacting on the tape as he sucks air in and out of his nostrils.

My thumb nail is starting to wear down, but after thirty minutes or so, I break through. It's just a small hole. but it may be enough.

Rolling my cocooned body to the right, I test the slack in the tape they lashed round the leather chair. It gives a little, as the padding and air recede to pressure. A few minutes of that, and the nail on my right thumb touches the seam at the angle of the seat cushion.

Stretching my protruding thumb through the small hole in the tape, I make contact with the plastic casing, just, but not enough to gain any purchase.

Getting there.

I take a break. It's hot inside the pillowcase and the tape. The music ceases. I wait for the next track, but it doesn't come. Eighty minutes is the maximum on a CD, but I'm guessing this one ran for an hour to an hour and ten. For once, it's nice to have the quiet. My head throbs. Miller managed to catch me directly on the spot where I walked into the tree branch.

Tony's breathing and the bu-bump of the record are the only sounds.

Tony and records, that's the way it's been for the past four years, at the exclusion of pretty much everything else.

Lanie.

She's a smart girl, she actually likes school and education. She gets that from her mum, and threw herself in to it. It was her escape from it all. Mine was sitting here listening to music. But it was't really an escape, it was a hanging on.

This is where I wanted to be, and now I'm desperate to escape it, because it isn't on my terms, and I've always had a problem with being confined and made to conform. And I vow that, when I get out of this, I will change.

I vow to embrace my ailment.

A lightness fills me. All I've seen for four years is darkness. A white dress shines so vividly in my mind's eye that I involuntarily squint so that I can see around it, so that I can see her face, her symmetrical beauty, the olive tan of her skin perfectly offset by that shimmer, the curl of her hair at the cheek, and the slenderness of her wrists through the flared cuffs at the sleeves. She's still wearing the necklace I gave her, green peridots catching that light and cascading in a million different directions.

I try to reach out to her, but my arms are stuck fast to my sides.

27.

A stylus has a diamond or sapphire at its core.

Diamond, from the Greek adamas, meaning unbreakable.

My thumb reconnects with the plastic casing of the stylus hidden down the side of my chair. The nail is sorely worn down, a blister forming on the tip. It was a fluke that I had it to hand, having set it on the chair arm on Saturday. I was going to ask Tony to fit it for me, the old one having accumulated too much grease and dust over time. More gentle acoustic records were sounding a little indistinct and less crisp as a result, female vocals had become lispy.

I can touch it, but I can't hook it. My concern is that if I push too hard, it'll slip further down, and that'll take it out of reach. Twisting my body as much as I can, and exhaling all the breath from my body, I strain with my thumb. I press against the side of my leather chair, the tip of my thumb and the leather making a partial sandwich of the stylus. The plastic casing is sharp where it joins the magnetic cartridge, having been cut at an angle.

I press as hard as I can and drive the plastic up and under my nail.

It hurts more than anything I've ever experienced in my life, and I've been shot in the head. The tender flesh that never gets exposed rips apart.

Deciding I'm only going to do this once, and therefore can't afford to let it slip, I drive it into myself again, further and deeper.

Slowly, I draw the plastic casing up. With minuscule movements, I bring it through the slit in the tape. It catches on my index finger and shifts away, as the snag eases it out of my flesh. Another shot of severe pain as all the goodness already begun by my body is undone to a certain extent.

But not enough to dislodge the object. That second driving of it into me has just been warranted. Arching my thumb as best I can, and tugging down with my finger, I open the slit up a little, and draw it inside as steadily as the throbbing will allow.

The next battle is removing the protective cover at the end of the stylus. Nothing's ever fucking simple, is it?

With a muffled groan of pain, I rest the plastic casing on my index finger inside the tape, and draw my thumb back the few millimetres required to dislodge it. The blood doesn't help, now gooey and adherent.

Pausing and drawing a few deep breaths, I know I have to use my thumb again, as much as I don't want to.

Sweating inside the tape, I wipe my thumb as best I can, given the limited movement. I arc it forward and insert what's left of my thumbnail into the crease of a gap between the dust cover and the main housing. I'm unsure which way round it is, so I start by pushing. Pushing, I figure, will be slightly less painful.

Nothing gives.

So I try pulling. The action pulls my nail away from my thumb, lifts it up, and tears open the wound.

Tears leave my eyes, tears of sheer pain and frustration. It's like performing surgery on myself.

But it shifts a little, the gap between the two plastic segments becomes wider.

The adhesive backing of the tape and the blood cocktail mix with the sweat. Hooking my nail in for another attempt, I shudder in anticipation and clench my teeth. I tense my body, every muscle, and pull back again on the casing. It comes away. Searing agony forces me to whine repeatedly through my nose, the whole chair rocking slightly with my convulsions.

It takes a few minutes for my system to settle, for my breathing to become regular and my pulse to come down from bounding and pounding in every fibre of my being.

And I start to laugh. I laugh because it's the only thing I can think to do. I laugh because it makes me feel better. I laugh in the same manner as people do when they stub a toe. It's a laugh through tight closed lips, so it comes from the depths of my stomach and forms in the back of my mouth, in my throat. Because it's un-amplified by the cavernous echo chamber of my mouth, and because the speakers my nasal passages offer are narrow and tubular, it leaves me as a tinny sound with too much at the top end and not enough bass. But it's unmistakably a laugh.

It must be close to two hours since I started this. The CD ran for an hour after they left, and it feels like the same amount of time without music. That makes it approximately eleven in the morning. Miller said they'd be back this afternoon.

Seizing up the stylus between my thumb and the edge of my index finger, I dab its diamond spade point on my numb middle finger to feel its impact.

Rotating it, I line it up so the wedge of the needle is running vertically, and facing outward. I begin sawing at the tape restricting my index finger. It soon cuts through and affords me more manoeuvrability. Now I can grasp the plastic tool in between the two free digits and cut along the top of my hand freeing up even more slack. After ten minutes or so, all of my fingers are free. Five minutes after that, my hand is clear of the tape. But I still have a problem.

My hand will only rotate and stretch a certain distance, so I can cut part way up my wrist, but can't free my arm. I cut away two strips of tape fastening me to the chair, and can now pull my right hip and thigh away from the leather. But I can't get free, not even close. And the stylus has had it, a quick touch-inspection tells me the diamond tipped needle isn't even there anymore. I'm now cutting with the stump left where it broke off.

The whole process is utterly exhausting. The heat adds to my fatigue, and I momentarily close my eyes, lulled by the rhythmic rotational bu-bump of the needle on the record. It's like a heartbeat, as though I'm inside a womb.

I snap my eyes open. I can't see, but that has nothing to do with the hood over my head and the tape over my eyes. I wouldn't be able to see even if they were removed. But I know the layout of this house, this room, this immediate vicinity. My blindness forces me to be consistent in placement of items. It ensures that I have things close to hand, whether that be the stuff I need, or simply the stuff I like.

Record dealers don't generally cater for blind people. Nick at the record shop is a great bloke, but his priority when packaging up vinyl is to protect it against damage in transit. Any damage will ultimately cost him.

The downside to this approach, is that the cardboard and tape used to encase all of the loose un-protected pieces, renders them as tightly bound and impenetrable as Tony and I are right now.

Anyway, the point is, I have to somehow penetrate those tape-bound packages without damaging the contents, which is not dissimilar to what I currently wish to achieve.

To do this, I have a cutting tool. To be fair, I had it even before I was blind. It runs on wheels, and has a sharp point of a blade that protrudes from the plastic casing by no more than a millimetre or so. It's designed to cut through tape and score the outer cardboard without penetrating it and damaging the records or the sleeves contained therein.

And if it's where I left it, it should be down on the floor by the right-hand side of my chair.

So I start rocking. The loosening up of the tape at my side allows me to get a little momentum. The chair, though heavy, starts to lift off its feet and clump down on the floor. Sixties leather and chrome art-deco styled chairs are built for their aesthetics, rather than their stability. Were I sat in some modern contraption, I doubt this would be possible. And the American styling, of jauntily angled arms that mirror the contours of their cars at the time, makes it top heavy.

To get past the tipping point, I know I need to fully commit. One huge push to the left, and I'm afraid the chair might go the wrong way. It's teetering on the edge, motionless. The moment I feel it start to tip back to the right, I know all the mass is at its maximum velocity. It could not start from a higher point and could not take better advantage of the earth's gravitational pull.

So I use it, and slam my body, such as it will cooperate within its confines, and will my internal organs to shift to the right. I keep on pushing through the bottom of the arc and up the other side. The chair comfortably achieves its over-exertion, and I brace myself for impact.

The downforce on the tonearm of my record player is one point nine grams. This is achieved via a counterweight. Just the right amount of pressure to read the data, but not enough pressure to damage that groove or pick up unwanted vibration that can be translated into unwanted sound or distortion. The anti-skate setting is right on two grams. This counteracts the forces acting on the arm as the record rotates. It best ensures both sides of the needle touch both sides of the record groove with equal force.

A man called Trevor calibrates that for me every few months. It's difficult to do if you're blind.

The point is, I have no counterweight. I am completely at the behest of force and gravity.

With that in mind, for the first time in a few hours, I'm glad of the tape holding me in place. It offers some protection against the table hitting the side of my head, the other side to where Miller clouted me. The table isn't substantial enough to stop me and the chair, or even alter the course. It slides out the way and crashes into something. Deduction tells me it must have hit the shelves of vinyl. The thought makes me angry.

The impact with the ground does nothing to loosen my constraints, as I'm left hanging in the chair parallel to the floor. The chair skated a little as it fell.

Deeming the operation a success, aside from the potential damage to records, I feel around the floor with my free hand. Nothing. Okay, so I was sitting in a chair that meant my hand was was about twenty inches off the ground. The side shift as I toppled felt like no more than two or three, maybe four inches. The box cutter must have been six inches to the right of my hand's starting point. Ergo, it should be about ten inches away from my hand, and beneath me.

By pushing down on my fingers and damaged thumb, I can raise the chair, and myself, fractionally off the floor. The trouble is, I can't do that for long, just long enough to drive down and push the chair about half an inch to the left. It has to be done like that, or I'll drag the cutter with me and defeat the purpose.

Four hand shuffles in and my palm's cramping up. Flexing and relaxing it, I try to shake it off as best I can. Dehydration probably isn't helping the matter.

Back to it. Two more and another rest, a quick feel around, but there's nothing.

Two more, and more feeling. Nothing. How many is that? I've lost count. Fuck knows.

Two more. Nothing. Fuck it. How long has this all taken? It must be about eleven thirty. I'm exhausted, both mentally and physically. It crosses my mind to give up.

That box cutter could be anywhere. Perhaps it wasn't even by the side of my chair. Janet could have picked it up and put it anywhere when she vacuumed up. It may even have been on the table I just sent flying. When did I last use it? Last week when the records came from Nick at the record shop. That's six days ago. It could be anywhere.

And there are no assurances that it didn't go flying away when the chair toppled. Or that it isn't smashed to pieces by the impact. All this effort for a potential nothing in return.

But I have to carry on, because there's only one alternative. To sit here parallel with the floor and wait for Miller and Sophie to return. And what then? They have to act, but they won't want any witness who can corroborate Tony's version of events. So they have to kill me, that's the way I figure it. They won't kill Tony, he's too influential with too many friends in high places. Questions would be more thoroughly asked, I feel.

Lanie. What about Lanie? It'll destroy her, to lose both her parents before she's out of her teens. No kid should have to endure that. She said as much on the phone last week.

With renewed strength I hoist the palm of my hand up until my fingers and thumb lock in position, much like I'm making a snooker bridge. I walk my thumb back half an inch, perhaps three-quarters. Then I slide my fingers the same distance towards it, and repeat. Three times. Five times.

Stop and rest. Feel around.

Got it.

28.

The cutting tool serves its purpose, more than its purpose. Once I have it to hand, it makes light work of the tape along the side of my body. And by twisting my hand under itself, I manage to free my arm almost up to the armpit. The wheels skim over the tape, and the tautness of the bindings are enough to offset the pressure applied and expose the small blade.

It's only when I feel the stinging that I realise I've pressed too firmly down my thigh and torso. My blood must be leaking out of the clean cut ruts. Go-faster stripes, I think to myself, and go slower, taking a bit more care. They sting like paper cuts all over one side of my body.

With my arm untethered, I can somewhat free my head. Slicing through the lashings that pin my skull to the chair, the sense of relief at being able to roll my neck is envigorating. I hadn't registered how the tight bondage was depriving my system of what it needed; fluids and oxygen.

Every joint aches, every muscle is starved and strained. As I relax mentally, so I begin to pick up all the pains, the bruises and welts on both sides of my skull, the excruciating soreness of my thumb, the stinging gashes down the bulk of the right side of my body and the sore cut on my tongue.

But I cut on, still nicking myself as I cut through the tape and my clothes beneath.

With both arms free, I brace myself before tearing the tape from across my neck and other exposed skin. Normally it would hurt, but it's insignificant in the league table of pain, thus barely registers. That done, I tug the pillowcase from my head.

The comparative freshness of the air on my face spurs me on to even greater efforts. Half cutting and half tearing, I pull the tape from my legs and left side of my body until I slump to the floor from my suspended position in the chair. The arm rest cracks into my ribs, certainly bruised, and I wouldn't be surprised to learn I've cracked one where the chrome made direct contact.

I run my hand over them once I'm sat upright. It's impossible to tell. The smell of my blood hits me, the unmistakable iron smell of sticky red bodily fluid. I rub my face with my hands, and the smell gets worse.

Raising myself up on unsteady legs, I stand still for a few seconds till the dizziness abates.

Unsure of my bearings, I tentatively step forward, feeling with my hands for anything that I might impact on, my paces smaller than the range of my bent arms.

"Tony?" I say, as I feel for something, anything.

He grunts.

It gives me a hint at where he is. I walk away from him. Eighteen half shuffles of my feet bring me to the cabinet where the bu-bump has now become a grind.

I hit the off switch.

Turning about face, I walk towards where I now know Tony to be, talking to him as I go, asking if he's alright, telling him that I'm coming to cut him free.

He grunts as I advance, more urgently as my steps and voice get closer. He starts humming. It's a tune, but I can't place it.

The man has no musical ability. Tone Deaf, I sometimes call him.

The humming becomes more of a whinny, more desperate as I get closer. What is that tune? "Hum-hum-hum, hum-hu-hum. Hum, hum! Hum, hum! Hum-hum-hum, hum-hu-hum."

Standing motionless in front of Tony, I hum along. I know the tune, so play it through in my head and try to lyricise it. He's trying to tell me something.

"'Don't Stand So Close To Me'..."

The Police.

"Are you telling me to get the police, Tony?"

"Hmm-hmm."

"Right, we need a system. One grunt for yes, two for no. Okay?"

"Hmm."

"Is that one for yes? Or was it just a grunt?"

"Hmm." A pause, and then, "hmm, hmm."

"Hang on. Hold up there. Is your name Tony?"

"Hmm."

"Do you run every morning?"

"Hmm."

"Are you running away from something?"

"Hmm, hmm."

"Are you running towards something?"

"Hmm."

"Good. Just checking it's you. So, you don't want me to come near you?"

"Hmm."

"Because there's danger?"

"Hmm."

"Danger aimed at me?"

"Hmm, hmm."

"At you?"

"Hmm."

I'm thinking. What could they have done? What would I have done?

"Does it involve electricity?"

"Hmm, hmm."

"A gun?"

"Hmm, hmm."

"Something sharp?"

"Hmm."

"A knife?"

"Hmm." Another pause, and then, "hmm, hmm, hmm, hmm, hmm."

"Either that was a poor version of a Wayne Fontana and the Mindbenders track, or you're telling me there are multiple knives, or sharp objects involved here?"

"Hmm."

"Two?"

"Hmm."

"Two knives. Okay, are they endangering you right now?"

"Hmm."

"And if I approach, I could make that situation worse?"

"Hmm."

"So the knives are pressing in to your person, and if I make a clumsy move, they could do you some serious harm?"

"Hmm."

"Oh shit, not your bollocks?"

"Hmm, hmm."

"Your eyes?" I choose next, logically, given my condition. Though quite why I went genitals as a first port of call is probably more telling.

"Hmm, hmm."

"Your throat?"

"Hmm."

"So, they've rigged you up in such a way that you're handcuffed, tape-strapped to a chair, and there are two knives pressing against your carotid arteries?"

"Hmm."

"That's unfortunate. They didn't bother with the knives on me. Nor the handcuffs. That was their mistake."

Tony doesn't respond.

"Physics. The knives must have a forward force for the set-up to work. They're pressing in to you from your front, so I need to approach you from the back?"

"Hmm."

"And the knives are mounted to something. Like a bar, some kind of bracket. How would they set it up to produce a forward thrust? With weights?"

"Hmm, hmm."

"No, the objective is to keep you pinned in that chair. So they mounted it by strapping it to the chair itself. That way, if you dislodged the chair, the knives would move with it?"

"Hmm." A decisive hum this time.

"I'm going to come up behind you now."

I take a wide arc, not wanting to trip on something, fall on him and kill the poor bugger.

Inching forward with my arms outstretched at the approximate height of the headrest, I gently make contact.

Taking the cutter from my pocket, I slide it down the back of the chair three or four times, making sure I cut any and all of the tape. My fingers begin at the top, feeling for the sliced former connections. The blade has split the leather, and I wonder how badly I've damaged myself. Very carefully, I start peeling the tape from both sides, ripping it from the chair and tentatively feeding it round and over Tony's head and face.

It takes about ten minutes to clear it away sufficiently for the mounted blades to come loose. They dangle down Tony's chest, and I notice his breathing is a lot calmer. Craft knife blades,I feel, nicking myself, honed along the long side, nasty little triangular points at each end.

"Wait," I tell him, and feel my way along the wall to the door. Counting my paces, I stride down the hallway, turn right into the kitchen, take four paces and execute a ninety degree left face. I step forward until the footprint of the kitchen cabinet meets my toes. Feeling, I find the knob and step back half a pace. I open the drawer, rummage, find the scissors and reverse the process.

Snipping the tape around the knives, I toss them on the floor and begin cutting Tony free. I leave the handcuffs. Scissors won't cut through those.

The whole process takes another half an hour. I've lost all track of time, but it must be getting on towards midday, even half past. This escape has been going on for at least three hours, that's my best guess. The palms of my hands are bruised and cramping at the scissor action, but it's better than using the cutting tool. I can better control the depth of the cut.

"Brace yourself," I tell him, "I need to take the tape off your mouth and eyes. Mouth first. On three, ready?"

Before he can hum a response I rip the tape from his mouth without counting.

He swears a lot.

"Eyes!" I call, and tear that off as well.

There's a ten second wait as I imagine him blinking away the pain and waiting for his pupils to adjust to the sudden shock of light after pitch black. I remember that.

"Jesus wept, Lorry, what happened to you?"

"How do you mean...?"

"You look like you've been in a fucking plane crash."

"Yep, that's kind of how I feel."

"No, not a plane crash. You know those shredder machines they have in offices? You look like you fell in one of them."

"I think I might have cracked a rib, Tony. It hurts when I laugh."

"Don't laugh, then."

"So what are we going to do now?" I ask, because it needs asking.

He snaps to attention. I can sense it. He suddenly got bigger and filled more of the room. Less air in here, more Tony.

"Now I sort this out," he says in a voice that leaves no doubt that he can.

29.

"You'll have to drive," Tony informs me, having resigned ourselves to the fact we can't get the handcuffs off his wrists, trapping his hands behind his back.

"Don't be fucking stupid..."

"Look, you don't have to drive, as such, just steer. I'll do the rest."

"Right, so you'll do everything except the most visual element?"

"It'll be fine. I press the pedals and you turn the wheel when I tell you to."

I keep quiet. I'm not convinced.

"...and you'll need to indicate. And change gear."

"For fuck's sake, Tony."

"We'll be in the cab. You know it inside out. And we only have to get to Gillian Grey's place. About three miles away."

"Can't we walk?"

"It'll take at least an hour. And then we'll have to get back to get the car. Besides, you don't look like you'd make it, and I'm not leaving you here."

"Can't we get a cab?"

"It is a cab."

"Another cab. With a driver."

"No phone. They cut the wire. No internet for the same reason. And they took both our mobiles. And do you really think a cabbie is going to pick up a handcuffed black man with blood oozing out the two puncture wounds in his neck, accompanied by a man in sunglasses who has to be escorted everywhere and keeps banging into stuff, who will puke up in his taxi..."

"I've never puked in the taxi."

"...and who looks like the love-child of Robinson Crusoe and Worzel fucking Gummidge?"

"They might."

"Would you?"

"Well, no."

"And they'll ring the police. We can't have that."

Drawing in a slow breath, I feel the pain in my ribs, and let it out even slower.

"I'll get my driving gloves."

"Get some clean intact clothes for yourself, whilst you're at it."

I count my steps out of the room.

"And we need to get you to a hospital, at some stage," Tony calls after me, concern in his voice.

"Ah, that can wait."

I don't like hospitals.

*****

The day I came out of hospital, it pissed down with rain.

Lanie and Tony wheeled me out in a chair, in line with policy. It was so bad, the rain, that Tony went and fetched his car, drove round and picked me and Lanie up at the door. It was like a monsoon.

But colder.

I sat in the front, next to Tony, with Lanie in the back. She volunteered. I'd never been a good passenger.

On arrival at the house, they led me in, Lanie at my elbow steering. It was something I'd have to get used to. Tony went ahead and cleared the path.

We sat, the three of us, having a cup of tea and a few biscuits. By this stage, Lanie called him Uncle Tony. He'd been a rock.

It would have been Kate's forty-third birthday.

After a while, Lanie led me through to the sitting room. In a fair world, any presents that day would have been for Kate. Instead, there was one large box over by the wall. It had sat there waiting for me for several months.

Running my hands over it, I felt the perfection of the triangles on each side, the neat lines along the seams, and the parallel tracks of ribbon running all around it. A metallic bow sat on the ninety degree angle they made. It was wrapped to mirror the book she'd given me in the pub that night.

That night.

'Brighton Rock 'by Graham Greene. One of my all-time favourites. An early edition hardcover, with the pink dust jacket.

I'll never get to read it.

"You alright, Dad?" Lanie asked, and I flinched at her hand on my back.

"Yeah. Yes, I'm fine."

"It's heavy, let me help," Tony offered, and stepped to the side of me. He took over.

"Pull here," he instructed, guiding my hand to the seam underneath.

The plush paper ripped apart. I remember thinking that perhaps it would be best left unopened, this anniversary present from Kate, the last thing she'd ever give me.

At some point in my life I'd had the discussion. Which of the five senses would you least like to lose? I may have even had that conversation with Kate, or a variation of it. Perhaps, which sense could you most readily do without?

In my experience, the sense most people would opt to keep above all others is sight. But not me.

It was always hearing. I'd even uttered the words, I'd sooner be dead than deaf. To live in a world with no music would be catastrophic.

I stand by that. As a blind man, I still maintain it.

My fingers felt the contents. They ran all over it. I could smell it was old, fifties, perhaps very early sixties.

"What colour is it?" I asked with a tremor.

"It's two shades of grey. More silver, I suppose. Mum had it fully restored."

My fingers continued to paint a picture. I added in the details as Lanie called them out, how it operated at thirty-three, forty-five and seventy-eight revolutions per minute. With her guidance, my hand found the switch that controls the speeds.

On the facing side I traced the letters, Rek-O-Kut. It was the thing I wanted more than any other. It was a machine that cut records.

Albeit, not with the greatest audio quality ever known, but the machine is iconic. And it didn't stop there. My hands were directed to other packages. I tore them open with my clumsy fingers. Extra cutting needles still in their packaging, and the lacquer disks on which to record, in a selection of sizes. They smelt wonderful, as only an acetate can smell.

A Rek-O-Cut creates a lacquer. It operates much like any other record player, but instead of gliding across the pre-cut groove and reading the notches and waves and translating those vibrations into sound, this takes an incoming sound, reads the vibration, and a heavier tone-arm with a cutting needle at its end cuts the required groove with all its peaks and troughs.

In short, it was the perfect gift.

"Brighton Rock..." I said out loud, as my hands continued to piece the operation together.

Tony asked and Lanie answered. "Why Brighton Rock?"

"Because there's a bit in the film where Pinkie makes a record for his girlfriend..."

"Rose," I interjected.

Lanie went on. "...Rose, at the pier in Brighton, on a recording machine a bit like this. And he says horrible things on it, tells her that he basically hates her and that he's just using her. But at the end of the film, after Pinkie dies, she plays it. It's scratched where Pinkie tried to destroy it, so it sticks and jumps back on itself, so all she hears is him saying over and over again, 'I know you want me to say I love you...'I love you...I love you..., or something like that."

"That's about it," I added, "but the film is different to the book. In the book, the last line is about Rose heading back to the flat after Pinkie dies and she goes to see a priest. And she wants to hear his voice, so heads off to play the record for the first time."

"So this machine can actually make a record?" Tony asked, more than a hint of scepticism in his voice.

"That's the idea," I said, "but let's find out."

Between us, we figured out how to set it up.

There's a forty-five rpm seven-inch record stashed in among the scores of one-off home recordings in the back room. These are the records that don't belong in any filing sequence. It has three names written on the label, and the date it was recorded, along with, 'For Kate on her forty-third birthday'.

I take the twelve-inch record from the turntable and run my finger over the completely worn through lacquer near the hub. Leaving the label unmarked, I slip it into a cardboard outer sleeve and follow Tony over to the shelves.

I slip the recording of Miller and Sophie in next to The Beatles 'White Album 'for safe-keeping, to best make sure we can find it if we need it, the recording on which Miller states his intention to set Tony up and destroy him, the one where I goad Miller into revealing his plan.

For the fourth time, I pat my coat pocket to check the recordable compact discs containing all that information are in there.

I light a cigarette and reach out and locate Tony's elbow, his hands cuffed behind his back; role reversal.

I follow him out the house, and down the lane to the taxi.

30.

"And there's no way of doing this, other than with me on your lap?" I ask Tony before climbing in on top of him.

"Can you think of one?"

"Not really, no."

"Okay, you're going to have to spread your legs..."

"Oh, for f..."

"Look, I need to operate the pedals. So, put your legs on the outsides of mine. That's it. Alright like that?"

"Not really. This isn't normal."

"It'll be fine. Just do what I tell you. Right?"

"You can't say right, unless you mean..."

"I won't say right unless I mean turn right. Okay?"

"Yep."

"Start the engine."

I turn the key. The reliable homely throb of the taxi coughs to life. It's good to feel the vibrations through the steering wheel, chugging up my arms.

"First gear, depressing the clutch...now."

Muscle memory, left and up, straight in.

"Handbrake. Releasing the clutch...slowly...get ready...pressing the accelerator..."

"Fucking hell...I can't see...this is weird!"

"Turn left. A bit more. And straighten up. Now, now, straighten up, second gear...go to second gear...second bloody gear, Lorry!"

I pull the stick back into second.

"Okay, straight bit of road down to the dual carriageway..."

"Dual-fucking-carriageway!!"

"It'll be fine. Dual carriageways are straight, right?"

"You mean okay?"

Tony chooses not to answer.

"We'll stay in second or third, no first gear. I can pull away in second with high revs. And definitely not up to fourth. Adjust slightly left, we're drifting. Not that much...back a tiny bit...hold it there. Look, I can actually do the small adjustments with my knees. Piece of piss."

"How far are we going again?"

"About three miles."

"To see...?"

"Gillian Grey."

"And who exactly is Gillian Grey?"

"The only person in the world, apart from you, I trust right now."

"Do you let her sit on your lap?"

"Shut up. Coming to a stop. Okay, put her in second gear. Good. I'm going to wait for a very clear stretch in the traffic, and then we're going to take a ninety degree left turn. We'll be on here for a bit, then we take a right turn. Ready?"

"Not really."

The traffic blasts by, a terrifying shum-shum of rubber on asphalt, thrum-thrum-thrum-thrum as a heavy goods vehicle with four axles hammers in front of us, jiggling the cab as a gust hits it broadside.

"Here we go, all clear...shit. Shit. It's stalled. Lorry, you're in fourth. The gear stick...it's in fourth! Get in second. Or first. Go for first. Leave the key. Leave it. Do the gearstick...fuck, a truck's bearing down on us...first gear, Lorry, now!"

I take a deep breath. I've driven my whole life. I drove professionally for a living. I used to love to drive. I can do this.

The problem is, I'm trying to drive like I can still see. My eyes are open behind my shades. They're open because I'm trying to look. That process of looking is tricking my brain because it's waiting for visual signals, it's stopping me from performing.

I close my eyes and picture the old cab in my mind. I visualise the stretch of dual-carriageway, the one I've travelled down hundreds, if not thousands of times.

Reaching down, I put it in neutral and turn the key. Old habits, as I engage first gear, fluidly reaching out and hitting the hazard lights to warn the approaching truck. Without pausing, I reach with my sore right thumb and press the down button on the electric window. The breeze is what I need, as a truck pummels past, its husky horn blaring.

"Excellent. And we're away, second gear, slight left adjustment...third gear. Okay, relax. I can keep her straight on my knees again. Well done."

It crosses my mind to light a smoke, but I think better of it. I adjust the mirror instead, just for effect.

"Approaching a tractor. We need to overtake, Lorry. If you could indicate right...splendid...and drift over one lane to the right."

I feel the white lines trundle beneath the wheels. They give me a clue as to road position - driver side, passenger side - and hold, as the clicking rumble of the tractor gets left in our wake.

"I got her again," Tony informs, and I feel the shift in his body under me as he raises his knees to re-engage the wheel.

"How fast are we going?"

"Just over forty. Another eight minutes or so to the right turn."

"Lying bastard."

"What?"

"You said it was three miles. If we're doing forty, and we're on here for eight minutes, that's about five and a third miles. Plus the bit down my road, and whatever we have to do after that..."

"Yes, but I was talking about 'as the crow flies'."

"Don't bullshit a bullshitter, Tony. You've already pointed out the straightness of dual-carriageways. Birds don't fly much straighter than straight."

"Look, I knew you wouldn't do it if I told you how far it was."

We drive along in silence for a few minutes, just the wind gushing through the open window, keeping me alert and blowing four years of cobwebs out of my head and body. All that dust that has settled on me, as I've sat in my chair waiting for, what? Kate isn't coming back. Is that what I was waiting for? And neither is my sight.

I lost sight of it all without Kate in my life, but I've possibly never felt more alive than right now as the traffic blows by and I'm back behind the wheel, literally and figuratively, steering a course and heading somewhere, signaling intent to move on and over.

Kate isn't gone. She's been in my life for all these dead years. She is Lanie, more than half of Lanie is Kate, and as the comforting click of the indicator accompanies a switch to the fast lane of life, I can feel my sore face hurt as my mouth first curls upwards at the sides, my cheeks stinging as my lips part and a wide-mouthed tooth-bearing grin opens me up, letting the wind enter me and blow all that dust away.

"Now, we need to make that right turn in about quarter of a mile. It's clear behind, indicate...and pull over to the outside lane. Nice. Hold it there...and I'm starting to brake, watch the slight pull to the left under braking...good."

"So, tell me about Gillian Grey?"

"Ah, we'll be there soon enough. You'll find out for yourself. Okay, good road position. Second gear...I'll keep the revs up...it's not quite a ninety degree turn. The road goes off at an angle, so understeer a bit. Ooops, left a little...make the adjustment. Good. Third gear, indicator off, and we're away. About a mile up here, and a left turn."

Tony shuffles under me and gets comfortable as we trundle along what feels like a country lane for a minute or so, the hedgerows swishing by, reflecting the sound of the wheels back at us.

"Left turn coming up. Indicate, braking, and second gear. Good. It's a bad turn, Lorry, back on itself, more like a forty-five degree angle. Twenty yards...ten yards...and turn left..."

Hang on, does he mean a forty-five degree turn, or a one-hundred and thirty-five degree turn? No time to ask.

"Left turn. Left. Left! Bloody left! More left than that, more left, more fucking left!. Shit, right, right - ditch! Bollocks."

The car stops, but I didn't feel a bang. I heard a horn, though, and the engine's still running.

"What happened?" I ask.

"Sorry, mate," Tony shouts out the window at someone.

"What the fuck do you think you're doing? You were on the wrong side of the road," an angry man shouts. He's not Scouse, but not far off. St. Helens, or thereabouts.

"Learner," Tony calls back, ruefully, "doing The Knowledge."

"On your lap?"

"It's how we do it."

"You know, he might do better if he took those stupid sunglasses off."

"I can't see without them," I add to the conversation.

It sounds like a van, a transit.

"Hey mate. you know you're bleeding from your head? And your cheek, by your ear? And your hands?" the northern man informs me.

"Yeah, it's The Knowledge," I tell him, in a voice that implies he's the one being stupid.

Wheels spin as the van takes off.

31.

"Made it! Neutral, handbrake on. Good...and turn the key."

Swinging my legs out of the cab, I stretch my arms up and quickly bring them back down. Every joint aches. I hear Tony stamp the feeling back into his legs, to get the circulation going now I'm off his lap.

Suddenly I'm moving, being swung round, Tony levering me with his leg wrapped around my waist. I'm slammed into the cab just as a horn sounds, deep and throaty, like a truck, confirmed by the hiss of air-brakes. The smell of diesel fumes pelts me.

Another set of bruises already form on top of the ones I have. I wonder if being hit by a truck could be any more forceful than being slammed into a taxi by Tony Alliss?

"Busy road, stay close to me," he snaps. I must have wandered into the traffic.

Taking his shackled arm, I follow him along the gritty lay-by.

It has to be a lay-by as I can smell the onions and meat. It's being cooked on some kind of grill. All meat like that smells the same; burgers, sausages, bacon.

It dawns on me how starving hungry I am, having not eaten since the pizza last night.

Not that I eat much. Prior to the past five days, I didn't ever do much, so didn't require much fuel. My stomach growls.

It seems as though I have my appetite back.

"Antony!" a voice wails.

"Antony?" I whisper.

"Shut up, don't embarrass me," Tony hisses back.

"We've been expecting you," the voice says as we get closer to the smells. I can feel the heat coming off a structure. It must be some kind of catering van.

"Hello Gillian. Hoped you'd still be here on Mondays."

"We usually aren't, dearie, but Colin thought you might come looking, so today we are."

"Well, it's good to see you."

"Likewise. Still as imposing as ever, I see. Well, apart from the handcuffs."

"This is..."

"Daniel Andrew Francis. Lorry. Yes, we know all about him. It seems you two are the hot topic of the day in the national security business. And, yes, Antony, it is a business, despite your idealistic notions to the contrary. Hello Lorry,, a pleasure."

"Gillian's holding out a hand, Lorry."

I fumble around, find it and shake.

"Are you a man or a woman?" I ask, because I'm confused.

"Lorry, you're a fucking embarrassment..." Tony starts, but Gillian Grey cuts him off.

"It's fine. I'm sure it must be very confusing for the senses you have available, Lorry. The answer to your question is, yes, I'm a man or a woman. I was born Graham Gill and was that person for the first forty-five years of my life. On the outside, at least. But inside, I was always Gillian Grey."

"Fair enough. Any chance of a burger?"

"Absolutely. Tony?"

"No, I'm good thanks. I need some info, Gillian..."

"All in good time. Patricia's pulling up everything you'll need. Give her a couple of minutes. Edward? Please cook Lorry here one of your special burgers. Oh, and let me have that package, please."

"Hello Eddie," Tony shouts out, but doesn't receive a reply.

I'm led into what must be a caravan. It moves with the heavy-goods traffic blasting by, and it has that caravan smell. It reminds me of being on holiday with my Mum and Dad and sister somewhere in Wales, the rain bouncing off the roof.

That's what we did when Dad wasn't working.

It seems that what former government employed spies do when they stop working is set up mobile catering vans on the sides of busy dual-carriageways, and essentially carry on working as government spies.

"Hello Trish," Tony says. "This is Lorry."

I say hello.

"Patricia has been my wife for over twenty years, Lorry," Gillian explains, the pride evident in his-her tone.

It's not a caravan, I decide, more of a mobile home. It's too heavy and too stable for something with one axle. There's a buzz of a generator and the smell of electrical circuitry. It's as though I can feel the radiation coming off it all, a bank of computer screens, I imagine.

Patricia's fingers click the keys, as everything becomes urgent.

"Lorry, I need you to sign this," Gillian tells me, before explaining, "it's nothing sinister. Official Secrets Act. It seems it was over-looked."

He-she guides my hand. I scrawl my name, Daniel Francis, or something approximating that.

"Right, first problem fixed. Patricia will insert a scan into the archive. We'll mis-file it under Francis Daniels, or something, an easy mistake to make. The original must have gone a similar way."

The ratcheting metal tells me the handcuffs are being removed from Tony. I expect he'll want to drive now. The mobile home shifts on its frame as Tony must flex his arms and loosen up his shoulders. He's been locked in cuffs for - how many hours?

"Thanks, Eddie," Tony says.

Eddie doesn't speak much. In fact, he hasn't uttered a word.

"In the bag, Tony," Gillian directs, "a thirty-eight. I know you prefer a nine mill, but it's the best we could do. And there's a little twenty-five there, just in case you should need a back up. They're clean, only ever been fired at the range, and as of last year, they're legally owned and registered to you. Shocking the way all this documentation gets filed in the wrong place..."

"How are you doing all this?" I ask, intrigued.

"Well, seeing how Patricia and I wrote all the security software for HM Government, we built in a few loopholes. It seems, Lorry, that my inability to tick one of two boxes on a form under the heading 'Gender', renders me undesirable as a direct employee. But it's fine for them to...not pay me, no, they'd never admit to paying me. Rather, they give me money by way of a pension, and retain our services."

"Right."

"It seems Sophie Hargreaves is my traitor and Miller's insider," Tony states, perhaps watching the computer screens.

"Yes, but our guess is not by choice, Tony, look here," Patricia responds.

A few seconds of silence follows, bar the grumbling generator, buzzing electrics and the traffic.

"What am I looking at?" Tony asks.

"This guy is her brother, and this is her dad. They were picked up in the past twenty-four hours on drug charges. And this," a pause while keys get pressed, "is Miller's computer access on those two people."

"So, Sophie's being emotionally blackmailed?" Tony pieces it together.

"That would be my guess," Trish agrees. "And we picked up this message from Marc's mobile phone, Tony. You ready?"

"Play it."

"Marc, it's me. I'm sorry about earlier. And yesterday. There's stuff going on. I need to see you. I don't want to do this on the phone. Where are you? I've done some really stupid stuff. Call me, Marc, please. Please just call me..."

"Why didn't she come to me?" Tony states sadly.

"The reasons are irrelevant. The question is, how far will she go?" Gillian offers.

I think again of what she said to me last week when she dropped me off. Family should always come first. That was it.

"What about the rest of my team?" Tony snaps, the anger rising in him.

"The gang back at HQ are on your side, Tony. We can see they've been working behind the scenes. All the history created by your computer accessing the B.E.N. site has been tidied up. Good old Colin, I trained him myself, many years ago," Gillian announces, the final comment directed at me, I think.

"Adam has been suspended, we gather, by Miller. He must have demonstrated his loyalty to you, Tony."

"And Marc? Lorry believes he's having a relationship with Sophie, so..."

"We only just got the information through on this, and it's why we had the message from his phone. I've been trying to piece it all together, but not everything's available, which is a worry in itself," Trish reports.

"What am I looking at?"

"Colin hooked us into your feeds, so this is Marc asking Miller if he can leave the office. Note the time, ten to eleven. He's lugging his dry-cleaning, which we assume to be his ruse. Miller waves him off, having gone from being obsessed with finding you at seven this morning, to seemingly not caring a hoot."

"Because he knew exactly where I was at that time. And thinks he still does."

"Correct. Marc leaves the office a couple of minutes later, and here we have him on a cash machine camera entering the dry cleaners. He drops off his stuff, and wheels away. We lose him for a minute, but he never appears on the other side of this bus, Tony. He vanishes. So, I did a street view and identified all the businesses between the dry cleaners and the end of the road. Six shops, a bank, a door to upper level offices, and this pub here, the Longshanks. That's where we figured he went. Now, this map shows that there's a back exit, with an alley here. We were figuring Marc slipped through and has gone AWOL."

"Why? Wouldn't it be better for him to be close to Miller at the office?"

"Slow down, Tony. There's more," Trish interrupts. "We 'were 'figuring that, past tense. This isn't...we can't prove what I'm about to tell you, Tony, so it isn't hard and fast. Please bear that in mind."

"Just tell me, Trish, please."

"We picked up police reports, but they've been shut down, and we can't verify anything. It seems a body, matching Marc's description, was discovered in the small courtyard at the rear of the Longshanks at eleven-thirty this morning. A single gun shot wound to the head. There were no reports of a shot being fired, so we assume a silencer was used. The police were saying that the barman discovered the body after he stood in something sticky. Thinking it was a leaky beer keg, he went to investigate..."

"Shit. Who did it? I need to know who did it."

"We don't know, Tony. We were lucky in even picking it up, and just happened to spot it on the suspected victim report from the police officers in attendance. That's the thing, Tony, this is being buried for now. Miller must be covering it. Nobody on the TERA team is paying it any attention, which must mean they don't know about it. But who could get that close to Marc? He was trained by you. From what we gather this was a point-blank shot to the head. Bearing that in mind, Sophie Hargreaves would be the best bet. She could easily get close to Marc."

"Or Miller." I get the feeling Tony doesn't want it to be Sophie. How would that reflect on his judgement?

"It's not Miller," I state categorically.

"Why not?" Tony snaps defensively.

"Because he's too cruel. This was too humane and clean."

There's a grunt from behind me. Instinctively, I look round.

"Relax, Lorry, it's Edward," Gillian informs me. "He's trying to tell you that you're right, except he can't. Because when he made one mistake and slept with a foreign agent who stole information from his computer, Miller cut away most of his tongue with a craft knife."

"I'm sorry, Eddie," I say in his direction, before thinking about the three wise monkeys.

"Besides, it wasn't Miller who pulled the trigger, because he was in your office for the whole time-window. Now, that isn't to say he didn't arrange it. It gets worse, I'm afraid," Trish continues, "they found what we think is your service weapon at the scene, Tony. The chances are, they're going to confirm that was the murder weapon."

"Where's all this coming from? Miller?"

"Miller's a middle-man, a puppet. So look at who pulls Miller's strings."

"Or has their hand up his arse, more aptly," Tony adds.

"We all know who Miller sucks off," Gillian ventures.

"The Home Secretary," Tony mutters, bitterly.

" Look at him now," Trish calls, but I can't.

"What's he doing?" I ask.

"He's pacing Tony's office, walking to the door and scowling at the name plaque."

"Anything to report?" I hear him rasp, playing his part, still pretending Tony's at large and a danger to national security.

"Look at him watching Maggie," Trish says, obvious distaste in her mouth.

"Lustily?" I ask.

"Oh yes," Tony comments, "ugh, he just rubbed his dick, the filthy bastard. That office is getting cleaned before I set foot back in it. If, if I ever get to."

"Maggie, isn't it?" Miller barks into the space.

She doesn't respond, but must look in his direction.

"Be a good lass, and tidy up the cup and plate in my office, will you? It could do with a wee dust while you're at it. I need to pop out for a wee while, pick up some pieces fae ma lunch."

I pick up the charge in Tony. He bristles through my arm as his hand finds my elbow and guides me down the steps leading from the mobile home. At the catering van he hands me a burger with onions.

"Anything else you need?" Gillian asks, as we walk back to the taxi.

"Just one thing. Lorry has a CD holding a recording of Miller. You'll work it out. Can you see it gets to who it needs to get to, please?"

"With pleasure."

"Thanks Gillian."

"Any time."

"Tony," Trish calls over. The tug on my arm tells me he turned round towards her voice, his fingertips holding me in check.

"I just put a trace on Sophie's car, via the Sat. Nav. She's at Lorry's house right now. Thought that might be useful to know."

"Thanks again, Trish."

32.

"It's constant, isn't it?" Tony mutters as we get to the taxi.

"What is?"

"The fear, the fear of walking into something."

After allowing him to load me in the back of the cab, I find the seat and wait. The engine starts and we pull away.

"What are we going to do now?" I call out after a few minutes.

"We aren't going to do anything. I'm going to drop you somewhere safe. A pub, or something. I don't suppose there's anywhere you can go? And then I'm going to go back to your house and sort this fucking debacle out. It's high time I had a little chat with Sophie."

"No chance, absolutely none. After all I've gone through today, there's no way I'm not seeing it through...or hearing it through, rather. Remember, if it wasn't for me, you'd still be strapped to a chair, bound with tape, handcuffed and humming Police songs."

"Look, Lorry, I can't do my job if I'm worrying about you. Besides, it's more dangerous now. It's not like this morning. Marc's dead... "

"Bollocks. The risk is the same as it was. Your understanding of that risk is all that's changed. I'm going with you. It's my house! What if they touch my records...?"

"Records," he mutters, "that's all you ever think about."

I don't bother to tell him how wrong he is, how it's all I ever talk about, because to talk about the things I think about is impossible.

He drives on with his thoughts for a few minutes, before pulling over suddenly and skidding to a halt. The cab rocks on its springs as his weight leaves it. He slams the door, and opens the back door with too much force, nearly swinging it off its hinges.

"Come here," he barks at me.

I shuffle over.

"This is a .25, a pistol, Baby Browning. USA manufacture, in the late-nineties, semi-automatic. Do you know what that means?"

"No. Well, some of it. .25 is the bullet size, right?"

"Hmm. Here's what you need to know. A .25 caliber will leave this pistol at between three and four hundred metres per second. It will make a loud bang, and it will kill a person if it hits in the right place from not too far away. Here, hold it. Fits in the palm of the hand, quite small. There are six bullets in the clip. Give me your other hand. This is the safety. Feel it with your thumb. Off. Ready to fire. On. Will not fire. Off. On. Got it?"

"Yep."

"Keep it on till you need it. Semi-automatic means it will automatically reload, or take a bullet from the clip and put it in the chamber ready for firing, but it will only fire one bullet per trigger pull. Understand?"

"Yes."

"One more thing."

"What's that?"

"Don't fucking point it at me. I appreciate that I shot you, but this isn't the time to get even," he tells me, batting my arm away.

"Okay."

"Right, where do you want to carry it?"

"There's a rip in the lining of my coat where I snagged it on something. I'll stash it in the inlay. That way, if anyone does get the jump on us, they might not discover it if they pat me down. Besides, they aren't really going to expect a blind man to have a gun, are they?"

"No, I suppose not. Any questions?"

I can't think of any.

*****

I eat my burger, and sit waiting for Tony to return from his reconnaissance mission. That's what he called it. I call it taking a look.

It occurs to me that I didn't let Lanie know where I was going. To be honest, what would I have told her? Besides which, Miller took my mobile phone.

Something tells me I've been abandoned. Not out of malice or disrespect, but I've been left here for my own protection with the gun in my coat as a little piece of insurance. He even told me to keep my head down below window level in case anyone came by, adding that if he wasn't back in ten minutes, I should try to find somewhere safe. I have absolutely no idea how I'd go about doing that.

Ten minutes.

So we're close to the house, we have to be. A couple of minutes for him to get there, a couple to scout about and a couple back.

With all that in mind, I decide to leave the taxi and head to the house. My house.

Now, which way is my house?

His footsteps went off towards the front of the cab, no question. I had the window open to shift the grilled food smell, so I heard them. But he may have done a loop approach. I assume that to be the correct term for such a manoeuvre.

Closing the cab door almost silently, I decide to blindly head off in the same vague direction.

After only ten small steps along the grass verge, I contrive to bang my head on a metal road sign. Most annoyingly, it connects with the exact same spot I hit on the table earlier.

There's a ringing in my ears which I try to shake away.

However, it's a stroke of luck, because I can reach up and touch the sign and trace the symbol with my hands. A triangle with a right bend shown.

My house is back the other way, but it occurs to me what Tony did. There's a gate just along from the sign. At least, there always was. It allows entry into a field owned by a local farmer. Lanie always wanted a horse, and that was where we were going to keep it, next door in the field.

The palms of my hands connect with the weathered wood of the gate. I feel the top to gauge the height and dimensions; about five feet. Bending down, I trace the structure with my fingers as I try to picture the gaps between the slats. I count them.

My reasoning is that it'll be faster and easier to climb than to try and work out the locking mechanism. It's probably chained and padlocked anyway, to keep the gypos out.

First step, left foot, second rung, right foot.

Five rungs up, and I'm at the limit of my hand reach. It's time to commit. Swinging my left leg over the threshold, I twist my body and sit on the top of the gate. I locate a rung on the field side with my left heel, and bring my right leg over to meet it. Given the angle of my knee, I deduce that my heels are a couple of feet below the top of the gate, or three feet from the ground. It's not a big jump.

Thankfully, I thought it through and had a predetermined plan to not try and land upright. Rather, I went for the land, crumple and roll approach I seem to remember parachutists using in war films.

It was a wise call, as the ground is rutted and sloping away on the field side, hard and bare where the grass doesn't grow.

Full of confidence now, I spring up and edge my way straight into a rusty old cattle feeder that was below the height of my outstretched hands. It clangs against my shins and I instinctively duck down.

I wait for a few seconds. I'm not sure why, it just seems the right thing to do.

It's September, so the trees are in full-leaf still, which should offer me plenty of cover from the house over to the left, should anybody decide to look over to the field. It's presumably why Tony chose the same route.

I walk almost sideways, leading with the outside of my right leg, resting my weight on my left, a bit like I'm playing a pool shot. My arms and hands are spread as though I could be holding a cue and making a bridge.

I count my half paces, twelve inches at a time, three making a yard.

My mind's thinking, remembering back a few years to around the same time Lanie first wanted a pony. We had the driveway leading up to the house re-done. A man came out and measured it. From the kerb to the step leading to the front door was thirty-six yards. If I lose four for the verge to the gate, I'm left with thirty-two. Times three, equals ninety-six side steps. That's what I need. I'll do a hundred and make sure I'm far enough.

Lanie springs to mind again, as I count them out, Kate, too, the three of us playing hide and seek, counting to one-hundred, coming ready or not.

How things have changed since I don't need to cover my eyes. She's more like the parent now, always worrying and fretting about me, nagging me to do this and that. Am I eating properly? Dad, wipe the Marmite off your face. Me telling her it's probably not Marmite. When did I last leave the house and get some fresh air and exercise? Did I remember to lock the front door?

Of course, I lie in reply to each one, I was out earlier today for a stroll round the lane, I tell her.

If she rings me later tonight, it'll all be true for a change. Except for the last one. I always forget to lock the front door.

Thank heavens.

Tony took my keys so he could get in at the back.

I reach one-hundred.

Taking a ninety degree left turn, I sink down on all fours and begin making my way forward. After each left and right crawl sequence, I pause and wave a stick in front of me - left and right, up and down. If it hits a tree, I navigate it, always moving right so as to hopefully come out at the side of the house where the brick wall will offer me cover.

Shuffling on, my stick rattles the wire fence, but no more than the wind does. Rolling up to it, I investigate with my hands. Taut metal cable about five feet high, too narrow to slip through, and too high to jump. It's too unstable to climb.

The widest gap is at the bottom. That's my best option. Tony probably vaulted it, one hand resting on a support post. I'm not sure I can manage that, given the run up I'd need.

There's nothing else for it, so I start digging with my hands, ripping the roots out and hacking at the soft earth with my stick. A flat stone I stumble across comes in handy.

But it all takes time. I have to keep stopping to flex my hands as they cramp up, it all taking longer than it should because I have to use my less adept left hand, my right too sore from the escape from the tape this morning.

This morning? That was all it was.

How many of my average days are contained in this one?

After a few minutes, I push my head through the gap. With a bit of wriggling and squirming, I drag my body through to the other side.

It's then a simple two paces to where I hope to find the wall of the house. Moving forward, I feel the mortar and brick pattern and trace it up.

Reverting back to my sideways shuffle, but leading with my left leg, I drag my hand along the wall and advance towards the front of the house.

At the corner I pause and peer round. No idea at all why I did that, not a clue. What was I hoping to see? Resting my shoulders against the brick at my back, I wrest the gun out of the inside lining of my coat. It's hardly a quickdraw.

I slide the safety off, before stepping out and slithering along the front wall till I detect the window with my hand. I drop down, just in case anybody's in the front of the house, and crawl through the damp soil. Standing up on the other side, I locate a low wall with my right shin and step over it. I teeter on the angle of a step, but catch myself and check my balance.

I make contact with the front door and use it as a screen, mindful of the net-curtain covered glass frame at its sides.

My hand rests on the handle. I take a breath before lowering it in increments. The door sighs a little at the relief of the block clearing the brass lined hole.

I use my strengths and listen. There's no traffic and no birdsong, there's nothing that can be amplified suddenly by a sound barrier being removed briefly. The wind is light, almost non-existent, and they don't know this house like I do. They won't notice the subtle little changes, the difference in the smell of the air, for example. They haven't sat imprisoned in this house for years.

Voices hit me as soon as I open the door, coming from the back.

Stealthily entering, I close the door quickly and gently behind me. Four strides and a left wheel. I duck into the kitchen with my back to the door frame. There are no doors in my house; can't trust the fucking things to stay open.

Listening.

"...why didn't you come to me?" Tony's asking.

"He told me not to. He used my brother and my dad, talked about people being got to in prison, Tony. And why wouldn't I believe him? Look what happened to those bombers last week!" Sophie emotionally tries to explain.

"What happened to Marc?" Tony roars in response, so fierce that things rattle on shelves.

"What do you mean? What about Marc?" Sophie pleads, "I've been trying to get in touch with him. Where's Marc?" She has a desperate tone, like someone's holding a gun to her head.

Adam fills the gap. "One of you needs to give me something here. I don't know who I can trust..."

"You've got this all arse about face, Alliss," Miller snarls, "you need to take that gun off me and put it on him."

"Don't listen to him, Tony, he's lying..." Adam talks over him.

Miller pushes on regardless, "I had to take you out the picture, Tony, so I could investigate your team and establish who the mole is, you know how this works..."

"Fuck off, Miller, don't try and worm..." Adam starts to say.

"What about Marc?" Sophie pleads.

"Tony, listen to me," Miller rasps, "you've got this all wrong, and you need to put a gun on Adam, not me and wee Sophie there. She's been helping me, that's all, get your head in gear Alliss. Ask yourself, who was left back at the office and free to cut that wee boy's throat on the Thames, eh? And who was unaccounted for today, who could have moved off the radar and pulled that off? No me, I was in your office at the time, ask your team if you don't..."

"It's bullshit, Tony!"

"What happened to Marc? Where is he?"

Adam shouts, "this is crap, Tony, all of it. Okay, okay, I was helping Miller, but only because he sold me on making the world a safer place, I've got a kid coming, Tony. I want that child to grow up in a safe..."

"Shoot me if you like," Sofa says quietly, "but I'm ringing Marc now."

I can hear her rummaging for her phone.

"His plan was to get the three bombers at the football, dress it up as German reprisals for the bombing, a hooligan thing, but Lorry worked it out, so I told Miller where they were being held..."

"That's bullshit, boy! Tony, I'm telling you. All I've done wrong here is secure you and your pal, so that I could conduct an investigation unhindered. That is all. Come on, you know how this works, that I needed you contained in a safe place while I undertook that. As much as anything, it was for your own safety! You know that I'm on your side, that I have nothing but respect for you and what you do. Christ above, Laddie, I've even taken Sophie here under my wing, I'm so impressed by her. Okay, so it took a wee bit of leverage, but...we know it was Adam now, so you and me can team up, Tony, we'll be unstoppable, you and me!"

I'm sat in a pub, our pub, with my beautiful wife on our sixteenth wedding anniversary. She's wearing a white dress, twirling a large glass of wine by its stem, smiling over the rim at me. All she sees is me, and all I see is her. From the instant I met her, all I ever saw was her.

We're having a conversation, about her work, about redundancies. She's telling me about a guy called John she worked with, an arrogant tosser who tried to undermine her.

Undermine. To destabilise by eroding from beneath.

But it failed, and he had to acknowledge, perhaps subconsciously, the strength of the foundations. Why was that? Because he either had to admit the strength, or concede his own weakness in failing to undermine. And people like that can never admit to weakness, it would destroy them.

So, in the face of a threat, he ran to the strongest location.

A toilet with no external windows.

"This is crap, Tony. Miller's the problem here, he's the one looking to take you down and destroy you."

"Where's Marc? Will someone please just tell me what's happened to Marc?"

"Tony, I'm on your side. You have no idea how well thought of you are. Why would I cross you, the shining light of counter terrorism? Aye, I admit, we want a bigger set up, but with you at the helm, Tony..."

"Shut it, Miller, you lying bastard," Adam screams over all the other voices. "Six people have died in the past week because of this man, and I have no intention of becoming the seventh."

33.

Just as I did when driving the taxi, and for the same reasons, I blink it all away and close my eyes.

The physical sweep of my lids rising and falling to meet wipes the slate clean.

Sophie's voice is strained. Yes, she's stressed, but there's another reason. It's because she's on the ground, lying horizontally. Lanie sounded similar when she called me the other night. She was lying on her front with the phone to her ear, ready to listen to the things she needed to hear.

That's how Sophie sounds. Tony must have her on the floor, face down, standing over her with the thirty-eight pointing at her head.

From the airiness of his voice, he's in the middle of the room. Not boxed in, but out in the open. I have to assume, given what Miller said, that Tony also has Sophie's gun, and is pointing that at Miller.

My best guess, therefore, is that Miller has a gun on Adam, and Adam has a gun on Miller. That would make sense, as they are the biggest threat to one another.

I add that image and build up the details, lay out the geography, the record deck to the left, the Rek-O-Kut turntable left of that, but further back against the wall. I add in the racks of shelves on the far wall, and the two art-deco leather chairs, both cut up and lying displaced on the floor. There's the table, toppled over and all the spilt items, flapping rolled up bundles of tape and two knife blades on a brace.

Miller is closest to me, but facing away from me. His voice resounds slightly off the walls and drifts along the hall to me almost as an echo. The wood floors and lack of soft furnishings allow the acoustics to be picked up. It's why the room's set out like that, sparse and a bit cold, designed for the optimum enjoyment of listening to music, the minimum amount of items for me to walk into and trip over.

Miller must have taken up a defensive position, whereas Tony came in on the attack. He took Sophie down, hence them spilling into the middle of the room.

Adam, meantime, is over by the wall to the rear of the house. His voice is direct, no echo as it comes to me loud and clear. He must have entered last, walked through the back door and stepped through the gap where a door once stood.

Which way would he go, left or right?

He's left-handed, Marc was right-handed. That was the main difference between them. Tony trained them, and taught them his way, to always be ready, to keep your sword arm free. Adam is my biggest worry, as he'll be facing me, but he'll be keenly watching Miller.

My time to move has come.

Taking one step forward I make a ninety-degree left turn and stride four paces along the hall, my new comfortable soft Brazilian-leather shoes silent on the wood flooring. Comfortable shoes are important to me.

The scene I painted springs to life in my head, Tony squatting down, turned slightly away from me, one gun on Sophie on the floor, and one on Miller by the wall where I hang my coats.

Adam, rigidly standing slightly to the left of the other point of entry as I look at it, but twisting his body to the left so he has a clean sight on Miller.

Sophie contorting her arm, feeling for where the hell she left her phone this time.

Miller, facing half away from me, his gun sighted on Adam.

I can see it all clearly.

Stepping one more pace into the room, I turn right, and aiming slightly down from eye height, I pull the trigger.

And shoot Miller in the head.

I think.

34.

"Dr. Haversham speaking?"

"David. Hi, it's Lorry."

"Aren't we supposed to be meeting at my office? Ten minutes ago?"

"Sorry, Doc, it's been a difficult week."

"It was a test, Lorry, to see if you could get yourself here. It was a challenge, by which I could gauge your progress, do you understand? Can you grasp how disappointing this is for me?"

"Yes, but..."

"I assume you have a good reason for not being here?"

I weigh up what I can tell him, and what I want to tell him.

He picks up on my pause and says, "the truth, Lorry, how would you feel about telling me the truth?"

"Okay. The truth is, I was helping Tony with an investigation last week, but it wasn't as it seemed, so Tony turned up at my place, we got taken prisoner, strapped to chairs, Tony with knife blades at his throat, but I managed to get free, and also freed Tony, but he was handcuffed, so I had to drive the taxi to see a man-woman called Gillian Grey, a former acquaintance of Tony's, who helped us get armed and informed, and gave me a really nice burger, cooked by a bloke called Eddie who had his tongue cut out, before we drove back to my place, where Tony left me alone with a gun before entering my house, so I had to make my own way there, and walked into a stand-off whereby it was unclear who was bad and who was good, but I used a small pistol and shot the really bad guy in the head, killing him, but I had to do that to save Tony."

There's one of David's long silences. "Lorry, if you aren't going to take these sessions seriously...you will only get out of this as much as you put in," he replies with exasperation.

"Erm, but...okay, the reason is that I'm heading up to see my daughter, Lanie, today, and couldn't get to your office as a consequence."

"Lorry, that's wonderful, why didn't you just say that?"

"Believe me, I wish I had."

"When did you last see her?"

"Four years ago."

"No, I meant when did you last spend time in one another's company?"

"Oh, it's been a fair few months."

"And how are you getting to - Scotland, isn't it?"

"Yes. Tony's driving us up."

"He's a good friend, isn't he?"

"Well, more of an acquaintance. I don't really do friends."

"Hmmm. Are you aware that you've mentioned his name at least half a dozen times during this short conversation?"

"Errrr, no, I wasn't. We're not gay."

"I'm not suggesting that you are, Lorry, but do you think you're a little too reliant on Tony at times?"

"How do you mean?" I ask, and regret the defensive tone as soon as I've said it.

"This is the same Tony who bought a machine to label up your records, isn't it?"

"Yes."

"Have you considered that his doing that perhaps offered you another reason not to learn Braille, for example?"

"Hang on, Doc, he did that to help me. Don't go there."

"Given your angry defence of him, would you now consider him a friend, Lorry?"

"Ha!" I scoff, relaxing, this is what he does, "yes, I suppose I must."

"Lorry," he starts, pausing to collect his words, "why do you have such difficulty expressing any emotion?"

My turn to pause and reflect. "I don't know, Doc."

"Bottling everything up is bad, like cancer, it eats away at you from inside."

"What do you want me to say, David?"

"All I want is for you to be honest about how you really feel, and for those feelings to be...unburdened."

For the first time in our sessions, he's not asking me questions.

"You want me to tell you how I feel about seeing my wife, who I loved more than life itself, shot dead in front of me, how I feel about the look of slight disappointment on her face just before that happened, and how I failed to keep her safe? You want to know about that last scene I bore witness to, and how I see it all the time because I can't supplant it with new images, how a bullet ripped through her chest and, in line with physics and biology, her insides took the path of least resistance, so spewed out of her nose and mouth before she buckled, and how her stunning new dress rode up and exposed her to...that's the bit that gets me the most, Doc, her nakedness. I don't know why. I can't get over that one, it fucks with my head, that nakedness. It was supposed to have been for me, something secret between her and I...something I never got to enjoy."

"Lorry, I'm so sorry for what happened to you."

"I have to think about the details, David, because I can't deal with the bigger picture. So I process it over and over, focusing on the minutiae, the build-up and all the things that could have been different, the physics and biology rather than anything more...more human. And I have to think of Lanie, and how, as her dad, I'm all she has left, and I know above all else, that I have to sort my shit out and step up and get on with life for her, because if I don't, that gunman will have taken three lives with one bullet. And, I must be honest with you, Doctor Haversham, I feel a fucking whole load better for having said all that!"

"Well, then have a great time with Lanie, and your friend, Tony. When we meet - in my office - next week, will you please be prepared to talk about undertaking a Guide Dog trial I'm now prepared to recommend you for?"

The words take a second to register.

He fills the space, "next week, then, bye."

"Wait, I've never had a dog, I don't understand how they work...David? Doctor Haversham?"

The line's dead.

*****

"Do you want me to drive?" I ask, holding the keys out, having remembered to lock the front door.

"No, you're alright," Tony says and snatches them from me.

I climb in the back. I actually prefer it as it doesn't make me feel so sick. Tony hands me an empty carrier bag, just in case.

The old taxi rocks on its springs as he gets in and closes the door. The engine starts, a familiar hum of reliability.

Off we go, heading north to Edinburgh and Lanie. We've arranged to stop a night in the Lake District to break up the journey.

See the sights!

"So," Tony begins, shuffling his large frame into a comfortable position for the long drive, "how do you feel about killing a man?"

We've not had chance to catch up in the few days since it happened. Tony had lots of reports to write and meetings to attend. That done, he has a few days off before heading back for Marc's funeral and Sophie's hearing.

"Oddly, very little. Perhaps not seeing what I did makes it different. I know I should feel something, but I don't."

"Hmmm, I should probably have you flagged up on some database as a potential nutter."

"That isn't to say I don't feel. I'm feeling happy that Sophie will probably just get a slap on the wrist for her part, that her brother and dad are safely out of prison, I'm gutted that Marc's dead, and angry at Adam for killing him, and for betraying us all."

"But you're not screwed up by shooting Miller?"

"No. Definitely not. Look, I even get why Adam did it, the kid on the way and wanting a safer world, his action man character and ambition as he approaches forty and reflects on his life and where he's heading. You don't think I've thought about it a thousand times, that if there were more resources, Kate might still be alive, that the gunman would never have slipped through the net and entered the pub that night and shot her?"

It must sting Tony to hear me say that, but I'm being honest and expressing my feelings.

"Good spot on Adam knowing there were six dead, by the way. I must start counting things."

"He even reinforced it by saying he didn't want to be the seventh victim."

"So he knew Marc had been killed, and had to have been involved. But why shoot Miller and not Adam?"

"I just felt Miller was the bigger danger. I knew Adam hadn't killed the kid on the bank of the Thames, because I'd heard Marc say that the killer was right-handed. He'd also described the murder weapon, and it tied in with the blades Miller was so fond of. And I just felt that if Miller was no longer in the picture, Adam wouldn't start shooting because he'd think he was off the hook. What do you think will happen to him?"

"Some clever family lawyer will enter a diminished responsibility plea, or something, and play up his family's proud military history. My guess is he'll get a stint in a low security nick, but he'll be out in less than ten years."

"It's his kid I feel sorry for, and his wife."

We both let that one drift away.

He pushes the button on the radio. It's ten in the morning, time for the news.

"...the latest news headlines at ten o'clock. Breaking news this hour: the Prime Minister is set to give a press conference outside Downing Street at midday, detailing his cabinet shake-up. In sweeping changes, both the Home and Foreign Secretaries are to step down with immediate effect, it was announced this morning. Political analysts are speculating that this has to do with the introduction of a new Homeland Security style bureau, mirroring that on the other side of the Atlantic, following last week's bomb explosion in London. More details as soon as we have them, and we will be interrupting regular programming to go live to the press conference as soon as it gets underway. In other news this morning, floods in India have claimed an estimated..."

Tony hits the off button.

"You ask me why I run," he begins, before taking a moment to reflect.

"Queen's Silver Jubilee. 1977. The whole neighbourhood got together to put on a bit of a street party. It was a nice day, I remember that. It was hot. I took my sister for a walk along the street, to let her see the flags and bunting and all the tables being set up. She was so excited, all dolled up in her best dress. It was white, with red hearts on. She was three years old, Lorry, I was nine."

Tony inhales deeply, and I feel the cool air wash over me where he opened the window. I keep quiet. As much as I want to smoke, I don't. I don't want to give him a reason to waver from what he's saying.

"I was supposed to look after her, that was what I was charged with that day. That's what I was charged with every day. About five seconds, that's how long I turned to look at something on a table. I can't even remember what it was, it was so unimportant. I let go of her hand. She saw a dog. She loved animals. We didn't have any, Dad wouldn't let us. She crawled under the table, a trestle table like you wallpaper on, and I couldn't see her because of the draped tablecloths, red, white and blue down to the ground.

"I span round looking for her, but I couldn't see her through the bunting and the flags. Maybe another ten seconds had elapsed, and I caught sight of her running after the dog.

"I remember the dog. It was black. Scruffy looking, but not a stray, just not well cared for. I was worried that if she caught it, it might bite her. I guessed it was there because of all the food being laid out, so it had to be hungry, right?"

"Right," I say, my mind building the scene.

"I vaulted a table and knocked a couple of things over, plastic rattling to the floor, the table collapsing under me. I was a big lad, even back then. Somebody shouted after me, told me to be careful, but I was running hard as soon as I felt the tarmac under my feet.

"She was nearly at the main road. It was busy because of all the local roads being closed for the parties. The dog disappeared, dashing between two cars, but she was so intent on catching up with it...she was looking at the dog, not the traffic. She didn't even see it coming...I couldn't get there in time."

"I knew you had to be running towards something."

"But I can never get there, Lorry. It was the same with Kate. I couldn't get there in time. The night Kate died..." he calls back over the noise of the wind rushing in as we pick up speed. The slip-road to the motorway, I should think, given the volume and speeds.

"I remember it..." I shout back, and nod at where I think the rearview mirror might be.

"I'm sure I saw that dog."

"What?"

He closes the window, as he thinks I couldn't hear him.

"I said, I think I saw that dog."

"Where?"

"Outside the pub. Before I entered, a dog came out of nowhere and walked up to me. I gave her a little fuss, rubbed her ears before shooing her away."

"The same dog? Over thirty years later?"

"I know. It sounds fucking weird, doesn't it? It's probably just a coincidence, my memory playing tricks. But it looked like the same mutt to me.

"I know how mad all this sounds. It even occurred to me that it was my sister, come back to warn me. Ha! How mad is that? But there was Kate in a white dress with the red blood, and it was like my sister... And if the dog hadn't stalled me, I'd have come in and confronted the guy before he killed Kate."

"Yes, and maybe he'd have killed you, still killed Kate, and then killed me as well with your gun."

"Maybe. The thing is, after we'd finished at the scene, and Kate had been moved away, I asked the guys. There was a van at the end of the street with two coppers in it. I asked them if they'd seen the dog, if anyone had seen where the dog went? They asked me, what dog?"

Because I don't know what to say, I don't say anything, and we speed along wordlessly for a couple of minutes.

"So, Lanie's excited about our visit," Tony states, changing the subject.

"Yes, she's...hang on. How do you know that?"

"She told me on the phone last night."

"Why...why...why were you talking to my daughter on the phone?"

"Because I can't do face-time from home till I get a new computer."

"Wait, wait wait. Back up a bit. You have face-time with my daughter?"

"Yeah! She's a lovely girl, smart, hell of a looker."

"No, don't even think about it, Tony."

"What?"

"Seeing her."

"Seeing her?"

"You know, dating her."

"Oh, why not?" A slight pause. "Is it because I'm black?"

"No, Tony. No. It's because you're two and a half times her age and you do a time-consuming dangerous job. Then there's the whole probable homo-erotic nature of this..."

"What?"

"She's half me, Tony. It's almost certainly a factor in what you covet. I haven't forgotten the whole taxi driving episode..."

"Bollocks, she's nothing like you. I already told you, she's a hell of a looker."

I continue through the giggles. "Besides all that, you just told me how you see dead dogs and couldn't look after your own sister .Why would I trust you to take care of my daughter...?"

He starts chuckling.

"Another thing," I call out through the partition in the cab, "this B&B in the Lake District...?"

"Yeah?"

"How many rooms have you booked?"

"Just the one. I need to keep an eye on you."

"No-no-no, Tony. No. We're not Morecambe and Wise!"

"It was cheaper..."

"This...this is what I'm talking about when I say homo-erotic. This is not right."

"Relax, it's a twin room."

"Oh shit, what will people think?"

"Hey!" he calls, changing the subject.

"What?"

"I brought the cricket bat."

"I don't even want to ask what you're planning on doing with it."

"Shut up, you're like a broken record."

"A broken record won't play at all, dickhead. You mean, like a scratched record."

"Shut up, you're like a broken record."

A smile lights me up inside, trundling northward with my friend, Tony, heading off to see my daughter, the thing through which Kate still exists. I can see that clearly now, how Lanie is the continuation of the song that I was happily playing for sixteen and a half years, how she continues that melody, and how everything else is nothing more than accompaniment, the harmony and rhythm that is everybody's life.

I'm looking forward to it all.

The end.

Beneath The Covers

Part One: Three Minute Hero

1.

"He's with me. Consulting," Tony Alliss barks before anyone can question my presence.

"But he's blind..." someone feels the need to point out, prompted, presumably, by my dark glasses, and the fact Tony had to help me out the back of the taxi before steering me here with a hand on my elbow.

"Is he? You ever thought about becoming a detective?"

There's an awkward silence, which Tony fills as soon as he feels his point has sunk in.

"What have we got?"

"University professor, named...Clifton, sixty-two, male, gun-shot wound to the head. It looks like a suicide, Boss."

"If it's a suicide, why am I here?" Alliss growls.

"Medical Examiner thinks she smells a rat."

"Who's the MedEx?"

"Stephani."

"Good enough for me."

We're on the move again, plastic tape catching the top of my hair as Tony guides me under it and in to a cordoned off area.

There are three concrete steps up, judging by the grind underfoot, then a bristled mat before polished wood flooring. Tony has to back me up to cater for the wide heavy door that opens towards us. It doesn't squeak.

I recall it from my last visit here, six years ago, before I lost my sight. My wife, Kate, was with me that time. I lost them both together, and I know which one I'd take back if both were offered but I could only choose one. Either way, I'm destined to never see her again.

We came for a lecture by Professor Clifton, me dragging Kate along. It probably bored her to tears, but she'd never have told me that. Rather, I remember chatting about it all the way home afterwards, continuing the boredom, as I attempted to explain the intricacies of defining what actually constitutes folk music.

Clifton is the world expert on such matters. Was. He isn't anything now.

"Steps heading down," Tony calls out, and tugs downward on my elbow for each one. I count them. I count everything. Not everything, just things I don't need to be able to see to tot up.

Seventeen steps and a half turn later, we push through another equally sturdy door, all done for soundproofing, and arrive in the subterranean space that was Clifton's place of work.

The whiff of music engraved on shellac and vinyl hits me, a familiar scent, but my nose twitches with a little recoil at the rusty smell of blood also present in the room. There are no windows, I suppose, no way of airing the place.

"Morning Stephoscope," Tony calls out, and I clock the softness in his tone and the slight release in pressure on my elbow.

"Morning Effing Tony," a woman's voice replies, a nickname applied in a derogatory sense as a rule, but she says it with affection.

The acoustics in the room are perfect, the panels on the walls and doors installed for the optimum music listening experience.

"Janine, this is Lorry. Lorry, meet Doctor Janine Stephani."

I hold my hand out in her vague direction, the room's structure not allowing me to pinpoint sound as accurately as normal.

"Best I don't take your hand, Lorry," she explains, "I'm covered head to toe in protective clothing, and you really don't want to come in to contact with the things I've been touching. I've heard a lot about you, though, so it's nice to finally meet you."

"Likewise," I reply, even though Tony has never mentioned her to me, but has evidently spent quite a bit of time with the woman, and not strictly business, it would seem. Why would he keep that a secret?

"What are you thinking, Janine, why am I here?" Tony interrupts my train of thought.

"Oh, I was just desperate to see you, Tony, so called you in." She's very flirty with him.

He laughs. He rarely laughs when he's working.

"The plod on the door says you suspect foul play."

"I do. Things don't stack up. Take a look at this, and tell me what you make of it."

"Don't move, don't touch anything," he snaps in my ear and releases his hold on my arm.

His footfalls are almost silent on the solid lowest level floor. If my memory serves, this whole set-up cost close to half a million quid, a chunk of change from the three million bequeathed to the University with the express purpose of employing Clifton, with a view to amassing the world's most comprehensive folk music collection. That was twenty-five years ago.

Having once sat in this area for two hours, I reconstruct it in my mind. We're currently in the main listening room, with its foam-backed panels and weird ceiling. Off to my right is Clifton's office, and it sounds as if that's where the body is, and where Tony has just walked to.

So, the climate-controlled perfect-humidity record storage facility must be directly ahead. It's probably the only chance I'll ever get to be in such close proximity to a few million pounds worth of the thing I'm somewhat obsessed with, so it'd be a bit churlish not to at least poke my head round the door, assuming I can gain access.

As I make my way along the padded walls, I hear Tony say, "it just looks like a splatter of blood and goo on a desk. What am I not seeing?"

"Well. that, Big Boy, is a picture of the victim's last breath."

She called him Big Boy.

"So...?"

"So, think about it. Put a gun to your temple, and pretend you're about to off yourself. My theory is that you'd either take your final breath and hold it, or you'd empty your lungs before pulling the trigger. But this gentleman was breathing heavily at the moment of his death. So much so, that in the fraction of a second between trigger-pull and the end, his final exhalation carried on it the blood and goo you so eloquently describe."

She sounds a little bit Asian, even though her name implies Italian. There's not enough for me to think she is, but I reckon she might have spent some time there.

Now that I think of it, Tony has been eating more rice of late, and he took me to a Sushi restaurant a few weeks back, justifying it by suggesting I might enjoy the different textures of raw fish. I didn't. I told him that fire had been invented for a reason, and made seal noises all the way home. 'Kiss From A Rose.' That kind of thing.

"There's more," the intriguing Doctor Stephani continues, "see here; angle of entry. And here; angle of exit. He must have moved his head at the vital second. Why?"

"How do you mean?" Tony asks.

"You wouldn't try and evade a bullet by moving your head, Tony, you'd simply not pull the trigger."

"He might have slipped," Tony suggests.

"That's almost certainly what a postmortem will conclude, and an open verdict will follow. But I'm just not sure. In the same way, an argument could be made that the pattern of discharge on the desk is simply blood and brain matter taking the path of least resistance, but I've done enough of these to know when it's slightly off. Something doesn't smell right here, Tony."

On reaching the opening I sought, I'm surprised to discover the door wide open, somewhat cancelling out the point of it, much like leaving your fridge door open all day. Still, seeing how it's ajar...

My foot catches on something as I step through, causing me to stumble, and before I can get my bearings again, a block of a door swings closed past my face.

At the same time as the lock mechanism engages, so a faint rhythmic pulsing begins.

2.

Using my ears and hands, I locate the source of the sound. It seems to be emanating from a bedside alarm clock attached via wires to a plastic box, and I can only presume that the door being open was holding it in check.

In short, by closing the door, I suspect I may have just activated a bomb of some description.

A low thrum emanates from somewhere, prompting me to make a noise at both ends of my body simultaneously.

With relief, I realise it's my mobile phone vibrating, and slip it free of my pocket.

"Hello?"

"Lorry, open the door."

It's Tony.

"I'm not sure I can, as I recall this door being like a safe door, and you need a combination number. Also, I'm not sure you want me to, as I think I may have just activated a bomb."

There's a short pause.

"Which bit of 'don't move, don't touch anything' was am-fucking-biguous?"

"It's not really the time for that, Tony..."

He's shouting, so I stop talking, and listen to him telling everyone to clear the building.

"Colin?" he snaps, obviously into his radio or another phone, "get me bomb-squad eyes on my phone right now. Don't ask, but I need them to see what Lorry's looking at - can you do that? Good. Conference them in. I'll tell him.

"Lorry, do you know how to operate the face-to-face app on your mobile?"

"I can have a go, but I'm not really..."

"Just do it."

My daughter, Lanie, got me the phone. She's a second year medical student in Edinburgh. She insists I take it out with me every time I leave the house. The thing is, I haven't really spent as much time learning to operate it as I might have implied to her and Tony.

The first button I press isn't right. Nor the second.

Nothing's happening, the bloody phone is supposed to speak to me, it's a special one for blind people.

Hang on. I have to end the call to operate the camera. That's right, I think.

"Tony, I need to end the ca..."

"Why are you still on the phone? Hang up!"

I hang up. As soon as I do, the device in my hand makes a different sound.

Praying I choose the right button, I stab my finger on the touchscreen. Promisingly, the noise ends.

"Lorry, can you hear me?"

"Yes."

"Okay. I can't see anything. Move the phone around a bit."

I wave it in front of me.

"See anything?"

"No. Try...hang on. Light. Find a light switch, Lorry. It's pitch black in there."

"Where is it?"

"How the f..."

"I've got my lighter," I recall, and grab it from my jeans. It fizzles to life.

"That's better. Point the camera at the door. You'll need to turn it around, Lorry, I have no desire to look at you right now. Or ever again. Right, the light switch is to the right of the door as you face it, at neck height."

The disposable lighter begins burning my thumb, so I release the gas lever and feel around. Locating the switch, I press it down.

"Dean, are you in the loop?"

"I'm in."

Deanamite from the bomb squad.

"Lorry, show us the device."

Aiming the camera and taking a step back to get a wider angle, Tony guides me down and side to side a bit.

"Shit," is all I hear someone say.

"Get out of there, Tony, now!" Colin shouts through my speaker.

"I'm not going anywhere. You hear me, Lorry?"

"I hear you. What's wrong?"

"Nothing, just relax."

Nobody sounds very relaxed.

Stephoscope's voice cuts in, "nobody knows the code, Tony. Apparently Clifton was a paranoid so-and-so, and kept it to himself."

"For fuck's sake. Dean, I need you to give me something here, pal..."

"Get out, Tony, you have thirty-eight seconds to clear the building..." Colin calls out.

"Give me a minute...a few seconds, I mean," Dean cuts in, before adding, "Lorry, I need you to kneel down and tilt the camera up so I can see the arse-end of this thing."

I do as I'm told, Dean steering me until I'm lying on the ground, but then say out-loud what's in my mind, "Tony, I need to speak to Lanie. Now."

"There's no time, Lorry. You can speak with her later. I'll make that happen."

"Twenty-two seconds, Tony, you need to get moving..."

I can hear the sweat in Dean's voice. "Lorry, tilt to the left. The other left. Hold it. Okay, fire-bomb, on a timer activated when the door closed, standard trigger, it gets power in when the alarm sounds and completes a circuit, must have been a three minute warning, enough time to get away, so...timer should fix it. Take out the timer, and it stops. No booby-trap that I can see."

"How sure, Dean?"

"Six fucking seconds…"

"Tony!" Janine Stephani screams.

"Ninety percent. Pull the blue wire out"

"Lorry, blue wire!"

"How the fuck does that help?"

"…the wire on the right!"

3.

"So, are you shagging that Stephoscope?" I ask Tony, as IT Colin works out how to re-set the code for the door.

""Shagging…" Tony restates in a tired voice.

"Yeah, you know f…"

"I know what it means, Lorry. I'm just amazed you'd use a word like that and ask me the question when everyone, including Janine, are still conferenced in."

"Oh no! Doctor Stephani, I'm so sorry, I didn't realise, I thought you'd logged out, but because I can't see the screen, I can't see who's…"

"Lorry. Lorry!"

"Yes."

"Relax, I'm winding you up. It's just you and me."

After quite a long pause, during which my face cools to a more normal temperature, I say, "that's out of order. That…that's taking advantage of my disability. I could report you for discrimin…"

The lock releasing on the door cuts me off.

"Shut up."

Fair enough.

People rush by me and I hear the device being examined.

"Why a bomb?" I say to Tony. "Clifton was dead, so why set up a fire storm?"

"I have no idea."

"It's not a bomb," somebody says, "just something made to vaguely look like a bomb. There's no actual trigger, no detonator, just a timer, two wires and a box of fire-starters with nails stuck in them."

"Why would someone do that?" I ask.

"Well, I suppose that's what we need to find out," is Tony's reply.

"It had to be a way to threaten Clifton. This must have something to do with the records," I add eagerly, keen for this to be an investigation I can be involved in.

"Or, perhaps Clifton killed himself, and intended to burn the collection but got out of his depth..."

"Why would he do that, this is his life's work? And he wouldn't need a timer on a bomb that wouldn't work. He'd just light a fire and go up with it."

"I don't know, Lorry, I'm just thinking out-loud. I can't believe a record, despite having known you for several years, is worth all of this."

"You'd be surprised."

"No, actually, I probably wouldn't." He calls out, "time of death, Steph?"

"Off the record, if you'll pardon the pun. late Friday night, early Saturday morning. That's going on provisional rigor-mortis levels and liver temp."

"Anything on the weapon?"

"It's a .38, and so is the slug. My guess is that they'll match, and the splatter pattern on it and the Professor indicate he was holding it at the time of discharge."

"Something's very off here," I decide.

Tony's less convinced. "I'm not so sure, Lorry; perhaps the guy just got sick of his life and tried to take it all down. But he couldn't get the bomb to work, so offed himself."

I listen to him communicating with IT Colin and Analyst

Maggie back at Scotland Yard, asking them to run background on Clifton; internet access, look for bomb making, all his financials, where he shops, what he does, what he eats, changes in routine, anything and everything.

"So, we're going to investigate it?" I ask, quite excitedly.

"No, I'm going to get my team to have a sniff around, and if they come up with anything untoward, I may involve you in any subsequent investigation, as a consultant. That means you don't fucking touch anything. You consult. Verbally. With your mouth."

Yes, we're back!

If I'm honest, I've been a bit bored these past six months since Tony's old department was wound up. Not bored, exactly, but a little unfulfilled. He comes round just about every Saturday evening, and sits with me, chatting and labelling up vinyl records on raised strips so that I can read them with my hands, but with Lanie being so far away, life can get a bit monotonous, all those hours spent sat listening to records.

"What was he listening to?" I call out, as a thought occurs to me.

"We don't know that he was listening to anything..." Tony starts.

Stephoscope cuts him off. "That record player was on when I arrived. The clicking was driving me mad where the needle kept rotating at the centre, so I turned it off. Downloads are so much more convenient."

"Leave it," Tony hisses in my ear before I can draw breath.

"Someone called Mick Stevens. Mean anything?" he calls out.

"Oh yes! Which album?"

"'See The Morning'."

"Bloody hell. An original, from the early seventies, on the Deroy label?"

"I don't know. It looks old, I suppose, if that helps."

"So do you."

"How would you know?"

Alliss's broad form and black stubbly face were the last things I ever saw.

"Give it to me. And the sleeve."

Tony places them on my upturned palms, and my remaining senses go to work, exploring the textured paper labels, weight and rigidity of the disc, the smoothness of the rim, and, most importantly, the smell of the sleeve and record itself.

"It's an original."

"What's it worth?"

"I'm not sure, as I've never heard of one coming up for sale. I think the book price is five hundred..."

"Pounds?"

"No, ounces...yes, pounds. Or do we have to use kilograms now? Anyway, as I was saying, it wouldn't surprise me if a mint copy were to sell for a lot more, maybe as much as two grand."

"Why?"

I suppose it's a reasonable question.

"There were only ninety-nine copies manufactured, I think, to skirt some tax law back then, and it's just a nice folky album with mildly psychedelic flourishes, on a label that's very sought after."

"You've got it?"

"Well, yes, but not an original. Most of this stuff has been re-issued."

"What's your point, Lorry, that robbery might be a motive?"

"Well, they didn't take the record that was most readily to hand. But perhaps they were looking for something specific, or stealing to order. There'll be much more valuable records than this in here, and the vault was open. But he didn't kill himself, I'm pretty certain about that."

"Based on what?"

"On the things the Doc has told us, but also on this. This isn't a record you play when you want to end it all, it's just not miserable enough. I might even describe it as uplifting. Even the title is optimistic, 'See The Morning'. I mean, it kind of implies you intend to be around to do so."

Tony lets out a long breath through his teeth. It goes on so long, I think he might have sprung a leak.

Eventually he says, "I know why you're doing this."

"What?"

"Trying to make this in to more than it actually is."

"I'm purely attempting to put right a potential injustice in the world, and catch the bad person or peoples!"

"So nothing to do with getting out of your guide dog examination later today, then?"

Bugger, he remembered.

"No," I say as earnestly as I can, so that my voice goes a bit high-pitched in the middle.

"It's important, Lorry, and I promised Lanie I'd make sure you got there."

"I know it is."

"Alright then, just so we're clear."

"It's fascinating," Janine calls, "it's exactly like listening to a married couple."

To move things on, I tell them, "he had loads of death threats, you know?"

"Who, the Professor?"

"Yep."

"I'm afraid to ask, but why?"

"Because he was trying to define what folk music actually was."

"And what is it?"

"Nobody really knows. Or, rather, lots of people think they know, but nobody can agree."

"Traditional, isn't it?" Janine chips in. I wonder how people can do that, have normal conversations whilst attending to dead bodies?

I answer her question with, "that's what the purists believe, yes. That folk music, in line with folklore, should be something passed down through generations via word of mouth, and as a result nothing contemporary can be considered..."

"Lorry, we don't need the history lesson. Get to the point please?" Tony snaps, and I imagine him and the doctor sharing a look.

"Well, Clifton expanded that when it came to the University's archive, and began including contemporary folk music."

"And people threatened to kill him because of that?"

"You'd be surprised how touchy people can be about music." I instantly regret the words.

"No I wouldn't," he mutters.

"I'm not sure that any of them would have actually done it, mind, but you never know. Clifton was a contentious figure in the beard-stroking, finger-in-ear world of seriously serious folk music aficionados. I mean, if you start including modern music, where does it end? Before you know it, all music could be considered..."

"Enlighten me, Janine, what more do you know about the gun?" Tony asks, cutting me off in my prime.

"Gulf War era USA service revolver. I've sent the serial

number in, but you know how those go; the trail goes off track after the war, and an undocumented history usually follows. Don't bank on anything there, Tony."

"Is there anything I can bank on? Who found the body?"

"The Professor's little helper, a student here...named James King. Prefers Jim, I'm told."

"I think we'll go and have a chat with him," Tony decides, and steers me back towards the door.

"Thanks Steph, when will I get the report?"

"Tomorrow, close of play."

"Today would be better."

"Tomorrow morning, first thing."

"I can live with that."

"Mind you, it'll mean me having to cancel our date tonight."

"We'll re-arrange, I'll call you later."

I knew it.

4.

"James, I'm Tony. This is Lorry. I'm sorry to do this now, and I understand you've had a tough day so far, but we just need to clear up a few things. It won't take long, I promise."

I'm trying to work out if Tony's being nice to the kid because he feels sorry for him, or because he's playing him, lulling him in to a false sense of security by treating him as a victim.

"It must have been a shock this morning, finding the Professor like that. I need you to speak out-loud, James, because Lorry here can't see, so nodding and shaking your head are no good to him."

He speaks. "What happened to him - his eyesight, I mean?"

A question, so he's deflecting. But is that done to hide any part in this, or is it done to negate the need to re-address what he saw today? By the same token, Tony hasn't asked any questions, it's all statements.

"He shot me in the head a few years ago," I answer.

"Why?"

"Because I wouldn't answer his questions." I hear a slight whimper carry on his breath. "Just kidding. It was an accident."

"So it was a shock finding the professor," Alliss pushes on.

"Hmm, yes. I came in as usual, at about nine, and...I, like, smelt it before I saw it, you know? And the door to the vault was open...and it never is. Clifton, erm, he was, like, paranoid about locking it."

"But you didn't close the door."

"No. When I saw, erm, the body, I just, like, left immediately, and called for help."

"But you knew it was a body, that he wasn't still alive."

"Erm, shit, I don't know. Yes, I suppose, the...blood and everything, and the gun. I kind of, you know, guessed what had gone on. Did he kill himself?"

"We don't know. Yet."

"It wouldn't surprise me, you know, if he had."

"Why do you say that?" I ask him.

"He was, a bit...down, a bit intense, and I think he was worried."

"Worried?"

"Well, yes, about it all coming to an end."

"What coming to an end?"

"The music, the, like, whole thing. There was no money left, really, so it couldn't continue, unless he could get funding. He said it was because of the economy and cutbacks, and so on, you know?"

"I know," Tony tells him. "You prefer Jim, right?"

"Yes."

"Jim, I know there's something you're not telling me. When you're ready to tell me, you call me on this number."

"No, I mean, there's, like, nothing to tell. I only worked for Clifton for...not even a year, I was just helping out, that's all."

"You can go now."

"We're done?"

"For now. Don't leave the country."

"Why would I leave the country?"

"I don't know."

The door closes on the classroom we're in.

"What do you make of that?" Tony asks me as soon as he's gone.

"He's shitting himself, but I don't think he could end a phone call, let alone a life."

"I agree."

"But you're not going to arrest him, bring him in for questioning?"

"No. I think I'll let him stew on what might have happened to Clifton. He'll come running when he gets scared enough. Besides which, I quite like the idea of him being out there and able to potentially communicate with whoever might actually be behind this."

Tony takes a second to ask Colin to monitor James King's communication devices, calls received and made, not content. It gets messy if you start tapping content.

"So, you now think it was a murder, then?"

"To be honest, I don't know. But we'll have a dig around, and see what comes up."

"Remind me of the motives for murder again?"

"Revenge, hatred, money, sex, power-gain, defence, psychosis, and to keep a secret. Those are the main ones, and what most others boil down to."

"Or more than one of those in combination?"

"Yes."

"Look, I can't see it being revenge, hatred, sex, power or any of those things. I know enough about Clifton, having attended his speech and once read a book or two, to think this is probably more to do with money and-or, what was the other?"

"Psychosis? This could just be random."

"Then why the fake fire bomb?"

"Perhaps that was Clifton himself."

"No. He wouldn't destroy those records, I'm certain of that. He wouldn't even have left the door open, he loved them."

We stand in silence for a moment, until I break it. "What are the motives for arson?"

"V-CREEP."

"Come again?"

"Vandalism accounts for fifty percent, The other half are Concealment, Revenge, Excitement, Extremism, Profit."

"That's impressive."

"Thank you."

"Where's the commonality?"

"Profit, concealment, and you can't rule out revenge."

"To keep a secret..." I play with those words in my mouth, to see how they taste, "why does that one feel right?"

"I have no idea. Right, come on Barbara Windsor, time for you to go dogging!"

"Do you mean Barbara Woodhouse?"

"Walkies! With me, heel..."

"Before we go..."

"You're not getting out of this."

"I know. But I wouldn't mind you talking me through Clifton's filing system."

"To what end? There's no way we can trawl through tens of thousands of records to see if any are missing. Besides, how would any of my people know? We'd need your eyes for that."

"No, I wasn't thinking of that. But I just want an understanding of how things work here. Besides, it'll give you more time with Stephoscope."

"If I agree to do this, that's not the reason why."

"Of course not."

"Right, come on. Ten minutes."

*****

Clifton was old school, as I thought he would be. Yes, he may keep his database on his computer, but he wouldn't completely trust that, so neither can I. One of several large volumes slaps down on a table and forces me to blink, and I hear the leather creak and taste the paper and ink as Tony flips it open.

"Okey-dokey," he begins, "so, we have a ledger of sorts, unique identification number, artist, title, etcetera, country of origin, price paid..."

"What sequence are they in?"

"Er, looks like date purchased."

"And this lists actual records, rather than individual tracks?"

"Yes. Why?"

"I'm just thinking that there must be another log of all the tracks somewhere."

"That's probably in the other files I noticed in the vault."

"Is this the latest one?"

"No, the last date in here is two years ago."

"Where's the latest one?"

"Ah, unfortunately it could be the one on his desk."

"Why unfortunately?"

"Because it's the one his last breath is spread all over, and we won't be able to take a look at that until Stephoscope's finished with it. Right doc?"

"Absolutely."

"So tomorrow?" I seek to clarify.

"Yep, but you'll need to come to my lab."

"Talking of labs, dog lesson time," Alliss authoritatively states, and pushes me out of the room with his hands on my shoulders.

5.

"Full name and address, sir."

"Why? I did nothing wrong. The fat kid kicked my dog."

"You see, expressions such as 'fat kid' aren't exactly helping your case."

The fat kid's family dialled 999 and summoned the law, throwing in words such as 'child' and 'abuse'. Those usually get a response when uttered in close proximity to one another. I suppose I can't blame the police for that.

"He says he only touched it gently with his foot by accident," is the contribution from the other policeman, a Constable, I gather, given that he calls the one questioning me, the prime suspect, Sarge.

"He couldn't touch anything gently. Gravity and its bearing on colossal mass would undoubtedly determine a certain amount of force."

"Well, when the canine retrieval unit arrives, I'll ask them to check the dog over for any bruising."

"Canine retrieval? You can't take the dog. It's not mine, I just borrowed it for two hours to see how I'd get on."

"Sir, I really don't think blind people loan out their guide dogs."

"I'm blind!"

"So you keep saying, but if you are, how could you possibly know that kid's f...obese?"

"Oh, for...it was just a lucky guess. No, you know what, I could hear he was fat because of the way the words formed in and left his fleshy cheeks. Add in that he sat there cramming salt and vinegar crisps in his face, and judging by how long he was shovelling them in for, I'm guessing he had a family bag all to himself. The frequent finger cleansing wasn't exactly pleasant to witness, either. Oh, and then there was the fact that when he sat down on the bench next to me and the dog, struggling for breath, I was nearly catapulted several feet in the air."

"And is that why you called him..." There's a pause while he checks his notebook and turns a page, "here it is, 'a thick fat wanker'?"

I could lie and deny it. The thing is, you never know these days. Someone could have been filming it all on their bloody phone for all I know. What will they charge me with then - perverting the course of justice, or something? Shit.

Okay, don't deny it, but don't admit it either.

"Look, the kid kept asking me if it was a blind dog. I tried to point out that a blind dog wouldn't be much use to me, and that it was a guide dog..."

"That you borrowed?"

"Yes."

"To try out?"

"That's right."

"I'm pretty sure they use sighted people to train guide dogs."

"I give in."

"You're admitting that you're not really blind?"

"No, I'm blind."

"I take it you're aware that this is a dog-free area, and that seeing-eye dogs are the only permitted type, sir?"

"Yes, I kind of thought that might be the case."

"It's also the area where the children tend to hang out on the climbing frames..."

"What? What are you implying?"

"Nothing, sir, I'm just looking to establish why a man might, and I'm not saying that you did, pretend to be blind so that he could bring a cute dog into an area of a park where children might be attracted to it, and then verbally abuse one of those children when they show an interest in the dog, because he isn't slim enough for him."

"I..."

"Now, sir, the family of the boy are saying that you offered him cigarettes. Anything to say about that?"

"I...didn't...no, that was...I lit a cigarette to calm my nerves after his father came over to ask why I called his son a thick fat wanker..."

"So you're admitting that?"

"No. Yes. Look, as I tried to explain to the father and mother, his 'blind dog' insistence told me he was thick, I think I've already explained how I knew he was fat, and the fact his voice had broken, so a certain sexual maturity had been reached, when coupled with the thickness and fatness, probably rendered him incapable of forming any kind of relationship based on physical or intellectual attractiveness, thus I presumed him to be a wanker."

"And you want all that in your statement?"

"Well, no..."

"Tell us about the cigarettes?"

I've had enough now. It's probably time to just get on with whatever is going to happen next.

"I lit a cigarette, and the parents started fussing about second-hand smoke. So I pointed out that I failed to see any difference between smoking and obesity, that's all. Both are a lifestyle choice, and neither are going to do you any good in the long run. I then went on to explain my theories about stress being the biggest killer in the civilised world, smoking being an appetite suppressant, and suggested they sit themselves down and take the weight off their feet, stop fretting and over-protecting their unhealthy child, and have a cigarette, as it might just save their lives."

"Sir, we're going to take you to the station now to be formally processed and charged. I urge you not to make this difficult."

"Charged? On what fucking grounds?"

"Well, let's see. There's threatening behaviour, offering cigarettes to a minor, using foul and abusive language in a public place - not to mention to me just now - there's verbal assault on a minor, and possibly even fraud, if you aren't actually blind. And if that is the case, I'll also be charging you with possession of a dog in a dog-free area. I'll see what else I can think of on the way back to the station. Constable, you stay with the dog and await the canine unit."

"Yes, Sarge."

Shit, Tony's going to kill me.

6.

"Alliss. A, double L, I, double S."

"And who is he again?"

"He works in Scotland Yard. I help them out occasionally. He'll vouch for me."

"Scotland Yard, eh?" He laughs disparagingly after he says it.

Disparage: To regard as being of little worth. To lower the estimation of. Demean. Denounce. Derogate.

Why would he do that? He's a plod from the suburbs, a Sergeant, one up from Constable, two up from trainee. Not that I'm judging. After all, I was a London cabbie prior to losing my sight, so hardly a high-flyer. It was Kate who had the career and all the talent and tenacity, and now I live comfortably on her pension and insurance. It's my cab Tony drives me around in. I'm not allowed in his car, as I have a tendency to be sick. I'm never sick in the black cab, though.

He must be forty, possibly older given his voice and the fact he had an eighties station tuned in on the radio in the car. He assumed control in the park even though he wasn't first on the scene, and he questioned me, the chief suspect, as he ordered the others about. I couldn't help noticing that he addressed by rank or nothing at all for subordinates, and first names for peers, but they all used his rank, or the abbreviated Sarge.

But he was the senior man, and it has to be on account of time served. And he very much likes being the senior man, as he ordered someone called Kirsty to fill out the forms and process my arrival as he chatted with the lads. No, not chatted with; talked at.

Yet, he speaks disparagingly of another division of law enforcement. I decide to test the theory a bit more, and read his reaction.

"Detective Superintendent Alliss," I throw at him.

He catches it in his teeth and chews it, before he decides he doesn't like the taste and spits it back out. It dawns on me that I've been spending quite a bit of time with dogs lately.

"Detective Superintendent, is he? Well, well, friends in high places. That must be nice."

Yes, I've got his measure, the way he slapped one of the young Constables on the back a bit too hard, forcing him to stagger forward and lose his breath. He's a bully, and he feels like his talent hasn't been recognised in life.

He'll have been overlooked for every promotion, and can't understand why. He sucks up to the right people, after all, but the moves he so fully believes he deserves keep eluding him. He may have even tried for a job at Scotland Yard, certainly in the Met, but always rejected.

Probably because he's a shit copper with no powers of perception, hence me being on a threatening behaviour charge. But that makes him dangerous. Ambition coupled with delusions of grandeur will always result in escalation. He'll want to overstate it and make it bigger than it is. The bigger it is, the more it will be noticed. The more it's noticed, the larger the credit. The larger the credit, the greater the recognition and broader the opportunities.

And he's an arse-licker. People who treat subordinates and peers like shit always are. They're too focused upwards. They have to distance themselves from the pack and become aloof. The way he barked at someone after I was booked in, to fetch him a cup of tea and see if there are any biscuits, there's a good girl.

He's a big guy. Sergeant Nicholson must be six-two, six-three in his police issue shoes. And he stood up straight and met every inch of it, he even tried to reach a bit more. His voice and breath came from about two inches above my nose as we stood in the park, and I'm five eleven in socks.

"Yep. Detective Superintendent Tony Alliss," I say, and lean back in the chair.

No cup of tea was offered to me, and not a hint of a biscuit.

He sips his brew and crunches in front of me. I bet it's a Hobnob. It has that mix of crunchy with chewy, as his jaw rhythmically processes it. The oats need to be washed down with a slug of tea, but it can't flush them all, so he uses the tip of his tongue and a bit of suction to clear the oaty debris left on his teeth.

You get to know the sounds.

I know he's watching me as he waits to see if I'll crack. Leave a silence, and people feel a need to fill it. I see no sense in disappointing him.

"So, what exactly am I being charged with?"

"My Superintendent..." he leaves it hanging, emphasis on the 'my', '...is reviewing the statements, and seeing if he agrees with my recommendation on that."

"Well, let's assume he's no smarter than you, so it could take a while. Any chance of a Hobnob...?"

"There! Got you. I knew you weren't really blind, or how else would you have known they were Hobnobs?"

What a tosser.

Somebody enters the room and wordlessly hands Nicholson some papers. I hear them rub together and note the slight creak of the chair as he anxiously rocks back and forth.

"It could be a welfare scam, Constable. Let's wait for the Super." He stresses the first syllable of Constable and makes it sound dirty.

"Why do you have a problem with overweight people?"

I can only presume he's talking to me, but decide to employ silence; taking the fifth, as they say in America.

"For all you know, that family you abused may have a glandular problem. But people like you have to persecute them for it."

Nothing.

"And if you turn out not to be blind, I'll be throwing the book at you. You'll do time for fraud. Claiming welfare fraudulently is a serious crime, you won't smart talk your way out of that one. There are people out there who genuinely need welfare to survive, and your sort bleeding the state dry deprives them of that."

I smile and say absolutely nothing.

The door opens and Sergeant Nicholson hits the table as he springs to attention. It'll be his Superintendent, then.

"Daniel Andrew Francis, I presume? My information tells me that you prefer to be known as Lorry, is that correct?"

I nod towards the voice.

"Knew it, benefit fraud," Nicholson mutters.

His high-sheen shoes creak as he swells up on the balls of his feet. They teach them that, for when they're on parade for hours. It's the same with soldiers; roll up on the balls of your feet and keep the circulation going. It stops you fainting.

But Nicholson just does it to make himself bigger, in the hope that he'll get noticed.

"Lorry, I'm very sorry for any inconvenience you've been caused today. Please accept my most humble apologies, and rest assured that the police officers involved will be admonished."

"What...?" Nicholson spits out.

"Where's the dog?"

"Your registered guide dog is safe and well, and has been

returned to the facility. Again, I'm very sorry about this whole...misunderstanding."

"But this isn't right, sir, with due respect..."

"Leave it, Nicholson."

"But he...how did he know I was eating a Hobnob? He couldn't have known that!"

I've had enough. "Look, it was fairly evident by the mastications that you were devouring something crisp yet chewy, something that the tea swilling wasn't enough to dislodge. I heard you hook what could only have been oats from your teeth. The clincher on that was one you unhooked and shuffled to the front of your mouth before nibbling it with your incisors. So, it had to be an oat based biscuit. Flapjack crossed my mind, but I deduced that you were taking them from a packet that you had to split down the side to gain entrance to, before levering them free with your fingernail. Flapjacks are either fresh from the bakery, or would invariably come in a flat plastic tray of some description, and the noises weren't consistent with that. Besides, Flapjacks are usually square or oblong in shape, but the biscuit you dunked in your tea tapped on the rim of the cup but still made contact with the liquid, because I heard you nibble that bit off and sensed you leaning in to it so it couldn't fall on your uniform, before rotating the biscuit ninety degrees and re-submerging it. It had to be circular. So, a round oat based biscuit in a cylindrical package - chances were that it was a Hobnob."

There's a resounding silence in the room, but I push on regardless.

"But far more worrying than all of that, is the way you're so keen to jump in and defend minority groups. You backed the wrong minority group, Nicholson, and should have gone with the visually impaired. Instead, you opted for the clinically obese and the welfare claimants you decided I was persecuting and defrauding, to use your words.

"Here's the thing, though. People who are too quick to jump in and speak out in defence of minority groups are always a minority group themselves. Except they can't speak out and defend that, they have to keep it hidden, and the frustration stemming from that leads to them being over-zealous when confronted with other oppressed groups, as they see them.

"So, I'm sitting here wondering what your secret could possibly be."

7.

The front door bell chimes, timed for the gap between tracks. Counting my steps, I make my way along the hallway through my uncluttered, one-level house. Swinging the door open, I wait for someone to say something.

"Good to see you, Lorry."

"I'd say the same, but I can't."

"Sorry, I shouldn't have come..."

"No, I mean I physically can't."

"Oh, I thought you meant..." She doesn't finish the sentence because she doesn't want to complete the thought. Sophie Hargreaves worked for Tony until seven months ago. The last time I had contact with her, she was lying on my living room floor with Tony pointing a gun at her head.

"Hello Sofa."

"Hello Lorry."

"Come on in. Cup of tea?"

"I'd love one, thanks."

"Me too, milk and one sugar, please!"

She sighs, but I think there's a smile carried on it. "Nothing changes, does it?"

"I'm only kidding. I'll do it."

"No, I don't mind."

"I'd like to, Sofe, I'm trying to do more, you know?"

"Good for you."

As I fill the kettle, gauge the weight and add a bit more water, I ask, "what can I do for you, Sofe?"

The small talk saves either one of us having to make big talk, but we're going to have to get there eventually.

"I wondered if I could pick your brain. There's this case I'm working on, and...that's a bit of a lie. No, it's true, but it's an excuse, really. I wanted to see you. And I wanted to come before now, but couldn't quite find a reason to. There, I said it."

"You don't need an excuse."

Draping three teabags over the edge of the pot, I let them slip from my fingers.

"And I wanted to apologise," she adds.

"You have nothing to apologise to me for."

"Yes, yes I do. I should have come to Tony and you. I should have trusted you two instead of allowing myself to be manipulated like that."

"Sophie, I'd have done what you did. If it was my family, if it was my daughter they were using, I'd have done anything."

"No, you'd have done the right thing. You're always bloody right!" she adds with a cheery northern flourish and a chuckle to herself.

"If only you knew the day I've had. Milk and sugar?"

"Just milk, ta."

After pouring the water in the pot, I jiggle it to expedite

the infusion process, gauge the level, and struggle to put the lid on where it has a bobble.

"How's Tony?"

"He's fine. I was with him this morning, as it happens."

"Working?"

"Yes, on a murder."

"God, I miss all that. It's nipple-numbingly dull out in leafy Surrey working on petty crime and traffic control."

Locating the top of each cup with my left hand, I add my sugar, spilling a few grains on the countertop, and try to ascertain the pour-angle of the milk carton. Half of it goes on my hand, but I think some of it went in the cups.

"Everything's so difficult, isn't it?"

"Ah, you adapt. I'm adapting, at least. I usually decant the milk, if I'm honest, but I couldn't find the jug. The home-help keeps moving things around. Deliberately, I think, to mess with me."

Cupboard doors open and close, until she eventually finds it, dirty, in the dishwasher.

"I'm doing better than yesterday. I ended up putting orange juice in my tea!"

We both laugh at that.

"I'm sorry about Marc, Sophie. And I'm sorry you missed his funeral. That was out of order, if you want my honest opinion, and I told Tony that."

"Thank you. Yes, it hurt, but we were only together for a few months. It wasn't really long enough to...fall in love, I suppose."

"I knew right away with Kate."

She's relieved to have the conversation moved on, "did you?"

"Yes. With hindsight, I knew the first moment I clapped eyes on her, and I certainly knew after a few minutes."

"You're lucky."

"Better to have loved and lost, than never to have loved at all, you mean?"

"Yes, I suppose I do. Something like that, anyway. How do you cope?"

"Without Kate?"

"Yes."

"Sometimes I wonder, but not lately. They made me see this Emotional Therapist, and that helped. But I hold on to her, I suppose, through Lanie, and through this house and everything in it. The records hold her, they hold my whole life."

"And through Tony?"

"Yes, and through him, I suppose. At the end of the day, he's the only other living-breathing person who was there."

"Lorry, the tea's going everywhere, let me do that."

I feel her hand on mine as she relieves me of the pot, and the contact makes my stomach kick.

"Tell me about this case of yours," I urge, moving away.

"Well, I thought of you right away. A couple got picked up on a drug possession rap, so I had a little sniff around. They claim to deal in popular culture..."

"Records?"

"Not really, but they do have a few. It's more toys and games, that kind of thing."

"And?"

"Well, they also claim to have earned about a million pounds doing that in five years."

"Hey, some of that stuff can fetch big money, Sofe."

"Oh, I know, I checked the internet. But they'd need to move an awful lot every year to make that kind of money. And their little warehouse unit isn't that well stocked. Look, I don't know enough about that stuff to really know, but I know there's more to them than meets the eye."

"A cover business?"

"That's my hunch."

I hear Sophie wiping down the kitchen surfaces and swilling the cloth in the sink.

"Two-hundred thousand a year, roughly?"

"Yep."

"Four grand a week average?"

"Exactly. Can it be done through toys and games?"

"Not a hope. So they're iffy. Tax?"

"Squeaky clean, which is a concern in itself."

She's right. You'd expect to find a little bit here and there. Too clean, and it's like the bloke driving home on a Friday night bang on the speed limit with his vehicle perfectly centered and strictly obeying all the rules of the road. He's almost certainly had a drink.

"What do you need from me?"

"Amongst other things, I need you to sleep with me, Lorry," she says in a way that is so matter of fact I have to replay the words over in my mind a few times to make sure she actually spoke them.

8.

Now, if I'm honest, the notion of having sex with Sophie Hargreaves has popped in to my mind on occasion. So it somewhat surprises me to find myself sat on the edge of my bed while she 'freshens up', fully-clothed and unable to move.

Emerging from the bathroom, she says, "Lorry, are you okay? Look, if this is too much, if you don't want to for any reason..."

"No, I do. I think I do. I know I do. I want to. But...are the lights out?"

She giggles, "it's daytime, Lorry, the lights aren't on."

"The curtains, then?"

"Oh god, you're serious aren't you? I didn't mean to laugh, I just thought you were being witty."

I smile, but it's a bashful sort of smile that forces me to drop my head and not look at my hands.

"I haven't had any intimacy with anyone since Kate." I feel like a virgin, but I don't add the last bit.

She's always been sensitive, it's part of the attraction, as she adds on my behalf, "...and I can see you, but you can't see me?"

"Yes. Stupid, isn't it?"

"No." I hear the curtains draw along the wooden rails.

She sits down next to me and takes my hands in hers. She opens my palms with her fingers, and brings them to rest on her face, so that I'm cupping her cheeks. Aside from Lanie, under very different circumstances, this is the first time I've touched a human face other than my own in over four and a half years.

It's terrifying, and I realise that I'm shaking, and Sophie must feel those tremors, so she places her hands back over mine and begins guiding me over her features. In my head I see a blind assumption, but as I explore her, so that image morphs into that which my fingers detect.

"What colour?" I ask, as I stroke her, surprisingly, longish hair. I had her pegged as being short cut.

"Dusky blonde with highlights."

"And these?" as my fingertips are tickled by her eyelashes.

"Blue."

Good, Kate was dark, olive skinned and tiny, not much over five foot tall, and her eyes were brown. Lanie's like her

Mum.

Coughing something away, I swallow it down from where it was gathering in my throat. I caught it before it could reach my eyes and exploit the one function they can still perform admirably.

Her nose is small and slightly upturned, button-like, and her ears match in size, if anything, perhaps a little too small for the face they're attached to, and her lips are nice, soft and fleshy, with lovely contours above and below between chin and nose, and a quite noticeable ridge down the centre of both. It must give her a pout, I imagine. She opens her mouth, and I feel her teeth, straight and clean, as her minty-fresh breath reaches me.

She's about fifteen years younger than me, seventeen younger than Kate, though Kate's frozen at the age she was that night.

The tips of my fingers find the outer edges of her eyes before tracing out to her cheek bones and down to her jawline, where they come forward before retreating to find the silky hairs on the back and side of her neck.

She's beautiful, I think.

My forearm inadvertently makes contact with her collarbone as I explore, and it dawns on me that she isn't covered, so my hands, barely touching her skin, sweep down following the concavity of her neck, my fingers like butterfly wings. I feel a shudder ripple through her that ends with a little hum on her breath, as I hear her lips part and close before she swallows.

Out I go, a sloping run along her shoulders before rounding and following her lean knotty arms down to her elbows, where they bend and lead me back in to where they rest on her naked thighs. She has goosebumps, so I take her hands instead of carrying on, her fingers interwoven with mine, and she guides me to her breasts where her erect nipples press in to my palms.

"Are you cold?" I ask in a whisper.

"No," she hushes in reply, as though anything more than a breathy barely audible voice will break something that we'll never be able to recapture.

Sophie lies back, my hands still cupped in hers, so that I have no choice but to twist my body and follow her, and when we stop moving my lips are on hers, and her tongue darts in to my mouth and draws me out of my shell.

The notion that the bed we lie on was once mine and Kate's stops me for a beat, but then I recall that the mattress has been changed following too many accidents with cups of tea, and the bedding itself was ordered by Lanie after she said it wasn't right for me to sleep in a room that had such a woman's influence on it. The quilt cover, I believe, is yellow and blue, and Tony spent a week in October last painting most of the house, including this room in a warm yellow. I wasn't sure of the point, but I was glad when it was done. I even helped by making the tea at regular intervals and choosing the soundtrack that he toiled to.

And Tony wouldn't approve of this, no doubt, as Sophie rolls me over on my back and takes my dark glasses off my face, prompting me to close my lids so that she won't see the pointlessness of my eyes, and, perhaps, the pointlessness that has lurked beneath them and within me for most of the past few years.

"Open your eyes," her light-breeze of a voice requests.

I can't.

"I don't know how I look," I tell her.

"You look fine, Lorry."

"No. I mean, I don't know how I look."

"Oh, you mean how your eyes appear?"

"Yeah."

"And nor will I, unless you open them."

It takes an effort, but I will my lids to part, and just as with every time I do that after a period of them being closed, I find myself willing this to be the time that I can suddenly, miraculously, see once more.

"Like I said," she concludes, "you look fine. Your pupils still react to light," she adds with some surprise.

"Yes," I confirm, "my eyes still effectively work. It's the processing of the images in my brain that got fucked up."

She leans down, her hair tickling my neck and face, and runs the tip of her tongue lightly over my re-clamped lids, and I feel my whole body relax and relent, so that I'm powerless to object or do anything other than comply when she hoists my long-sleeved Henley-collared top over my head before picking at the button-fly on my jeans and levering them off my legs.

And by the time she hooks her fingers beneath the waistband of my jockey shorts, having already tugged my socks from my feet, I'm willing it to happen.

The not being able to see is the most exhilarating thing.

With Kate, I always wanted to see her, and to read the pleasure on her face as I savoured her body. The visual element was equally as important as any other to the whole experience, but not knowing how or where somebody is going to touch you is mind blowing; so much so, that when Sophie wraps her mouth around me it comes as such a shock that four and a half years of pent up frustration come pouring out of me.

Sophie doesn't miss a beat, almost as though she was expecting it.

"I'm sorry," I try to say, "it's been so long, and you're

so..."

"Shhhh," is the only sound she makes, as she straddles me and guides me in.

9.

"Thanks for coming, Tony."

"Why wouldn't I come? What's wrong with you? Why are you being so nice to me?" he rapid-fires as he swings through the door, "got any beer?"

"In the tall cupboard, where it always is."

"You having one?"

"Please."

"Hey, that Professor Clifton was financially in the shit, by the way," he calls back at me as I wait for him to encounter Sophie in the kitchen, and the subsequent explosion that, much to my surprise, doesn't materialise.

"You all right, Sofa?" is all he says, as calm as you like.

"Yeah, are you?"

"Depends."

"On?"

"On why you're here. After all, the last time you were here you pointed a gun at my face and handed me over to that bastard Miller. So, why are you here?"

Psst-plunk goes a can of beer before being thrust in my hand, and then repeated for himself. I notice he doesn't offer Sophie one.

"I have a case that I need to pick Lorry's unique mind on."

"Then why am I here?"

"That was my idea," I tell him, because it was. In fairness, Sophie wasn't keen.

Deciding they need to talk, I slope off to the living room and line the stylus up over the run-in groove of the LP already sitting on the platter. I don't know what it is, Haydn, I think, lute and strings, or some such malarkey. I've been enjoying classical music of late, as long as it has no singing on it and isn't piano based. It chills me out and makes all my cares melt away. Besides, I'm hoping the relaxed vibes will transcend to Tony and Sophie.

Over the music I can hear her apologising and attempting to explain, as Tony keeps quiet and lets her speak. It'll make my life a lot simpler if they get on, all assuming Sophie wishes to repeat our tryst today.

I feel good. And younger, as though ten years have been taken off me, and I like myself a little more. Surprisingly, I don't feel disloyal to Kate. I think I've mourned for long enough, and I'm pretty sure she'd have wanted me to move on. That's what Lanie has said for the past couple of years, at any rate.

Sophie says something about fetching the file from her car, and I hear the door open and close.

"Are you shagging her?" is all Tony says to me.

"Shagging...?"

"Yeah, you know..."

"Yes, I know. Why would you think that?"

"Ooooh, let's see now. Let me close my eyes and walk in to things, perhaps that'll help. Terrifyingly, I noticed the increased humidity in the kitchen, caused by the slight dampness of her hair when I arrived, and couldn't help but perceive that you both smelt of the same shower gel. Oh, and, I don't know, there's something light and fucking airy in the way you're suddenly walking, so I reached the conclusion that you've relieved yourself of a great deal of something you had going on. But the real clincher was the fact I came by your house earlier, saw her car on the driveway, ran the plates, ascertained who she was, snuck round the side of your house to ensure you weren't in trouble, just in time to see the bedroom curtains being drawn by a naked woman."

All I can think to say is, "why were you here?"

"Oh, well, you know, it possibly had something to do with me receiving a phone call from a fellow Superintendent about you getting arrested!"

"That was a misunderstanding," I try to fob it off.

"No, Lorry, no it wasn't. It was you being a dick. So, are you getting a guide dog?"

"Ah, a slight problem there. I have to re-sit the test in a few weeks."

"Right. Well done."

Sophie re-entering saves me. I hear Tony leaf through some files and make a couple of grunting noises.

"Possession rap was dropped?" he asks.

"Yes. Too small a quantity for the CPS to give us an intent to supply charge."

"It's got to be drugs, hasn't it?"

"That's their history. The guy got three years, released five years ago. He copped for the full charge to save her doing time, by the looks."

"He and her?" I ask.

Tony drums out the details. "Craig and Debbie Russell, our baddies turned goodies, from drugs to toys and games. It looks like they're the ones playing a game."

"That's what I figured," Sophie says, as she settles on the floor between my legs, a hand on my thigh.

"You went to their industrial unit?"

"Yes, but there was very little there. And I mean next to nothing there. There just wasn't enough stock to even warrant renting the unit, Tony. It's the kind of business you could comfortably run from home, especially as their home is a four bed place, mortgage paid, out near Reigate, and they have no kids."

"Lorry, what do you make of it?"

"I agree that it sounds iffy. Look, you can make good money dealing records and toys and games, but four grand a week? It's tough, and imagine the turnover you'd need to generate that amount of profit. Remember, the right stuff has to be bought, and that's not so easy to get now everyone can look up the price on the internet. That's why half the second-hand record shops went under. It wasn't because of the demand not being there, it was because the shops couldn't get the stuff through the door in the first place."

"Sophie, I don't see an inventory of stock here..."

"No, the warrant only allowed us to search for drugs. Anything else was deemed irrelevant."

"Home and workplace?"

"Yes, but there was no trace of anything in the home. All the business side was in the unit."

"People do that," I offer up, "they segment their lives so that, in their minds, one isn't tainted by the other less salubrious one."

"What do you want to do?" Tony asks, I assume, of Sophie.

"What was that you just said, Lorry, about segmenting life?" she asks me.

"Ah, Kate used to talk about it. She said you should never blur the lines between work and home, that the two should be totally separate entities, and as soon as one impinged on the other, you'd end up hating one or both of them in time."

"She was smart," Sophie states, and pats my leg. "With that in mind, I think we could do with taking another look in Craig and Debbie Russell's place of work."

And Tony adds, "more importantly, I think we could do with Stevie Wonder here not taking a look in that unit."

"We'll never get another warrant," Sophie muses.

"Oh, I wouldn't worry about that," Tony tells her.

"What's the deal with Clifton?" I probe.

"As broke as can be. The guy had even re-financed his house to plough in to the archive. It looks like a suicide, Lorry. The more chance I've had to think about it, the more I think the guy intended to torch the archive, claim the insurance and begin again, but couldn't bring himself to do it, so popped himself off instead."

"It's not a suicide."

"Because you don't want it to be."

I take a few seconds to reflect. If money is as tight as it appears and he were faced with being shut down and the collection being flogged off to service debt, it might have pushed him in that direction, but I still don't buy it. That Mick Stevens LP on the turntable just doesn't fit.

"Look, there are people out there who would gladly burn Clifton's archive because of his inclusion of certain tracks. But on the other side of that coin, he was petitioned and lobbied to include Nick Drake, for example, and received death threats for, initially, refusing to. A new category of 'Baroque Folk' had to be invented to accommodate it."

"Do people really get that het up about music?" Sophie wants to know.

"Wait till you know him better," Tony jumps in, before continuing, "it's not enough, Lorry, I'm sorry. Unless Janine comes up with something more in her Medical Report, or James King coughs up some new angle or insight, there's not enough here. Everything Colin, Maggie and the team found points towards suicide. The professor hadn't even drawn a salary for over two years, he was so desperate for it to continue. He ran out of options."

"Can't we lean on that King kid?"

"Not without reason. Look, he was a shifty little shit, and he's hiding something, but he's no killer. You said that yourself. We're monitoring his calls, and there's nothing there. Besides, we've got Sophie's case to keep us occupied. Let it go, Lorry."

10.

We take the cab, as it can move inconspicuously any time of day or night, and it's about half past one in the morning. Tony drives, with me and Sophie in the back, looking like a regular fare as she snuggles up to me and I loop my arm round her shoulders. I don't know if she's acting a role, or whether she'd have done that anyway. Is she happy to be seen with me in public, and is this a relationship we've embarked on?

Or was it a one-off to scratch an itch we both needed to rid ourselves of?

Tony brings my wandering mind back in line with, "so, to recap, the alarm system will be off between two and twenty past, which means we go in at five past, and we're out by quarter past. Remember, the security patrol swing by every hour between half past and quarter to, so there's no leeway on this. Ten minutes is all we have, and we need to use it wisely. I'll take the computer and hook Colin in remotely, leaving you two to look at the rest of the facility. Sophie, you need to keep Lorry close. He'll ask you questions, so try to give him what he needs. We leave no trace, okay? This is dodgy, and nothing we find will be admissible as evidence, so we're on a reccy and nothing more. Don't take anything, don't move anything, don't break anything. Lorry, are you paying attention?"

"Yes."

"You don't leave Sophie's side, understand?"

Just for tonight, I want to ask?

"Understood," I say instead, before adding, "how does all this happen?"

"Don't ask."

A few minutes later, the cab shudders to stillness, just a ticking remains as something cools in the engine.

"I'll go first," Tony outlines, "and trigger the security light. Let it burn for thirty seconds and keep your eyes and ears open for any attention it might draw. Most people just assume it's a cat or similar, so ignore them after an initial glance. After thirty seconds, if all's well, I'll have the door open. The light's on for a minute, so you then have thirty seconds to get to the door and for all of us to get inside. We don't want that light coming on for a second time prior to us leaving. Got it?"

"Can't Colin just stop the light coming on?" I ask, because it seems a more logical thing to do.

"Not without killing the power, and we need the power on for the computer. He's also put the security cameras on a half hour pre-record, so it'll look good should anyone subsequently take a look."

We walk across a flat slab of hard ground, and come to rest at something that smells of rotting waste. I presume it to be a skip or similar.

"What about the window at the front?" Sophie asks of Tony.

"It's small enough for me not to worry about it, and it looks like it's covered with something anyway."

"To stop people seeing in?"

"It seems that way. I wonder what they wouldn't want people seeing?"

"Shall we go and find out?"

"Mark the time, Sofe."

"Got you."

After a few seconds, I have to ask, "has he gone?"

I didn't hear a thing.

"Shhh," Sophie breathes, "okay, Tony just triggered the light. Keep your ears open, Lorry."

I strain them in to the night. When I was cabbing, I chose not to work many night shifts, preferring to curl up with Kate every chance I could. I'd do a few, when she was away on business, or on the rare occasion I felt the need to escape. It probably amounted to no more than a hundred nights over sixteen years. And, for the past few years, each one of those nights has left me feeling rueful. I could have been with her. Yet, there was something attractive about working the graveyard shift. I always liked the stillness of the night, as I'd sit waiting on a rank somewhere in London with the radio on.

The radio was part of the magic, I recall, and hearing a song you love but didn't expect to hear. It would overwhelm you under those circumstances, in the pitch black silent night, with its crisp air and stillness. Without other sensory distractions, it ratcheted up the intensity of the music, just as, in this moment, all I hear is Sophie breathing softly as she clocks the seconds.

"Let's go," she hisses, and I allow her to re-point and drive me forward.

"Flat ground all the way, then two steps up in to the unit. Okay?"

"Yes."

My heart is pounding in my chest, a sudden requirement

to fuel my muscles, and I'm warm in my dark blue jumper and black jeans where just a moment ago I was chilly in the cool night.

"Two steps coming up," Sophie tells me as I shorten my paces in readiness.

"Now," she instructs, and my left foot locates the first, my right the second, before stepping in.

Shit, I'm pitching forward, my left shoe tip having caught on something - a metal strip across the threshold I think - and Sophie's hand tries to pull me back, but I slip from her grip and bring my hands out to absorb some of the impact as I pass the point of no return.

A large plate of a hand finds my chest and effortlessly stops my fall, before just as easily taking my full weight and standing me back squarely on my feet.

Tony. It's always Tony.

"All right?"

"Yeah. Thanks."

The door closes behind me with a soft metallic clunk, before Tony growls, "go," before adding, "Colin, we're in, get ready to do your thing."

The click of a torch precedes a few seconds of silence, before Sophie begins. "Two desks with office chairs in the middle of the room, one with a computer on, the other with papers and files. There's a sink and a bit of work surface on the right against the front wall, where there's a kettle and a small fridge. Close to there is a vacuum cleaner, a heater and a tool box, by the looks. Aside from a fire exit door at the rear right, it's metal shelving along all other walls, most of which is empty."

"No other chairs?"

"No."

"So they don't receive visitors, we can hazard a guess.

Anything else not on the shelves?"

"No, it's clean."

Spotlessly clean, I can smell the bleach and furniture polish.

"A tool box, you said?"

"Yes, why?"

"Tell me what's in it, Sofe."

The lid opens, and she details, "sheets of sandpaper, a few tools. There are a couple of screwdrivers, a craft knife, a hammer. There's one of those handheld electric grinder sets. My dad has one, it comes with lots of different attachments. It's standard stuff you'd find in any shed, really."

"Right, tell me what they have on the shelves that are occupied."

She walks me to the left, and I notice nothing grinds underfoot.

"I need to let go of you now, Lorry, so I can rummage and hold the torch. Take hold of my waistband here, and stay to my right."

She begins calling things out, "several boxes of Action Man, and similar, some still in their packaging. A scuba-diving Action Man here, Six Million Dollar Man doll, with bionic grip, it says on the box. There's also a Bionic Woman...Oscar Goldman...and a Venus Space Probe, which sounds a bit rude."

"All in the boxes?"

"Yes. Why, is that good?"

"Doubles the value, at least. I wish I could see those. I had that Six Million Dollar Man when I was a kid. Red overall suit, right?"

"Erm, yes."

"He had a pump on his back that raised his arm, and

bionic vision if you looked through the back of his head..."

"Get on with it, you two," Tony snarls.

"There are several boxes of Doctor Who stuff, and Star Wars. Star Trek. What's this? Starsky & Hutch dolls. Evel Knievel toys, lots of that, only some of it in boxes. James Bond here, and Scalextric, Matchbox cars. Some boxes are marked pre-69, others Superfast. Whatever that means..."

"It's to do with the wheels. Superfast were launched in 1969 to rival Hot Wheels in America. Go on."

"Board games, lots of them. You want a list?"

"Yes, as many as you can, especially ones you've never heard of."

"That'll be most of them, then. There's Kerplunk, which I've heard of, Test Match, lots of Subbuteo in these boxes here, Dungeons And Dragons. Good grief, what's this? Stock Car Smash Up. Two of those."

"Oooh, do you think they'd miss one?"

"Probably. There's Battleship, Escape From Colditz, loads of Top Trumps...Panini Football stickers. What have we got here? Cluedo. I've heard of that! Magic Roundabout Game, Scoop, Totopoly, Haunted House. Lorry, that's most of them."

"Okay, I get the picture. What else have we got?"

"That's pretty much it, aside from a few boxes over on the other side."

Sophie drags me across the unit, my finger having located and hooked through the belt loop on her jeans.

"There's not much here, Lorry, these boxes are half empty. There are a few books in this one, mostly price guides."

"Toys and games?"

"Yes, and records. There are two vinyl price guides that I can see."

"But hardly any records?"

"Indeed. Ah, in fact, this box is partly full of the white sleeves that records come in."

"How do you mean?"

"You know, the ones inside the jackets, if that's the right word?"

"Inner-sleeves, Lorry," Tony snaps from across the room.

"Really? Can you hand me a few?"

Sophie must look to Tony, as he calls out, "go on, but put them back exactly how you found them. Three minutes left, you two."

Unhooking my finger, I take the sleeves she guides to my hands. There are perhaps half a dozen, and as I thumb through them, I can tell that a couple have the plastic static reducing inlay, where the others don't. But they all smell old. To confirm it, I bring them up to my nose and draw in the unmistakable aroma of aged paper.

"Okay, I've seen enough of those," I say to Sophie, handing them back. "What else?"

"Records in a couple of boxes here."

"How many?"

"Hard to tell, but no more than thirty, I'd say."

"Hmmm. What do we have, Sofe?"

"Okay ,this record is by someone called Billy Nicholls. There's another here by Comus. Is this someone called Mungo Jerry?"

"Yep, keep going."

"Kaleidoscope, Chris Farlowe, one by Tommy Histon, called 'Three Minute Hero'. This is by...Kip someone? No, make that 'Kip Of The Serenes' by Dr. Strangely Strange. Is that right? Bloody strangely strange names, if you ask me. One by - it looks like a compilation - 'You Can All Join In' or something. This one's by Duane Eddy. More?"

"No time, you two. We have to go," Tony says urgently, "Colin, are you done?"

"Give us one more minute, Tony," I plead. "Sophie, hand me the compilation you found, 'You Can All Join In'."

It makes contact with my hands. There's no time to ask questions, so I press the sides to billow the open edge and stick my nose in. I suck the essence up.

"Thanks, Colin," Tony says, and disconnects something, "we need to go guys, this is getting too close."

I ignore him.

"Tony, get me a sample of what's in the vacuum cleaner! Sofe, quick, the Billy Nicholls." I repeat the process.

"And now the Tommy Histon..." She does it, with Tony hissing at us, but doing as I asked him.

"One more, the Duane Eddy."

Tony has the door open a click tells me. "Now, or I lock you in."

Sophie stashes the records back in their box, and we're moving to the door, fast, my feet clumsy, Sophie with her arm round my waist, her body pressed against mine like a crutch.

"The sink area," I implore, "clock what's there, memorise it!"

"Move!" is all I hear Tony say, as my feet leave the ground and I'm bent forward over his broad shoulder, my arm catching the doorframe as we exit, and I feel the cold air on my face.

"Did you get the vacuum sample?" I pant out as Tony runs back to the taxi at a sprint despite me being on his shoulder.

"Yes," he states, and I realise that I'm breathing harder than he is.

"And what was in the sink area?"

"Nothing, Lorry, just a jar on the side with cleaning pads inside."

11.

"Lorry, that's not normal. And it can't be healthy," Sophie tells me, because she cares, which is nice to know.

Removing the vacuum cleaner bag shard from my mouth, I test it between my fingers again.

Tony enters the room. "Here's something to get your head round."

"Go on," I urge him, nibbling on the shard again.

"That's disgusting. Are you hungry?"

"A bit peckish, if I'm honest. What do you want?"

"Colin just called. He's been through the Russell couple's internet history."

"Oh yeah?" I say, raising my head, which strikes me as a rather pointless act.

"They spent over half an hour looking up a certain Professor Clifton."

"Really?"

"Really."

"Okay, I didn't see that coming."

"It could just be coincidence."

"You don't believe in coincidences."

"No, I don't. What do you reckon, Sofe?"

"You trained me. If it looks like a coincidence, it probably isn't. And what's the other one; trust your gut? My gut told me there was something awry with Craig and Debbie Russell, and now my gut tells me it ties in to this Clifton shooting."

"I'm with Sophie," I state, because I think I am.

He goes quiet.

"Well, what about you, Tony?" Sophie asks.

Drawing in a large breath that whistles through his nose, he growls a little, before stating, "as of now, the Clifton case is a murder investigation, and the Russell case comes under my remit as part of that. Sophie, I'll arrange for you to be seconded to me for the duration. Are you okay with that?"

"No problem, and thank you, Boss."

"Lorry, you're on it as a consultant, in the way that we spoke about. Now, I need you, as a priority, to find me a more tangible link between the two, because we can't use any of the information we discovered via the search. So, you two need to get on this, and don't expect much sleep tonight. Sophie, can you stay with Lorry, and bring him to the Medical Examiner's office for nine?"

"No problem. What are you going to do now, Tony?"

"I need to get to the station and get this moving, and then I'll catch up with the Medical Examiner first thing. We need her report, and we need that ledger book she took with her. See you in a few hours, kids, play nice."

"Thanks for tonight, Tony," Sophie calls after him.

"No problem. And, Lorry? I haven't forgotten about the guide dog shambles, and nor have I forgotten that you have a cricket match on Saturday."

Shit, he remembered.

As soon as he's gone, Sophie leans down over me, and pecks me on the forehead. I raise my mouth towards her, but she pulls away. "Sorry, I didn't mean to be forward..."

She laughs. "Lorry, you've been sucking on the contents of a Hoover bag! You aren't kissing me until you've brushed your teeth. Twice. Go. I'll get us a beer."

Brushed and swilled, my beer tastes like crap as a consequence, as I dig out an album to play from the ones labelled up.

Her cheery Lancashire accent has always had an ability to put a smile on my face, as she places a plate on my lap, and says, "here you go."

"What is it?"

"It's a cheese sandwich. It was all I could find in the kitchen."

I pretty much live on cheese sandwiches. In the winter I even attempt to toast them. It's not easy, but I worked out I could better monitor them by slapping them in a dry frying pan and toasting them over the hob. I cook them until they begin to smell right.

Whilst we eat, I let my mind go blank, just the rhythm of my jaw for company, so that all I see is black.

The Russell couple are faking records, I'm sure of that. The cleanliness of the floors first made me think it, somewhat confirmed by the subsequent scrap of vinyl discovered in the bag. I presume the sandpaper to be for scuffing up the centre labels, plus the craft knife and grinder tool for adding hairline scratches, smoothing the rim and centre hole, and adding the spindle marks. It all points to that. Then there's the scouring pads in the jar on the sink. I bet they're steel fibre ones, and I'm equally as sure they're sitting in vinegar, so they oxidise up and can be used to age outer jackets. Throw in the old paper inner sleeves that will obviously pass as being period, and all the pieces are in place.

But the clincher for me, was the copy of 'You Can All Join In'. It was an original, but it's not an expensive record. It's the kind of thing you can track down on the internet for a few quid, or stumble across in a record shop or car boot sale for not far off the price of a new record, or less than a tenner.

However, the important thing about it? It dates from 1969 and is on the Island label, so has the pink label design with the eye logo that people covet.

It's a similar thing with the Chris Farlowe record on Immediate. I didn't get to smell it, but I'd wager it's an original copy, dating from 1968, but worth not-very-much.

Offset those against the Doctor Strangely Strange and Billy Nicholls records. They're from the same era, respectively, as the other two, and therefore have a very similar layout and design, but worth a bit more.

The Strangely Strange LP is worth hundreds of pounds, but the Billy Nicholls record is worth thousands. It was withdrawn on release, so is as rare as just about any record you'd care to mention.

I have them, but only on re-issue. Call me tight, but I'd never spend what it would cost me to own originals. But people will pay the big money, especially for those rare records from the psychedelic sixties or progressive seventies. The folk, blues and jazz aficionados are the same, and it's a similar story for rockabilly and Beatles collectors. But it has to be the the right thing, and-or it has to be in the right condition.

And Clifton would be one of those people, in the folk genre.

I've heard of Billy Nicholls 'Would You Believe?' LPs selling for seven or eight grand. The mint condition book price is about three thousand pounds.

Ah, but all of that is small-fry compared to the Tommy Histon LP, which happens to be one of the most sought after records known to exist. And it just so happens to have been on the same label as the Duane Eddy LP Sophie handed to me, and that was an original and worth all of about twenty to thirty pounds, and probably not even that.

The Histon LP is the one everybody wants. It's beyond collectible. Officially, it was never released, neither in the USA where it was recorded, nor in the UK where it was scheduled for release.

It was psychedelic folk music before the concept had even been conceived. It was the most tripped out slab of vinyl pressed up to that time, and, arguably, still could be.

I say pressed, but it barely was. Just a handful of copies slipped out before it was pulled, and all in the UK, where an edict from on high arrived a few minutes too late, or so legend has it. And very occasionally, a copy pops up in the UK, a rogue disc that was never destroyed, and smuggled out by a far-sighted employee most probably. No promotional or demonstration copies have ever been seen. The label had such little faith in the record, they neglected to send any to the press and radio stations. The best guess is that less than twenty copies exist.

It's so sought after for a number of reasons. First up, it's mind-blowingly good, which always helps. But it also appeals to a few sectors of the collecting community. There are the psychedelic music collectors, an obsessive group if ever there was one, and the strange-folk fraternity, not to mention the rockabilly, and even country music rabble, where Histon had his roots. It appeals both in the USA and the UK, as well as the rest of the world, and pre-dated the summer of love by five years, but encapsulates it.

Rumours abound, with some saying Histon got blotto stoned on LSD for three days, and recorded the whole LP during that time, having no recollection of that process once he came down. Others claim he did it purely as a piss-take, to fulfill the contractual obligation he had, to supply his label with one more record.

It was all hard to verify, as he was dead within two

months of recording it. A drug overdose saw to that. Another certainty is that nobody liked the record at the time, certainly not the label, who were more than happy to acquiesce to the family request 'not to release this piece of garbage that will stain the memory of a great musician, and much loved son and brother'.

Vitally, though, it contains hitherto unknown traditional folk songs, that Histon tried to pass off as his own compositions. They were tunes he'd picked up as a child, living in the Appalachian mountains, and were dark, full of apocalyptic imagery dressed up in a sunshine and flowers kind of way. Musically pretty, but lyrically gritty, was how I once read it described.

"Wow! Where have you just been?" Sophie asks me, as I come back to the here and now.

"Sorry, I do that."

"Thinking about the cases?"

"Yes."

As the current situation comes back to focus in my mind, I become aware that the record has finished playing, and may have ended some time ago. I stand to put on the other side, forgetting that my plate was resting in my lap as it rattles to the floor.

"Stay still, Lorry," Sophie calmly directs, "the plate broke in half."

She takes my hand as she sinks down to collect up the pieces.

"Sorry."

"It's fine. Everything's so difficult, isn't it?"

"Is it too difficult, Sophie?"

"I'm here, aren't I?"

I want to ask if she's still here because Tony told her to be, or would she be here anyway, but I don't.

"I've got an idea, but I need your help," I say instead.

"Go on."

"I need your eyes."

"Then they're all yours."

"And I need them to look on-line."

"I didn't think you liked the internet?"

"I don't, but other people do."

"And is that it, just my eyes on a screen?"

"I think so. For now."

"Good, then we can do all that in bed."

She collects up the broken crockery, and I hear the pieces being discarded in the bin.

12.

"Morning campers!" Tony greets us, far too bloody cheerfully.

I'm not a morning person. He probably got two hours sleep, and went running at six thirty this morning. With that in mind, I just grunt and take the cup of tea Sophie hands me, though despite having stood undisturbed for twenty minutes in its styrofoam container with the hopelessly inadequate lid with the pop-up spout that I can't deal with, is still a few hundred degrees from being a drinkable temperature. It shouldn't even be liquid.

"He's grumpy in the mornings," Tony feels the need to state out loud.

"He was fine with me. It must just be you."

To move things along, I say, "did you get what I asked for?"

Tony confirms that he did. What I requested were copies of the final few pages of Clifton's ledger.

"And did you go through it looking for what I detailed?"

"I did."

"And?"

"It's there, purchased for fourteen thousand pounds three weeks ago. What does it prove, and, more importantly right now, how does it link the Russell couple with Clifton?"

"It doesn't prove anything in itself, but it establishes a connection."

"Go on."

"We spent quite a bit of time on the internet after you left, a healthy chunk of which involved reading about Professor Clifton's latest acquisitions for the archive. It seems he's been more active in the media of late than historically, presumably because he was touting for funding. Anyway, he was quick to announce his latest jewel, a copy of the legendary Tommy Histon LP."

"And how did he come across it?"

"He didn't say, but the ledger should."

"You're thinking that he bought it from the Russells, and the ledger will prove that, establishing a link?"

"Yes."

"Sorry, Lorry, but you're wrong. The ledger says it was purchased from a charity auction house based in France."

"Really?"

"Really."

"Bollocks. I was sure..."

My annoyance has me instinctively reaching for a cigarette, which I hook with my lip and tug from the packet, my hand occupied with the tea.

"I need that link, Lorry, if we're going to open this up."

"I know. We discovered something else. Three copies of that album have sold via on-line auction houses in the past few months. Two were sold by the same seller, and the third by a different person. They were all sold from here in the UK."

"And the point is?"

"Do you have any idea how unlikely that is?"

"No. I mean, you said it was rare but..."

"The odds on that happening are so slim it's...to put it in context, we could only find one prior example of that LP selling in the entire history of the internet."

"But it's not impossible."

"No. In fact, it just got more remarkable, because you just told us of a fourth copy. But here's the other thing, the seller who sold two copies, netting a sum of fifty-one grand incidentally, has the seller identity 'CrabbieSell'."

"Craig and Debbie."

"Exactly. Now, I believe that they're faking records, making new ones look old. My thinking was that Clifton bought a copy of the Histon LP from them, recognised it as a forgery, challenged them and threatened to blow their scam wide open..."

Tony completes my line of thought, "so they showed up here looking to retrieve the evidence..."

"By kidding him that they intended to destroy it, hence the pretend fire bomb."

"...but they got their information from Clifton, retrieved it anyway, the gun went off, perhaps accidentally, so they panicked and fled leaving the toy bomb in place."

"Yes."

"It makes sense."

He's thinking about it. I can hear his hand rubbing his stubble.

"So, if I go and check the archive," he concludes, "using the reference number in the ledger, the record shouldn't be there."

"That's my thinking."

"And that's why we met here, and not at the lab."

"Well, that and because we need to have another chat with James King."

"The Professor's little helper?"

"The very same."

"Talk of the devil... Oi, you little shit!"

Sometimes it flashes in to my mind that Tony could do with working on his interpersonal skills.

*****

The four of us are in Clifton's studio. Tony probably chose here to unnerve King, by bringing him back to the scene of the crime. He's quiet as I sip my luke-warm tea. I pause and suddenly state, "Jim, tell me which records you've removed from here and sold via the internet?"

"Er, what? Erm, I don't know what you're talking about..."

"Let me ask that another way; which records have you sold on the internet having removed them from the archive?"

"No, I..."

"Of the top twenty selling items on internet auction houses, three were sold by a certain 'GuyFawkes95'. 'GuyFawkes95' is shown as being located in Bristol, which, I'm reasonably sure, is where your slight accent hails from. It's easy enough to check. But let me guess, were you born in 1995?"

His silence answers the question.

"Jim King, or King James The First. What do I know about him? You see, you pick these little snippets up, driving a taxi around London for years, it's the same with the accents. 1605, rings a bell, the Gunpowder Plot, Guy

Fawkes and all that. How does it work, Jim lad? No, let me guess. This is how I'd do it. You steal records Clifton replaces with upgrades, because I can't imagine you having the balls to take his primary copies. That way, there's no risk of Clifton accidentally buying them, as he already has better ones. How close am I?"

"You've got it wrong, I swear!"

"Then put me right, Jim, but don't dare lie."

"The Professor knew what I was doing, it was his idea!"

Sophie jumps in with, "but he's conveniently dead."

"No! I mean yes! You're not getting it!"

She pushes him a little more, "and right now, you're our number one suspect."

"No, look, there was no money left, but Professor Clifton couldn't resist buying things when they came up. He was addicted, and just like any addict, he couldn't stop. So he came up with the idea of selling the surplus copies of records we had, to raise funds."

"Why didn't you tell us that yesterday?" Tony barks.

"Because I knew how it would appear. And besides, what we were doing was illegal, we were selling property that belonged to the University. That's why Clifton asked me to do it anonymously."

The kid's nearly crying, and all the hesitation present in his speech yesterday is gone. I believe him.

"Tell me about the Tommy Histon album, Jim?" I coax gently.

"Ah, shit, you know about that?"

"Yes, but I need you to tell me," I half lie. There's no sense in volunteering my half a theory.

"Look, Clifton was desperate, and this record came up for sale in France..."

"The Histon LP?"

"Yeah, 'Three Minute Hero'. It's an iconic record, and you just never see it for sale. A couple had come up recently, and Clifton had lost out on the bidding. They went for an insanely high price."

"Twenty-seven and twenty-four thousand pounds, respectively," I fill in, as much to let him know that I know as anything else.

"Yes, and it was Clifton who pushed those prices up, but on both occasions he got outbid. I'd never seen him so livid. And depressed, he was terribly down about those. So, when a third copy came up... You see, with hindsight, we should have smelt a rat; the odds on three copies of that record coming up in the same decade, let alone in the space of a few months, well, it should have had us seeing red flags."

"Go on."

"Clifton got a tip-off from the auction house in France, as he'd bought things from them before. He was determined not to let this third chance slip by, especially as the record was described as being in Excellent condition with a Very Good Plus sleeve."

"He already had a copy of the album in the archive?"

"Yes, from years back, but it was in pretty bad shape. The sleeve was messy, torn and split, and the vinyl would be hard pushed to be graded Fair. You couldn't play it, really, not without skips and masses of background noise."

"But you still managed to sell it for the best part of ten grand."

"Yes, that was an incredible price, really, given the state of it. The superior replacement copy from the French site only cost fourteen grand, so we were only four down on the deal, and with a few other pieces being sold, we could cover it."

"But..."

"Clifton fucked up...sorry, I didn't mean to swear, or speak ill of him."

"It's fine, go on," Sophie tells him gently.

"Well, he was financially screwed, and didn't have the fourteen grand to pay for the auction he'd just won. They insist on payment within two weeks. So, he took a gamble, and asked me to list up and sell the Histon LP we already had. Look, he knew it was risky, letting one go before the other was in his hand, but he didn't feel like he had a choice."

"So you listed it and bailed him out by, what, pushing the money directly to the French people who sold the record?"

"Yes, Clifton couldn't have it showing on his accounts."

"Go on, what happened next?"

"We thought we were home and dry. As soon as we had a tracking number from the French, Clifton relaxed."

"Until the record arrived?"

"Precisely, and he knew immediately that it was a fake. I mean, he knew practically before he'd even taken it out of the box."

"How?" Tony asks.

"The weight, the smell, everything was off. And as soon as he clapped eyes on it, well..."

"Where is it now?" Tony snaps.

"That's the thing..."

"What's the thing?"

"I can't find it. Clifton had me insert the fake in the archive, just in case an audit were performed, while he worked out what to do."

"And it's gone," I say more than ask.

"Yes. When I came in yesterday, and saw what had happened to the Professor, I sensed it was something to do with that record. Well, either that, or I thought he might have borrowed money he couldn't repay from people who wouldn't take that lightly. Anyway, I went to look for the record last night after everyone had gone, seeing how I had the reset code, and it wasn't there."

"Convenient for your story?" Sophie suggests.

"It's not a story! Shit me, how could I even begin to make all of that up?"

He's got a point.

"Is there anything else you can tell us, Jim, anything that might help us find who did this?"

"Not that I can think of. I just can't believe he's dead over this. It wasn't suicide, was it?"

"No, Jim, no it wasn't," Tony informs him.

"The tragedy is, the record is worth nothing as a forgery, so the Professor died for nothing."

"Why do you say that?" I prompt.

"I assume someone came here to steal it."

"Not the forgers looking to cover their tracks?" Tony asks.

"But nobody knew it was the fake copy," Jim King muses, "except for me and the Professor. And besides, if it had gone through an auction house in France, how could it be traced back to the people that faked it?"

He's quite a smart lad, for a student.

"Jim, I need you to go with a couple of officers and make a formal statement back at the station," Tony informs him.

"Am I being arrested?"

"No, but we need to dig around some more," Tony mutters.

He summons two police officers who walk Jim King from the room.

"Hey, one more thing, Jim..." I call after him.

"What?" he asks gloomily.

"That French auction place; do you happen to know how they came across that copy of the Tommy Histon LP?"

"Hmm, I can't be certain this is the case, but in the past, I know they get stuff from the parcel companies."

"What, undeliverable stuff?"

"Yes, you know, either that or the stuff that people won't pay the import duty on."

13.

IT Colin fills us in on speakerphone. "It all stacks up, Tony. I can follow the money, and it's all as the kid said. So, you still have no tangible link between Clifton and the Russells, other than the fact they looked him up on the internet."

"And there's no law against that," Tony continues, "after all, they deal in a few records, and he collects them."

"Talking of which," Colin pushes on, "regarding the record sold in France; I spoke with the auction house owner, who confirms he sold it as a charity fundraiser on behalf of one of the international shipping companies. They have a semi-annual sale like that, and he gets his fifteen percent."

"Got you. Thanks Colin."

He punches in another number, and waits a few seconds. "Janine, anything?"

"Nothing, Tony. I submitted my report to the Coroner, but he's saying inconclusive, probable suicide."

"Shit, so we can't even officially call it a murder?"

"I'm afraid not."

"Alright, thanks."

"What now, Tony?" Sophie asks.

"I don't know. Lorry, give me something, will you? Give

me an in, anything?"

My mind keeps hitting brick walls. I know he didn't kill himself, that Clifton was murdered, and the motive for that lies in that record. I'm sure of it. We can't go after them on the forging, because we aren't supposed to know, and the only way we can demonstrate that we know is by admitting to an illegal search of their premises.

What am I missing?

Thinking out-loud, I begin, "they forge records, plural, and the Histon LP must have been done months ago. But that unit had been scrubbed clean recently, so it's reasonable to presume they've prepared a new batch in the not-too-distant past, correct?"

"Yes," they both answer.

"Sophie, we only looked at the completed listings. Can you get back on line, and do a search on the current active ones?"

"No problem."

"Tony, remember yesterday when we were going through the motives for murder and arson?"

"I do."

"What was that acronym again, and what did it stand for?"

"V-CREEP. Vandalism, Concealment, Revenge, Excitement, Extremism, Profit. But it's an irrelevance, Lorry, because it wasn't a real bomb."

"I know, but they rigged it up for a reason. Look, how many copies of the Histon LP have been sold recently?"

"Four."

"No. What if it's actually only three."

"How do you mean?"

"We know one copy sold was by Jim King, and that it was a very poor original pressing. Agreed?"

"Yes."

"So that leaves three others. My thinking is that there were two fake copies, and that one of them never reached its destination. Hence the carrier company selling it off via the place in France."

"So,' Tony continues, "one of the Russells fakes was sold twice. Once by them, and again to Clifton from France."

"Exactly. If this is about profit, they had to reclaim the disc to send out, or be faced with having to issue a refund. But nobody would wait months for a refund or the product, particularly given the price and nature of it. Does that make sense?'"

"Yes."

"Then it has to be about concealment."

"I'm inclined to agree."

"But as young Jim said, the likelihood of that record being traced back to them was extremely remote, if not impossible. After all, if it could be tracked either way, we have to presume that the shipping company would have tried to return it on failing to deliver it."

"Ah, so the delivery address and sender details must have been lost."

"That's my thinking, that the contents got somehow separated from the outer packaging. It's the only explanation."

"But the intended receiver would seek compensation from the sender."

"Exactly, and the sender would seek compensation from the shipping company."

"And if that were the case, the shipping firm would have connected the dots and returned the record."

"So no compensation claim was ever filed," I decide, and meet no argument.

Tony continues the brainstorm. "And that was because they didn't want to be tied to it for some reason; they didn't want it being traced back to them."

"Precisely, so why even bother to retrieve it?"

"Off the top of my head, to conceal something else."

"What?"

"Not a clue, Lorry. But I agree with you, there's something about that record, something more than meets the eye."

Sophie interrupts us. "Hey gentlemen, I'm looking at the active listings, and our friends with the cleanest unit in Britain are currently listing just about everything I recall seeing last night on the toy and game side, plus a couple of records."

"Which ones?" I need to know.

"The Billy Nicholls one, and another we must have not got to last night, by Catapilla Changes, I think it is?"

"Catapilla is the band, 'Changes' the title. On Vertigo swirl, UK pressing, correct?"

"Erm, yes. How did you know that...?"

"Lucky guess. Indulge me, please, and run through all the toys and games they have listed."

She reels them off, covering everything I remember being told about last night, plus a few we must have missed in the rush.

"When are those records due to end, Sofe?"

"Give me a sec...tonight, at ten'ish."

"Any bids on them?"

"Twelve on one, seven on the other."

"Prices currently?"

"Er, the Billy Nicholls is at nine hundred, and the Catapilla is sitting at six-fifty."

"What's the maximum amount of expenses I can claim in

my line of work, Tony?"

"You don't have expenses. You barely have a line of work. We buy you tea, the occasional sandwich and the odd pint of beer."

"Okay, but isn't there a pot of money, you know, like petty cash sitting in a tin that I can get access to?"

"No," he says in a way that implies he has no idea what I'm talking about.

"Well, how much are you going to authorise me to spend, then?"

"How much do you think you'll need?"

"It shouldn't take much more than two grand...plus shipping."

"I can't sanction that, on a hunch!"

"But you'll get it back. As soon as we prove the record's a fake, you can re-claim it."

"What if it isn't fake?"

"Ah, well, in that case, can I keep it?"

"No."

"Fair enough. Are we on, then? Me and Sophie can handle it."

"I'll be round yours at nine-thirty."

"To be honest, Lorry," Sophie adds, "I need to get home and change my clothes and stuff."

"Okay, Tony it is, then."

"Well don't sound too fucking happy about it," he snaps.

14.

"So, how was your night on the Sofa?" Tony asks, as we sit and eat the chips he picked up on the way.

"Not bad at all. How was it having a Stephoscope hanging off your ears?"

I can sense him smiling, his teeth rub on his lips as they part.

"Hey, I hope you don't mind, but I asked Janine along to the cricket match on Saturday."

"Why?"

"Because she was asking what you did, and I mentioned the cricket. She lived in Sri Lanka for a couple of years, so got in to it."

"I suppose it doesn't matter, in the great scheme of things. Just tell her not to expect much. What was she doing in Sri Lanka, anyway?"

"She took some time off to help the poor and needy there."

"Good for her," I say, popping a chip in my mouth. They could do with more salt.

"That's what I thought. Hey, she wants us to go to the Maldives."

"Us?"

"What? No, me and her, you nob-end."

"Oh, right. That'll be nice."

"I've not had a proper holiday in years."

"You did say you'd think about taking me to America..." I remind him. Subtly, I thought.

"Ah, we'll get round to it. It's been difficult with work, and the new department."

It's no more difficult than going to the Maldives, I think.

"Right, five minutes till auction end," he states, screwing his chip wrapper in a ball.

"Is Colin all set?"

"It's Colin, what do you think?"

There's no music playing, the realisation of which baulks me. I've played less music over the past two days than any other two days I can think of in years, probably since I came out of hospital.

That has to be a good thing, doesn't it, indicative that I'm moving on? And it must relate to Sophie being around.

I like the feeling, the knot in my guts and a nonchalance about everything. It's early days, but it feels good. And, yes, it reminds me of first meeting Kate, and the early days of that, the thrill of discovery, I suppose. And it was just nice waking up to a house with someone else in it. I didn't need to play music, because I didn't have a void to fill, and there was no urge to occupy the senses that still function, because they were otherwise engaged.

Tony brings me round, as I fold up my chip wrapper and hand it to him. "So we're going for the Catapilla album?"

"It should be the cheaper of the two."

"And what 'should' it sell for?"

"Given the condition? Book price is seven-fifty, but we know it isn't Mint, VG+ to EX at best, but Vertigo label progressive rock is hot at the moment. A grand would be a fair bet."

"And we're going to bid?"

"Two grand."

"Because it's a stupid amount to pay?"

"Exactly."

"Proving?"

"Proving that if we get outbid, there's more to it than meets the eye."

"And if we don't?"

"Then I don't think we'll ever see the record, and they'll refund us. How long?"

"Three minutes."

"Then let's be naive, and bid too early."

"How much?"

"Straight in with a grand."

"In. Current high bidder. Hey, I've just noticed that the two records were on three day listings, whereas all the toys are either thirty day Buy Now, or ten day auctions. Mean anything?"

"Probably. Any bids on the toys and games?"

"Let me scroll, through...yes, on a couple, but nothing exciting. Nowhere near the records anyway."

"How long?"

"Two minutes. We're still the high bidder. This may be as good a time as any to let you know I'm logged in under your account name."

"What? How?"

"Colin. So you'd better be sure about your theory."

"I was, when I thought I was playing with someone else's money."

"Yep, that's what I figured."

"Have you ever done this before?"

"What, an on-line auction?"

"Yes, in real time?"

"Nope, this is my first. You?"

"I used to. But it's harder to do now."

"I suppose. One minute. Still the highest."

"Any serious action on the Billy Nicholls LP?"

"Loads, it's up to five and a half thousand, and thirty-one bids. Ah, hold up, we've just been outbid!"

"Re-bid, and go...fuck it, two grand."

"Lorry..."

"Just do it."

The keys click, and I sense his finger hovering over the return key. "Sure?"

"Yes."

"It's your money." Click.

"High bid...twenty seconds to go...ah, outbid notice!"

"Go three grand."

"Lorry, this is insane..."

"Trust me, Tony!"

The numbers click, four taps on the number keys, and a definitive slap on the return.

"Highest...ten seconds. nine, eight, seven...shit, I'm sweating!"

I'm buzzing, and so's Tony.

"Outbid! Five seconds to go..."

"Five thousand and one, Tony, now...!"

15.

"Did we win?"

"I don't know, it's sorting itself out. Here we go, 'Congratulations, you won Catapilla 'Changes' LP etcetera', 'Pay Now'."

"Pay."

"Lorry, you don't have to do this."

"How much?"

"The full five thousand and one."

"So, someone went five thousand, and we pipped them with the extra quid."

"Wow! That was amazing. Look, Lorry, whatever happens, I'll make sure you're not out of pocket."

"Just make sure Colin's doing his bit."

"He will. I need your credit card, Lorry."

"Bedside table, in wallet in drawer."

As he goes off to get it, I hear his phone chirp. "Colin, what did you get?"

Through speakerphone, Colin reports, "Lorry was right, Tony, I'm sure of it. Despite the privacy setting on the account, the first and last characters of the username are visible when the auction's active, and the winner of the Billy Nicholls LP - for nearly ten grand, by the way - looks like the same person who was bidding against you."

"Track the bastard. I want to know who it is."

"You've got it."

"Anything else?"

"Yes."

"Go on."

"I'm getting my old vinyl out of my mum's attic tomorrow, I may not need to work for a living."

"Good man, Colin. Thank you," Tony says.

Once the transaction is complete, we sit back and wait to see what will happen.

Tony kicks off the inevitable point. "So, why would someone pay five times the going rate for a record, Lorry?"

"Money laundering?" I suggest.

"That was my inclination."

"We know the Russells have a drug background, right?"

"Yep," Alliss confirms.

"So, perhaps, as Sophie suspected, they're still in the game, and this is how they cover the financial..." a sudden thought stops me in mid-flow. "In the game?" I repeat to myself.

"What?"

"In the game!"

"What, are you thinking that the drugs get smuggled inside toys, such as the Action Man stuff in the unit?"

"Maybe, but I'm thinking not. After all, they went to Clifton seeking to reclaim or destroy a record, not toys, but there's something I can't put my finger on. Run through the toys and games they have on-line again, please. I'm missing something."

Colin calls in. "Tony, I can't get hold of anyone in a

position of authority at the auction place, so things are going to have to wait till tomorrow without a warrant."

"Can't you hack it?"

"Probably, but the firewall's good, as it needs to be. It'll be easier to wait and pick it up again tomorrow. We don't want to compromise the case with anything illegal. This isn't the terrorism business, remember, we can't get away with things in the name of National Security."

He's impatient, but agrees, "first thing, Col, go and get some rest."

"Night gents."

"Night Colin," I call out.

"Here we go," Tony tells me as he goes back to the computer. "The seller has refunded your payment, blah, blah, blah, and there's a note added explaining that the record, on inspection before packaging, isn't an original, sorry for any inconvenience caused, and thanks for bidding."

"Told you."

"Phew! Well done. But we still don't have enough to act, do we?"

"No, but we will come tomorrow."

"We will?"

"Yes, because we know which shipping company they use, thanks to the French connection, so if you trot off now and find out what time that company is due to collect from that unit tomorrow, we're laughing!"

"Right, I'll toddle off then."

"Thanks for the chips."

"I'll ring you in the morning."

*****

Sophie showed up fifteen minutes after Tony left. She brought a toothbrush with her, I gather, as I found it in the pot. I may have used hers by mistake, so I dried it on the towel in the hope she wouldn't notice.

She didn't say anything when she came to bed.

"I did what you asked," she begins, her head resting on my chest.

"I know, I'm still recovering."

"No, the other thing! I was following your crazy bidding on the internet. Mine wasn't nearly as exciting."

"Which one did you bid on?"

"Oh, I don't know, one that was cheap."

"Bugger, if I'd thought it through, I'd have told you to go for something good and worth keeping."

"Well, I won, so I paid and contacted the seller via email. I gave them some story about heading up north tomorrow afternoon, for my nephew's birthday, and that the toy was a present for him. Anyway, I asked if I could drop by and pick it up to take with me, because by the time it'd arrive in the post, it would be too late."

"Good work; so it gives us a nice convenient excuse to spin by."

"Debbie Russell got back to me, gave me the address of the unit, and said I could call in between ten and midday, no problem."

"Brilliant!"

"Is it?"

"Yes, as long as the courier calls between those hours."

"Well, I figure they must, which is why the Russells will be there then."

"Hmmm. You're a very clever girl."

She giggles, and the word 'girl' triggers a thought I've been having.

"Are we...are you my girlfriend?"

She bursts out laughing, and I feel utterly stupid for even asking.

She must spot my anguish, as she spins round and sits on and facing me with her hands on my shoulders. "Oh, my love," she says, "nobody's said that to me since I was about thirteen! It's so sweet."

"I didn't know how else to term it."

"Do you want me as your girlfriend?" she asks, seriously.

I nod.

"That'll mean you aren't allowed to see other women..."

"I can't see the one I've got!"

"...then ask me again."

Self-consciously, I mumble, "will you go out with me and be my girlfriend?"

"I will. But, as such, I'm allowed to come and watch you play cricket on Saturday. Deal?"

I sigh. "Tony?" is all I need to say.

"Yes, he's told everyone. I think he's proud of the fact you've made the final."

"We came tenth..."

"Well, that's good. Top ten!"

"...out of ten. Everybody makes the final, and because we finished bottom, we start by playing the top team. You know, the one that went unbeaten all season."

"I don't care, Lorry."

"I'm not very good."

"It doesn't bother me. We still have sex, don't we? Look, you're my boyfriend, and I like to support my men."

"Men?"

"Man, then."

With a heavy breath, I decide, "okay, you can come."

"Excellent! I used to go with my dad to Old Trafford when

I was a kid. They'd let me sneak in for free, and my brother and sisters hated cricket. I've always loved..."

"Hang on, what do you mean, we still have sex, don't we?"

16.

Quite how Tony knew to show up with three teas and muffins worries me, and I wonder if he's had Colin install surveillance equipment in my house.

"We're all set. The legal rep has given us a green light. However, we're not there for drugs or anything to do with Clifton. This is about fraud through fake records, and nothing more at this stage. Understand?"

Sophie and I confirm that we do.

"Good. You and Sophie will arrive at ten thirty to collect the toy. The parcel pick-up could be any time between then and a quarter to eleven. I've got discreet eyes watching, just in case he gets there early, but I'm assured he never does. If anything, it's far more likely he'll be late. Sophie, you're sure the Russells won't make you?"

"No. I went along for the search of the unit, but was never involved in the interviews, and they were in those interviews when we did the search. It's all good, Boss."

"Fine. Now, listen, both of you. These people may have already killed one person, so we aren't talking petty criminals here. They're prepared to do what it takes to protect their lucrative scam, so be wary, and keep that in mind. Sophie, you look after him, alright?"

She must nod as she squeezes my arm.

"And as soon as you get a fix on the record being in the shipment, you give me the signal. What's the signal, Lorry?"

"I say 'the cab's waiting', and you make the interception."

Outside, it's great to feel the sun on my face. It epitomises how I feel inside; brighter, and with a glow at my core.

Good god, I'm happy! That's what this is. I'd forgotten how it felt. And I'm confident!

"Have you spoken with Lanie?" Tony asks me as we head to the taxi.

"Not since Sunday, no. She's got these mock exams this week, with a view to choosing her specialty."

"So, she doesn't know you're doing any of this?"

"No."

"Lorry, I thought we had a deal? You tell her, or I do."

"I'll call her tonight."

"Make sure you do."

As before, Tony acts the role of driver, with his fares in the back.

"Colin, give me an update on the courier; on schedule?"

"Within a couple of minutes, Tony, you're good to go."

"Thanks."

"Is Lorry with you?"

"I'm here Colin, what do you need?"

"Just to let you know that Maggie and I are looking forward to the cricket on Saturday."

"Oh for Christ's sake, Tony!"

The cab sways with laughter, and eases the tension out of us all.

A hush descends as we get close to the unit, just Tony coordinating with Colin so we time it right.

"ETA, three minutes."

I swing the door open as soon as the cab comes to a halt, and hop out, almost stumble, but catch hold of the roof to steady myself.

As I hold the door open for Sofa, I hear Tony tut.

"Shan't be long, driver," I shout, probably too loudly,

"keep the meter running!"

"What the fuck are you doing?" he breathes in my earpiece, followed by, "shit, the truck's gone the other way. Stall them."

"Take my arm," I tell Sophie, "but not like I'm blind, like I'm your husband."

She does, and we bump hips before finding our rhythm, as she points me towards the unit.

"Hiya," she calls, "I'm Sophie, I contacted you about picking up the toy I won on the auction?"

"Oh, yeah, hello. I just need to grab it for you, and I'll pop it in a box. Give me a minute."

"Take your time."

"We need more than a minute, guys, at least five," Tony communicates.

There's no invitation to come in, but I nudge Sophie in that direction. Two steps and a metal strip, I recall, and negotiate them effortlessly.

"If you can just check this is the right one, I'll tape the box up for you."

Following Sophie's lead, we walk towards where I think the desk without the computer sits on the spotless floor.

Sophie takes thirty seconds to examine the item, before telling Debbie Russell that it's fine.

"Is the paperwork done for the pick-up?" a man mutters from a couple of yards away.

"Alright, mate?" I say in his approximate direction.

"Yeah, you?"

"Not bad. Lovely weather."

"It's alright."

"So, this is what you do, is it," I begin, waving my hand about the space we're in, "toys and games, and stuff?"

"And stuff, yeah," he says, but not aggressively.

"Money in that lark, is there?"

"You'd be surprised. What do you do?"

"Me? I'm a pilot."

I feel Sophie flinch next to me, just as Tony hisses, "truck's picking up a big load from a unit round the corner. Keep stalling."

"I don't suppose you have gift wrap, do you?" Sophie jumps in, "it's just, we're heading straight to the station, and getting a train to Manchester."

"No, sorry."

"Ah well. Tell you what, forget the big box. I'll struggle with that on the train. Can you just slip it in a bag, or something?"

"Erm, yes, I suppose. We have some lying around somewhere. Craig, can you help, please?"

"What do you want, my love?"

"A bag for these people."

I hear the tape being ripped from the box. Smart move, I let Sophie know, by pressing her arm against my ribs.

"Truck's on the move. Three minutes."

"Here, that'll do it," Craig says.

"Strewth, is that 'Escape From Colditz'?" I exclaim, looking over my shoulder at absolutely nothing. "I had that when I was a kid. I loved it. How much is that?"

"Er, that one's not for sale," Craig informs me.

"Ah, really? I'd buy that." I begin a move towards it, so Sophie has to release her hold, spin, and take my hand instead. "What does it sell for?"

Sophie steers me, so we're standing in front of it.

"That one? It's in great nick, so about seventy-five quid, or thereabouts."

"Really? Shit, that much. You know, I used to read Warlord comic when I was a kid, I loved all that war stuff.

Peter Flint, I think it was. I had a secret agent wallet, with a code book and ID card. Great, it was. So, I suppose it was natural I'd like the Colditz game."

"Truck's pulling in," Tony tells us, but the rumble of the engine through the open door had already done that.

"Like I said, it's not for sale," Craig Russell growls, suddenly a little anxious.

"Hey, come on, love," Sophie says, "that cab's waiting."

I ignore everyone. "Yes, it had a book inside. That was the best bit about it, that book, as it had all this cool information about the POWs, and there were loads of pictures of how they pulled the escapes off. Do you know," I say to Sophie as I resist her attempts to move me towards the door, "I even did German at school, because I thought it might come in handy if I was ever caught behind enemy lines! Ha!"

"Yeah, whatever, mate. Like I said, it's not for sale. Time you were off." There's a threat to his tone.

"Parcel driver approaching the door!"

In for a penny, I figure. "Yes, one picture showed how they'd have forged documents smuggled in to camp. Can you guess how they did it?"

They must think my question's rhetorical, as all I hear is Debbie Russell telling the driver, "it's the nine packages over there."

"Inside records! Can you believe that?"

"I'll take that," I hear Tony bark, presumably at the driver.

I'm suddenly alone and in the dark, as Sophie pulls away from me, and snaps, in a voice that leaves no room for misinterpretation, "move a muscle, and it'll be the last one you ever move."

"You bloody idiot!" Tony shouts. He must mean me.

17.

Tony adds a beat, tapped on the table top, as I whistle the theme to 'The Great Escape'.

Craig and Debbie Russell sit opposite us, with Sophie observing through the one-way glass.

He's cocky and she's quiet. "Are you going to charge us with anything? And where's our Solicitor?"

"Do you know why you're here?" Tony asks.

"Not a clue. For selling a toy, which I don't think is a crime. We pay tax on earnings, so I have no idea."

"Yes, you're very good on your taxes. That was a red flag, by the way, you should always be a little bit out," I tell them.

"Can you see anything wrong here, Lorry?" Tony acts his part. He's James Garner, I'm Donald Pleasance, or Blythe The Forger.

"Why, I can see perfectly! I can see...that record down there!" I bend to retrieve it from where it's propped against the table. It's the Billy Nicholls LP that sold the previous evening.

"So what?" Craig snaps, but there's stress in his voice this time. I bet he's sweating.

"It's all wrong," I tell them.

"What is?"

"Everything. The sleeve is too shiny, and the record too heavy. Far too heavy. Even the spine is too square. Records back then weren't like that. I can tell that you tried to make it look period, and that would be enough to fool a bloke at customs and have them ask no questions, but, take an expert...take Professor Clifton..."

"Never heard of him."

"Lorry, be careful," Sophie says in my earpiece, "we can't go there yet."

Tony kicks me under the table.

But I push on. "Oh, really? Well, he was an expert when it came to records, and now he's dead. Anyway, Clifton would have known before he even touched it that it was wrong - that it was fake."

"Fine, so it's fake. How were we to know that? We sold it in good faith."

"Well, you knew the record I won from you last night was fake."

"That was you? Well, that one was obvious."

"But this one wasn't?"

"I'm no expert."

"How did two fake records, both highly collectible, wind up in your possession?" Tony wants to know, quite rightly.

"I bought them years ago."

"From?"

"A car-boot sale."

"So, it'll be pointless me asking who sold them to you, or if you have a receipt?"

"Obviously."

"How many years ago, just roughly?"

"At least ten. And what's any of this got to do with Debs?"

He's a cocky shit, but she's as quiet as a mouse, and he's protective of her. Is she just subservient to him, or more nervous, and more likely to crack, therefore? He called her 'my love' in the unit. I wonder if he does.

"I had a sandwich the other day," I begin.

"Good for you."

"And I dropped the plate from my lap. I'm always doing things like that. I have to get a new set of crockery every couple of years. Anyway, it broke in half, and my girlfriend had to clean up the mess. It was that, I think, that first sowed a seed in my mind."

"Right. Why would I give a shit about any of this?"

"Tony, may I ask you to utilise your incredible strength to break this record?"

Craig tries to delay the moment with, "you'd better be sure that's what you think it is, or you'll owe me ten grand."

There's an odd sort of flexing noise, followed by a crisp snap.

"Well, well, look what we have here."

"Sadly, I can look but cannot see, Tony. You'll just have to describe it to me."

"Well, encased inside this record, Lorry, a record that was being shipped to an address in France that we now know to be linked to a very bad man, are three seemingly brand new EU passports."

"I have no idea how they got there," Craig claims, but not very assuredly.

"So we won't find your fingerprints on these, or, perhaps, a fibre or hair or skin fragment that will link either of you two to them?" Tony asks, as I hear them hit the bottom of a plastic evidence bag.

There's a period of silence, which Tony breaks.

"Talk to me, Craig? Debbie? It's not you we want, you're the link, we know that. and I'm much more interested in getting the people responsible for producing these things. Give me that, and we'll put you through the regular legal system, and keep you off the Homeland Security side. I mean, you don't want to go down that path, I promise you."

They must be thinking about it, as Tony pushes on, "you really don't want to be done for treason, and stuck with the extremists and suicide bombers, do you?"

"No," Debbie barely says, and I think she might be close

to tears.

"Shush, Debs, it's all okay, I'll take care of this..."

"Split them, Tony, now," Sophie says in our ears.

It makes sense. Make him sweat on what she might be telling us. But my gut tells me to keep them side by side.

I go with, "I mean, I hope for your sake none of these passports helped people gain access to America, or you'll end up being extradited. But, then, there's still the murder charge, of course..."

"Murder?" Craig starts.

"What?" Debbie adds.

"The Professor. Clifton was murdered," I tell them.

"No...no, no, no. You're not pinning that on us," Craig whines, suddenly sounding like he's the one about to crack.

"Why not?" I ask.

"He killed himself. I took the gun along, but only to shit him up."

Got them!

"And I suppose he rigged up a lookalike bomb to destroy his life's work, did he?" Tony shouts at them, suddenly getting horribly aggressive. He's pushing their emotions, confusing them. I keep quiet.

"No, okay, that was me, but it was just a threat, I never planned on setting it off. I wouldn't know how. He gave me what I wanted," Craig Russell pleads back at him.

"And what did he give you, Craig?"

"The location...in the archive! Okay, okay. I just wanted the record back. That was all."

"How did you find out about Clifton?" I ask.

"He did an interview in 'Vinyl Addiction' magazine...fuck. He was boasting about his latest purchase, looking for donations. I knew it had to be our missing copy when he said he'd bought it in France."

"So, how the hell did he wind up dead?"

"He thought we were going to destroy his records, so he got his book out and told us where to find the one we wanted..."

"The Tommy Histon LP, 'Three Minute Hero'?" I seek to clarify.

"Yes. But I think he still thought I was going to torch the room, so there was a struggle, and he managed to get his hand on the gun, and it went off."

"An accident?" is all I ask.

"I don't know," Debbie says quietly, "I was holding the gun on him, but it was almost as though he pushed his head in front of the barrel before he squeezed the trigger."

Debbie Russell breaks down, and I hear her sobs become muffled as she must bury herself in Craig, as he mutters soothing words.

After a minute or so, Craig Russell states, "we'll give you everything you want, everything we know, as long as you promise you won't charge Debs with murder."

"Let me see what I can do," Tony says, and we leave the room.

An hour later, and we have a signed statement outlining the whole process, from the former EU passport office employee who Craig met in prison, a conversation about the stock of passports he'd hidden before being arrested, to an idea forming whilst incarcerated. Craig had a plan he could enact as soon as he'd served his time, feeling like one of the characters in a game he played as a kid; 'Escape From Colditz', the picture in the book from which he remembered just as I did.

"How did he get the records pressed with the passports inside?" I ask Tony as he drives back to my place.

"A willing accomplice situated on the same industrial

estate. Craig paid him five hundred a pressing, and the bloke asked no questions. He's already been picked up and charged."

"What'll happen to them; the Russells, I mean?"

"They'll serve time, Lorry, but we'll try to keep the murder rap off her, and push the rest through the criminal courts as promised. My best guess? They'll both serve a ten-stretch, minimum."

"And do you believe their version of what happened?"

"To Clifton?"

"Yes."

"I don't know, Lorry, and I doubt we'll ever know. To be honest, he's dead either way, and I can't find anyone who'll care much about that."

"How do you mean?"

"Well, he had no family that we can trace, and no friends have come forward. Even his colleagues at the university struggle to portray any real sympathy."

"Poor bastard."

"It's what happens when you forsake everything for an obsession, Lorry. The same as any addiction, you end up losing everyone."

An almost shameful smile flicks across my face, hopefully unseen by anyone, prompted by the realisation that I'm no longer like that.

18.

"Tony, is this cheating?"

"That's a very harsh word, Lorry,"

"What is it, then?"

"Oh, it's definitely cheating, but it's a very harsh word."

"And you see this as levelling the playing-field with the

partially sighted players?"

"Yes; who's to say they aren't exaggerating their condition to gain a competitive advantage?"

"I'm not sure they'd do that, Tony."

"You want to impress Sophie, don't you?"

"I think she's already impressed."

"Right. Let me put it another way; do you want to look like a twat in front of a lot of people?"

"No."

"So we're doing it?"

"Of course we're doing it, I just wanted to know if what we're doing is cheating."

He fits the tiny receiver in my ear. It tickles a bit, so I jiggle it with my finger.

"It's one-way, so you won't be able to speak to me, and don't try, or someone might smell a rat."

"Okay."

"Let's recap the rules."

"I know the rules. But knowing them doesn't seem to help me."

"Just to be sure. You're allowed to touch the stumps to ascertain position, so make sure you do that, even though I'll be guiding you, or it'll look a bit odd. A minimum of two bounces before you swing, and the ball has to be in the air. The bowler must shout 'Play' as he releases the ball. What else?"

"I can't be stumped, and I have to be LBW twice. That's about it, I think."

My batting scorecard reads like this: 9-0-0-0.

The bowling's worse: 4-0-62-infinity.

"You can open your present now," he tells me.

"Present?"

"Here." A box lands on my lap.

It's loosely wrapped with the minimal amount of tape, done by somebody thoughtful who knew I'd struggle to pick open anything tightly bound. As the paper parts, I pick up the smell of aged cardboard, and hear the crinkle of the see-through plastic panel.

"Is it...?"

"Six Million Dollar Man. Sophie got it via the auction. Strictly speaking, it's evidence, but she thought you might like it."

"Fantastic!"

"So, er," Tony begins, a little reluctantly, "I got the final Medical Report on Clifton this morning. Everything stacks up, Lorry."

"He killed himself?"

"Yes. There was his partial print on the trigger, and looking at blood pattern on him and on the clothes Debbie Russell was wearing, there was a struggle, but not in the way you thought. She was attempting to get the gun away from him, and he pulled it towards himself, hence him breathing hard and the movement of both the gun and his head at that moment."

"But he wouldn't have done that if they hadn't threatened his collection..."

"We don't know that. Looking at the state of his funding, he was screwed, and there are too many ifs and buts for the CPS to bring any charges. A half-smart solicitor will tear any case apart. Besides, I did a deal with them, and they gave up the information we wanted."

"So that's it?"

"That's it."

"What about the bomb, didn't they attempt to murder me?"

"We had to give them something, Lorry, and it wasn't a

real bomb."

"I still don't think this is right. If they hadn't taken that gun in there, he'd still be alive. They should be charged with murder, Tony!"

"You can't know that."

"It's not right," I mumble, as I try looking through the back of the Six Million Dollar Man's head, but to no avail.

"Come on, let's do this."

The taxi door whines wide, and I step out. Tony connects with my elbow and weaves me along a winding gravel path towards the field of play.

Sophie greets me with a kiss. I think it was Sophie, anyway, and she's taken my hand. I can't imagine IT Colin doing that. At least seven people say hello, including Doctor Stephoscope.

"Hello Dad!"

It takes a second to register. She sounds like her Mum, and it totally disarms me. Instinctively, my hand pulls away from Sophie, and my arms reach out before enveloping her as she comes to me.

"How?" is all I can say, knowing that if I try to even say so much as her name, I'll fall apart.

"Tony told me you had a big game, though it would have been nice if you'd mentioned it, and seeing how my final exam was yesterday, we drove down this morning."

"We?"

"Dad, this is Ollie; a friend."

Ollie? Friend, as in boyfriend?

Instead of saying that, I hold out my hand and opt for, "Ollie, pleasure, any friend of Lanie's..."

I have no idea what any of that actually means.

Maggie the analyst saves me, "so, Lorry, I'm confused."

"Go on," I encourage her.

"Well, Tony said that you don't bowl, is that right?"

"They tried me on bowling, but it didn't pan out."

"Then why are you batting at number eleven?"

"Maggie, have you met my daughter? And her friend, Ollie?"

"Anyone fancy a drink?" Tony bawls, "bar's over there."

"I'll have a pint," I say.

"You'll have nothing until after the match."

Sophie isn't holding my hand. I miss her touch. I suppose she doesn't want to...shit, should I have introduced her, as my friend? My girlfriend? I've not had a chance to tell Lanie about her. I would have done it this weekend on the phone, but she's here now.

"Sofe?" I call out.

"She's gone on ahead, Lorry," Tony says to me as he takes my elbow.

There are too many people for me to get any kind of grip on what's going on. Crowds do this, they scatter everything so it's hard to get a fix without visual signals. I need to get Lanie and Sophie together and do this properly.

But before I can, I'm summoned to the team.

I half listen to the bluster coming from Ken, the manager, my mind all over the place. Ken lets me know I'll be fielding at straight hit. Using powers of deduction, I guess this to be behind the bowler, the hope being that the bowlers will stop anything before it actually reaches me.

Instinctively, I pat my shirt pocket to ensure I have my cigarettes and lighter.

*****

Ten of the twenty overs in, and I've fielded the ball four times. It's bigger than a standard cricket ball, and has ball-bearings in it. I like the sound it makes, and spend quite a chunk of my time fitting songs to the percussive rattle. Sixties Motown seems to fit quite well, along with Spector girl groups.

"Lorry, you hear me?" Tony's voice says in my ear, "scratch your bollocks if you can."

I scratch my bollocks.

"Good. I managed to slip away for a while. There's some stuff I need to tell you, and this is...this is probably as good a way as any. You know we fitted a tracker in the re-assembled package sent to France? Well, we got what we wanted, and busted up a major operation, Lorry. You, actually; it was you who pieced it all together. The whole set-up wasn't simply about sneaking in illegal immigrants, but we kind of already knew that, as the passports were too real, and the cost too high. It turns out they were being used to bring in would-be terrorists."

He pauses, before adding, "did you hear all that?"

I scratch myself again.

"Look, I wasn't sure whether to tell you this or not, but I figure you have a right to know. It was the same method that allowed the man who shot Kate to enter the country. We know that without doubt, Lorry. You just helped us shut down a major operation that has direct links to the murderer of your wife."

It's good news, is the thought that looms at the fore of my mind, but there's something lurking behind it that nags, a notion that it always comes back to that, and a further thought about how many other bastards were involved who have never paid a price?

A gun-shot crack jolts me upright, my head clearing like a light being switched on, and I remember where I am, with grass beneath my feet and people shouting. It was the crack of ball on bat, leather on willow, assuming those materials are still used, or is that just some antiquated expression based on how things used to be?

"Ball's in the air, Lorry, and coming right at you. Hear it?"

No, I don't. I don't see or hear anything, just a mishmash of people shouting, and the vision of Kate, in the white dress I'd never seen before, but have seen constantly since, and the spread of red blood over her heart as she crumpled, that dress snagging on the wall and riding up, her empty shoes pointlessly waiting for her to reoccupy them and walk away, her leg twisting out as she sank to the floor to show her nakedness.

That's what I'm left with. That vision, all the time. But no, not so much lately, thanks to Tony, Lanie, Sophie...

I hear the slight rattle.

That night, I tried to lunge, forward and to my left, to block that bullet.

"Shit, I'm at the wrong angle, Lorry - it's about five feet to your left and heading for a six, neck high..."

I dive, up and over.

The ball slams in to my chest, but I don't feel a thing. I hear it as it impacts and begins to drop, slightly above me.

Hard earth connects with my hip and left side, I'm unable to break my fall as I need my hands, open and cupped, my little fingers touching.

The ball finds them, and I cradle it, snatch it to my body and hold it tight and close.

"Spec-fucking-tacular!" Tony roars, as cheers erupt from all sides of me.

Standing, I roll the ball back to where I believe the field of play to be. I pat my shirt pocket, and feel the crumpled remains of my cigarettes. I should give in, anyway.

"Dad!" Lanie calls from over my shoulder, "that was the

best thing I've ever seen!"

I turn my head and smile at her. An announcer over a tannoy informs me that they're seventy-four for seven in the twelfth over. That's not bad by our standards; the match is usually unsalvageable by this stage.

"Hey, Dad!" Lanie calls again, "I'll see you in the break. Sophie seems really nice, by the way, you dark-horse!"

And just like that, everything in the world seems right.

"Hey, Lanie!"

"Yep?"

"Would you ask Sophie to please come and collect me as soon as we've rattled this lot out?"

"I'd better get back then, I don't think it'll take long."

"Oh, and Lanie? Where are you staying, the spare room's a mess, as Tony stayed there last week, and..."

"Dad, relax. Ollie and I are checked in to a hotel. We wanted it to be a surprise."

"It is."

"A nice one?"

The match recommencing rescues me.

19.

"There's more," Tony speaks in my ear, as I sit and wait for the twenty overs to be up, or for us to chase down the ninety-seven runs required to win, or, heaven help all concerned, I have to go in at number eleven.

Surely it'll be done and dusted by then?

"I've requisitioned Sophie on a permanent basis, so she'll be back working with me from now on. Okay?'

After a suitable period of pensiveness, I scratch the plastic box encasing my knackers.

"Was that a yes, or just a reaction to thinking about

Sofa?"

I giggle, and have to swallow it.

"Are you okay with what I told you earlier, about the passports?"

I let him know that I am.

"Oooh, shit, another wicket! That's sixty-six for seven. It's looking like you'll get a knock."

Bugger.

"Did you get a chance to say hello to Gillian Grey, Trish and Eddie?"

I did. They're former spies, now running a burger van as a cover while they continue to spy, off the radar, for the government.

"Typical Gillian, Colin mentioned your match, and they snaffled the catering rights."

The smell of those rights drifts over the field at me, setting my stomach off grumbling. Tony would only let me consume fruit, water and cereals before the game.

How my life has changed. These are the people I know, where prior to losing Kate, I knew nobody but her. Even Lanie was a bit of a mystery to me.

"Here we go...out! Seventy-five for eight. Have you done your warm up?"

I lie and scratch myself, which makes me sound like a dog.

"Good luck, Lorry," IT Colin says from behind me.

"Thanks," I reply.

"Hold out your hand, Lorry, I just ran and fetched this out the car."

"What is it?" I ask, taking a tub of something.

"I noticed you were scratching down below a lot. Pop some of that powder on, and it'll stop the irritation."

"Erm, right. Cheers for that. Why did you have that to

hand?"

"How do you mean?"

"It's for athletes," I point out incredulously.

"Right. And because I'm named Colin and I work in IT, I can't be active?"

"No...well, yes, I suppose."

"Break a leg, Lorry!"

I'm not sure that's the right expression given the circumstances.

I drift along with the smells and sounds for a while, Tony silent in my ear. He's probably spending a bit of time with the others before he has to slip away and give me some pointers.

Everybody's fine. The notion hits me harder than that ball earlier, and it's undeniably the fact. Despite everything, we're all doing fine, myself included. Even this, the cricket; I'm enjoying being a part of something. To a man, my teammates congratulated me on the catch I took after the innings, even though half of them couldn't even see it.

I tap my bat against my foot, a bat Tony bought me as soon as he heard I'd joined the team.

Crack, rattle-rattle-rattle, and a roar as I piece it together and mentally chalk up another boundary.

What's that, eighty-one for eight? As long as the penultimate wicket falls on the final delivery of an over, I might still be able to get out there and not have to face a ball.

How many overs is that? Seventeen? Tony and Colin talking messed up my counting.

"Oi, you awake?"

I jiggle myself.

"Two overs to go, eighty-two for eight. Someone needs to start swinging the bat, a four-and-a-half run per over average is no good now. It's more than a run a ball..."

I can work the numbers, that's never been the problem with me.

The match carries on, me counting down not up, ticking off the balls, each one lifting my spirits as the innings comes closer to its end.

Two balls in a row bring runs, but I can't gather how many, and then I hear the appeal.

Given.

Bollocks.

"Here we go. Are you ready?"

I was already nervously straightening my box, so figure that'll serve to answer his question.

"Five balls to go, twelve runs required. Piece of piss."

Ken leads me to the crease, and chunters in my lug-hole as we make our way, saying something about simply getting bat on ball and nicking a single, getting Richie on strike.

A cheer accompanies me all the way. All eyes on me.

Reaching behind me, I locate the stumps and shuffle to my left. I bring my bat down and tap-tap against my shoe.

"Batsman ready?" the umpire calls.

"Ready," I shout out, even though I'm not even close to being so.

"Play!" the bowler shrieks, and I hear the ball chink-chink as it bounces.

"Coming at your ankles, swat across!" Tony raps.

But I'm too slow, and it slams off my pad. It's LBW, but I get a reprieve. One more.

Twelve runs from four balls required.

"Move more to your left this time, get your feet clear of the stumps, and step in to the shot."

"Batsman ready?"

"Ready."

"Play!"

Chink-rattle-chink-rattle, like the start of a Siouxsie & The Banshees track I can't piece together as Tony snaps, "straight down the middle. Hit the fu..."

My left foot jumps across the worn down grass, my right coming to meet it, and the bat, face full on, sweeping down at a slight angle, and for only the second time in my life, I hit the ball.

The shockwave rises up the bat and tingles my elbow as the rattle-rattle speeds away from me.

"Go on, carry!" Tony shouts, so loud that I feel sure the umpire and wicket-keeper must be able to hear him through my earpiece.

"Four!" the man in, I presume, the white coat calls.

The cheers collide in my head, coming both through the air, and from inside my ear.

My breathing's hard, even though I haven't had to run.

"Lorry, can you hear me, I hit the microphone in my excitement?"

I can, so I let him know that in the agreed manner.

"Good work, but we're not there yet."

The cheers subside, just a nervous rumble remaining.

"Batsman ready?"

"Ready!"

"Play!"

"He's a foot wide, to your right..."

I step forward and swing, sinking down on one knee as I sweep at the ball.

It connects, but not as true as the last one.

"Run!" is all I hear.

So I do, as fast as I can with all the bloody gear on.

"Just take a single," Richie calls to me as his footsteps

thump by.

"Turn!" is my next instruction from Ken and Tony simultaneously, and I mess up, because I thought I would only have to run one, but now we're going for a second, so my foot slips as I try to make the adjustment for the turn, and all I can think to do is use my bat like an oar, like a crutch, and keep myself upright.

And I'm falling forward so I have no choice but to keep on running, Tony and everyone else roaring me on.

"Safe!" is the call from the umpire as I land on the ground and slide along on my chest, my breathing heavy, my mouth dry, my heart racing. My cigarettes wrecked.

"You've just taken six from two balls, Lorry. Same again, and you're the hero," Tony reports to me.

And for the first time, I start to actually believe that I can do this.

"Batsman ready?"

"Ready!" Because I am.

"Play!"

"Pitched short, in-line, above your hands!"

All I can do is bring my bat up and fend it. Shit. A disappointed rumble matches the dull clunk of the ball as it falls in front of me, and goes nowhere.

"There was nothing you could do with that one, Lorry. He tossed it in short knowing you'd have to go defensive. Sorry, pal, but you need a six off the last ball. It's do-able."

A chant goes up from over on my right, where I know Lanie and Sophie, Janine, Colin and Maggie to be congregated. "Lorry, Lorry, Lorry," it echoes, as people all around the ground clap along to it. They don't know the words.

"Hey, you can do this, you hear me? Listen to them, Lorry, they all want you to do this. Which is why I'm not going to do it for you. This one's yours, and yours alone. Pull it off, and I'll take you to America..."

And my ear goes silent.

I feel senseless as a hush takes over the whole ground to an almost painful extent. My face flushes as vulnerability fills me so full that my nose seems blocked.

In an attempt to clear it, I snort and draw oxygen into me. It's so sharp it lifts my head and straightens my spine.

I scratch myself, desperate for Tony to come back on line, but there's nothing in my ear.

Standing tall, I'm not blind, I simply stopped looking as soon as it became clear to me that I could never see Kate again. I could never watch her play with her hair when she teased me, or the way she'd twist her lips before delivering the line that always served to keep me in check.

Oh, and how proud she'd be of me right now, stood here facing life full on, in front of an audience. She tried to make me better, but I always resisted. Yet, perversely, it was her who made me resist, because I resented anything that came between she and I, even our own daughter at times.

And I'm so sorry for that, all of it. I was selfish, and I wanted Kate all to myself all of the time, and as a consequence, eschewed anything external.

She told me, that last night as we sat in our old pub celebrating our wedding anniversary; she warned me of the dangers of isolating myself. Is it enough, she asked me, if something happened to her would the records and the music be enough?

"No, Kate," I say in a whisper.

But, then, I didn't think anything could be. Not really. But I think I was wrong, and she was right as usual. It takes more to fill a life.

Stepping forward, I raise my bat and tap down an

imaginary divot in the grass. I hear a ripple of laughter.

"Best get on before the light goes!" I call out loudly, and hear a few people chuckle, as I touch the stumps and gain my position.

"Batsman ready?"

"Ready!"

I know what'll happen next. The bowler will try that high ball again. It forces a defensive shot, that it's difficult getting the purchase on the ball when it comes in above the hands on the bat. At the end of the day, he'll take a four off this one, and they still win. With that in mind, I shuffle half a pace backwards just as he shouts, "Play!"

The first bounce confirms it, as I imagine him releasing the ball early so that it pitches well inside the line painted across the middle of the wicket, a heavy clunk, and then a gap as it rattles through the air.

But I don't wait for it. I'm sick of waiting for shit to happen.

Instead, I step towards it, my stumps left unguarded - after all, I can't be stumped - and I start my swing early, twisting my wrists ever so slightly away from me to angle the face of the bat upwards, a sweeping shot with my bat pretty much parallel to the ground.

The second bounce is so close I'm sure I can feel it in my feet as my hands tighten on the handle, already fully committed to whatever happens next as my legs begin to extend from their bent posture.

A resounding crack shatters the silence and I think I might have broken something as, what feels like the sky, comes crashing down.

Part Two: Number Cruncher

20.

"Is New York your final destination?" a woman with what sounds like adenoid problems asks.

"No," I reply, "we're going to a place called Harburg in south west Virginia."

"Yes," Tony adds quickly, "we're driving down to Harburg from New York. Lorry, she's only bothered about where we're flying to."

"Did you pack your bag yourself, sir?"

"Lorry, she's talking to you."

"Pack it myself? No."

"Lorry, what the f...?"

"Well, I didn't."

"Er, who packed your bag, sir?'

"My girlfriend, Sophie, we've been together for about a month now, and..."

"Yep, Lorry, that'll do."

"Okay, and has anyone else had access to your bag, apart from you, and has it been out of your possession since you...since your girlfriend packed it for you?"

"Yes."

"Lorry, half the men standing in this very long queue didn't pack their own bags, but nobody admits to it!"

"Well, I'm not going to lie. Sophie packed it for me, though I kind of told her what to pack, because she can fold things better than me, but we did that yesterday afternoon, partly because we were out last night, but also to save time this morning, so anyone could have gained access to it during that time. After all, it has no lock on it, because Sophie said it was best not to do that, or the security people just cut the lock anyway, with bolt cutters, especially if they detect any metal in there, which they will because I packed a portable record player and an acetate, which is a record cut into a lacquer spread over a metal plate. I wanted to bring that as hand luggage, but Sophie said it was a bit sharp, and could be used as a weapon, so she wrapped it in one of my jumpers to protect it. In addition, Tony here had access to my bag for the past few hours, and could have done anything to it without my knowing. I'm blind, you see. To be honest, you could have just slipped something in there, and I wouldn't know."

"Right, erm. what about you, did you pack your own bag?"

"Yes."

"That's a lie, isn't it, sir?"

"Yes. Okay, okay, I submit! My girlfriend, Janine, helped me."

"Could you just step to one side, please. Gentlemen, just step over here, thank you."

I hear her say Code One-One into a radio or phone.

About a minute later, during which Tony doesn't say anything but seems to be breathing quite heavily, a man approaches, and trills, "Tony Alliss, as I live and breathe! How are you?"

"Hello Doug! Long time, no see."

"Code One-One, very good! Who's this?"

"A mate of mine, Lorry. Lorry, meet Doug."

"Ah, Lorry. Would that be AKA Daniel Andrew Francis, the man who took down Miller?"

"That's me."

"Then it is an absolute pleasure," he says, taking my hand and shaking it a bit too firmly so that my fingers pinch together.

"What can I do for you, Tony?"

"I think this lady summoned you, Doug, not me, I'm afraid."

"Why?"

"They haven't packed their own bags."

"So? Nor have half the men in this line."

"I know, but they usually say they have."

"In fairness, I did try to claim I had," Tony pleads.

"He did, but the other one was adamant that he hadn't."

"Just check them in, will you? Where are you off to, Tony?"

"America."

"Business or pleasure?"

"Neither. I'm with him."

"Listen, I've got to run. Have a good trip, and give me a shout sometime."

"Will do, Doug."

We stand around for a few minutes.

"There you go, all done," the woman behind the desk says, "will you be requiring a wheelchair today?"

"Why?" Tony snaps curtly.

"I think she's..." I start to say, but Tony cuts me off.

"I'll deal with this, Lorry, you've done enough."

"Well, I just thought Mr. Francis may find it..."

"What are those?"

"Legs, sir."

"Right, so he's perfectly capable of walking. He's blind, not paraplegic!"

"Sorry, I didn't mean any offence."

Alliss grunts as I smile in the vague direction of her voice. Or at her nose, in other words.

It's only when we reach the security screening that it dawns on Tony you aren't allowed to take trolleys through.

ANDY BRACKEN

It takes his brain a few seconds to calculate that he won't be able to handle both sets of hand-luggage and guide me.

He steers me back to the lady who checked us in, and meekly asks about the possibility of getting a wheelchair.

*****

The advantage to being disabled is that we get to board the plane first. The disadvantage is that it means we have to sit in the cramped space for longer. Tony just about fits. I'm by the window. Not for the view, but because Tony can contain me better from there.

"What now?" is all I hear him say, the exasperation evident in his voice.

"What?" I ask, lifting the spongy earphones from my head, and taking a break from repetitively elongating and retracting the strap of my seatbelt.

"There's a woman pointing us out to a security guard. Was there anything dodgy in your luggage?"

"As previously explained, how would I know?"

"Antony Alliss?"

"That's me."

"And Daniel Andrew Francis?"

"That's him."

"DS Alliss, I need you to come with me, please, sir."

"What's all this about?"

"If you come with me, I'll explain everything."

He's reluctant to say what's going on with too many people around, but he's clearly aware of who Tony is, so this is something, I'd guess, work related.

Tony stands, and I gather he's making the security guy carry our hand luggage.

"Come on," he says to me, resting his hand on my

382

shoulder.

Raising myself, the headphones round my neck pull tight as I forgot to unplug them. The action of them releasing suddenly propels my head up so it smacks on the air outlet nozzle, which hurts like a bastard. Something breaks, but we don't have time to dwell on it as the man clears the aisle and we disembark.

"Does this mean we're not going to America?"

"I have no idea, Lorry."

We walk the incline and push through a door, I'm guessing to the main area we sat and waited in prior to boarding. I'm bundled on board an electric powered vehicle, and we're whooshing along, a constant beep clearing the route.

Pulling up, Tony helps me clamber down, and we enter an office where all the noise from the terminal disappears.

"Sorry to do this to you, gentlemen, but I'm simply doing as I'm told. You need to switch your phone on. Your bags are being pulled from the plane, and we'll get them back to you. If you need anything, I'll be outside the door, so just shout."

I hear Tony switch his phone on. It rings instantly.

"Go on," is all he says, the display evidently showing the caller.

There's a long period of silence during which I don't hear Tony breathe.

"We'll be there as soon as we can. Don't move."

His phone snaps shut.

"We're not going to America, are we?"

"Not this time. Sorry."

"What's going on?"

"Three bodies found."

"Where?"

"Separate locations in London."

"And why do they need you?"

He takes a fortifying breath before he answers.

"Because one of them is Maggie."

21.

The acidic bile rises up in my throat as the car, sirens blaring, powers towards central London.

I swallow it and groan.

"Hold on, Lorry, we're nearly there."

As soon as the car skids to a halt, I'm tugging on the door handle, but it won't open. Tony leaps from the front, his weight leaving the chassis, and the door my hand's on levers open. I dive out, head first, and vomit.

"Are you okay?"

"Not really, no."

"No, me either. Get out the other side, Lorry, or you'll get it all over your shoes."

I slide across the leather seat.

"You've got my address?"

"Yes, sir," states the security man. "I'll leave the bags inside, and arrange for your suitcases to go there, as well. What do you want me to do with the key?"

"Drop it back to me at The Yard when you're done."

"You got it. And I'm sorry for your trouble, sir."

Tony doesn't audibly respond, and we're moving before the sentence is even finished.

"Are you up to this?" he asks me.

"Yes," is all I have to say.

*****

Sophie's filling Tony in. She'll get to me when she can, but right now, there are more important things.

My head's spinning, I'm completely in the dark, I need input, information, to stop the spiral.

Her hand takes mine. I already know how it feels, and she squeezes, just enough to let me know that she knows I'm here, that simple acknowledgement enough to bring me back.

My mouth feels like the bottom of a shoe, my throat as though I've been swallowing glass. It's even in my nose, the puke, so it's all I smell.

Janine's here, just arrived, having pulled herself off one of the other murders to attend this one; Maggie.

"Let me through!" she bellows, and immediately after, "oh, Christ, no!"

As much as I don't want the details, I crave them. I need them to occupy me, to stop this taking me back to that night, as selfish as that is.

Only one other person I've cared about has lain dead in my presence before. I'm glad that I'm blind and don't have to bear witness to this one.

"It's a serial killer, Tony, or some kind of spree," Janine Stephani states.

"Sure?"

"No doubt. Different MO, but this tells me it is. It was on the other bodies."

"What is it?"

"A number, written on the chest."

"What does it say?"

"I don't know. We'll need to clear away the blood to read it properly. But on the body I've just come from, it read '84', and the MedEx at the other scene thinks he has an '86'. If I didn't know better, I'd say this one reads '83'."

"Where's 85? A tally?"

"I don't know, Tony. If it is, I hope it isn't counting upwards, because that's a lot of bodies out there."

"Cause of death? It looks like a suffocation gone wrong."

"I've just got here, Tony! The plastic wrap certainly indicates that to be the case, but there's an awful lot of blood, and her head has almost been sever...I don't know."

Despite them all being able to see, Janine describing it silences everyone.

"Tony, are you okay?" Sophie asks.

"No. No, I'm fucking not."

"Look, don't take this the wrong way, but do you think you should be leading this one..."

"What?"

"I'm just thinking..."

"Why would you want me off this one, Sophie? Tell you what, let's pursue a line of inquiry; this happens a few weeks after you worm your way back on to my team through Lorry. Explain that to me."

"Fuck you, Tony. Maggie was my friend!"

"You wouldn't even have known her if I hadn't taken you on in the first place. I've worked with the woman, the gentle caring woman, every day of my life, for fifteen years. Time of death, Steph?"

"Jesus, Tony, give me a chance!"

"I need a best guess. Now."

"She's been dead at least twelve hours, and no more than twenty-four. That's the best I can do."

"Sophie Hargreaves, where were you between ten yesterday morning, and ten last night?"

"With him. Right, Lorry?"

"That's right."

"It doesn't mean you didn't get someone else to do it."

"Tony, this is ridiculous! It's too personal, you should not lead this..."

"Listen to me very carefully. If this comes back to you, in any way, shape or form, even indirectly, I'll end you."

"If this comes back to me, you won't need to, because I'll end myself. She stayed in touch, Tony!"

"Who did?"

"Maggie! She called me twice a week for months after you'd written me off. Check her fucking phone records. She helped me cope with Marc being killed. She offered me support, Tony, when I had no other bastard. Least of all, you. So don't dare..."

I want to reach out to Sophie, but she's moving around and I can't get a fix. She's close to crying, and I should be there. And I want to reach out to Tony simultaneously, and bring them back together. Along with Lanie, they are my life, and it's all falling apart in front of my ears.

In any event, I don't have to. "Shit, Sofa, I'm sorry. That was out of order."

"Fucking right it was!"

"Everyone, listen up! I'm annoyed. Know that. In fact, know that I'm fucking livid. Maggie was one of ours. She may not have been out on the streets, but she got her hands as dirty as any of us. She was an analyst, that's all. Well, it isn't all, because I know that some of the things she came up with saved our lives. So, we owe her. Pull out the stops on this one, please. Let's do this. Sophie, can you get on to Colin? I want to know every move Maggie made in the time leading up to this. And we need to get profiles on the other two victims; see if we can find any link."

"On it, Boss."

"Lorry? Are you okay sticking around? I can get you dropped off at home, if you'd prefer."

"No. Less than a month ago, she was watching me play cricket, Tony, and she was happily chatting to, and charming Lanie. I want in on this one, if that's okay?"

"Of course. Consulting?"

"Consulting."

"Come on, let's get away from this."

"Where are we going?"

"There's a cafe just up the road. I don't know about you, but I need a cup of tea and to clear my mind."

"Me too."

"Sofe, as soon as you're done here, meet us in the cafe at the end of the road. We need a plan."

We head up the street, me lighting the first cigarette it's occurred to me to smoke since we entered the airport at about seven this morning. When was that, three, four hours ago? Something like that.

"Sorry about that business with Sophie, but I had to stress her. I knew she'd have been with you, and I was as certain as I could be that she was clean, but I'm going to need her on this one, Lorry, and I had to be absolutely sure. Fair enough?"

"You do what you feel you need to do."

And I reflect on something Kate used to say about blurring the lines between your work and home life.

22.

"Why the numbers, Lorry? You count everything, why?"

"I do it now because I need to. I mean things such as steps, and so on. But, the truth is, I've always done it."

"Then why?"

"I don't know. There's something comforting in tallying things up."

"Up, not down?"

"Ahhh," I reply, thinking about it, "yes. I tot things up."

"Why, Lorry?"

"Kate used to ask me that. I like symmetry, and certain numbers offer me that."

"How do you mean?"

"For example, in my head it makes me feel more comfortable if there are even numbers of things rather than odd, and I like multiples of twelve."

"That's a bit odd, to be honest with you."

"Well, you asked..."

" I did. But these numbers appear to be concurrent. Shit, I don't even want to think about Maggie being the eighty-third victim."

"Unlikely, isn't it?"

"Amazingly, not as unlikely as you might think. If you knew how many people simply go missing each year, and drop off the radar. And if our killer has been at it for years, no link may have come up."

"But wouldn't the numbers have been spotted and documented - surely someone would have noticed a link?"

"Yes, almost certainly. But perhaps the numbers are an escalation."

"If they are, then he's getting bolder, which either means he's getting complacent or he wants to be caught."

"And he's obviously not being so careful about disposal of the remains, and he seems to have killed three people in quick succession," Tony adds.

"Poor Maggie. Strewth, I can't even think about what she went through."

"Then don't think about it."

"Is that how you cope?"

"Yes. I'm not going to lie to you, every body I see takes me back to my sister being killed. Did it make you think of Kate?"

I nod.

"You don't have to do this..."

"I already said, I want to."

"Fine, but if it gets too much, you let me or Sofe know. Lorry, I mean it. Talk of the devil..."

"Hey guys, you want another drink?"

"Please," I say, and Tony must nod.

"I'll give you a hand," he says, and his chair legs scrape on the linoleum flooring.

As they make their way to the counter, I hear him say something about needing to know he could trust her, before adding in his soft and gentle voice, "and Maggie asked me if it was okay to ring you, and I told her that I thought it was a good idea, if that means anything to you."

Numbers. To count, make a total, or reach an amount. To denote or organise, to sequence, distinguish, serialise, brand, designate, score or rate.

Score or rate?

"Any sexual abuse?" I ask, as they return.

"We don't know yet, and you might want to say that a little quieter," Tony answers.

"It could be a score," I tell them, because it was in my mind.

"What, like eighty-three out of a hundred?" Sophie seeks to clarify.

"Exactly."

"And we just happen to have found the ones scored eighty-three, four and six? Not likely, Lorry," Tony adds.

"No, you're right."

"But those numbers are the only connection we have."

"Well, let's hope the background checks reveal something

more," Tony says.

"When will we have them, Boss?"

"Assuming we can ID all three bodies, late today or early tomorrow."

"Irony, isn't it?" I say, as I sip the tea Sophie sugared for me.

"What's that?"

"That the person we could use right now, the analyst, has just been killed."

There's a gap for reflection, before Tony mutters, "yes, this is what Maggie was exceptional at."

"Could that be a motive?" Sophie throws in.

"I don't know, Sofe, I just don't know. We're working blind here, until we get more information."

The numbers are consuming me. "If this is counting down, then down to what?"

"To zero."

"And you'd start that countdown at a round number, right?"

"Like 'Ten Green Bottles'?"

"Yes."

"Even if it starts at one hundred, we're sill looking at a minimum eighteen bodies so far."

Every way we look at it, it's sobering.

"I'm sorry to ruin your trip to America," Sophie says to, I presume, both of us.

Neither of us reply.

"Hang on. It's Colin..." Tony says, and takes the call.

After a minute of silence, he thanks him, and tells us, "it appears that Maggie was killed on her way home from work. She was logged in until nine last night, and scanned her pass out at five past. Going on Janine's provisional time of death, it stacks up."

"Could she have just been unlucky," Sophie asks, "the wrong person in the wrong place at the wrong time? Or was it more targeted than that?"

"Something against the police?" Tony suggests.

"Yes, or against..." she pauses, "you."

"If the other victims have any link to me, I'll go with that. But, in the meantime, we have to assume not."

"Why was she walking?" I ask.

"She always walked, and where we are now is between work and her home. She said she didn't see the point of having a car in London, that she could walk just as quickly."

"And she did it to keep in shape, Lorry," Sophie adds. "She once told me that if people walked to and from the gyms they went to every day in their cars, they wouldn't need to pay to attend a gym!"

"Was she married?"

"She was, but it went awry. Another woman, I think, a younger woman."

"Any motive in that?"

"Unlikely. It was years ago."

"How old was she?"

"Sixty-two."

"Really?"

"Yes, why?"

"I don't know. She seemed younger, to chat with. Her and Lanie got on great the other week, despite the difference."

"Trust me, Maggie got on with everyone."

"So, no enemies?"

Sophie ends the thread with, "Lorry, I never heard anyone say a bad word about her, and she was squeaky clean. I suppose that's why this one is so hard to take. If there's one person I've known in my life who didn't deserve...that, out there, it's Maggie."

"Agreed," is Tony's contribution.

"Was she happy?"

Again, it's Sophie who picks it up. "Yes, and I know that, because she told me how happy she was. She'd had some crap happen to her, such as the divorce and her parents passing, but as she herself put it, 'I have my faith and my friends, my health and my work, in that order'."

It makes me smile.

23.

The large busy space is full but silent, excepting the buzz of strip-lighting and computers. Until Tony Alliss' voice cuts through it.

"Nine PM, or twenty-four hours since Maggie left this room and headed home. As you all know, she never arrived.

"Let's begin. We have the MedEx team conferenced in, and for anyone who doesn't know him, this is Lorry, a consultant. And yes, he's blind, but don't let that fool you.

"Victim Eighty-Six. From the Medical Examiner's report, we know that, of the three bodies we have in the morgue, he was killed first. His body went undiscovered for several days until yesterday lunchtime..."

"Are we looking at a murder a day, Tony?" someone asks, but I don't recognise the voice.

"Hold fire, Dave, I'll get to that. Let's go through it first, okay? There are a lot of people here, pal, but I'll take all questions at the end of the briefing.

"He went undiscovered because he was killed in his home during early afternoon on May 29th, and he wasn't missed for a while because he was off-duty until yesterday morning. When he didn't show, and his pager went unanswered, someone went to check. He was a Senior Registrar, specialising in anaesthesiology, at Higham Hospital, North London, and lived out that way in Crouch End. Aged forty-eight, it appears that he was rendered semi-conscious after being hit with a bottle. That same bottle was then...look, some of you may not have encountered stuff like this before, so if anyone feels the need to leave the room, don't be embarrassed."

I don't hear anyone depart.

"Okay. The still full and intact bottle was shoved in his mouth with force, narrow end first, and we think it was then stamped on repeatedly. I won't go into the full extent of the injuries, but we all need to have a feel for what we're dealing with here. Cause of death was brain trauma. The bottle was a white rum, pictured here, and available at every off-licence and supermarket in the country.

"Victim was homosexual, and of Asian descent, having been born in India. His name was Doctor Anish Kamala, and here's his picture. He had no criminal record, and wasn't politically motivated, other than with gay rights, somewhat at odds with his Hindu upbringing. He had no perversions, and had been in a relationship until recently. It seems he kept his sexuality hidden from his work colleagues, but most had guessed.

"He was a nice guy, people, by all accounts. We can't find anything on his computer untoward, and he loved field hockey. That's about it. He had no connection to either of the other victims, as far as we can see."

"Victim Eighty-Five. We haven't found it yet, but we presume there is one, and that he or she was killed on May 30th."

Another unknown voice cuts in, "what if there isn't an

eighty-five? What if eighty-five is significant because it's been missed?"

"It's a good thought, and worth exploring, Paula, but hold-fire. Victim Eighty-Four. Meet Carol Marsh, also known as Trixie. Time of death, approximately three in the morning, May 31st. Carol, or Trixie, was a twenty-three year old dancer at a club in Soho. Before you ask, not a stripper, more of a nightclub, and not on the game as far as we can tell. She was an aspiring actress, but didn't seem to get the breaks, so took to dancing to keep a roof over her head.

"She's no saint, but we think she was trying to sort herself out. She headed to the big city after leaving school at fifteen, and we know the home she left was violent, and possibly sexually abusive. Originally from Stoke On Trent, she has two raps for drug possession, marijuana, one for drunk and disorderly, and a further one for shoplifting.

"She had a steady boyfriend, and a three year old son from a previous relationship. Both the current and ex have been interviewed, and their alibis stand up. We don't consider either to be suspects. Look, she kept some dodgy company, but nothing too heavy.

"She was attacked as she smoked a cigarette in an alley by the club, her body then hidden in a skip. It was quick and brutal, a blunt force trauma to her head. MedEx believe it to have been inflicted by this tree branch pictured. The first blow was enough to kill her, so we're dealing with a powerful assailant, almost certainly a man, but that first blow didn't stop him hitting her a further four times.

"There was no sexual abuse on Trixie, just as there wasn't on the other victims. Her breasts were exposed, but we believe that was because she was clad in her dance costume, the club having recently closed, and happened when our killer applied the number to her chest.

"Either our killer is a lucky man, or he chose his locations carefully, as none are covered by CCTV. It may be indicative of him having a security, or even military background. But that's just my theory.

"Trixie was white, with no political or religious affiliations, and spent her time on-line looking at showbiz and gossip sites, and applying for reality television roles. None of which she got.

"Is everybody okay?"

A few people mumble that they are.

"I'll press on, and we'll all grab a tea or coffee and I'll take questions.

"Victim Eighty-Three. Margaret Dawlish, Maggie."

Tony has to pause, and I hear the crunch of a plastic bottle of water in his grip as he sucks a draught out of it.

"Sixty-two year old female, who worked here at Scotland Yard, having worked in counter-terrorism for six years, which she joined from the Met. She was an analyst, and a bloody good one."

"Hear-hear," someone calls, and a spontaneous round of applause strikes up.

"Thank you, she'd have appreciated that. She had top level security clearance, and as such, underwent regular background and profile checks. She was as clean as it's possible to be. A religious woman, Catholic, she was divorced, but as amicably as any. I met and spoke with her ex-husband this afternoon, and he's pretty devastated by the news, and not considered a suspect. She lived alone, no kids, just a cat, Mister Misty.

"She loved to walk, to read and to hold tea parties for her circle of friends, mostly attached to her church. She baked a lot, and I know most of us can vouch for her ability in that department!"

A little chuckle patters its way through the room, and I find myself smiling, even though I know Tony's doing that to soften what he has to do next.

"There's still some of her homemade bread left in the kitchen, Boss," a woman calls out, "she only brought it in yesterday."

The woman's voice cracks at the end, and Tony pauses for a few seconds to allow everyone a moment.

"Maggie was walking home from work last night, June 1st, and we can see her on CCTV crossing the bridge. We have her again on this still-shot walking along the South Bank to the East at nine-nineteen. As she cut through towards Waterloo area, she was seen by a man smoking outside this pub. Neither the man, nor the CCTV picked up anyone following her. The man isn't a suspect because he never left the pub vicinity.

"Maggie almost made the one and a half miles to her home, and given that she was a brisk walker, we estimate her time of death to be just before nine-thirty. As she cut through this small square, she was attacked from behind, a plastic sheet stretched across her face. She was forced down and forward, and a heavily serrated blade, probably that of a saw, was drawn across her neck. A provisional count by the MedEx on those cuts indicates that..."

Tony has to clear his throat.

"...it shows that she was alive when the cutting was done, and that the saw was drawn back and forth by a right-handed person sixteen times.

"Here's a picture of what that did."

There's a general din as people express their revulsion, and I hear hands being clamped to mouths.

"I'm sorry, but we all needed to see that. I'm going to take that one down now, and replace it with this one. For Lorry's benefit, this is a picture from her sixtieth a couple of years back, when we had a party for her, with the biggest pink cake I've ever seen. She asked if it was big enough to accommodate a naked man!"

I find myself laughing along with everyone else.

"To summarise. We don't have much, ladies and gents. There's no connection between the victims, and demographically, geographically and psycho-graphically, there's nothing. There's no clear motive, because it wasn't robbery. Nothing, as far as we can tell, has been taken from any of them. Aside from the numbers and the extreme violence of the attacks, there's no commonality that we can see."

"Is it just a random psychopath, Tony?"

"I don't know, Ellen."

"Are we sure it's just one person?" someone else calls out.

"No, I'm not ruling out anything until it's ruled out."

"But isn't the randomness almost a pattern in itself?" I call out.

"How do you mean?"

"Well, nothing's truly random. But this smacks to me of someone deliberately trying to make it look as random as possible. We have different areas of London, north, south-east, and west. We have one Asian, two Caucasian. One man, two women. One gay man, one perceived tart, and one clean-living woman. We have attacks by glass, metal and wood. We have plastic used on one, and even the method beyond that is deliberately varied, from a foot on the bottle, to a saw on the throat to a club wielded. Like I said, it's too random."

"And, what? In that lies a pattern?"

"Yes. I'm betting the next victim you find will be in a

different post code area, won't be Asian, probably not female, may tick an ethnic box not yet accounted for, will be from an age group not covered, and so on. Even the time of day or night is deliberately varied; nine-thirty PM, three AM, lunchtime."

"That's an awful lot of options, Lorry, but it's a fair point. Let's look at missing person reports that don't match any of our known victims, and concentrate police presence in the areas where bodies haven't been found."

"And the killer must be moving around, but he doesn't appear to stand out," I continue.

"So, he's either someone who knows how to blend in, or he's someone expected to be in the places he is. Perhaps he has a job that takes him to those places at varying times of the day," Tony continues my thread.

"Like a Cabbie," I say, because I once was.

"Exactly. Or someone in uniform, perhaps, in a position of trust, or someone doing something synonymous with London, something that would seem perfectly natural. Anyone?"

"Street cleaner," is one suggestion.

"Priest, vicar, rabbi, Muslim cleric," comes another voice.

"Bus driver! That's what the numbers could be, the routes!" a woman shouts.

"Tony, perhaps the numbers relate to Biblical passages, or the Koran!"

"That's a good thought. They're all good thoughts. Colin, can you get that checked, please, the religious passages and the bus routes?"

"It's not a cop, Tony, is it? It couldn't be one of us."

"No, I don't believe it is, Dave, but we're not ruling out anything. Look, there's not much here, but we might have something on the DNA and forensics come tomorrow.

Anything on that, Doctor Stephani?"

"Nothing yet, Tony. It's priority, but with three bodies, there's a tremendous amount to analyse. But we're keeping the Lab open all night, so we'll get any info to you as soon as we have it."

"Thank you. I'm worried about the level of violence, people. Our killer's committing some of the worst acts I've witnessed, and it doesn't seem to be satisfying him. The next crime is just as fierce as the previous one."

"But controlled." Sophie adds.

"Yes, precisely. That amount of anger, but coupled with such control, that's a scary combination."

"I keep thinking military, Tony," Dave says.

"Yep, that would be where I'd put my money right now, but we don't close our minds to anything. Hey, one more thing from me. I know I have no right to ask this, because it implies you don't do it normally, but I need to ask you to go the extra yard on this one. All of you. Not for me, and I know I don't need to tell you why, and, like I said, I have no right to ask.

"Right, any more questions?"

The questions come, but they're mostly recapping and confirming details. I'm handed a cup of tea by Sophie, as it suddenly hits me how completely wiped out I am.

It also occurs to me that, unless we get very lucky, more people are going to have to die before this case is solved.

24.

"Lorry, wake up!" I can hear Tony saying.

I must have nodded off.

"Why are you here?" I slur.

"Lorry? Lorry!"

"What?"

"You're in my office."

It all comes flooding back.

"We have another body. Why don't you stay here, get some rest? Sophie and me will head out."

"No, I want to come."

"It'll mean a fast ride in a police car."

"It isn't as though I've had chance to eat anything to bring up."

"Sorry, I should have fed you."

"Don't worry, my appetite went as soon as we got the call this morning."

"At least you didn't have to eat the airplane food in the end."

It's scant consolation, if I'm honest.

It takes the short journey to clear my head, a window down and the cool breeze slamming me.

"Number Eighty-Five. Nineteen year old student, Vincent Husband. He's an American national, black, over here for an interview at a university. Extremely bright, I'm told, a bit of a star in the world of mathematics."

"Could that tie in to the numbers," Sophie says, before adding, "and Maggie was an Analyst?"

"Good point, so they had those kinds of minds. I can't see Trixie being a number cruncher, but can you check it?"

"Will do."

"The American Embassy in London has been notified, and they're informing his family back in the USA. We already have a media blackout on this, until my statement, which is due later today, but this one has to stay that way until his family can all be contacted. We know that Vincent stopped posting on his Blog on May 30th, his last entry being at eight in the morning. His social networking tells us he intended to visit the Tower Of London that day, and we have him on CCTV there in late morning. Colin and the team are isolating all of that footage and assembling a timeline."

"Have any of the other victims used social media to potentially inform the killer of where they might be found?" I ask.

"Maggie didn't do social media."

"The others?"

"I'll get it checked. Incidentally, there was no correlation we could find between the bus routes or taxi cab registrations, and the biblical and other religious texts are too general. Psalms kind of connect, and there's something about Psalm 83 that may link to Maggie having her face covered. Here, Colin sent it through;

"so pursue them with your tempest

and terrify them with your storm.

Cover their faces with shame, Lord,

so that they will seek your name"

"But there's not enough for us to think it might be relevant. Also, Colin checked military unit numbers, and found nothing of note."

"What the hell do these numbers mean?" I find myself stating, rather than asking.

"Back to Vincent Husband. He was killed sometime during the afternoon as he walked north past Aldgate, back towards the hotel he was staying in. The hotel is close to Spitalfields, but he never made it.

"He was, we assume, forced or coerced into this building which is due to be demolished next week. Again, it's a location that has no CCTV surveillance. Death was quick and violent, with no obvious sign of sexual abuse, though that's a bit tricky to fully determine. He was hit with a piece of pipe on the back of his head. It seems he's using what he finds, rather than anything pre-determined, with the exception being Maggie. I think it's unlikely Maggie would have been carrying a saw..."

"Shit! Tony, a thought. What if it wasn't a saw?" I beat out in his gap for breath.

"What are you thinking?"

"I heard someone say that she'd brought in home-baked bread the day she died."

"The bread knife?"

"Exactly."

"Then where is it?"

"How do you mean?"

"Well, in every other case, he left the weapon behind, but not that one. Why?"

Sophie joins in, "because it might have incriminated him."

"Go on, keep going..." Tony tells us.

"Prints," I say.

"Or blood or DNA," Sophie follows on.

"Maggie fought back," it dawns on Tony, a hint of pride in his voice.

"She must have pulled that knife to defend herself after he placed the plastic over her face, and he ended up using it on her. Was the plastic from the scene?" Sophie seeks to confirm.

"We think so."

"Then where would he have put that knife?"

"More importantly, did he bleed at the scene, and can Stephoscope and her team isolate it?"

"It was a blood bath, Tony," Sophie reminds him.

"Yes, and I'm thinking even that was deliberate. There's something inconsistent about Maggie's death..."

"Tony," I prompt, "did the blow with the metal pipe kill Vincent Husband?"

"No, but it would have knocked him out. He was killed by having that same pipe inserted in to his rectum, before he was raised up and hammered down on it."

"Jesus..." is all I can say.

"Sorry, are you okay?"

"I just can't imagine..."

"Look, I've been doing this for a long time, and I've never seen anything like this in all those years. I mean, I've seen violent deaths, but they're usually isolated heat-of-the-moment stuff. This is anger like nothing I've experienced."

"What? So I shouldn't have nightmares, as this has never happened before?"

"Something like that. If you want out, Lorry..."

"No, that's not what I'm saying."

"There's no shame in it," Sophie adds and holds my arm, "some people don't have the constitution, and that's fine."

"I'll survive. Can we get out of this building, please?"

"Yeah, there's nothing more to see, anyway," Tony growls, "come on, we all need something to eat, and to take stock."

Ten minutes later, we're in an all-night cafe having ordered more food than the three of us would normally eat in two days.

It's difficult to eat, and impossible to switch off from the case. I don't know how Tony, Sophie and the rest of the team do it. How is it possible to live a normal life when you're having to deal with this kind of thing? I've always had jobs that were menial and fairly insignificant, the type that you showed up, did your shift, and went home, not giving it a thought until the following shift.

Professor Clifton comes to mind, a man who lived for his work, and, it seems, killed himself rather than lose that reason for his existence.

Shit, as usual, every path I go down in my mind delivers me to Kate. That last night of her life, as we sat in a pub, she was talking about taking a redundancy package from her work. We were okay for money, having inherited from parents, and Kate's salary was high with a good pension. And we didn't live extravagantly. As long as I had a few quid in my pocket for records, I was good, and Kate liked her clothes and nice things for the house, but nothing high-end. Lanie was taken care of, any money needed for her education set aside.

Bugger, I haven't called her, and it's too late now. Too early, rather, as it must be two in the morning.

"What's the time?" I ask.

"Just before five."

I have no appreciation of time in the way that I once did, since I have no visual reference with regard to the light. I go to bed when I'm tired, eat when I'm hungry, have a drink when I'm thirsty. Some people might, quite rightly, use that to define freedom.

"He kills at different times every day?" I say.

"That's right."

"Then it either ties in to his work, or he doesn't work."

"Agreed, and that's part of the profile we're looking at."

"He lives in London, and he knows his way around this city. I'm betting he's a Londoner, born and bred."

"Okay."

"He knows how to kill people, as daft as it sounds to say that."

"No, not daft, and I agree," Tony bounces off me.

"And he knows how to disable people prior to killing."

"How do you mean?"

"Well, I wouldn't have a clue how to immobilise someone

with one blow, which he did with the iron bar and rum bottle. I'd probably hit them several times to make sure, but he's sure."

"Yes, that makes sense."

"He's trained, Tony, no question."

"Trained as...?"

"A soldier, a policeman, a...bouncer. I don't know, but he knows how much force to use for what he wants."

"Except Maggie," Sophie adds.

"Yes, except Maggie. He's also cool, and doesn't seem to panic. If we assume we're right, and Maggie fought back, he had the ability to modify his plan, use what he was confronted with, and pretty ably cover the scene."

"Again, agreed."

"He thinks and acts like you, Tony."

"Well, it isn't me, because I was with you, but I know what you mean."

Come on, think, process this. Why can't I get a fix? I set my mind to nothingness, a black screen, and build up what I know, what I've been told, and try to add to it, to connect the dots and establish a pattern. It's what I do.

What am I missing?

The numbers are blinding me, as they're all I can see in my head. Could they simply be a red-herring, therefore, tossed in to the mix to achieve exactly what they are achieving, to divert our minds and focus away from all the other details?

Nothing's random. Everything is done for a reason. Jim King chose his auction seller name based on his real name, for example; there's always an element of truth in the seeming randomness.

"Tony, pick four numbers at random," I snap out.

"What?"

"Go on, four numbers, now, don't think about it."

"Four-eight-one-one."

"Right, why did you pick those?"

"They were the first numbers that came in to my head, Lorry."

"No, it's never random. Why?"

"Errrr, I suppose, four-eight is my age..."

"And one-one?"

"I don't know. I suppose because that was the code the woman gave at the airport yesterday morning."

"There you go, it's never truly random."

"And how does it help?"

"I have absolutely no idea."

25.

Tony takes a call as I stand unattended, drawing in the fresh morning air. It's set to be a warm day, and I wish I could have seen the sunrise. It must have risen as we sat in the cafe, at around five in early-June. If I could have my eyes back, I'd get up every day and watch the sun nudge over the horizon. And then I'd go back to bed.

"We've got another. Number eighty-two."

"He's made an early start today."

"And, once again, a different time to all the other killings."

"Where is it?" Sophie asks.

"Down near Croydon. You want to come, Lorry?"

"Yes, but I might head home after we've been. I need to call Lanie, and I could do with a shower and a change of clothes."

"No problem."

"Do you want me to drive, Tony?" Sophie offers.

"Thanks," Tony replies, and I hear the keys rattle in her hand.

We've been using a police car, Tony's car left at my place, parked up next to the taxi. Sophie dropped us at the airport before heading to work and being told about Maggie.

Sophie calls out the bends to me, much like a navigator in a rally car, and it helps.

We make good time, heading against the influx to the city, and carve through the traffic around Croydon thanks to the siren and flashing lights.

The rough terrain, solid but pitted with potholes, buffets the car, and as soon as the door opens, I can smell the grease and candy-floss, the toffee-apples and fried food. It clings to the wood and metal, drawn out by the heat of the day.

I've always hated fairgrounds.

I recall visiting one when I was about six, and my dad dragged me along despite my protestations. Prior to shooting Miller in the head eight months ago, it was the only other occasion on which I fired a gun, albeit an air rifle. And much like the latter incidence, I hit what I was aiming for, laying down all of the metal strips and winning a prize. The bloke running the stall handed me a record, a seven inch single, and I was made up with that, but my dad had to stick his beak in and told the guy to give me a fluffy toy.

To this day I've wondered what that record was. I have a vague recollection that it was some reggae disc from the early seventies. It could have been Desmond Dekker, for fuck's sake. That was my dad all over. He never knew me, and his arrogance dictated that he always assumed I was just like him.

And when my family spoke out about Kate, and it being

rushed, and her trapping me by falling pregnant, I cut them off. They're dead now, but I have a sister somewhere that I haven't seen in years. I don't even know if she's aware of Kate being killed, or me being blinded. Moreover, I don't much care.

By way of sharing all of that with the others, I say, "I fucking hate fairgrounds."

Tape drags across my head again as we enter the scene. It's too problematic for me to advance all the way, so I'm left with my hand resting on a railing, with Tony and Sophie promising they won't be long, adding "don't move, don't touch anything."

Apparently, the body is beneath one of the attractions.

*****

"Two bodies," Tony informs me as Sophie hands me a cup of tea rustled up from somewhere, I presume one of the catering vans.

"Two? And two numbers?"

"No, just one, eighty-two. The other body's a dog."

Tony doesn't like dogs. That's not true, he likes them, but he's somewhat haunted by them. I tease him about it. He's especially plagued by black dogs, which I suggested was a bit colour prejudiced on his part.

"Black dog?"

"No, brown."

"You and dogs, eh? What is it, a fairground dog, for security?" One's been barking since we pulled up.

"Apparently not, though this lot aren't exactly forthcoming when it comes to assisting the police. It seems we have a homeless person and his canine companion. There's no identity on the victim, but he looks to be mid-forties, and he was killed at approximately five this morning."

The dog continues barking incessantly some way off, and I begin walking towards it, Tony catching me and taking my elbow.

"Take me to that dog, Tony."

After fifty yards or so, he tells me, "it's in front of you, but chained up, and it looks a bit vicious, Lorry, be careful."

Stepping forward, I squat down on my haunches and offer it the dregs in my cup of tea, its tongue lapping greedily at the slightly sweet and milky brew. As it's otherwise occupied, I reach out my left hand and find an ear that I rub forcing it to tip its head over.

"What you doing with my dog?" a defensive voice snarls.

"He or she?" is all I ask, still rubbing the ear.

"He. What of it?"

"Well, I figured he sounded thirsty, with all that barking."

"Yeah, well he barks to warn us about unwelcome visitors."

There's a slight accent, but nothing I can pinpoint. Amidst the mish-mash is a hint of something more eastern; King's Lynn, not Kuala Lumpur.

"And did he bark at around five this morning?"

"He barks all the fucking time."

"Then you must get a lot of unwelcome visitors."

There's a pause. He's weighing me up.

"You a copper?"

"No."

"Are you blind?"

"Yes."

"How'd you know that dog was soft as clarts?"

Interesting phrase.

"I didn't, but I figured he wasn't straining at any tether to get to us, but guessed he would be tied up. There was no rattle of a chain, and no thwack of a rope tautening. His claws didn't scratch the ground, and his bark was as much a cry for help as anything threatening, as I detected no growl in the lulls. I decided he sounded inquisitive as much as anything else. In fact, he sounded like he was summoning, not warning off, so I thought I'd indulge him."

The dog is now lying on its side with its nose inside the empty cup, as I rub his tummy.

A door opens and closes, and I hear footsteps descend metal steps. Light, belonging to a woman or child.

"So, hear or see anything at around five this morning?" I persist.

"Listen, I was jiggered out. Busy night last night, and we only pulled in yesterday morning."

"Get back to Lincolnshire much?" I suddenly ask.

It baulks him, but he covers it with, "not often, no, if I can help it."

He doesn't ask how I know that, and I see no sense in informing him. It's better that he thinks I know more than I do.

So, I decide to say, "no, I imagine you want to leave that behind you."

He weighs up my bluff.

"Okay, look, I heard the dog go barmy at some point, but I didn't look at the clock, and I certainly didn't see anything."

"Was it daylight?"

"Erm, now you mention it, yes. But it was early, I knew, because of the way the curtains were lit from low down."

"What do you do here?"

"How do you mean?"

"What's your job?"

"Handyman, and I run the Helter Skelter. And my missus does the fortunes."

"Did you hear a vehicle when you woke up?"

"Sure, I remember hearing a car."

"A car?"

"Yes, look, first night in a new area, and some of the younger lads like to go and check out the town, if you know what I mean."

"I'm not sure that I do."

"Hey, nothing bent, I'm talking about pubs, a club, and a sniff round the local women, nowt more. They know to behave, or we get banned."

"And the car?"

"I just thought it was them coming back. Like I said, I was jiggered, and out of it."

"But you said car..."

"Taxi, if you want the truth. It sounded like a 2.5 litre diesel engine."

"The rattle?"

"Yes, that, and I just know. I've been around engines and motors all my life. You get to know. But I never got up, and I never saw nothing."

"Fair enough. Thanks for your time."

Giving the dog a final rub, I raise myself, and feel a hand on my arm. Assuming it to be Sophie or Tony, I go to walk away.

"Sorry for your loss," an Irish voice says, a woman's voice.

I nod at her, low down but directly in front of me.

She continues, by saying, "I don't understand, but she says something about taking care of the lane?"

Sharply, I pull away and almost lose my footing on the uneven surface. The dog barks, protectively. Tony steadies me, and begins walking me away.

"Enjoy your trip on the air-o-plane!" she calls after me.

"Are you okay?" Tony asks.

"Bloody freak," I say, the spot on my arm lingering warm from where she touched me.

"Should we be checking that guy out?" he asks me.

"No. I suppose you'd better tell me how the latest one was killed."

"The man or the dog?"

"Both."

"The dog was pummeled, multiple fractures in all four legs, his ribs broken and massive internal injuries. His jaw was broken, and his muzzle tied up after the break. It looks as though he was repeatedly thrown against a wall or dropped from a height. There's no sign that any of that happened here.

"The man was throttled with the length of chain that appears to have been an improvised dog collar. It seems our killer used all his anger on the dog, because number Eighty-Two had it quick and easy compared with the others."

I tell Tony, "I'm guessing that he didn't need to make this one suffer in that sense, because he was made to watch the dog getting tortured. That was suffering enough. This is all about causing others to feel the pain that he feels."

"And he's using a cab?"

"It appears so."

"Why would he bring those bodies here? Why would he take that risk?"

"Because it ties in to whatever it is he's angry about."

"Fairgrounds?"

"I don't know, Tony. I need to re-charge now. And I need to call Lanie."

I need to take care of the lane.

26.

"Hi Dad! How's the US of A?"

"I don't know, I'm at home."

"Shit, Dad, what happened? Are you okay? Wouldn't they let you in?"

She always does this; twenty questions and no room for answers.

"I'll tell you if you give me a chance; yes, and no."

"They wouldn't let you in?"

"What?"

"Dad, what did you do?"

"I didn't do anything."

"Then why are you at home?"

It's impossible.

"We got pulled off the plane..."

"Where, in America?"

"No! Here."

"Why?"

For Christ's sake.

"There's been...you know the lady you met at the cricket a few weeks back?"

"Which one? Gillian Grey?"

"Well, Gillian's actually a man...look, don't worry about Gillian. Maggie, you remember Maggie?"

"Yes, the older lady, loved to bake. She gave me a recipe for Welshcakes like Gran used to make!"

"Well, she was killed the day before yesterday."

"Killed? What, murdered?"

"Yes."

"Oh, Dad, I'm sorry. She was so sweet. Who'd kill her?"

"Well, that's what we're trying to find out. Lanie. There

have been five murders so far, but you won't have heard about it in the media..."

"The Number Cruncher?"

"The what?"

"I've just heard it on the news on the radio, Dad. They're calling the killer the Number Cruncher."

"Who is? How did it get out? When did this happen?"

"Bloody hell, Dad, one question at a time! And, I don't know. I heard it about ten minutes ago."

"Right. Well, Maggie was one of his victims."

"Was it random? You won't be next will you? What about Uncle Tony?"

Strewth.

"Did you get your exam results?"

"No, tomorrow. I told you that."

"Ah, sorry, I've forgotten what day it is"

"You sound tired."

"I am, Lanie. Tony and I had an early start yesterday to the airport, and I've only had an hour or two sleep since then. I popped home to give you a call, and get freshened up. I'll see if I can grab forty winks before I head back out there."

"Dad, don't push yourself. Be careful."

"I will. Don't worry. Anyway, are you okay?"

"Fine. I'm glad the exams are behind me, and I'm looking forward to the summer break..."

There's more coming, but she doesn't know how to tell me.

"...I might head off to Europe with Ollie for a bit of a holiday, Dad. In the summer, I mean."

"Right, so you won't be coming here, then, coming home...?"

"Of course I will. But it might not be for the whole six

weeks. I need to study, and Ollie's parents have a place in Spain, and we want to go horse trekking in Italy..."

It's a hammer blow. But she's growing up, she has a serious boyfriend. Before I know it, she'll be working full-time, and having a family of her own.

"You should, Lanie. You should do that."

"I will come and stay, Dad, I promise. We'll still get a couple of weeks together, and we can go to Brighton and do the record shops, like we said."

"I'd like that."

"I've got to get to class, Dad!"

"Yes, go, I just wanted to let you know that I was here."

"Take your mobile, okay, when you go out?"

"Yes."

"And lock the door behind you, you know what you're like."

"Yes."

"And are you eating properly?"

"Yes."

"And I'll ring you tomorrow, as soon as I get the results."

"Please."

"Speak to you later."

"Bye."

"Love you, Dad."

"Yep..."

And silence returns.

I'm glad of it. I need to give my senses a break. Not just from Lanie, but from everything. I work my remaining four senses so hard to compensate for the one I'm lacking, and it can be exhausting.

*****

Standing motionless in the shower with the water slightly too hot seems to have largely washed the stain of death from me. But it lingers, and again, I don't know how homicide police do it day in and day out.

My problem, and I would think it the same for Tony, Sophie and the gang, is that so much information has come in during a twenty-four hour period, it's difficult to harvest it all. My disadvantage is that I can't write it down, and tabulate it and sort it in to some semblance of order. It all needs to be retained, because I can hardly look up a detail.

And coupled with that, aside from the numbers, I can't get any connection. And maybe that's because there is no connection. But, no, nothing is truly random. And why would he have moved the body of the tramp and his dog to that specific site?

The kettle clicks off, and I pour water in my mug. It's not worth doing a pot for one, so I settle for a Tinker's cup.

Tinker; a traveller, a Gypsy, or other person living in an itinerant community, an act of attempting to repair, a person who makes minor mechanical repairs.

Was the Tinker woman's 'lane' comment just a lucky pick? Did I mention to the dog I was fussing that Lanie would like him? Most people have lost someone, so that was a generalisation, and besides, it was the best part of five years ago, so she's hardly current. And what about the airplane bit at the end? Well, she was wrong there, because I didn't actually get off the ground.

Yet, the first thing she said was "sorry for your loss", and I knew she was referring to Kate, not Maggie. I shake the cloudy thoughts from my head, and re-set back to the clear sky that mirrors the reality outside.

The taxi is the first break we've had, and I know the vast resources at Tony's disposal will be all over that. I hope it's not a cabbie, but somebody posing as one. Anyway, there are a lot of vehicles with 2.5 litre diesel engines, but a black cab does have a distinctive rumble.

Deciding to sit outside and make the most of the decent spell of weather, I pop one of my frozen bacon and egg stuffed pancake pockets in the microwave, and set about finishing my tea.

As I add milk and drop the teaspoon in the sink, I count the time in my head, ticking off the seconds, to ensure I pressed the right numbers on the microwave.

I count up, inserting 'little elephants' between each, but picture that bright green display in my mind, and recall that it counts down.

To what?

To the end, to the point at which things are complete. And then it stops.

I take my snack and tea to the garden, set them on the wooden table, feel around for one of the laid-back chairs, and calculate that the sun will be high in the sky and slightly to my left. So I point it that way, eat my food, and lay my head back, eyes closed and no sunglasses, so that the warm tongues of fire can kiss my lids.

They no longer glow orange in the light, but remain black.

And I think of Sophie kissing me that first time as I drift off to sleep, my tea barely touched.

For the first time, in the half a second before I completely drift off, I don't think of Kate, and I sense that it's a good thing, and that she doesn't mind.

27.

"What happened to you?" Tony asks before hello.

"How do you mean?"

"Your face."

"What about it?"

"Lorry, you're bright fucking red!"

"Oh, I nodded off in the sun."

There's quite a long pause.

Eventually, I say, "are you coming in?"

"Oh, sorry, I was waiting for you to turn to green..."

Tosser.

"Any joy with the taxi angle?"

"Not yet, but do you have any idea how many black cabs there are in London?"

"Approximately twenty-one thousand."

"Er, that's right. Lorry, that's annoying."

"There are nearly fifty thousand people in the Met, and over thirty-one thousand sworn officers."

"Again, annoying."

"Well, you just give them one each."

"Yeah, Lorry, life doesn't work like that. They don't actually all report in to me. Some of them even have other things to do, other crimes to investigate. Besides, we have to be low-key. I don't want our killer knowing that we're on to his mode of transport."

"I'm just saying."

"And to be honest, I've had to send a lot of people home. Some haven't slept in sixty hours, Lorry. So we've set up three eight hour shifts, with Sophie and me trading twelve hour supervisions."

"How did the media get a hold of it?"

"I let it leak."

"Why?"

"Because the public need to be warned, and they need to be vigilant."

"Number Cruncher?"

"It seemed apt."

"How much information have you put out?"

"As little as possible."

"Good."

"Any other questions?"

"I think that covers it."

"Glad to hear it. Look, we have to assume he's done his killing for today, and it was an early morning kill. I took advantage of that, and gave people a break. Come midnight, and for the duration of tomorrow, we'll have double presence on the streets, and cabs will be a focus. We're also concentrating the bulk of those resources on the areas he hasn't yet operated in. But with him pushing out to Croydon, that's a wide circle, Lorry."

"I know. Needle in a haystack."

"Exactly. And Colin has written a programme that allows us to follow your 'deliberately random pattern' theory. It pulls in all the data from the murders we know about, removes what he's already done, and leaves us with a shopping list of what he might do next. But it's still a long list. It's the same thing with the geography. But it helps. At least it narrows it down a bit, and allows us to focus the resources."

"Is it surprising that the killer hasn't made contact?"

"Not really. They do that on television, but not so much in real life. Besides, it tells us something about his motivation."

"What, so he's not doing it for attention?"

"Exactly. There's no politics involved, no statement to make or great cause he's championing."

"What are those murder motives again?"

"Ah, with serial killers it's different..."

"Really?"

"Yes. There are four, that can overlap to varying degrees. I'll fetch the beers, you get the crisps."

"What flavour?"

"How are you going to tell the difference?"

"I'll bring a few packs."

"So, the widely taught belief is that serials are either Visionary, Mission-orientated, Hedonistic, or Power-Control," Tony tells me.

"Visionary?"

"It's the hearing voices thing, God told me to do it, and all that. Psychotic breaks with reality is the official line.

"Mission-orientated is ridding the world of undesirables, culling societal injustices, and so on.

"Hedonistic is about thrills and pleasure. It's self-serving.

"Power-control is self-explanatory. These are the ones who are sometimes abused as children.

"Now, there's also a loose fifth option, which is Media driven murders, and they're on the up. But most Media attention seekers are one of the other four."

"Right, I've got it. So we can rule out Media..."

"Don't be hasty. Media can be the trigger, not the medium they court for attention."

"So, it could be any of them, Tony."

"Well, no, I have my theories. This guy is too in control to need to seek control, and for the same reason I don't think he's a Visionary. So, I think there's an element of Hedonism about it, but the tallying his victims would, to me, point at Mission-orientated."

"But what's the mission?"

"Not a fucking clue. That's where I'm hoping you can help, because if he doesn't get in touch to tell us what the goal is, I don't expect him to stop until he reaches it."

"And more people die."

"And more people die."

"How will we know when he's finished?" I ask as the notion occurs to me.

"The numbers kind of suggest that he's working towards something, so I'm hoping we'll know."

Tony's teeth process the crisps, and I sit back in my leather armchair and swill the acidic salt and vinegar flavoured fragments from my mouth.

I was hoping for smokey bacon.

"Another beer?" I offer, knowing he'll fetch me one and save me the bother.

"No, I need to drive in a couple of hours, one's the limit."

I wait, toting my empty can.

"Do you want me to get you one, Lorry?"

"Oh, erm, yes! Very kind of you, thanks."

"Don't be embarrassed about asking."

"Why would I..." I begin, instantly wishing I could retract it; the sunburn.

"Sorry, I thought you were blushing. Hey, can I take the cab tonight?"

"Of course. Why?"

"I'm set to relieve Sophie at midnight, and I thought it might be a good test of the system to drive in to the city in a black taxi."

"Good idea. So, are you getting me that beer?"

I hear him rise from the chair and pace through to the kitchen.

28.

"Hello?" I say in to what I hope is the right end of the phone.

Tony left less than half an hour ago, so it must be close to eleven at night. I'm hoping it's Sophie saying she's coming round.

"Mister Francis?"

"Yes, who's this?"

"I'm so sorry to call this late," says a posh voice.

"It's fine. Who's calling?"

"It's Ollie...Oliver Crutchlow, we met a few weeks..."

"Is Lanie okay?"

"Oh, yes. God, sorry, I didn't mean to give you a scare."

My breathing recommences.

"What can I do for you Ollie?"

Oh Christ, he's not about to ask me for her hand in marriage, or something, is he?

"I feel bad asking, but the truth is, I'm coming to London tomorrow, and I heard about the killings - this Number Cruncher thing. Well, Lanie's a little worried about me, and I wanted to reassure her. She mentioned you were involved in the investigation, so, I thought you might be able to give me a couple of pointers. You know, things I should avoid, and so on?"

"Ah, yes, she worries about me all the time, as well."

"And there's something else. I wanted to ask if it were at all possible to have a brief meeting with you, as there's something I'd very much like to ask you?"

Shit, there it is.

"Of course. Swing by the house at, let's say...four? Call first, though, to make sure I'm here."

"Absolutely, thank you."

"Do you have the address?"

"Yes, from Lanie."

"Right, well you'll see me tomorrow, then."

"And the pointers on visiting London?"

"Don't be alone in places off the beaten track. Under no

circumstances use a black cab. Stick to the areas where bodies have already been found, so central London or Croydon, and match yourself as closely as possible to one of the already reported victims. And keep your wits about you. Actually, you should be okay; he already killed a student and a doctor, so I think you might be covered."

"Thank you."

"You're welcome."

Cowardly little prick.

29.

"Number Eighty-One. Paolo Adams, thirty-eight year old restauranteur, UK citizen of Italian descent. Approximate time of death, one this morning, June 3rd, or...about four hours ago."

"He's getting earlier and earlier. Keen to get to his next quarry, perhaps?"

"No idea, Lorry. My thinking is that he knows we're getting closer..."

"Are we?"

"Yes. We know about the cab, for example. He must know that the more he kills, so the more data we gather. So, he got in early before we could act on it."

I can smell the baked bread, stewed tomato, garlic and olive oil, but the aroma of charred meat cuts through it all.

"I'll be brief on the profile, because it doesn't tell us much. He was hard-working, and opened this Italian restaurant two years ago. He has debts, but was working all the hours trying to pay them off. As well as the table service, they offered a local delivery, and sometimes used cab companies to cope with demand. That's being checked."

Even Tony's getting jaded, I can hear it in his voice.

"Ah, what else? There are no cameras on the premises, because he couldn't afford them. Ironically, he was getting quotes to get them installed..."

"Could that be a link, Boss?" someone asks.

"Good point. Get it checked. In fact, a fucking good point. If he's in the CCTV business, he'll know where they are and aren't, and can avoid them. Good work, Jamal."

"Thanks. I'm on it."

"Mister Adams was clearing up, having sent all staff home. It seems someone gained entrance through the back, and attacked him. There's no money gone from the till, and there was only a float in there. His wife had already departed with the night's takings. He was married, to Heather, and had four kids..."

He has to stop and clear his throat.

"...aged two to eleven. All girls. The family are getting all the help we can offer, and, as you can imagine, they're completely devastated.

"The family have lived peacefully in Wickford for years, and Paolo worked in an Italian there before opening this place in Romford. We don't suspect any of his competition, nor do we have any sense that his former employer holds any grudges, going on the information we got from his wife.

"His face seems to have been held against the hot grill until he passed out. You can see those marks here. After that, his unconscious body was dragged to the meat mincing machine, and you can see the result of that. Finally, he was stuffed inside the freezer cabinet over there. We don't honestly know which of those injuries was the fatal one."

"Fucking hell," comes from my left in almost a whisper.

"Yeah," Tony acknowledges, "that's the only phrase that fits, because anything more civil, anything more human doesn't apply to this.

"You're more than earning your salaries on this one, and I appreciate it. We have to keep going. That's six bodies in six days, eighty-six through eighty-one, and we have no idea where or when this stops. We have to continue. This man will fuck up, and when he does, we'll be there. And I'm giving you the authorisation right now; when you get the chance, you take him down. Do not hesitate. Do not negotiate. End this, and if there are any repercussions, I'll take the heat. Are we clear?"

There's a loud and definitive yes.

As Tony steers me out of the premises, he asks, "can I get a smoke off you, Lorry, please?"

Silently handing him the packet and lighter, he adds, "I haven't had one in thirty years."

Clutching at straws, I say, "he cooked, Maggie cooked?"

"Lots of people cook. And none of the others did. A doctor, a dancer, a student, a tramp. There's no connection there, Lorry."

"We can't give in."

"I'm not giving in. Shit, I haven't even seen Janine all week. She's working flat-out, twenty-four-seven. This one's eating me up, Lorry. I've never been like this before."

"Because of the gruesomeness?" I ask.

"No. I've had some grim ones, and I've read all the files on the worst ones. This is an eight, maybe nine out of ten on that front. It's the lack of anything, I've never known a case so closed. I can always get a toehold..."

"Still nothing forensically?"

"No, that's the thing, there should be. Nobody's that good."

He coughs, the smoke evidently having caught in his throat.

"Boss!" someone shouts.

"Talk to me. Don't worry about Lorry, you can say anything you want."

"MedEx Stephani has just been on to HQ. They might have something."

Tony carries me to my taxi, the cigarette flicked out instantly.

"At fucking last!" he gravels in my ear.

I'm tossed in the rear of the cab, the door closed before I can locate the seat, and we're moving before I can fasten the seatbelt.

"It's Tony. Talk," is all he says; name and command, and no time for anything else.

Stephoscope's voice fills the cab through the speaker. "Tony, we got something."

"I heard."

"At least, we think we have."

"Go on, Janine, give me something."

"Matched DNA at three scenes, Tony..."

"Please, say you found a match on the database..."

"Sorry, Tony, no go."

"Okay, but it'll put the bastard there when we do catch him. It's proof, Janine, right?"

"It's the best we've got. I'm running the other three scenes as priority now that we know what we're looking for. But there's a potential problem."

"Go on."

"Well, we don't have Lorry's DNA on file, and he visited the three sites, so..."

"We'll be there before you know it."

*****

"If it isn't Lorry, run the familial analysis, Janine, see if we have anyone related to this bastard on a database," Tony says as I dab my tongue on the spot where my mouth was swabbed.

"You've got it."

"How long will it take?"

"Given the hundreds of samples from six murder scenes, plus the regular backlog we have anyway..."

"This has to be priority."

"I know, and I'll rush it through, but we need to get it right."

"Understood. Just give me an idea, please?"

"You'll have it sometime today, first thing tomorrow, at the absolute latest."

"Thank you."

"Why so long?" I ask.

"It isn't like it is on the television, Lorry. Average wait on testing is a week, and can be fourteen days. Expedited is twenty-four to seventy-two hours," Janine explains, "and that's just for the most basic identity test. Any further analysis takes even longer."

"How are you holding up, Janine?" Tony asks, the softness back in his voice.

"Knackered, but we just keep going. You?"

"Yep, about the same. Go on, don't let us stop you."

A call takes Tony away from me for a second. It gives me a chance, as I sit in a high chair in the lab, to build a map in my mind. Being a cabbie for years affords me a certain familiarity with London. As such, I construct a mental depiction of Greater London, and begin adding the six murder scenes in order.

The first four were all clustered around the centre, around the bullseye on a dartboard; the City Of Westminster, within walking distance; north, then east, west, then south. Victims five and six are further afield, south in Croydon, and east in Romford. I think of them as doubles on the board. The first two bodies were inside, in buildings, the next three outdoors. Why? Because he wanted to buy a little time before they were found, presumably.

What else? He knew, as soon as the news broke, that the concentration of police resources would be around the centre, so he took his crimes further out. Yes, that makes sense. He also probably knew that killing a cop, if he actually knew she was, would up the ante.

Five bodies were left where they were killed, except the tramp at the fairground. Why? That has to be significant.

How did he move the body? In a cab. Okay, that's possible. After all, who'd bat an eyelid at a cab on the streets at any hour of the day or night. He'd cancel his light, and nobody would wave him down, assuming he was either off duty, or already had a fare.

North-east-west-south-south-east. The first four make a neat pattern around the hub, like spokes on a wheel. It's a pattern, but he mixed it up by jumping across right to left, rather than continuing round. He was mindful not to repeat the pattern by pushing further south. Can I presume he'll go north or west next? Not if he wishes to play the apparently random game he's been playing.

What would I do? I'd go in the trough, where the treble beds lie on that dart board, because I haven't been there before, and I'd go east again, because that would be the least likely given the prior locations.

Again, I'm stumped by the fact we simply don't have

enough information, and that to gather it, he needs to kill more people.

"Let's go. Now!"

Tony really doesn't sound very happy.

"What's happened?"

"Have you told anyone anything about this case?"

"No, I haven't seen a soul."

"Think about it."

I take a few seconds. "Oh, shit."

"Talk to me."

"Ollie...Lanie's bloke. He rang me last night, late, said he was heading down to London, that Lanie was worried..."

"Fuck it."

"What's he done?"

"Gone to the media. The morning news is running with everything we have, from the black cab to details of the victims, to the geographic changes. Oh, Lorry, what have you done?"

The honest answer to that, though neither of us bother to state it, is that I have probably just cost people their lives.

30.

"Thanks for meeting with me, Mister Francis."

"No problem. Come on in."

I wait for Oliver Crutchlow to brush by me. He's tall, six-one or two, I know from my previous meeting, but skinny with a wimpy milky handshake.

Rather than the habitual offering of tea, I go for, "what can I do for you?"

We're stood in the hallway, by the entrance to the kitchen. I had all the doors removed, for obvious reasons.

"Well, I simply wanted to catch up with you, to explain

about Lanie and I going to Europe in the summer. I assure you, my intentions are honourable. She's been working incredibly hard this year, and I thought..."

"It's fine with me. It'll be good for her."

"Ah, splendid."

"There was no need for you to come all the way out here to explain that."

"Well, it seemed like the decent thing to do."

There's more to come, so I don't bother to thank him for his decency.

"Oh, hey, it just occurred to me..." he starts, and I hope he can't see my eyes roll beneath the cover of my sunglasses.

"Oh, what's that?" I reply with a fake tone of intrigue that matches his.

"Well, I have a friend at Uni who's specialising in criminology. You know, it might be very beneficial for him to have a chat with you..."

"Really? I can't say I know very much about all that, to be honest. I'm not sure what I'd have to offer."

"Well, he's only out in the car. Why don't I bring him in, and you two could have a chat about things? He's a friend of Lanie's..."

I think it's the using Lanie's name that makes me snap. My head flushes with rage, and a kind of fizziness bristles inside me. So much so, that I decide to ignore Tony's instruction to wait for him.

"Okay," I say, "but before you fetch him, could you pop the kettle on for me, please?"

"Of course, with pleasure!"

Stepping to the doorframe, I gesture for Ollie to enter, and as soon as he's level with me, I reach out with my right hand, cup the back of his head, and ram his face in to the frame.

Something cracks, and I hear him hit the floor. Sinking down, I gather he's on his side, so I bring my knee, leg bent, down on the side of his head. Hard, so there's another crack.

He's whining, making whimpering noises.

"Shut up!" I bark, in my best Tony Alliss voice.

Tony should be listening to all this through the microphone and receiver we kept after the cricket.

Judging by the car door slamming shut, and the roar of his voice, Tony has hold of the freelance journalist posing as a fellow student. God help him.

"Listen to me, you sneaky little shite. You ever pull a stunt like this again, and it won't be me on you, it'll be Tony, and you really don't want that to happen. Ask your mate out in the car, as soon as he can speak again, and I'm sure he'll tell you that.

"Now, here's what's going to happen. You never see my daughter again. Understand?"

There's no response, so I press my knee down on his head. "Understand?"

"Yes! Okay, just let me go!"

"I don't care what reason you give her, but you don't mention any of this, and you do it gently. Get it?"

He does, so I release my weight from him and stand up. I sense him raising himself up to hands and knees, and then a groan as he finds his feet, his shuffled staggering steps let me know he's woozy.

"You broke my bloody glasses!" he whines. "And you've chipped my tooth!"

Just for the tone, I want to hit him again, but I'm not sure of his exact location. He could take me now, if he had any bollocks.

"Fuck off," is all I can think to spit at him, as I become

aware that I'm shaking with anger.

Tony enters the house. "Lorry! Are you okay...bloody hell, good work!"

As Ollie leaves my house, and scurries across the driveway with a helping shove from Tony, I ask, "what did you do to the other one?"

"Not much," he says walking back to me, "I showed him my weapon, and he pissed himself."

"You might want to rephrase that."

He chuckles, which might mean I'm somewhat forgiven.

"It'll be a pleasure ditching your daughter, Lorry," Ollie calls from the idling car, "I mean, she was hardly in my league. Still, a half decent shag, and not a bad looking girl, so I can't complain. She must take after her mother..."

Tony vaulting down the steps and sprinting after the wheel-spinning car ends any further communication.

31.

"We believe this to be his seventh victim, and she bears the number eighty. Joyce O'Malley, aged seventy-three, retired widow, and a volunteer at the Canine Protection Society. She ran a fundraising arm called 'White Collar', which aimed to get donations from businesses in central London with a view to opening a shelter here in the city centre.

"She was killed in the middle of the morning in broad daylight in a closed down pub, and as most of you can see, she was hung from the rafter running the width of the ceiling. She was hung alive, people, and MedEx believe she was left like that for a few minutes, prior to force being applied to her legs to speed up the process. The number eighty is indelibly written on her chest as with the other victims.

"Joyce was a grandmother to seven, and had recently become a great-grandmother. She loved animals, and on retirement from the publishing profession, dedicated herself to that.

"This bastard's thumbing his nose at us, following the media leak. Look at the map here, and you can see he just hit the bullseye, the geographical dead centre of London. The last two killings were out here and here, practically Surrey and Essex. He knew we'd be focusing our attention on the fringes, and he smacked us in the mouth.

"We have to assume, as well, that he's ditched the taxi following that being announced on the news."

I hang my head guiltily as Tony talks about the leak, and hope he didn't look at me.

"So, we're back to square one," somebody muses.

Tony ignores the comment and continues. "Joyce was hit once, but not tortured prior to being strung up, and the Medical Examiner has identified these marks on her neck. They aren't caused by the rope, and on checking the other victims, similar marks were found to be present on three of them, including Maggie."

"How did they miss that, Boss?"

"Ah. come on, Mike, they're drowning over there. And our victims are so badly mangled, particularly Maggie's neck, it was missed. It happens, and I'm not about to roast them for it."

"Fair point. Why do we think this one wasn't as vicious as the others?"

"Best guess; because he didn't have the time. It was daylight remember, Mike, and in a busy place. He took more of a risk with this one, but couldn't afford to piss about or risk being overheard."

"But he got away with it."

"Indeed. He was proving a point to us."

"The point being?" Mike pushes on.

"That we're miles away, and that we can't stop him."

"What are these marks like," I call out.

"Red strip circling the neck, eight millimetres in diameter, and believed to be caused by plastic..."

"So, like a plastic coated cord of some description?" Sophie asks, having come on shift an hour or so ago. We've not had chance to interact.

"Exactly. Like a washing line, was how it was described to me."

"Dogs..." I say, louder than I'd intended.

"What are you thinking, Lorry?"

"Well, the tramp's dog was beaten to a pulp, and this woman worked in that field. Is there a dog link to any of the other victims?"

"Maggie was a cat person," Sophie contributes.

"It's a long shot," I begin tentatively, "but what if those marks are from one of those poles with a loop on, the kind they use to restrain dogs?"

"Go on," Tony encourages me, the room silent.

I can't because I don't know where I'm going with this.

Sophie saves me, "he might have something here, Tony. Think about it. A dog patrol van wouldn't draw attention, and the guy could, presumably, cover his face with those mesh guards. And he'd be in a uniform of sorts."

A thought occurs to me. "Is that fairground still in Croydon?"

"Er, yes, until tomorrow, I think."

"Then as much as I don't want to, I think I need to go back there."

"What are you thinking, Lorry."

"I don't know. But there's something to this."

*****

My taxi bucks side-to-side on the pitted surface and coughs itself out.

"Is that dog there? The one from the other day, I mean?" I ask before we leave the cab.

"Yes," Tony tells me.

"What's he doing?"

"Nothing. Just lying with his chin on his legs watching us."

"Okay, let's go and see him again."

Tony steers me over, and I sink down on my haunches as before. The dog didn't bark once. I think he remembers me, as he pushes his head firmly against my flat hand, and my fingers go to work on his ears. He's so at ease, he rests his snout on my thigh. Soft as clarts.

"Can I help...ah, you again, eh?"

"Us again," I confirm.

"Come back to see the dog, have you, the daft bugger?"

"Kind of, yes."

Being here makes me uneasy, and I hope the fortune teller doesn't show.

Because of that I push on, "he didn't bark."

"No, he doesn't some of the time. I figure he gets tired of it."

"But he did the night the body was dumped."

"I already told you that."

"Tony, can you call in back-up, please?"

"Ah, come on, what is this bollocks? I've done nothing..."

A car pulls in, and the dog jerks away from me, sniffing the air to my side. His barks come in bursts of five, rar-rar-

rar-rar-rar, increasing in intensity as the car doors open and close, ratcheting up another level as the footsteps chew their way over the gravelly surface.

"I've done nothing, you have no right..."

"Relax," Tony says affably, as I hold my hand up.

"Send them back, Tony."

He shouts, "that'll do, thanks."

The footsteps retreat, and the dog settles down, looking for my hand, as the car pulls away.

"I've had to learn a lot about dogs in the past six months. To be honest, I knew nothing about them before then," I begin, speaking rapidly, "but I'm down for a guide dog, so there were loads of courses to attend, one of which was Canine Character, which detailed how dogs are a reflection of their owners, in the same way that children are their parents. As such, dogs will be afraid of the same things their owners are, or become excited by the same things, if you follow, and I know that you're wary and untrusting of the police, understandable given your history, so the dog has inherited that from you. He barks at people in uniform, and at cars with stripes along them, and with lights on the roof."

"Bugger me! I'd never noticed."

"I'm right though, aren't I?"

"Christ, well, yes, now you mention it."

"Sorry to bother you again," Tony tells him, and helps me up.

We begin walking away, but the Irish voice I'd been keen to avoid calls from inside the caravan.

"Some bloody father!" she shouts. "Blind to it all. Couldn't keep an eye on her! Not a father at all!"

"Lorry, ignore her, close your ears."

Tony loads me in the taxi and shuts the door to cut her

off. I fucking hate fairgrounds.

"It wasn't a taxi," I begin, as soon as he hops in and closes the door. I try to light a cigarette, but can't get a flame.

"Give it to me," Tony says, and lights it for me before handing it over. The filter's slightly damp from his lips.

"He's not thumbing his nose, Tony. He's laughing at you."

"So, he wears a uniform."

"Dog Catcher, Tony. The engine was, as our friend from Lincoln said, a 2.5 litre diesel, as commonly used in cabs. But this was a van. Even the rattle can be explained by the metal cages I bet are fitted in the rear. It's brilliant, if you think about it. Who'd look in the back of a van like that? Who'd think twice about a van like that being around the streets? I can even see how Maggie would have fallen for that. He plays the card, 'vicious dog loose, I'll keep you safe', and they'll instantly trust him, and be watching for a dog to attack, and therefore off guard when it comes to the actual threat. Maggie must have smelt a rat at some point, hence the knife, but you can see how it all fits together."

"Dogs. I'm plagued by fucking dogs. But you're right. I think we have something. And now we know what we're looking for..."

"As long as it's kept out of the media," I add, and turn my head to the open window.

He calls in and asks Colin to check all CCTV footage for a van and man matching the description.

I doubt we've barely got out of Thornton Heath before Colin's back on, saying he's got one in the vicinity of three of the scenes so far, around the time of the killings.

"Why'd they miss it?" I ask, because it seems to be a question asked quite a lot.

"It's a lot easier to see something when you know what you're looking for, Lorry."

After a period of silence, he adds, "and don't pay any attention to that old hag at the fairground, okay? You did what needed to be done with Ollie, and Lanie will understand that."

"We'll see," I reply, unconvinced.

"You have this guide dog re-sit this afternoon, I hear?"

"Yeah, they called to say I could join the group. Someone cancelled, so it'll save me waiting another month."

"Right, well that's good."

"I suppose."

"Look, Lorry, if we'd been in America as planned, this wouldn't have been possible, so take it. And then you'll have some good news to tell Lanie; soften the blow."

32.

I can't do this. A few weeks ago, I was locked in a room with a bomb. Okay, so it wasn't a bomb, but I wasn't to know that. The point is, it was nothing compared to being outside with a guide dog, with traffic streaming by two paces away. A stumble, one trip on a raised paving slab, and I keep having visions of a truck running over my head.

And I felt terribly self-conscious, as though everyone was staring at me; an irony, of course, given that I'm incapable of staring at anything with any purpose. Since I lost my sight, I sometimes get a feeling that I imagine is claustrophobia, but can just as easily be regarded as agoraphobia. There's simply too much going on in the world at large for my remaining senses to be able to deal with. My nature is to perceive, so that I overload my mind with all the data I'm guarded against.

So, I'm not sure it's agoraphobia in the true sense, as it certainly isn't the wide-open spaces that terrify me, it's more all the things that I sense close by me in an environment that I can't control. Now, if I could see at this very minute, I'd look up the definitions of both on the internet to satisfy my desire to understand.

Anyway, the net result of my excursion is that I sought safe haven in a pub, as directed by a man I smelt smoking outside an office building. Even the instruction, "three doors down on the right" didn't help me much. I could smell the acidity of the spilt beer and the whiff of fried food, but the dog led me to the neighbouring door of a hairdresser, judging by the ammonia smell and daytime radio playing within.

Eventually, we made it, and having been repointed to the front bar on account of the dog, the back bar being full of lunchtime diners, I'm now getting stuck in to my second pint. The dog is as happy as I am, I think, to be off the streets, as he lies contentedly by the leg of the chair. I think he does that so he can close his eyes and rest, but feel any movement of mine through the wood. He's clever, there's no denying it.

All things considered, I struggle to understand how a guide dog is going to improve my life. After all, he only serves his purpose if I know where I want to go, and can somewhat steer him accordingly. To my mind, he requires guiding even more than I do. Yes, he stops at pedestrian crossings, and kerb-sides more generally, but it isn't as though I can instruct him to take me to the record shop on the High Street. He isn't a taxi.

That's the thing. how often would I utilise him? Twice a week, perhaps? It would be nice to go record shopping once a week, and pop out for a pint now and again, but there really isn't anywhere else I care to visit. He can't get me to Lanie, and if I were with Lanie, I wouldn't need the dog. As for the rest of the time, I have Tony and Sophie.

And even if he got me to the record shop, how would he go through the racks? He hasn't got thumbs.

"Another pint, love?" the woman serving behind the bar calls out, I presume to me, as I don't sense anyone else in this side of the pub.

"Please," I respond, even though I know I shouldn't.

The damage is done now. Another pint won't make any difference. I'm unsure of the hour, but I know the time for reconvening back at the starting point is come and gone.

"There you go," the woman says, placing my pint on the table, "anything else I can get you?"

"No, thanks." I hand her a bank note. I think it's a tenner, but I've lost track. It's either that or a fiver or a twenty, and she'll either rip me off or not.

I suppose I should have asked for a drink of water for the dog. That's the thing; it's all extra responsibility. I'll still need to pick up his crap, and so on, and that isn't going to go well. I've never had a dog. I'm not a dog person. Some people are, and some aren't. Not that I dislike dogs, but I've never desired that unconditional love that comes with them, having always been fine, in the main part, in my own company.

It's conversation I crave...

My phone ringing stops me.

"Hello?"

"Mr. Francis?"

"Yes!"

"It's Jeremy...from the guide dog centre."

"Ah, yes Jeremy, I may have got a bit lost."

"Where are you?"

Towards the bar, I call out, "what's the name of this pub?"

"Red Lion."

"The Red Lion," I unnecessarily relate.

There's a sigh. "Don't move. I'll be there in ten minutes."

Perfect; just enough time to finish my beer.

33.

The way she says hello tells me she's down. I put off making the phone call for twenty-four hours, hopefully giving Ollie time to get back and do whatever he intended doing, to say what he wanted to say.

In addition, I was hoping to lead off with good news about the guide dog, but it didn't go well.

"What do you want, Dad?"

"I wanted to hear how you are."

"How do you think I am?"

"Not happy."

"No, well that'll have something to do with Ollie coming to see you, and showing up back here with bruises all over his face, and..." She can't finish.

"And what did he tell you about that?"

"That he came to chat with you, and was attacked by you and Tony. He dumped me, Dad."

"I know. Oh, Lanie, I'm sorry."

"I didn't think you were like that."

"Like what?"

"Like your own parents. I thought you were smart enough not to repeat their behaviour."

"This is nothing like that..."

"Yes it is, Dad. They didn't accept Mum, so you cut them off. Perhaps I'm a lot more like you than you think!"

"No, no, no, Lanie, don't do that. You don't know what happened."

"There's no excuse for what you did. I've never been

dumped before, and I thought it was special..."

I don't know what to do. The words from the shrew at the fairground echo in my mind, 'some bloody father! Not a father at all!'

How else could I have handled it? Okay, I shouldn't have hit him, but I was angry. His actions will almost certainly cost people their lives. He played on my love for my daughter to get the information from me, saying that it was Lanie who was worried, and I presume he did it all for financial gain.

This is where I fail. Kate and I chatted about it, that final evening of her life, how I couldn't communicate with my own kin. It was in relation as to whether she liked her name. Kate said I should ask her, but I told her I couldn't. I blamed it on her being fifteen, a funny age, and a girl, and Kate being better suited to it as a woman.

All I can do is tell the truth. Besides, she hasn't hung up on me, and she did answer the phone in the first place, and she must have been able to see it was me calling.

"He used me, Lanie, and he used you, as well."

"Just fuck off, Dad."

"No. Please take a minute to listen to me, and if you want me to never contact you again after that, you have my word that I won't."

"One minute."

Speaking fluidly, I tell her everything. There's a long silence when I've finished.

She breaks it. "Shit, Dad, he didn't tell me any of that. You're serious, aren't you?"

"Yes."

She connects the dots, and reaches the same result I got to. "People will die because of what he did, won't they?"

"Possibly. But, as it transpires, he may have done us a

favour."

"Can you tell me?"

"Secret?"

"Secret. Cross my heart, on Mum's grave."

"We discovered today that he wasn't using a taxi, and we made a giant stride in the right direction. The leak made him bold, Lanie, and he made mistakes as a consequence."

After a short reflective period, she says, "good. You catch this bastard, Dad, you hear me?"

"I hear you."

"That piece of shit!" she suddenly exclaims, "I'll bloody rip his head off when I see him on campus!"

I have to laugh. Perhaps she is a little like me, after all.

"Talking of campus, have you got those mock exam results yet?"

"Yes, yesterday."

"And...?"

Modesty stalls her, but I can hear her smiling through the phone line, so I know she did well before she says, "well, it's only a mock, and probably easier than the finals, but I got all As and one B."

"Well done!"

"Thank you."

"What was the B for?"

"See, you have to do that!"

"Well, I'm just surprised you didn't get straight As."

"Of course you are. They picked me up on my bedside manner. It was first thing in the morning, and I may have been a grumpy bugger."

"Yes, you're definitely my daughter."

She laughs heartily for the first time, I imagine, in a day or so.

"I'm proud of you, Lanie. I wish your Mum..."

"I know."

Keen to move the conversation on, I ask, "so, what's the deal now? You have choices to make, right?"

"Yes. Next year is about hospital placement, and I've been asked to think about medical specialty."

"And what are you thinking?"

"Well, I've drawn up a top five, but it's really a top three. I'm sure I want hospital work, not General Practice."

"Great. Let's run through your choices."

"Okay. At number five is pediatrics, four is oncology, three is ophthalmics..."

"Because of me?"

"Hmmm, kind of. It was your condition that pushed me in this direction remember, and all those weeks spent visiting you in hospital chatting to the doctors?"

"I remember. But there's other areas you're keener on?"

"Number two is general surgery..."

"And this week's number one!" I throw in, attempting to sound like a seventies DJ.

"Number one is neurology."

"Brains?"

"Brain and nerves, yes."

"My daughter, the brain surgeon."

Again, I'm stalled, because I know what I want to say, but I can't seem to say it. David, my Emotional Therapist, has raised this in his subtle way on occasion.

Falling back on the old safe ground, I go for, "hey, guess what song I was listening to last week?"

"Which one?"

"'My Little Girl'. It always reminds me of you. You'd dance to it when you were little."

"I haven't heard that in years. The Crickets, wasn't it?"

I nod and smile, which I realise is meaningless.

"I might download that," she says, and I resist the temptation to scoff and tell her to get it on vinyl. "I'm sorry I got mad at you earlier."

"That's okay. I'm sorry you got dumped, Lanie."

"Hmmm. Sounds like I dodged a bullet. I hope you hit him really hard!"

"Hey," I suddenly think, "I'll make you a promise."

"What's that, Dad?"

"I'll take you pony trekking this summer."

"You'll get on a horse?"

I hadn't really thought it through, but reluctantly state, "yes, I'll go on a horse."

"But you don't like horses, you don't trust the way they move."

"For you, I'll go on a very sedate, docile old nag that can run no faster than me."

"I'm counting down the days."

Lanie's words stun me. I'm aware that my mouth is frozen in the position it was as I was about to speak. I don't blink.

When I eventually speak, I opt for, "oh shit! Oh ruddy nora! Lanie, I have to go!"

"Dad, what's up, are you okay?"

"What? Yes, I'm fine. You're a genius, Lanie!"

"I get it from Mum. Though, I have no idea what I've done."

"I'll tell you later."

"Okay, go...save the world, or something! I love you, Dad."

"I..." but she's gone.

34.

Why isn't Tony answering? He always answers when I call. He knows how much effort it takes to dial the numbers and press the right button.

In the midst of trying to ring Sophie instead, my phone chirps to life. It confuses me for a moment, but I work out it's an incoming call. It's probably Tony calling me back.

"Tony?"

"No, Lorry, it's me."

"Sofe, where's Tony? It's important."

"That's why I'm ringing you..."

"How do you mean?"

"To see if Tony's with you?"

"No. I haven't seen him since we went to the fairground yesterday."

"We've got another body, Lorry, and Tony's gone AWOL."

"Tony wouldn't take off in the middle of a case. Have you tried Janine?"

"Yes. No word since last night."

Something dreadful shudders through me. "The latest victim; what do you know?"

"Not much. The body was found fifteen minutes ago."

"Don't tell me it's a black male..."

"Relax, Lorry. Female. A teacher in her mid-thirties."

"Where?"

"A church in Harrow."

"Sophie, I think I know where this is going. Can you pick me up?"

"No can do, Lorry, I'm running lead with Tony gone."

"Shit, I need to get there."

"Where? The church?"

"No, the incident room. I need the info we've got, and to borrow your eyes."

"I'll sort it out. Just stay there."

"I wasn't thinking of going anywhere."

"No, sorry. Just wait for me. It might be an hour."

And she's gone.

It's a countdown, all the way to number one, the biggest hit, the top of the chart, the top ten, top five, top three biggest sell-outs!

That's what all of this is about.

*****

"First victim, number eighty-six, give me all the data again. Just blitz through it, please," I beat out urgently.

Sophie does the talking. "Doctor, male, age forty-eight, lived in Crouch End, worked at Higham Hospital..."

"How did he die?" I interrupt.

"Blunt force trauma to the head, bottle inserted in mouth and rammed home."

"The bottle was?"

"Erm, hold on...a white rum."

"That's what I thought. Colin...Colin?"

"Here, Lorry, I'm here."

"Look up Doctor & The Medics 'Spirit In The Sky'."

"Got it."

"Number eighty-five," I tell Sophie as I spin half a turn back in her direction and nearly lose my balance.

"Student, killed in East London, near Aldgate, having visited Tower Of London, pipe inserted in rectum and, again, rammed home...."

"Age?"

Colin interrupts. "Eighty-six! Number one single in 1986, Lorry."

"Was it the biggest selling single that year?"

"Give me a second....no!"

"Shit. What was?"

"Erm...Communards 'Don't Leave Me This Way'."

"Fuck it, I was sure I was on to something..."

"Lorry, you still might be," Sophie snaps, and brings me back in line.

"Okay, yes. What else on the student?"

"He was nineteen, American..."

"Paul Hardcastle 'Nineteen'!"

Colin clicks some keys. "Yes! 1985...but it wasn't the biggest seller either. That was...Jennifer Rush, 'The Power Of Love'."

"And the biggest seller of 1984 must be Band Aid, right?"

"Yes."

"Okay, that's not part of it, but the songs still have to be. Give me the next one, Sofe."

"Victim eighty-four, is twenty-three year old Carol 'Trixie' Marsh from Stoke On Trent, a dancer...had a son aged three, a couple of drug raps. What else? She was hit with a tree branch."

"I'm looking at the number ones from 1984 now," Colin tells us. "Perhaps it is Band Aid, Christmas tree?"

"Let me see," Sophie says, moving across the room.

I wish I could see the screen.

"Hang on...the club she worked in was called 'Whammy!'. Wham had two number ones in eighty-four, 'Freedom' and 'Wake Me Up Before You Go-Go'."

'Go-Go dancer," I say, "that's what she did, right?"

"Yes, I suppose."

"And I think I've already sussed number eighty-three, dear old Maggie. Try The Police and 'Every Breath You Take'. My old man had 'Synchronicity'."

"Yep, 1983. I guess taking breath explains the plastic over her face," Sophie states.

"Who was number eighty-two?"

"He was the tramp with the dog, Lorry."

"At the fairground. Yes, I remember. Run through the tracks from that year, please. Just the titles will do."

"Okay, it goes, 'Don't You Want Me', 'Land Of Make Believe', 'Oh Julie'..."

Sophie interrupts. "Stop, Colin. It's that one."

"Madness 'House Of Fun'. Why?"

"Because that was the ride the body was beneath," Sophie says.

"That's why he transported it there," it dawns on me. "Was our tramp a care in the community victim - was he mad?"

"We don't know. We haven't managed to ID him."

"He will be, and that fact might help you identify him," I tell her.

"Is this enough, Lorry, or are we seeing what we want to see here?" Sophie asks, reasonably.

"We'll know in a minute when we've done the other three. Where the fuck is Tony?"

"We don't know. I've got people trying to track him down, but nothing so far."

"I'm worried about him."

"Me too, Lorry love, but let's get on with this, eh?

She takes my hand and massages it as she passes.

"Number eighty-one, Paolo Adams, thirty-eight year old restauranteur..."

"Adam & The Ants," Colin buts in.

"What track?"

"There are two, 'Prince Charming' and 'Stand And Deliver'."

"Well, they did delivery, so I'm assuming the latter. What's the name of the restaurant?"

"Ah, that's it" Sophie calls, a dawning apparent in her voice, "Adamant."

"Move on. Number eighty; that was the dog woman, hung in the pub. Name of the pub?" I ask.

"The Old Ash. Anything in the chart Colin?"

"Yes, I've got 'Ashes To Ashes' by David Bowie."

"How does it relate to our victim, though?" I want to know.

"How do you mean?"

"Well, all the others are more than just the place name, from what we can tell."

There are a couple of minutes of silence as they both, I presume, scan the board.

"I'm not seeing anything."

"Me either."

Nor am I, but I move on, "let's assume it's the Bowie track. What about the latest victim, number seventy-nine?"

"Thirty-five year old teacher, called Heather Mason..."

"It could be Ian Dury & The Blockheads 'Hit Me With Your Rhythm Stick'," Colin buts in.

"Why?" I have to ask.

"Blockhead might refer to a dunce, and being hit with a stick was a school punishment."

"I never had you pegged as a bad lad at school, Colin."

"How does it tie in to the church?" Sophie asks.

"Well, it might not," I propose, "after all, some of the other sites were irrelevant."

"It could just as easily be 'Ring My Bell' or 'I Don't Like Mondays'," Colin quite rightly announces. "Actually, even 'Another Brick In The Wall' had school kids in it, if I recall correctly."

"It did."

Sophie's the first to cast a bit of doubt on my hypothesis.

"That's the point, isn't it? We've just managed to crow-bar four songs to fit. What if we're doing that with all the others?"

"Then we have nothing," I concede.

"Is that a photo of the victim, Sophie?" Colin asks.

"This one?"

"Yes."

"Yes, that's her."

"Oh shit. She's a blonde."

"What's your point, Col?"

"Blondie 'Sunday Girl'. That's my point."

"Why was she in a church, Sophie?"

"She was a Religious Education teacher, and she held a Sunday school at the place in which she was killed."

"Lorry," Colin begins, "I just noticed something."

"What's that?"

"They were nearly all number one about now."

"How do you mean?"

"Late-May, early-June...they were the number one singles in the UK this week."

"That's it! That's the link. So tomorrow's victim will be somehow connected to...Col, what was number one this week in 1978?"

"Already on it, Lorry. It was...Boney M 'Rivers Of Babylon'. Hold fire, I'm just checking that I'm right on this."

"The only one that wasn't, is the Bowie 'Ashes To Ashes'."

"So, what was the number one that year this week?"

"MASH 'Theme From MASH (Suicide Is Painless)'."

"He hung her, like a suicide..." I toss in.

"And the pub name was Ash, so it's in there."

"Slow down, gentlemen," Sophie interjects, "strewth, Lorry, you're a genius!"

"Well, I didn't like to say..."

"The dog rescue centre she was raising funds for?"

"Yes..." There's a rustle of papers being sifted through.

"Midtown Animal Shelter. Or MASH, to use the acronym!"

35.

Five-word fragments reach my ears every couple of minutes as I sit in a swivel chair in the open-plan office at Scotland Yard. Where on earth is Tony? Where the fuck is Tony? Any word from Tony Alliss?

Sophie kicks things off. "At last, we have something solid, thanks to Lorry. Here's a list of song titles, all of which were number one this week between 1986 and 1977."

"Why only ten?" the man called Mike asks.

"Best guess is that he's working to a chart of his own, and a top ten countdown seems to fit," Sophie replies.

"Why not top forty? That's how the chart works, isn't it?" There's a challenge in his tone, as though he feels he should be up there doing the presenting. This is no time for internal petty power plays.

I jump in. "It won't be forty, because he knows we must be gathering information Besides, the singles chart was only begun in the fifties. Forty's too much to pull off at one a day, unless he relocates, and if he relocates it'll no longer be your problem. I considered twenty, but I still think it's high. Ten makes sense. It also implies that he's counting down to the 'big one', the real purpose to all of this, which gives you a day and a half until he gets to that. So, June the seventh, and it links to the year 1977."

"It all seems a bit speculative to me," he adds, his voice projecting in my direction.

"Got anything better have you?" I snap at him.

"So," Sophie continues, "alongside each year is an explanation of how the song relates to the murder. 1978 was Boney M 'Rivers Of Babylon'. Any ideas on that? Come on people, let's brainstorm this, don't be worried about shouting out something stupid."

I hear a click as a top must come off a marker pen, and I follow the squeaks as the song title is written across the top of a wipeable board.

"Given the other killings are all in greater London, it must be the Thames."

"It's in Iraq, isn't it?"

"Hanging gardens."

Jamal adds, "it means the gate of God."

"Is that Arabic or Persian?"

"Hebrew."

Jamal adds, "Euphrates river."

"I think they have artifacts from there in the British Museum."

"Saddam Hussein."

"Lion of Babylon."

"Babel."

"Elton John!"

"What?"

"He did a song called 'Tower Of Babel'."

There are a few snickers.

"This is pointless!" someone shouts.

"It's all we've got," someone else counters.

"But it could be a kebab house or a bloody restaurant for all we know, anywhere near the river. It could be Kew Gardens, or any of the parks..."

Sophie raises her voice, "he's right! It could be anything. But if we can narrow it down, we can focus our resources."

"He's had six kills north of the river, so my hunch is he'll go south," I add seamlessly on the end of Sophie's plea. "And he hasn't gone south west as yet, so it could be out there. Then again, if his main objective lies there, he'll avoid it and save it for the following day. And we have to assume he's still using his dog catcher guise. That hasn't come out in the media, has it?"

"No, we left them thinking we're still looking for a taxi."

"Good. You know what you're looking for. This can be done."

"I know everybody's exhausted," Sophie continues, softer now, "and I know we've hardly had any sleep in five days since this started, but we owe it to Maggie to keep going, and to up our game. Nail him tomorrow, and June seventh becomes an irrelevance. And my gut tells me he'll be more vigilant on that final kill, so our best chance is tomorrow. He'll have planned his big one for a long time, and I'm still sure his other killings are more spur of the moment."

"How do you think he's choosing his targets?"

"Internet, or even a local paper, but Colin and the team can't find a single source that lists them all."

"And what's his objective?"

"He's angry, so it's righting a wrong, or addressing some kind of injustice as he sees it. This is a Mission Orientated serial killer, and he isn't going to stop until he feels he's achieved his goal. And the key to stopping him, is to discover what that goal is."

"Any significance to the June 7th date, all assuming that is the end day?"

"Well, D-Day is the obvious one," Colin picks up, "and in 1967 Israeli soldiers entered Jerusalem..."

"Muslim extremists dislike dogs, don't they?" Dave suggests.

Jamal answers, "yes, some do, but many don't. They're seen as unclean, but the Koran says nothing bad about them. It came later."

"Could that be something?"

"It's possible, Dave, good thinking," and I hear Sofe add it to the board.

"In 1981 the Israelis also destroyed the Osiraq nuclear reactor in Iraq, so there's another link there."

"But if it was anything to do with that, wouldn't some message have been sent?"

"That's usually the way, but we can't rule anything out."

"What comes after 'Rivers Of Babylon', Sophie?"

"Rod Stewart. I've written it here, but it's a tricky one, as it's a double a-side, 'I Don't Want To Talk About It' and 'The First Cut Is The Deepest'. Now, we don't want to focus on that yet, as I'm hoping we won't need to, but have it in mind, please, and let Colin know of any thoughts. Right, anything else?"

"Oh, and it was the Queen's Silver Jubilee in 1977, of course," Colin adds, almost as an afterthought.

And I feel all the blood drain from my head.

*****

"Lorry, what's wrong? You don't look well. Colin, get a doctor..."

"I don't need a doctor. I need Tony. Now!"

"He's not here, you're going to have to tell me."

"Fuck it. I have to be wrong about this..."

"About what, Lorry? You aren't making any sense."

"Is it just you, me and Colin?"

"Yes, as you requested."

"Col, I need you to look up Tony Alliss' personal record,

and find out about his sister being killed."

"What? You've lost your mind, Lorry, Tony never had a sister. And I know that for sure, because last year when Miller got us to pull everything on him, there was no mention of it," Sophie confusedly informs us.

"But he told me...why would he make that up?"

"I don't know, Lorry. But he never had a sister."

"No, he wouldn't do that, why would he...? He told me that his sister was three, he was nine, and they went out to see the bunting on June 7th 1977, it was hot and she was in her best dress, he was supposed to be looking after her. He told me the whole tragic story."

"And what happened?"

"She saw a dog, and ran after it, but it ran in the road, and his sister was killed. He told me all the details, last year after the Miller thing. It was as we were driving up to see Lanie in Scotland."

Colin, evidently looking at the record says, "there's nothing on file, Lorry."

"There has to be!"

Sophie comes close to me. "Lorry, I need you to think now. Has Tony played you? Was it all some sort of cover for something he was planning?" She pauses before adding solemnly, "do I need to consider him a suspect?"

"Don't be fucking ridiculous..."

"Lorry, I have to consider it!" she tells me, placing a hand on my arm.

I shrug her off. "He wouldn't. And he couldn't, because he was with me or Janine at the times of the murders."

"Was he? Can you be sure of that?"

No. No I can't. But I can be sure of the man.

"He's given me everything for nearly five years, Sofe."

"I know, I know that. But things can happen to people."

"He wouldn't have killed Maggie."

"Perhaps she knew something. Where's your cab right now?"

"Er, Tony's got it."

"Has he had it quite a lot over the past week or so?"

"Yes, but only because it was convenient, because I'm sick in his car, and we were working on the case, and I don't have any use for it."

There's a long silence, much like, I imagine, waiting for a V1-bomb to land.

"Didn't you say something about Tony not liking dogs once?"

"No, he likes dogs, but he's haunted by them. Because of his sister. Shit," I add to myself, as things worryingly begin to click in to place.

A thought occurs to me, "what about the DNA samples at the scenes?"

"No match, and no familial match, I heard earlier today."

"Then it can't be Tony."

"He could get close to Janine, and switch samples easily enough. He has the clearance. And any other on-scene evidence would be dismissed because of his presence as an investigator."

My world is falling apart. Until this moment, I hadn't really appreciated what Tony is to me.

"I know you don't want this to be true..." Sophie starts.

Colin's very quiet.

Why? Because he has nothing to add? Colin always has a take on things, he's great like that.

Without warning I snap, "you're quiet Colin?"

"Give me a second, Lorry, I'm looking at something."

"I'm taking you off this, Lorry," Sophie tells me, "you're too close. I'll get you a ride home."

Now I'm angry, as angry as I can remember being since the night Kate died, and I've been pretty angry for a lot of the time in between.

"No you're not, you can fuck off Sophie. That's what this is, eh? You tried to have Tony taken off the case right from the start, and now this..."

"Lorry, don't say things you'll regret."

"Bollocks. That man has...I don't think I'd be here without Tony, and I'm not talking about him saving my life after he shot me. You should have a bit more fucking faith!"

"Then where is he?"

She's got me there.

"Right, if you two lovebirds can stop squabbling, I have a newspaper report here of an RTA on June 7th 1977, somewhere on the main drag in Merton. a young girl, aged three, killed after being struck by a car. Her name was Gabby Alliss. There are no other details, the papers taken up with the jubilee celebrations, and the police accident report is missing."

"There, now do you believe me?"

"But Lorry, my love" Sophie says, softer now, "that just gives him motive."

36.

Somebody I don't know takes my arm and begins clumsily leading me out of the room. Nobody says anything.

Just before the door closes behind me, I hear Sophie state, "priority is to find Tony Alliss. He's now our lead suspect..."

We reach the car, where a male voice says, "mind your

head."

I'm loaded in the back like a prisoner, like a criminal, and I wonder if this is what Tony will have to go through.

We've barely gone half a mile when I have a thought.

"I need to go back!" I say blindly.

Nobody responds.

"Oi! I need to go back," I shout, reaching forward and connecting with a mesh partition that I thread my fingertips through and attempt to shake.

"I've got my orders, sir."

"It's important."

"Orders are to take you home."

Bollocks.

Fine, I know what I have to do.

"I feel sick."

"Of course you do."

"No, I get really sick in cars, because I can't see where I'm going."

"We won't be long, sir, depending on traffic. Soon have you home."

I will my guts to churn, and breathe hard, but to no avail. So I stick my fingers down my throat, retch, try it again, and chuck up all over the back of the drivers seat.

"Oh, for fuck's sake!" comes from the front. "That bloody stinks...ugh!"

"Sorry. I did try to warn you."

"Christ, I can't drive in this for an hour. We'll have to go back and change cars."

*****

As luck would have it, he had to take me back in with him to get allocated a new vehicle and pick up the keys.

We enter the main door and a secondary secure door, and he sits me in a seat to the right and says, "won't be long, don't move."

It's not like I'm high-risk, so I'm unrestrained. As soon as I hear the cracks of his feet depart on the tile floor and another door click closed, I'm up and counting my paces at what I hope will be an approximate thirty degree angle from twelve o'clock.

Seventeen strides on, during which I sense people moving to accommodate me, I turn another sixty-or-so degrees right and drag my hand over the wall for the push button for the lift. If anyone's observing this, they must think I'm mad.

Sliding along, I brush over the metal sealed doors, and find the buttons. I hit the higher one of two, figuring it'll be for 'Up', and step back.

After the longest twenty-two seconds I've ever experienced, each of which I count out in my mind, I hear a ping, and a door to my left whooshes open.

People disembark, and I wait until I hear no more footsteps or chatter before walking forward, where I'm confronted by a gap in the wall.

The sliding doors start to close. At the same instant, I hear, "hey, get back here!" from the copper who was assigned to run me home, his feet now slapping hard on the tile.

Twisting my body, I slip through the narrowing gap mindful not to activate the automatic door open sensors, and drag my hand quickly down the wall to the side of the door looking for buttons.

My hand connects with a panel, my heart racing in my chest, as I let my fingers read them like I do my phone. It's imperative I don't hit the door open or alarm buttons, so I go for the second row down, button on the right.

The lift begins ascending, and I let go of a devious little chuckle.

I know Tony and Sophie are based on the fifth floor, but I have no idea how to locate that. Phone! Bugger me, why do I always forget I have a phone?

With that in mind, I let the lift take me wherever it's headed, and step out as soon as it comes to a halt.

"Hello?" I call out, but receive no reply.

I'm completely in the dark, the only directions I can be sure of are up and down. So I begin shuffling forward, skipping my left hand along a wall until it finds a door. I knock. There's no answer, so I lever the handle down, relieved when it relents and opens, and step inside.

Feeling my way forward, I stumble in to a chair, build a picture of it using my hands, and sit down.

My fingers are shaking as I press Sophie's number in to my phone and hit call.

She answers after one ring.

"Lorry?"

"Yes."

"Where are you?"

"I'm not telling."

"Lorry, don't be bloody..."

"Do one thing, and then I'll tell you."

"Lorry, I don't have time for this."

"One thing."

She's mad at me, as she huffs through her nostrils.

"What?"

"Ask Colin why the death of Tony's sister isn't in his file."

"What will it prove, Lorry?"

"Just do it, please. If we meant anything, I ask you for this one favour."

I'm aware that I used the past tense; meant.

I hear her asking Colin. She must have switched to speaker mode, as Colin echoes back, "because somebody removed it. Illegally."

"Did you do it, Colin?" I ask him.

"No."

"Could Tony have done it?"

He laughs, before stating flatly, "he could barely log-on."

"Could you have done it, if asked?"

"Erm, yes, I could, but there'd be a trail."

"And there is no trail?"

"Correct."

"Who could have done that, Colin?"

I already know the answer before he says, "there's only one party I know of."

"Gillian Grey?"

"Yes."

"And, to the best of your knowledge, would Gillian ever do anything to facilitate a crime?"

"Not knowingly, no."

"Thanks, Colin."

"Where are you, Lorry?" Sophie insists.

"No idea. Somewhere on the second or third floor from the top, left out the lift, first door on the left. Oh, and I appear to be locked in," I add as I try the handle.

"And I've a bloody good mind to leave you there!"

*****

"We have to go and see Gillian Grey." I tell Sophie as soon as she releases me.

"I can't go anywhere on a whim, Lorry..."

"Look, you're right. This has something to do with Tony.

But he's no bloody serial killer, Sofe! Fuck me! It's madness to even think it. We need to go and see Gillian."

"How would we even find her? Not that I'm agreeing to this."

"Colin will know."

We stop moving at the lift, and I hear no depression of a button, no chime indicating it's been summoned.

She needs more convincing. I try by asking, "Tony's involved somehow, so how do you best solve this?"

She knows the answer. "By finding Tony."

"And Gillian and Trish, not to mention Eddie, are our best bet of achieving that. But they won't talk to you, Sophie, not given your history. But I think they might talk to me."

She hits something hard, and the chime sounds.

"Colin, it's Sophie. Find me Gillian Grey. I need to see him...her, now. Call me with the details, and I'll get to my car. Lorry's coming with me."

I scrabble around for her hand, but she pulls away. "Not now, okay. Just...not now."

37.

"Can you remember how to get to where you first met Gillian?" Sophie asks me.

"I think so. It's close to my house. Get me there, and I can guide you."

"Don't be sick."

"Relax, I've already done that."

My shoulders being pulled back on to my seat, my head pinned to the headrest, tell me we're shifting suddenly.

The first time I met Gillian and the team, Tony made me blindly drive there after we'd been taken hostage, and he was handcuffed. When I say I drive, I only did the more visually dependent elements such as steer.

We went a bit slower than this, which throws me on distance, but I find the sharp left turn, almost back on itself, and am thrust against Sophie's shoulder as she takes it at a speed I wouldn't have thought possible.

"At the end of here is a slip road to a dual-carriageway, correct?" I ask her.

"Yes."

"Take the left lane, merge in, and you should see a lay-by with a catering van parked on it after a few hundred yards."

I feel the bends, the forces acting on my unprepared body.

"I see it." she announces, as we slide to a halt on gravel and grit. "Nice welcome," she adds.

"How do you mean?"

"Well, a man with terrible looking scars on his face just flashed a gun at us, and now he's motioning for us to get out of the car."

"That'll be Eddie. He has no tongue, so keeps himself to himself."

Opening the door and alighting, I ask, "is that you Eddie?"

It was a stupid thing to ask a man who can't speak, I realise as soon as I've done it.

"Hello Lorry," calls the slightly haughty not-male, not-female voice of Gillian Grey, formerly Graham Gill, also formerly a government spy. His-her wife, Trish, is the IT queen, though I probably shouldn't use that term.

A car pulls in, and someone calls through a lowered window, "all clear" before the car speeds off.

"We had to be sure you weren't followed, Lorry. Not that I don't trust you, but little Miss Sophie here does have some history of being disloyal where Antony Alliss is concerned."

"I'm clean," Sophie says, but I hear Eddie patting her down anyway.

"How are you, Gillian?"

"Not at my best, Lorry. We've been monitoring things at our end, and I'm deeply concerned about Antony. He's like a son to me, you know? Have you seriously got him pegged as a suspect?"

"I haven't," I state decisively, but flinch at the unspoken inference that Sophie and others might.

"Allow me to take your arm, Lorry. Hungry?"

"Er, a bit peckish, yes," I report, as she begins walking me towards the smell of food.

"And what about you, Ms. Hargreaves, do you think my Antony would perform such horrendous acts?"

"I don't want to, but the evidence isn't looking good."

"Yes, well, all you see is evidence. Whereas Lorry here, he can't see, so he sees the person, I suppose."

"I take it you're backing him to be innocent?" Sophie asks, as we arrive at the trailer emanating heat carrying on it a blend of meat and onions.

Gillian's grip tightens on my upper arm. "Oh, I know he's innocent. It's with you, young Sophie, that my doubts lie."

The sound of metal leaving metal shrieks out, and ends with a metallic clunk as it hits, I hope, wood.

It must make me flinch, as Gillian explains, "it's only Edward chopping onions, Lorry. It's funny, but they usually end in tears, don't they?"

On previous exposure, I'd not noticed how terrifying he-she is. There's a calmness in the oddly pitched, genderless voice, and a complete and utter confidence.

"Tea, Lorry?"

"Please. Milk and one sugar, thanks. Any chance of a

bacon buttie?"

"Oh, yes! Edward, please give him anything he requires. He loves cooking bacon. If you could see him, Lorry, he has a real smile on top of the one permanently cut in to him."

"Thank you, Eddie."

No offer of food or drink is made to Sophie.

"Whilst we wait, let me tell you something about Antony Alliss. He first came to my attention when he was, oh, let me think now...about eighteen. He played football for the police when he was training, a centre half, not to mention captain of the team. They won a game 9-1, and Antony left the field with a face like thunder! Well, his coach asked him what was wrong, he wanted to know if he was injured. Antony was angry because he felt the goal they conceded could have been prevented. He takes things very personally, but does that sound like a man who could butcher eight people and counting? Now, what else do you require today?"

"We need to find..." Sophie starts.

"I was speaking with Lorry!"

I fill all of the silence. "Whilst I don't believe for a second that Tony could perpetrate any of this, or be in any way knowingly involved, it has something to do with him. That's clear, if nothing else, by his absence. And I believe it ties in to his sister's death on June 7th, 1977."

"I agree. But I asked you what you required, Lorry. After all, you're here for a reason, and I hope you haven't jeopardised our security simply to confirm things you already knew..."

"Absolutely not. I'm here for Eddie's cooking."

It lightens the mood as Gillian chuckles, suddenly sounding more manly.

"Ketchup or brown sauce?"

"Neither, thanks."

"Why not?"

"Because I want to taste the bacon, not have it covered by something else."

"Well, you're making Edward happier and happier today! I wish you could see his face."

"Sophie's right, though, we need to find Tony."

"Yes you do. To pick up on your bacon comment, you need to get to the flesh, not have it hidden under a smeared mask of assumption."

"Do you know where he is?"

"No. We've been trying to locate him since first thing this morning. He's gone very dark, Lorry, and if he doesn't want to be found, you won't find him."

"Would that be a different answer if Sophie wasn't here?"

"Hmm, interesting. So, you'd rid yourself of Sophie to help Antony?"

Fuck it, I've dug myself a bit of a hole here.

"In the short-term, yes."

Gillian's thinking, as I'm handed a napkin containing my sandwich, and my tea that has no lid and is of a perfectly drinkable temperature.

"Fair enough. But the answer's still the same; we don't know where he is."

"Can you tell me where Tony's sister was killed? The exact spot, I mean."

"Ah, clever man. That's the right question. Patricia!"

"Hello Lorry," Trish says, as she emerges from the mobile home to my right.

"Hello Trish."

"Come with me, please," she says, and takes my arm.

The jolt slops my tea, and it runs down the knuckles of my left hand, my sandwich almost gone. I cram the last of it in my mouth, and set about wiping myself clean with the napkin.

I don't really want to leave Sophie, but I think she'll be safe as long as she keeps quiet. And she's smart enough to work that out for herself.

Once inside the caravan, the buzz and whirr of electrics and cooling fans tells me I'm in the hub I visited once before with Tony. As soon as the door's closed, Trish hands me a piece of paper and tells me a location that I commit to memory.

"It's on the paper should you forget it, along with a map, but you'll require eyes to read it and to take you there. Make sure those eyes are attached to someone you trust, Lorry. As much as Gillian likes and respects you, if you're instrumental, albeit even innocently, in any harm coming to Tony, even God won't help you."

"Understood."

"And take this."

"What is it?"

"You'll work it out," is all she says, as something that feels like a cigarette lighter is pressed in to my palm. "Good luck."

"Thank you."

"Oh, and Lorry, we deleted the record of Tony's sister from his file many years ago. Gillian thought it irrelevant, and didn't want it to soil his CV, so to speak. People could have interpreted it as him being, well, damaged."

I nod my understanding.

Affable Gillian's back as he-she walks me to the car. "How is that wonderfully gifted daughter of yours, Lorry?"

"She's fine. Thank you for remembering her."

"Splendid! Be sure to send Delanie our very best regards."

"I will."

"Such a pretty girl. And don't worry too much about the B on her grades this week."

"How on earth…"

"Take care, Lorry. I hope to see you again soon under less stressful circumstances."

"I owe Eddie for the sandwich and tea," I call out.

"No you don't."

I'm in the car, and we're moving before I can settle, my empty tea cup occupying my hands. It stops them exploring the items in my pocket.

"Where to?" Sophie snaps.

"Just head back to London, towards Merton," is all I say.

38.

I can't stand the silence. It's why I sit listening to music so often when I'm alone, or why I have the radio on.

Silence was always welcome in my world, even sought out, when I knew it would be eventually shattered. But when there's potentially no end to it, it's a different matter. When there's no wife to come home from work, no daughter to swing through the door after school, and after the phone stops ringing and people forget to remember to check if you're okay, or simply don't wish to remind you of the thing that you've lost, it starts to haunt you.

So, I fill the void, and drive away the ghosts by using sound.

"Are you okay?" I ask Sophie when I can stand it no longer.

"Fine."

"Sure?"

"Yes. I know you had to go there and say the things you said to get the information. I get it."

I need to be honest, so I tell her, "and I said them because they're true, Sophie."

"Yes, and that. Gillian was right, wasn't she?"

"In what way?"

"That you'd rid yourself of me for Tony. He'll always come first, won't he?"

"No. Lanie will always come first," is my truthful, but diplomatically evasive answer.

"That's different, Lorry. I wouldn't have that any other way. I just want to be somebody's bloody priority in this world, just once."

I think back to the things Tony told me about Sophie last year. How she was the third of four children, two older sisters and a few years gap to her younger brother, despite her parents not really getting on.

She was never really wanted, let alone a priority. Her mum and dad have a girl first, and that's fine; as long it's healthy nobody's really bothered by the gender of the firstborn. Then they try for a boy, but get another girl. Again, they convince themselves that it's fine, that they can be playmates, and one can inherit the others clothes and toys.

They go for a final stab at it, the law of averages says this one should be male. But out pops Sophie, another bloody girl.

They leave it for a few years, thinking that's their lot, but decide, before they get too old, to give it one last go. And lo and behold, out pops a son and heir!

It was the final one that screwed Sophie up even more than being unwanted, because the little boy would have been doted on, spoilt to bloody death. That's why he wound up on drugs, and why Sophie ended up doing what she did in order to protect him. If she hadn't, her parents would have really hated her.

It's also, I reason, why she'd go to cricket matches with her father; to try and earn his love and fill the void. And it's almost certainly why she does an all-action job, and knows about tools, and so on.

"Sofe, the last month has been the best in years. And that's down to you. Tony has been there for me for nearly five years, and I owe him, but it's you who's made the past month so wonderful for me."

There's a gap.

"Thank you," she says softly, and I want to lean over and kiss her, but we're moving too fast.

She calls out the bends, and my guts settle back down. Not that it was the travelling that was making me feel a little churned up.

"I was thinking about that thing you told me, the first day we got together," she starts.

"What was that?"

"It was something you said Kate said, about mixing your work with your personal life, how you always end up resenting one of them."

And I don't know if she means from her or my perspective, and which one of those two life elements she might be beginning to resent.

*****

Sophie punches the address I relate to her in to the Sat Nav. In Tony's absence, she's the only person available to help me, and I have to show her trust. She needs to be trusted.

"Ah, right, we're only about three minutes away. How do you want to play this?"

"I have no clue. We don't even know that he'll be there, but I can't think of anything else, and Gillian seemed to think it was the right call."

We drive on in silence until Sophie says, "okay, this is the spot."

"What do you see?"

"Not much; there's a railing on my left with a gap for a pedestrian crossing. Same thing on the right. Do you know which way she came from?"

"No, but it might be on here," I say, handing her the piece of paper.

"Ah, okay..." I sense her spinning her head and neck round to read the street signs. "We need to be on the other side. Sit tight," and we're moving again.

"Any sign of Tony?"

"I might have mentioned it if there was."

We take a right turn across the traffic, my body braced for a u-turn so I impact lightly with the centre console when the car unexpectedly straightens.

"What are you doing?" I ask.

"Swinging round the side street, so we can park up away from the traffic."

"Is that the street Gabby Alliss would have run up that day?"

"Yes."

"Can you describe everything to me, please?"

"Er, yeah, no problem. Here, if I park up, we can walk it, and I'll tell you everything. It's hard to do when I'm driving, and I could use a stroll."

It feels nice to have her close again, her arm linked through mine, like a normal couple. We fit one another. It was the same with Kate. We could walk like this, and not bump hips all the time, despite the height and stride difference. I don't know if that's a natural physical compatibility, or whether it's indicative of two people willing to accommodate one another, so therefore compatible. Either way, it's comfortable.

We could be idling along a country lane, until Sophie describes, "lines of terraced houses, but not a bad size compared with up north. Decent gardens, as well, and most of them are neat and tidy. A few scruffy ones, but it's not a slum by any means. Some are painted white, some brick, and the odd pebble-dashed one. It makes it a nice mix. Being a cul de sac, it's quiet, and it's the middle of the day, so I suppose people are at work. And it's a school day."

On the black screens of my eyes, I paint the picture. I know the area a bit from cabbing, down at the end of the Northern Line. Even though Tony was born in Tooting, his family moved here when he was about five.

I can also recall and visualise that day in 1977. I'm sure it was a similar patriotic picture up and down the country, from Tony down here, to me in Oakburn, and up to Sophie in Lancashire. It dawns on me that she wasn't born in 1977.

Has she ever owned a vinyl record?

Shaking that thought away, I add the red, white and blue bunting, the union flags and trestle tables draped in matching tablecloths. I ratchet up the heat and glare from a hot sun that day, even hotter than this day, and I add in sounds of things being readied and prepared; from the clatter of cutlery being laid out, and china plates being stacked, and bowls of trifle, platters of cakes, and sandwiches stacked high, and crisps being emptied in to bowls. There are the coordinating calls from neighbours, asking if they have something, any more garden chairs, perhaps, and the laughter of children, excited and off school and loving all this!

From houses come the smells of baking, sausage rolls and bread and cakes, and the sweetness of the icing makes my mouth water. Music fills the air, as a man tests a hi-fi system, the radio, the current number one, by Rod Stewart, a cover of a Crazy Horse song, the other side a cover of a Cat Stevens song. Horses and cats! And dogs are barking in the street on that day in 1977, as a nine year old black boy holds his three year old sister by her tiny dimpled hand and walks her along to see all the sights. He walks, at least, with a cocky swagger, but she skips playfully at his side.

He's big, even for nine, and could be taken for older, if it wasn't for the boyish grin. He's wearing his blue football shorts and a red t-shirt with white capped sleeves, fitting in despite his skin colour being different to most people round here. And his sister has her best dress on, the new one, white with the red hearts, and her mum has tied a blue ribbon in her wiry hair, so that it sticks up like a pony's from the top centre of her head, pulling back her fringe to show her cherubic face with huge round brown eyes and skin that shines with health and happiness.

Oh, and something catches the boy's eye, as he peels off to take a look at the item on a table on the corner of the street, where it branches off to the right and leads up to the main road they aren't allowed to cross.

But his sister doesn't want to look at that, because it's boring, so she slips her hand free of his, and skips along on her own, like a big girl.

He only looks for a few seconds, five at the most, before he smiles and nods at the man setting up the music, and swings back to catch up with his kid sister.

But Gabby Alliss isn't there any more.

The street is busy, people bustling back and forth, and Tony hops on his feet, leaping up to better see over the head of the crowd. No sign of her. He sinks down, and scans through the legs and tables, a desperation starting to rise in his chest and throat.

He uses it to shout her name, his voice shrill and unbroken.

The big smile leaves his face, and a frown creases in two lines between his eyes. He shouldn't have to wear that then, aged nine, and carry it for the rest of his life.

He's lost sense of time, it feels like an hour, but he knows it's only about twenty seconds since her hand was in his. He can still feel the warmth of it.

He spins, looking all around him, the scene stretching out in his mind and leaving him a little disorientated where he failed to blink and re-set.

"Gabby!" he calls again, but it goes unanswered.

Something catches his attention and holds it in its jaws.

A dog. A black, scruffy looking thing. Not a stray, he doesn't think, but not well loved either.

Gabby loves dogs.

He sees her, and the relief allows him to breathe again for the first time in that hour, the dog running up the road, his sister chasing after it. And he knows that was why he couldn't see her, because she'd crawled beneath a table, the long draped tablecloths covering her up.

He smiles again, and shakes his head.

He's moving, though, before his brain has time to process his actual thoughts, as his bearings come back to him, and it dawns on him that Gabby Alliss is chasing a dog towards the main road.

Resting a hand on a trestle table, he vaults it, the table giving way beneath him and causing him to almost fall on landing, but he just manages to keep his feet and keep moving; running to stand up.

He can see the traffic speeding along at the top of the road, the side streets closed for the parties, everyone in a hurry to get to where they need to be.

The sound of their wheels fizz by, not deflected back the other way because of the gap between the houses. His training shoes pad lightly on the road surface, the sound of each step only reaching his ears after his foot has left the ground, such is his pace.

"Gabby!" he calls, but regrets it as it cost him half a stride.

He's gaining on her, the distance half what it was when he set off, but he knows it isn't enough, so he digs in, his arms piston-like at his sides, his hands pointing forward straight-fingered so he might carve through the air.

Long distance is his event, anything 800 metres and over. He's too bulky to be a sprinter, too heavy in the frame.

He's ten yards behind her, and she's three behind the dog, as it turns and looks at Tony advancing, blowing out a breath, his face taut, his immature muscles knotty along his arms and legs, a frown of worry creasing his face.

A freeze-frame might have him appear angry. More so when he shouts her name again, "Gabby!"

Perhaps it's that, as well as the footsteps, that make the dog turn and dart through the dog-leg gap in the metal railing at the end of the road.

He hears a car horn moan, but sees the fleet mongrel negotiate the similar chicane on the other side of the street. In his head he perhaps thinks, "thank God she didn't have to see the dog get killed."

Because she's only a yard in front of him as he eases up and gets ready to grab her.

But she takes one more step, a skip of a dance step down the kerb, and a blur of silver metal wipes her from his world.

39.

"Any sign of Tony?"

"No," Sophie informs me, as we stop and I locate the railing with my left hand.

Un-attaching my arm from her, I tug my cigarettes and lighter from my pocket, and spark one up.

"Lorry, you're shaking," she needlessly points out to me.

I nod, and double-draw on my smoke.

"What do we do now? I have to get back, Lorry, I'm the lead detective on the murders, remember?"

"I know. Look, if you want to go, I'll stay here."

"I can't leave you here, Lorry."

"He'll come here. I need to stay."

"How long for?"

"For as long as it takes."

"Okay. I'll get someone out here. They can stay with you, and I'll shoot off as soon as I'm relieved. How does that sound?"

"That's fine. Thanks, Sofe."

"Hang on. There's a black cab parked on the opposite street. Is Tony using your taxi?"

"I'm not sure, to be honest. I've lost track. He may be."

"It's facing away from us...and I can't see the plate through the railings," she tells me, and I sense from her voice being strained that she's stretching up on her toes.

"Is there a sticker in the rear window, looks like a vinyl record, with 'I've got 12 inches!' written on it?"

"Erm, I can't read the writing, but yes, I'd say that's what it looks like."

"That's my cab."

"Here we go, the door's opening. It's Tony."

"Go away!" is all he shouts across the road at us.

"No," I reply with a shake of my head.

"This is my problem, Lorry. I need to deal with this."

"Yes you do, but you don't have to do that alone."

"You worked it out, then?"

I'm unsure what I'm supposed to have worked out. Is this a confession?

"Yes. We need to talk about it, Tony?"

Traffic speeds between us, causing an almost staccato effect on our words.

"I got it late last night," he bawls.

What does he mean by that, got what?

"How?"

"A combination of things. The dog link, and some of the injuries mirrored what happened to my sister. I couldn't shake it, so I went to my dad's house. He wasn't there, and hadn't been for a while, but there was a shrine laid out to her. And I found a list..."

"Of song titles?"

"Yes. You?"

"Lanie gave me a countdown of her top five choices at medical school, and it clicked in to place."

I hope he can't see the relief I feel. It's his dad doing this!

"I went to his allotment, Lorry."

"And?"

"Dogs."

"How do you mean?"

"I don't know how many, but I started digging, and came across at least a dozen bodies buried. The brutality..."

"I know, Tony. Come back now, mate, please."

"I can't, Lorry. How can I come back after this? Sophie, I'm sorry for doubting you."

"Oh, Tony, no! That's fine. You were doing your job, that's

all."

"But I told you what I'd do to you if this had anything linking it to you. I'd be a fucking hypocrite if I didn't apply that same rule to myself, wouldn't I?"

"No, Tony. You said something at a very stressful time. Maggie was lying butchered just a few feet away from us..."

"But I meant it. I found the knife."

"Knife?" Sophie shouts.

"The bread knife. The one he used on Maggie. It was in his shed at the allotment."

"He's not your dad, Tony!" I shout suddenly.

"What?" he calls.

"Yes, what?" Sophie whispers to me.

"The man you think is your father, isn't."

"What do you mean?"

"Janine ran the family check. You're on the database for elimination purposes, but no match came up."

There's no immediate reply. I don't know if that revelation is a good or bad thing for him to hear. It changes things, I'm pretty sure of that.

"I still don't know what that means," he calls eventually.

"it means that you were either adopted, or your mum had an affair, Tony. Either way, that man isn't your father."

"It's still personal. It's still to do with me."

"You were a nine year old boy, Tony. What the fuck were you meant to do?"

"She was on my watch."

"So was Kate. So were my eyes!"

"Yeah, and I've tried everything I can to put that right."

"So that's it? It was all simply you putting things right - easing your fucking conscience?"

He doesn't answer.

"Just leave me alone to do what I need to do."

"And how are you going to do that? Have you got any idea what the next song title relates to?"

"Have you?"

"No."

"There you go, then. If I'm off the clock, I don't have to play by the rules."

"And what, end up in prison?"

"If that's what it takes."

I've had enough of the self-pitying dross. My ears tell me there's a lull in the traffic coming from my right. With a sudden motion, I drop my cigarette on the floor and step in to the road.

Something locks up, a heart-stopping whine of rubber on road, but I don't alter my pace as I rapidly stride towards the centre point. A horn blasts in my ears, and an angry shout comes from a lowered window, just as Sophie screams my name.

My toe catches the lip of the low kerb at the centre, but not enough to trip me, so I keep going, judging things wrongly and planting my foot squarely on top of the kerb down to the other carriageway.

"Lorry!" Sophie screams again, as something heavier and less able to stop locks its wheels to my left, a shriek coming from someone female who must be observing.

I'm slammed in to, lifted off my feet, and flung backwards. I rotate half a horizontal turn in midair, and come to rest on top of Tony Alliss, his back and shoulders taking all the impact, his beefy arms absorbing the shock.

"Fucking idiot," is all he hisses in my ear.

"Is this that homo-erotic thing manifesting itself again, Tony?"

For any number of reasons, I start laughing. Mostly I do it because I don't know what else to do.

Tony joins in, our bodies sandwiched on a narrow strip of pavement at the centre of a busy road, his arms clutching me to him. In that clinch we both reverberate with a kind of perverse mirth.

He lifts me off him, and sits me on the ground, him rising to a sitting position next to me.

"Shall we go and catch this bastard, Tony?"

"Yeah," is all he says, pulling me up on my feet.

"Are you back, Boss?" Sophie calls from her side of the street.

"Sofe, get back to HQ, and run that end. I'll take Lorry with me, and see what we can come up with. Note the time; six-thirty in the evening. We have five and a half hours until it's game on for victim number nine. 'Rivers Of Babylon'. Focus all resources on the river..."

"We already are, Tony."

"Contact me on Lorry's phone."

40.

"I keep thinking of things," Tony tells me, as we sit in the cab and try to fathom what to do next. Or, rather, what our killer is likely to do next.

"Like what?"

"Things I should have noticed before now, things that might have got us to where we are sooner."

"Again, like what?"

"My sister loved pop music. She'd dance round the living room with the radio on. She'd make me dance with her. She loved the chart show on a Sunday, Lorry. That was her favourite thing. We'd sit and listen to it, from start to finish. It was the only thing that could hold her attention at that age. Christ above, it's how she learnt to count.

"And the injuries were similar, as well as other factors. My Dad...Frank Alliss. Now that I think back on it, he was angry at all the things I've been seeing, the tube down my little sister's throat, and the one up her behind. That's what he did to the doctor with the gin bottle, and the student in the derelict building. It was mirroring what they did to her, but escalating it.

"She didn't die immediately, she was a tough little thing. She hung on for ten days in a coma, as they tried to ascertain the level of brain damage and likelihood of recovery. There was no chance, but they have to give you hope."

"I'm sorry, Tony."

"Ah, it was a long time ago."

"Do you think he went for Maggie to get at you? Is this all done to get at you?"

"Probably. He blamed me."

"What about your mum?"

"She was...she had depression, Lorry. It was a pretty shit time all round, really. She married the wrong man, and they were too young...he was hard. On her, and on us kids. Ah, what a fucking mess," he breathes, and goes quiet.

I need to keep his mind working, not allow him to sink.

"So, in addition to the songs, we have a link through the type of death?"

"Er, yes, from what I can gather. And, in some cases, a link through the choice of victim."

"Explain."

"Well, we have a doctor for starters, and Frank blamed them for not doing enough. It was a busy day, with the jubilee celebrations, and at one point he went ballistic because she was being tended by a student."

"Go on."

"There was a dancer in the hospital. She was screaming in pain, driving him insane. She'd fallen off a float and twisted her ankle, that was all, but she was making a meal of it. He went mad, shouting about his little girl being really hurt. The police are an obvious one, and he wasn't happy with the investigation. He felt the driver should have been prosecuted. He wanted someone to pin it on. Apart from me, I mean.

"The tramp and his dog, I think he targeted because he believed the dog to be a stray living on the streets. He spent months looking for the dog, Lorry, months. He'd make me describe it to him over and over again.

"What else? The restauranteur matches the driver of the car that hit Gabby. He was on his way to work, opening up for the lunchtime trade, having delivered stuff to a party somewhere in Sutton, I think. He was running late, but I don't think he stood a chance.

"The MASH woman is obvious, because of the stray dog connection, but I think the suicide bit relates to the people who he felt let Gabby down. He said that if they had any conscience, they should hang themselves for failing his little girl."

"And what about today's victim?" I ask.

"Blondie, 'Sunday Girl'." he confirms. "There was another girl on life-support, in the next room to my sister. She was the same age, and had been brought in a couple of days before. She survived, and the day they switched off Gabby's machine, we walked past her door, and saw her eating ice cream."

"Ice cream?" I ask, confusion in my tone.

"There's a line in the song about ice-cream. And she was a little blonde girl. Frank was convinced race played a part, that they neglected Gabby because she was black."

"Wow. I hate to say this, but it's really well conceived, isn't it?"

"He isn't stupid, my old...Frank."

"When did you last see him?"

"About twenty years ago, at mum's funeral. He was still angry at me, but I was big and ugly enough not to have to worry about him by then. Or so I thought."

"How old is he?"

"He'll be mid-sixties, Lorry. My Mum was only sixteen when she had me, and he was a year older, I think."

"And is he trained - to kill people, I mean?"

"He was military, Lorry. Joined up when he was sixteen, straight from school. He had it hard. There weren't many black squaddies back then. I think it was that experience that made him so mean. Anyway, he did eight years before he was released."

"Released?"

"Yeah. He had some trouble, but it was kept quiet, and they shipped him out. There was no big deal about it. They wanted him gone, and he'd had enough. I know he was in Yemen in 1967, and I think he was in Borneo prior to that. He'd never talk about any of it, and there isn't much in the files. Trust me, I've looked."

"He must have kept himself in shape."

"Oh yes. He was always a fitness fanatic, strong as an ox."

"Sorry to ask this, but I need all the pieces..."

"Go on."

"You said the injuries he's inflicted relate to Gabby. Can you be more specific?"

"I suppose so. We've covered the bottle and the pipe. Head injury to the dancer is obvious, Maggie was supposed to have been suffocated, which is what happened to Gabby when they switched off the machine and she couldn't breathe unaided. The tramp's dog, we now believe, was dragged by a car, which is what happened to Gabby. The burns on Paolo Adams' face match those on my sister's face when she was dragged along the road surface. Also, the mincing of his hand matches Gabby, who lost hers. The hanging, I think is asphyxiation again, and I don't have any details on today's victim, but I bet it'll be similar."

"Right, he's reaching the end. What isn't covered?"

"She lost an eye. I just had another thought; Paolo was sealed in his freezer, just as Gabby was after she died. There were so many clues, Lorry, and I missed them all..."

"Well, if we're going to find him, we need everything you remember."

Drawing a breath, he tells me, "she was a mess, Lorry, a right state. There wasn't a bit of her that wasn't bruised, grazed, cut or missing. And that was just the bits we could see. She was mangled inside almost as badly. The worst bit of it all for me was her hair. She was so proud of her..."

I give him a few seconds to regain his composure.

"She loved her hair, and my Aunt would braid it for her. She wouldn't leave the house without having her hair tidy, even at that age. And half of it got scrubbed from her head, the rest following when they operated on her brain."

I have no idea what to say to him. Carrying on in the same thread is all I can do.

"Did her hair wind your...did it annoy Frank particularly?"

"Yes. Yes it did. He told them to put her hair back."

"What else made him angry, Tony?"

"Me, I made him angry."

I go to dismiss that, but suddenly realise that I can't, that Tony could well be a target in all of this. Moreover, it's probable that he may be the ultimate objective.

"Do the Boney M and Rod Stewart tracks mean anything to you personally?"

"The Rod Stewart one, yes. I took the radio in on the Sunday when Gabby was in hospital. It was stupid, but I thought she might...I thought it might help her to listen to the chart show. Frank sat there fuming, chewing his fingers till they bled. Mum was drugged up to her eyeballs, so I felt as though it was all on me, do you know what I mean?"

I nod.

"Here's a thought," he says.

"What?"

"The place where I get my hair cut; it's called First Cut."

"What's that, like a salon?"

"Yes, why?"

"Do you get your manicure-pedicure-bikini-wax done whilst you're at it?"

He chuckles, and throws in, "well, it looks like you cut your own hair!"

That's better. He's taking the piss. It can't be a bad thing.

"Sophie goes to one of those places where fish eat the dead skin on your feet."

"So does Janine!"

"I told her, if I did that, I'd be left with stumps!"

"Talking of stumps, are you going to play cricket again this year?"

"I don't know. I took a catch and hit a six. It's never going to get any better than that, is it?"

"Good attitude, Lorry."

"Well...says the man who was all set to throw away his career and liberty for vengeance."

"I'm serious. Look, you sat around moping over Kate for over four years, but then you opened up a bit, and Sophie enters stage left."

"It's not better than Kate, Tony."

"No, but I know from how you've been that it's good. It's different, that's all. It doesn't have to be better or worse."

He's right, of course.

"Hey, how did the guide dog trial go?" he suddenly remembers.

"Ah, well, you know...okay, I think."

"Lorry?" He waits fruitlessly, and adds, "I'll find out anyway."

"Not great, if I'm honest. I freaked out, and spent the time in a pub. They had to come and find me."

Before he can react, I add, "besides, it's no big deal now, as I have Sophie!"

"I'm not sure the harness will fit her."

"No."

"And it'll shred her knees shuffling around on all fours."

"Yes."

"And given what you told me about what happened today, she may not be around, Lorry."

"No," I concede.

"So, you could probably use a guide dog, then..."

"Yes."

"You're a fucking idiot."

"Yes. Thanks. You bastard."

"Apparently."

41.

"Well, it's one minute after midnight," Alliss feels the need to point out.

"I know. The news is on the radio."

We're sat in the cab, me eating a banana I made Tony inspect for brown bruises before getting him to pick off the stringy pith.

"I've got Sophie concentrating all our resources along the river, with most of them to the south. We have no tangible clue as to where he might strike, so we have to get lucky."

"That's about the size of it. Did you track down the people linked to your sister's death?"

"Some of them. The guy who was driving the car is in an old people home in Crawley. A lot of them are dead, Lorry. It's been half a lifetime. Anyway, we have police presence where we know them to be."

"It's probably a waste of time, anyway. He's not targeted anyone directly linked up to now."

"This is the bit I hate, the not knowing, the waiting for something to happen."

"I spent four years doing that."

"Get some shut-eye, Lorry, this could be a long night."

*****

"What time is it?" I mutter through a sticky mouth. I need to brush my teeth.

"Ten past seven."

"Nothing?"

"We're still sitting here, aren't we?"

"Don't you need a cup of tea?"

"Not really, but then, I wasn't snoring for several hours."

"Aren't you hungry?"

"I haven't got much of an appetite, Lorry."

"Don't you need to use the toilet?"

"I'll find a cafe, Lorry!"

*****

If my eyes worked they'd be bleary, as we sit in the greasy spoon, me having devoured six rounds of toast that Tony had to butter for me, my hands cradling a second hot mug of tea.

"He knows we're waiting, doesn't he?"

"Yes."

"And he knows it's driving us mad, doesn't he?" I add.

"Yes."

"It's the perfect power-play, if you think about it. I don't think we'll even find the body today, given that train of thought. He could commit his crime, and keep us hanging on way beyond his ten day countdown."

"I'm not so sure. I think he'll want to show me that he's better than me, that I can't keep people safe."

"Why, because you failed to keep Gabby safe?"

"Exactly. He wants me to feel powerless."

"And he wants it to hurt you, just as he was hurt."

"And that."

"Shit. Janine might be a target!" I suddenly think.

"Relax. I've already thought of that. I'm having her watched."

"Gabby must have been his daughter, correct?"

"I don't know. I suppose. Until yesterday, I thought he was my father."

"Do you think he knew that you weren't his biological son?"

"He told me I wasn't. But I thought he meant it in a disowning way, not literally."

"When was that?"

"When my sister died, when I was nine."

"What did your mum do?"

"Nothing. She was out of her tree, Lorry, as I told you. And she was scared of him. She'd just sit around staring at nothing all day."

"How did she die?"

"Overdose."

"Accidental?"

"I have no idea."

"You didn't investigate it?"

"No. It wasn't a bad thing that she died, Lorry."

Strewth, what do I say to that?

Thankfully, my phone rings, and he snatches it up.

"Go on, Sofe...nothing at all? Alright, thanks. Keep going."

Bizarrely, 'Rivers Of Babylon' comes on the radio in the cafe. On reflection I suppose it isn't that strange, as some music database will have flagged it up as being number one on this day, so it was inserted in the playlist.

We sit listening to it for a minute, neither one of us bothering to point it out.

"Bone!" Tony exclaims.

"Hey?"

"Boney M..."

He's thinking it through.

With a click of his fingers, he says, "Frank got really mad at the guy who came round to ask about organ donation. There was something about bone marrow."

"Boney M."

"Yes. It's a long shot."

"But worth sniffing around."

"It's better than sitting here doing nothing."

He's on to Colin, asking him to locate any donor centres or administrative places close to the river.

It takes Colin all of a minute to give him what he needs.

"Woodbridge On Thames," he raps in my ear, as he helps me up, "we went there for a day once as kids. It was Frank's idea of a family holiday. Shit…"

"What?"

"It was on the weekend before the jubilee."

*****

"We're probably wide of the mark, Lorry, and nothing's been reported from here," Tony tells me as he unloads me from the taxi, "but we may as well have a sniff around."

To be honest, it's nice to be out of a seat and have chance to stretch my legs. It's shaping up to be another warm June day. So far so good, on the summer weather front. Still, give it time.

"Do you know the name of this building?" he asks me as we walk over an even surface.

"Obviously not, but go on, enlighten me."

"The Riverside."

"Okay, it ties in."

"Morning," Tony calls out as we enter a building.

"How can I help you, gentlemen?" a woman asks.

"DS Alliss, Metropolitan Police."

"Any identification?"

"Not on me, no."

"And he is…?"

"Blind."

"O-kay."

"My office should have been in touch, to see if everything's all right."

"Ah, yes. We did get a call. Normal day here, as I told them, so it seems you've had a wasted journey."

"Anybody not show up for work today?" I ask.

"People don't clock in and out, sir, and we run flexible shifts, so it's almost certain some members of staff won't be here."

"How many staff?" Alliss snaps. He gets impatient so easily.

"Full-time?"

"Start with that."

"Fourteen."

"And part-time?"

"Approximately two dozen. Mostly field based on commission."

"Security?"

"Yes, we have an alarm system, and a man who patrols the premises between eight in the evening and six in the morning. Look, I should really insist on seeing some identifi..."

"Who's the guy in the picture?" Tony wants to know.

"Our CEO."

"Where's he from?"

"Er, Iraq, originally."

"What's that?" Tony asks suddenly, prompted by nothing that I can see.

"It's an organ transportation box..."

"The number - is that right?"

"Number 78. It could be. It's just an empty box that needs sterilising."

"How did it get here?"

"A courier dropped it off half an hour ago. Look, it'll be empty, I can show..."

*****

I'm on the ground. No idea how I got here. My head rings with a constant screech. I taste dust in my mouth. And blood. I think I taste blood. Or rusty metal. I can't think for long. The noise in my head...

Everything's truncated. I feel my eyes move. But I remember that they don't work. I sense it's dark, anyway.

I can't move. My arms and legs won't respond to my will. I take a breath. But it's acrid. I cough it out of my lungs.

I feel hot. But as soon as I've thought that, I feel cold.

Over the screech I hear my pulse. It rises in my ears, boom-boom, boom-boom. Above the ringing. My fingertips begin to tingle.

Am I dead?

No. There would be no noise, no screech, no pulse.

There's nothing when you die. But I don't know that. Not for sure.

Am I dying?

Yes, I think I am.

If I die will my eyes work again?

Will I see Kate? Waiting for me.

There's a crash, weight coming off me, and I'm moving. Upwards. Ascending. I'm being wrenched by the strong hand of something. Pulled up, out and clear.

Floating, in fact.

Have I left my body?

No, it's still here. Along with the screech in my head.

The tingling's receding. I move my fingers. My toes.

And I breathe. Cool air, that floods in to me, and clears my mind. It's like dirt, thick mud, being hosed off a window, the removal of which allows me to see in the way that I've been seeing for the past four and half years, since I was blinded, by Tony Alliss, the night Kate died, on our anniversary in our pub...Lanie!

Tony is carrying me one-handed, I sense, given the strain on my abdomen and the tautness around my testicles. He has his hand down the back of my jeans, my leather belt in his grip, and he's running with me like that, I gather from the motion.

He's simultaneously shouting in to a phone.

I weigh one-hundred and eighty-six pounds, or thirteen and a quarter stone, and he can carry me like that, and run. And think and act and speak.

He drops me, and I feel fresh soft grass on the side of my face, as he barks, "don't move!" His voice sounds very far away.

His feet depart, back the way we've just come, and I have no intention of going anywhere.

42.

"Why are you listening to Ray Charles, 'The Spirit Of Christmas'?"

"How do you mean?"

"Well, it's June the sixth."

"I know, but I pulled it out by mistake. You must have mislabeled it."

"I haven't."

"To be honest, it didn't register. It was just on."

"Are you feeling okay?"

"Yeah, I'm fine. You?"

"Good as new. Has the ringing in your ears gone?"

"Just about."

"That was a close shave, Lorry."

"Yes, I got that impression."

"Did you call Lanie?"

"Yes. Thankfully she hadn't seen the news. How many dead?"

" Two. And another two in hospital. I need a beer."

"Me too." I don't volunteer the fact I had three as soon as

I came through the door, to steady my nerves.

"I don't get it," Tony calls from the kitchen.

"What don't you get?"

"Why an explosion?" he says, entering the living room and handing me a tin can, "where's the violence in that?"

"Oh, I thought it was pretty fucking violent."

"But not in the same way. It wasn't hands-on. He didn't see it, and get to exact revenge with his own hands like before."

"So a complete change of MO, as you lot term it?"

"Exactly. It's unusual, Lorry."

"Perhaps he knew we were getting closer, so shifted tack."

"Maybe."

"But you're not buying that, I gather from your tone, Tone?"

"I don't know. Why else would he do that?"

"You know him better than me."

"No. Apparently, I don't know him one bit. Do you mind if I change this album? It's doing my head in, Christmas music in June."

"Knock yourself out."

He doesn't change the album at all, but switches it off. He wants to talk, I gather from that.

I begin with, "he's only got one more hit after this one, so perhaps he wanted more impact, more devastation. Two dead and two hospitalised is a decent score."

"Maybe. Doesn't it strike you as odd that the explosion happened when we were there?"

"That you were there, more pertinently?"

"Yep. Was he sending me a message, Lorry?"

"What, that he can get you?"

"Something like that."

"How did he know you'd be there just as that box was

opened?"

"He couldn't."

"I mean, how did he even know the police would twig it, and even if they did, that you'd be the officer in attendance?"

He thinks about it, as he takes a swig of his beer that he sucks through his teeth. "You're right. It must have been coincidence."

"You don't believe in coincidences."

"No, not usually."

"You're not thinking of an internal leak, are you?"

"I don't want to think that."

"No. It couldn't happen, Tony. You only twigged the link as we sat in the cafe and the song came on the radio. Half an hour later, we were there. And the box only arrived half an hour before we showed up. There was no time for him to have done all of that."

"No, I suppose not. I'm getting paranoid."

"Besides, who knew?"

"Colin, Sophie..."

"So, coincidence, then?"

"It must be," Tony confirms.

"Anyway, what's done is done. It's what comes next that we need to focus on."

"Agreed, and given this escalation, it could be anything," Tony says.

"Just a thought..."

"Go on."

"Well, this whole explosion thing could be a bloody clever move."

"Why?"

"Because...I don't know what I'm trying to say. Look, it's got us confused, and it's resulted in our minds going in a multitude of different directions."

"So, what? It's a con?"

"Yeah, why not. A cover, if you like. I think he always had a final target in mind, and by dropping a bombshell like today, it looks like he's escalating, whereas in fact, he has no intention of doing that. Does that make sense?"

"Yeah, I know what you mean."

"Then let's take a step back, and think individual again. We have two tracks, 'I Don't Want To Talk About It' and 'First Cut Is The Deepest'. What do they mean to you, and, moreover, did anything happen that day you took a radio to the hospital so Gabby could listen to the countdown, something that could relate to either song?"

"Well, the obvious one is the surgeon who told Frank there was no hope. Surgeons cut, right?"

"Right. And what was Frank's reaction to that?"

"What do you reckon?"

"Bad, eh?"

"Oh yes. He put the man on the ground, face down, and threatened to kill him."

"Really?"

"I remember it like it was yesterday, Lorry. Every detail."

"And where's that surgeon now?"

"Dead. Natural causes, before you ask."

"Does he have a daughter?"

He's on to Colin before the words have stopped sounding in the room. Two minutes later, Colin calls him back.

"No, two sons. But get this..."

"What?"

"He has a three year-old great-granddaughter."

He contacts Sophie, and I hear him detail what needs to happen to make the family safe.

"Lorry's fine, Sofe. I'm at his place now," he reports in.

"She's worried about you," he tells me, hanging up.

I smile. It's nice having someone worry about me like that, even if I don't know how we stand at the moment. I've not had chance to see her since we parted at the road where Gabby died.

"What about the other track?" I push on.

"It doesn't spark anything. I mean, he made it clear he'd never speak to me again, but I didn't see that as a bad thing."

"Was there any sort of grief counseling?"

"It was 1977, so not really. I mean, it was offered, kind of. I went to see some psych-doc a couple of times, and there was a bit of that at the school, as well."

"What about Frank?"

"No. He'd have seen that as weak. Besides, he wouldn't have wanted anyone exploring his mind."

"Too many demons?"

"Yes. And he was that kind of bloke, Lorry, the sort who intimidate by silence. I always got a sense he did it because he had nothing to say, and that it made him look wiser and smarter than he was. He'd shout, and he'd use his fists, but he never expressed any emotion."

"Other than anger."

"Other than that, yes."

"Who else did he blame?"

"He blamed everyone, from me and Mum, to the local authority for closing the street and allowing the party, to the bleeding school for giving Gabby a day off. I mean everyone, Lorry."

"But mostly you?"

"Yes. Mostly me."

"And not himself?"

"No. Not that I saw."

"And who do you blame, Tony?"

He doesn't answer.

Instead, he rises from the leather chair, puts Ray Charles back on, and heads off to get more beer.

"Christmas music in June," he scoffs, "completely inappropriate."

43.

By the time it registers that I'm awake, I'm already sitting upright in bed. My joints and back ache; my throat's parched. I need water. The last remnants of the ringing still exist in my ears.

"What's the time?" I say aloud, even though I know I'm alone.

Tony headed back to the office in the afternoon. He's due to collect me at ten thirty tonight, so that we can get to London for the new day, and await what will happen.

It must be before midnight, I gather.

Desperately, I hang on to the thought I was having in my semi-conscious state. It was about that Ray Charles LP I was playing, the Christmas one.

I swing my feet down and find the floor. Touching myself, I ascertain that I'm naked. There's no time to shower, so I pad through to the bathroom, splash water on my face and hastily brush my teeth.

My clothes were clean on yesterday after the explosion, so I re-dress in them, all the time thinking my thought, the one I have to hang on to.

Stepping in to my shoes, soft leather uppers and durable soles, I locate the door frame and exit my bedroom, silently negotiating the corridor and hallway that deliver me to the kitchen.

I gulp down a glass of cool tap water, followed by another, and fill the kettle, my throat still parched and raw from the dust. As it boils I drop a bag in a mug and add sugar; a Tinker's Cup.

Keep the thought in mind.

With feathery movements of my fingers, I locate the radio and switch it on. It's some shitty pap-pop current hit by a bloke with a vocal effect making his voice sound alien, but, no doubt, better than it actually is. He's probably some pretty boy, which more than makes up for his lack of talent. Not to me, it doesn't, as all I can do is hear him.

The kettle clicks off, so I pour the water. The awful song ends, but there's another one cued up and ready to follow on. The DJ must have nipped off for a slash, I think to myself.

Ensuring the spoon isn't sitting on the teabag, thus killing the infusion process, I stir things up, and squeeze the bag against the side of the cup as best I can. I want a builder's cuppa, something to wake me up and sharpen my mind.

I stretch, my shoulder-blades stiff, my spine opening up as I raise my hands above my head and roll my neck. I feel like a building fell on me.

The tuned-in radio gets tuned out in my head. I vaguely know the song, a cover-version of something that should be too recent to warrant a cover-version. Then I remember that it's over twenty years old, and was in the charts when I met Kate. The knowledge makes me feel old, not helped by my aches and pains.

Milk gets added to my brew, and I take a tentative sip. It's a good one. Some are, some aren't. It's luck of the draw.

The cover-version winds down, and I'm glad of it. Very seldom is a cover better than an original. Some are, The Stranglers doing 'Walk On By', for example, as much as I love the Dionne Warwick version.

The DJ's blandly droning on about the artists he played when he went for a pee, so I decide to have one myself.

It's easier to sit than stand, particularly first thing after rising, so that's what I do.

And as I'm sitting on the seat, in mid-flow, the radio presenter's voice registers in my ever-sharpening brain, and, for the second time since awaking, I utter out loud, "what's the fucking time?"

I'm up before I've really finished, straining to hear the broadcast as the ditty they play before the news reaches my ears.

"Did he say four...? Did you say four?" I shout, despite the pointlessness of it.

It'll be easier to wait than try to locate my phone. Wait for the news to finish. They always tell you the time at the end.

"...and that's the news, at three minutes past five."

It has to be in the evening, correct? It felt as though I'd been asleep for longer than an hour, but perhaps not. Could I have slept for thirteen hours? It's possible, but unlikely.

No, because Tony was picking me up at half past ten...oh, fuck it! I was supposed to call him.

The DJ I heard is the one who does the graveyard shift, but perhaps he's standing in for the regular drive-time guy. Yes, that would make sense. It's holiday season.

On the house phone, I locate the bobble on the number five, and call Tony's number. On the third attempt, I get the number right, and it rings.

"Yeah, Lorry?"

"Is it yesterday, or today?"

"What?"

"Nothing. Er, what time is it?"

"Just after five."

"Morning or afternoon?"

"In the morning, Lorry...are you alright?"

"Fuck it, Tony. Why didn't you come and get me?"

"Because you didn't ring, and I guessed you needed rest after yesterday."

"It's not Rod bloody Stewart...it's nothing to do with that!" I shout.

"What, slow down?"

"It's the Sex Pistols, Tony! 'God Save The Queen'! That was the best seller that week in 1977, but they rigged the chart because it was deemed completely inappropriate on jubilee week!"

"I'm on my way - give me fifteen minutes, tops."

And he's gone.

44.

"There," Tony Alliss snaps decisively, and thuds his finger on a table.

"Where?" I have to ask.

"Boat on the Thames," Tony informs me, "midday, sailing from Tower Bridge to Parliament."

"It sounds about right, and it's what the Sex Pistols did that day in 1977," I confirm. "Three miles?"

"Just under."

"That's a hell of a lot of river to cover, Tony," Sophie points out, and meets no argument.

"And the crowds won't help," Colin adds.

"Can it be cancelled?" Sophie suggests.

"No. There's no real proof of a direct threat, so they won't act. We can up the security level, but it'll be as high as it gets, anyway. It's the Queen. It means we have six hours to either find Frank Alliss, or to protect Her Majesty. Lorry, any thoughts?"

"It's all speculative. If he's true to form, it'll relate to the song, so I would think a pistol will be the weapon used, but I can't be sure. The explosion yesterday has thrown a spanner in much of the supposition we were working to. It isn't violent in the same way as the others, but the act itself is all that's important here. He's blaming everyone, so why not the Queen? In his mind, if there was no jubilee, his daughter wouldn't have been out, and if there wasn't food around, the dog wouldn't have been there, and so on. She's the catalyst. Take the Queen out, and all other factors become an irrelevance. He'll be well planned on this one. It's what he's thought about for decades, so it won't be improvised like the others. All of that was him exorcising his anger. This time he'll be cool and calm. He'll know he only has one chance, so it'll be well planned."

"What else, Lorry? Come on, give us everything you've got."

"Okay, erm, he'll not care about himself once this final act is performed. He may even use that pistol on himself. This smacks of a final hurrah. Why now? He may be ill, something terminal, or he might simply have had enough of life or encountered some other trigger that's brought it all back to him. He knows he can't get away with this. I think all the other killings, to some degree, have been red-herrings, and this was always the objective."

"Then why didn't he simply perform this one and not alert us to his presence and state of mind through the other nine attacks?" Colin asks, I presume, of me.

"I think that probably has something to do with Tony, Colin. He's showing that he's the better man, that Tony can't keep anyone safe. It's a way of apportioning blame, of highlighting what he believes to be Tony's failure, whilst confirming to himself that it wouldn't have happened on his watch. The truth of it is, Frank Alliss feels a huge amount of guilt for what happened to Gabby, but can't process and deal with that. Okay, so Tony was with her, but more pertinently, Frank wasn't," I drum out, a lot of it taken directly from my Emotional Therapist in relation to myself. "What was he doing that day, Tony?"

"I'm not sure, but he had no intention of partaking in the celebrations, that I do remember. It was our mother and aunt who tied the ribbon in Gabby's hair, and got us ready. He was probably watching television, or brooding with a bottle of rum. To be honest, I don't even remember him being at home that day. He was probably out, seeing how the weather was so nice. Or down the gym working out."

Nothing in Tony's recollection triggers any thoughts, so I push on. "He'll need to be close in to pull this off with a pistol, and he'll know he'll only get one chance. So, what, within a few feet? How would someone get in such close proximity? Is she doing a meet and greet?"

"Yes, but with a select group on disembarkation, and they will have treble-vetted everyone there," Sophie tells us.

"Get the security to re-check anyway, Sofe, please," Tony instructs.

She does it instantly.

"As a boat crew-member?" Colin suggests.

"They'll have checked them, as well. But, yes, Sophie - same thing."

"Media?" I say.

"No, it's a very closed event, and the only press there are the regular couple of elite royal correspondents," Sophie answers.

"How would he do this, Tony? You know him better than

any of us."

"I don't know."

"Okay," I ask, "how would you do it?"

He takes a brief period to compose his thoughts.

"Another boat makes no sense, security will be too tight, and it's extremely difficult making a shot over two moving craft with a pistol. It's the same thing with an air attack via a drone say, or from underwater. It feels overly-complicated. Does he want an audience for this? Not necessarily, no, I don't believe he does. It'll be enough for him to achieve his objective. If he wanted plaudits, we'd have heard from him through the media by now. This is purely mission-orientated. So, if all that matters is the ultimate objective, I wouldn't use a pistol at all. And if that's the case, we can't rule out anything."

"Do you think he knows that we've worked out the link?" I ask Tony.

"He's an arrogant bastard, so he'll think not, but he's a planner with a military background, so he'll have allowed for that."

"We have to go with the pistol," I suggest, "because, in all honesty, we don't have anything if we don't. It makes sense. All the other killings have been linked to the songs, one or two a little crowbarred in, but this one was his starting point, I reason, so it'll have been the focus all along. I honestly believe he'll use a pistol on the Queen at the river today."

"Then we go with that," Tony states decisively.

"Agreed," Sophie confirms, as he must look to her.

"It makes sense," Colin adds.

"Right," Tony growls, rising from where I imagine he must have been half-sitting on a desk, "Sofe, you take the Tower Bridge end, with Dave and his team. I'll have Jamal and his section with me at the Westminster Bridge end. Colin, you run Funnel from here, and let's string everyone else out along the bank, north and south."

"What about me?" I ask.

"You stay here with Colin."

"No, not a bloody chance! I've been practically blown up, my trip to America cancelled, which has cost me quite a lot of money incidentally, then there was almost being run-over, the business with Lanie's bloke, I've been..."

"Shut up. You come with me, but you do as I tell you."

Alliss takes my arm, as I begin singing 'God Save The Queen' in my head, matching the beat to my steps, or the other way round, so that I'm pulling Tony more than he's pushing me along the corridor and in to the lift.

"He might use a bomb, Tony."

"Why?"

"Because he already has once, and it's in the lyrics."

"Okay."

He snaps my idea in to his radio as we exit the lift and our feet continue to crack out the beat on the tile.

"Does the boat have a figurehead?"

"It's an old sailing vessel, so it may."

"Get it checked. It's in the song."

Again, he's on to Colin through his radio.

As I reflect on the fact Sophie barely greeted me, and never once took my hand.

45.

Crowds were something I didn't like even when I could see. Gather together more than six people, and it makes me a little uncomfortable. As a consequence, we move down to the river bank and settle at a railing.

The inaction allows self-doubt to creep in.

"We could have this all wrong, Tony."

"Well, it's this or Rod Stewart."

"Are you not a Rod fan?"

"Actually, I don't mind him. You?"

"I don't own a record by him, which probably says a lot. That said, no, I don't mind him at all."

I can only guess that Tony's receiving information via a receiver in his ear, because he tells me, "no problems on boarding, the party's on board, the vessel on the move and heading our way. ETA, on schedule, twelve minutes. Colin, have you got eyes on us?"

He must answer affirmatively, as Tony goes back to watching the crowd behind me, his hand twisting on my elbow as he does.

We're down a slope from Westminster Bridge at the pier. The briny Thames reaches my nostrils; that in-wash from the sea.

This is where Kate and I were going to walk that night; close to here, at least. We probably wouldn't have crossed the river at Waterloo Bridge, but we may have used the Jubilee at Hungerford. It would have depended on how much fresh air Kate fancied, but we may have made it down as far as Westminster, and then grabbed a cab home.

We never made it. I opted for another drink, and to use the toilet, delaying us until the moment Kate's killer arrived.

That's how it works. I play it over and over, going through the details and identifying all the little things I could have done differently; the multitude of circumstances that, had they been off by just a fraction, would have had a huge impact on what transpired.

And I imagine that's how it is for Frank Alliss.

I readily concede that, given a chance, there are no measures I wouldn't take to punish the people who allowed that to happen to Kate. To the point that I wanted Debbie and Craig Russell charged with murder for their role in the passport scam.

My problem with all of that, is that it was Tony who let the gunman slip through his fingers. That's a confusing one. As far as I know, he's only ever taken his eye off the ball twice, and it resulted in everything happening right now, from Frank to my presence.

"Are you okay here for a couple of minutes?" he speaks in my ear.

"Where are you going?"

"There's quite a crowd behind us now. It's always like this. Word spreads. I want to go and have a sniff around. Plus, I'll be able to see better from off the bridge."

"Yeah, go."

"Two minutes. Don't move, don't touch anything."

I tut by way of reply.

My guess is that seven or eight minutes have passed since the twelve minute countdown. All I can do is wait for a crack of a pistol shot, or the safe arrival of the boat.

*****

True to his word, Tony's back within a couple of clicks, as he takes my elbow.

"Anything?" I ask him, but he must be listening to the reports as he doesn't reply.

The hand's wrong, I realise. It grips me too tightly, and pulls rather than guides. It holds me back and pulls me down, instead of making me feel light and supported.

Over the aroma of the water, I detect the whiff of stale

skin and hair, a man who hasn't washed in a while.

"Frank?" is all I say.

"Keep quiet," is his reply, his sour rum-soaked breath hitting my face.

I ignore his advice. "So you knew he'd bring me along?"

"That was a bonus."

"Where's Tony?"

"He's having a lie-down."

"Dead?"

"No. I want him to live with this."

"We're being watched. You won't get near."

"We'll see about that. At the moment, given the surveillance being above us, all they can see is a large black man in a black suit and white shirt keeping a blind man company. The dyed hair's a good match. He should really vary his wardrobe."

"So you knew he'd be here?"

"I hoped he'd piece it together."

"Do you know who I am?"

"Another victim of my son's...his negligence."

"He's not your son, you fucking idiot," I bark without warning.

His hand clenches even tighter on my arm.

"I disowned..."

"No!" I cut him off, "he's not your son. He never was. You really are stupid, aren't you? No wonder they kicked you out of the military."

His breathing's harder, a slight growl carried on a breath.

"You should stop talking."

"You should stop breathing."

Coming tighter to me, he jabs the end of what feels like a pistol in my flank.

He's about Tony's height, I gather now he's close, and I

would think a similar build given the force of his killings so far.

"Ha!" I scoff, "you'd probably miss from there. After all, you missed your daughter that day, ignoring your responsibilities. A nine year old boy left to tend a three year old sister. That was irresponsible. A mother driven to depressive instability by a bully of a husband. It's all on you, Frank. I don't know how you live with yourself."

"You really need to shut the fuck up now."

I can hear the boat approaching, as the crowd volume rises in anticipation, drowning it out.

"She really was your daughter, by the way. You managed to sire one of them, at least."

Frank moves me a few feet to my left, along the railing until it ends. If my memory serves, there's a covered walkway, and an open area where a car will be able to pick people up. That's his window of opportunity; between the two.

The displaced water laps and slaps up the concrete beneath my feet, stirring up the ocean smell even more.

Cheers emanate from the gathering a few dozen yards off behind me.

And my phone rings.

46.

"I need to take that," I calmly say to him.

"Leave it," he snarls, driving the gun in to the soft flesh under my ribs.

"It'll probably be my daughter."

It stalls him just a fraction, this knowledge that I have a daughter, just as he once did.

"I said leave it."

"No. If I'm going to die today, I want to hear her voice one final time. Even you must be able to understand that one, Frank."

Again, I feel him flinch as I nip a raw nerve.

I begin wrestling my phone from my pocket.

The truth is, it's probably Sophie or Colin wondering why Tony isn't communicating.

Hang on...he didn't know I had a daughter.

"Show it to me," he snaps, as the phone comes free of my pocket.

I do as he asks.

"Other way up."

I twist my wrist.

"What's your daughter's name?"

Shit, which way do I go on this? Lanie was going to set up different ring tones for people when she comes down in the summer.

"Sophie," I tell him.

"Okay, take the call, but be very fucking careful what you say."

"Hello darling!"

"Lorry...?"

"Yes, hi. Is everything okay?"

"Can you put Tony on the phone, his comms are down?"

"No, no, nothing much, just sitting in the garden."

There's a long pause while she processes what I said.

I fill it with, "yes, I had my cereals, and some toast. Don't worry about me."

"That's not Tony with you?"

"No, I've not heard anything."

A jab of the gun in my flesh sends a message that I should end the call.

"Shit, Lorry, I'm coming..."

"No problem. I love you..."

But she's gone.

"I never got to say that," Frank mutters as I place the phone back in my pocket.

My fingers hook up the small lighter-size article Trish slipped to me in the mobile home.

The boat's engine falls silent as the crowd behind us become more audible, speculating that they can see her, that she's coming. I hear a chain being unhooked as cameras click.

Cradling the item in my hand, and holding it against the side of my leg, I press the button.

A searing pain shoots through me as the blade unexpectedly materialises from the wrong side and slices in to my palm. Containing it, I bite down on my lower lip and almost silently allow the blade to fully open.

Louder cheers and a round of applause come from over my shoulder, and I feel Frank readying himself.

The way I figure it, Maggie was in a similar position, with Frank behind her, plastic being pulled over her face. She took out the bread knife in her bag, a bag she carried on her left hip, I know from being guided by her. My guess is that she drew it with her right hand with the business end sticking out past her little finger, her thumb locking it in place, and stabbed Frank on his right front side.

That's what I do.

And just as Frank wails out in pain, I hear a roar as Tony bellows, "Lorry, sweep shot!"

I sink down and forward, three gunshots snapping out, screams from the crowd, and a kerfuffle to my left as everything coming through the covered walkway gets backed up, voices urgently shouting "cover" and "down".

But I have nowhere to go, as my hands pointlessly flap at

the air looking for purchase.

47.

The water slaps my face, hard like a scolding, the surprising coldness whipping the breath from my lungs. Instinctively, I try to replace it, but draw in frigid brackish filth instead.

When I opted for cricket, swimming was one of the options I could have gone for. I didn't, because I can't swim.

Something in my brain tells me that the water here is only a couple of metres deep, but it's an irrelevance because I'm being pressed down or pulled down by a weight.

I don't know which, because all of my sense of up versus down is lost. I begin coughing, spluttering in more water that fills my nose and mouth and forces me to gag, letting in more and more, causing me to panic and convulse, as my clothing gets heavier and something continues to keep me beneath the surface.

I'm willing myself to relax, as I figure that will force my body to float upwards, towards the light I can't take in, but the air that I can.

Nothing happens.

Something taps my face, so I swipe at it, an image in my mind of eels crawling all over me, leeches attaching themselves to my skin, but my fingers tap on my sunglasses, those shields for my eyes, and send them away from me.

Reaching back over my own shoulder, I come in to contact with the opened up face that until recently belonged to Frank Alliss.

It's unknowable to me whether the fragments that filter

514

through my fingers are his brains or weeds from the water.

All sense of time is lost to me. I could have been here for days. I have to breathe, and more salty filth fills me fuller.

Every bit of me is full now, every cavity and hollow and nook.

48.

Her lips are on mine, soft and warm, and I can see her, still beautiful.

The light stings my eyes, that thing I haven't seen in years. That's what it is, light washing in to me and filling me, not water at all. And I should suck it all in, drink the whole river's worth of the stuff. One final time.

It brims me, and rushes out of me, before filling me again. My heart beats in flutters as I go with the tide. I count the beats, I count everything. It would drive Kate mad, that counting, and she'd tease me for it. Ten times my heart pounds, before stopping. She fills me again, twice, and then another ten beats.

"Lorry?"

It isn't Kate. How could it be? She's dead, her heart scrambled in her chest, her limp pointless body lying on a tacky pub floor.

That image makes me sick, literally, as all of the bile inside me spews forth. I feel it leave my nose and mouth and come back down to land on my face.

Violently, I'm whipped over on my side, and it all pours out of me, clearing the way for air to enter. It's only as that happens that I notice the tingling recede from my lips.

I cough. I should really give up smoking.

"Tony?" I susurrate, as I'm rolled back on to my back.

His is the first name that I think of in the real world.

"Tony?" I rasp again, louder.

"Yes, Lorry, I'm here," he replies, and I feel the water dripping from him on to my face, and know that they were his breaths that filled me with the stuff and will to carry on.

49.

"Is New York your final destination, Mr. Francis?" asks a man who, if he isn't gay, should be.

"It is," I reply in my most serious voice.

"And did you pack your bag yourself, sir?"

"I most certainly did."

"And has anybody had access to your bag since you packed it?"

"Absolutely not. It hasn't left my sight."

"Well, that was easy, wasn't it! Will you require a wheelchair today, sir?"

"That would be very helpful, yes please!"

"I'll arrange that for you. It should be here by the time I've checked your travelling companions in."

"Thank you, most kind."

"Oooh, you're welcome! Right, who do we have next...Miss Hargreaves?"

*****

"Where are we?" I ask from my seat in the minivan, a plastic bag tucked under my hip for emergencies. So far, so good on the sickness front.

"We're ten minutes south of where we were ten minutes ago when you last asked," Tony mutters from the driver's seat which is where the passenger seat should be.

"Do you feel sick, Dad?" Lanie asks.

"No, I'm fine. I just wondered how much further, that's all."

"According to the Sat Nav, about twenty minutes," Janine Stephani tells me from the actual passenger seat.

"Or ten minutes less than the half an hour it was ten minutes ago," Tony feels the need to clarify.

"And when are we going pony trekking?" Lanie calls out generally, a wind-up tone in her voice.

"Tomorrow!" Tony and I tell her in unison.

Sophie stirs from her slumber next to me, which I'm pleased about because my arm was beginning to go numb. She sits upright, and I sense she's set to ask how much longer, but before she can I hear Tony ask softly, "everything okay?"

Janine replies almost in a whisper, "just got the test results through from the lab."

"Well, go on," he tells her.

"Perhaps we should wait till later…"

"No, come on, tell us all at once. It'll save me having to re-tell it."

"Are you sure?"

"Yes."

"Okay. Well, your mum was your biological mother, Tony."

"Good," is all he says.

"And your sister was your half sister."

"Same mother, different father?"

"That's how it works."

Nobody says anything for a while.

"Are you alright, Tony?"

"Yes, Lorry, I believe I am."

"It still makes you my Uncle Tony," Lanie adds kindly, before ruining it all by adding, "hey Dad, if you and Sophie have kids, can I get my order in now for a baby brother?"

"You don't want one of those," Sophie quips.

"Oh, for fu...," Tony starts, "imagine it, Lanie, a mini-version of him!"

"I might not want kids," Sophie suggests, before adding, "with him."

"At least he'd have someone to inherit all his bloody records," Lanie says. "I'm terrified he's going to leave them all to me. Hey, Sofe, if he marries you, will you become his next of kin?"

"Er, yes, I suppose I will, unless I sign a pre-nup, or he makes a will accordingly."

"Good. You can have all the records then!"

"Are they worth much, Lorry love?" she asks, hooking her arm through mine.

"Some of them are, as you'll find out in...how much longer, Tony?"

"For Christ's sake...sixteen bloody minutes, Lorry!"

"And when are we going pony trekking?" Lanie wants to know.

*****

Charlene Kendrick seems like a gentle lady, as she hands us each a glass of lemonade she made herself.

Her and I are sat on the lowest rung of the wooden steps leading from her front door. I have a feeling it's her only door.

A solicitor called a lawyer and also known as Ian Cooper met us at Ms. Kendrick's home. We're outside because we can't all fit inside the house that shifted slightly under my weight as I used her fresh smelling bathroom.

She offered to make us all something to eat, but we told a

little white lie, and said we'd already eaten on the journey. I know from the information I was given that she's in her late sixties, and I like her southern accent; the way she says 'y'all' and makes a 'hmm-mm' sound by way of acknowledgement of a thank you.

Charlene is the daughter of a man named Charles Kendrick, a blues picker back in the post-war years. He wrote a song titled 'Beneath The Covers', though prior to this day that was debatable.

"He always said it weren't about nothing dirty," Charlene tells me.

"It's about books, isn't it?" I reply.

"Hmm-mm. That's right, though he made it ambiguous in the lyric, you know?"

"I know."

"And you good people came all the way here from England just because of Papa Charlie? It's quite amazing, after all these years."

"He wasn't always blind, was he?"

"No, sir. He was born with good eyes, but a childhood illness left him blind, when he was...oh, let me think, now...he'd have been about fourteen, I guess, when that happened."

"Could he already play guitar?"

"No! He spent months in a bed getting well, and to relieve the boredom, someone gave him a beat-up old guitar. Well, Papa just took to it like a duck to water."

"Why did he write a song about books, when he couldn't read them?"

"Ah, well he loved to read. He was ej-cated - a very smart man was Papa Charlie. And he missed them words real bad when he lost his eyes on the world."

"Yes, I miss that."

"I'd read to him. Lord knows, that's how I learned to read."

"Well, I hope you can read this," I say, and hand her the acetate I've had for at least fifteen years.

I picked it up at a yard sale in Colorado, part of a small batch in a box that I think cost me considerably less to purchase than they did to have posted back to England.

Kate was there on business, and we took a walk round a quiet neighbourhood one Saturday morning and stumbled across the sale.

"Oh, my good lord," Charlene Kendrick gasps, and I can tell by the breaths that she's nearly in tears. "That's my Papa's mark on the label."

"There's a date there, as well."

"1959, five years before he died. But it don't say what tracks is on it..."

"Well, the important one is "Beneath The Covers'."

There's a silence whilst Charlene takes a few moments to weigh up what I'm telling her. Not because she's daft, but because of the import of the revelation.

'Beneath The Covers' became a huge hit in the early sixties. Scan a list of who covered it, and it reads like a who's-who of popular music. It crossed over, from its blues-R&B base, to pop and country, and stood the test of time. It's a classic.

"How?" is all she can manage to ask.

"It's a long story, but I picked it up on a visit to the States, and didn't think much more of it. I just figured it was another, albeit very good, cover version of the track. But, about three years ago, I was listening to the radio back in England late one night, and heard a tale about Papa Charlie and his insistence that he'd written the track. So, I had Tony here dig it out, and got in touch with Mister

Cooper, who authenticated and dated it."

"Yes'm, Papa always swore he wrote it, but the people at the record place in New York said there weren't no proof of the fact."

"Well, there is now. Hey, help me out, will you?"

"Anything, honey, you just ask. Papa would be so happy!"

"Can you read this for me, please?"

There's a faint click as she unfolds her glasses, and I catch the breeze off her arm as she slides them over her eyes.

"It say...well, it's a cheque..."

"Whose name's on it?"

"Er...that's my name there, I reckon..."

"And how much is it for, Charlene?"

"Well, that can't be right..."

"It's right."

"Well, mercy me, it says here 'three hundred and twelve thousand dollars'!"

"And change."

"Yep, and change."

I'm unsure who starts it, but a small round of applause breaks out.

Her voice is away from me, as she asks, "is this for real?"

"Yes, ma'am," Ian Cooper confirms, "with all future revenues to come, along with any more back royalties we can track down."

"I'm going to kiss you now," Charlene informs me, and I feel her moist lips on my cheek, as my arm enfolds her and she buries her face in my neck.

A loud pop breaks the moment, along with a chorus of whoops, and I hear the fizz of champagne being poured in to the robust glasses we had our homemade lemonade in.

"You should keep the rekkid," Charlene says to me, "after all, you bought it fair and square."

"No, I couldn't. It was your father's."

"Now don't you be disagreeing with me, after we was getting on so well! I want you to have it, and so would Papa. In fact, can you...Tony right? Can you help me with something, please?"

I hear Tony say he will, and feel the steps vibrate as he follows her up and in to the house.

"You did a good thing, Lorry," Sophie tells me, and Lanie and Janine reinforce the statement.

After a couple of minutes, they re-emerge and Tony places a heavy wooden case on my lap.

"You may as well have them, as well. I can't play them, and it ain't gospel, which is what I like! Them was all Papa's."

"Charlene, you don't have to do this. That acetate of your dad's is probably worth hundreds, maybe even a thousand dollars."

"Well, it ain't like I needs the money now, is it?"

"Tony?" I ask.

He knows what I want.

"Sunnyland Slim 'Highway 61', Howlin' Wolf 'Gettin' Old And Grey, 'Corn Liquor Blues' by Papa Charlie Jackson...was he your dad?" Tony asks.

"No, honey. But he was an acquaintance of his. They all were, back in the day."

"These are worth a lot of money, Charlene," I plead.

"Well, good. Because I already have a lot of money. Look, one of them tracks was called 'Gettin' Old And Grey', and the truth is, I am. And I don't got no kids or family, so it's better you have these," she says, tapping the box.

After a pause, she adds, "and you got a little girl there who don't look no more than about twenty or so, so I reckon these rekkids is in good hands for the future if I gives them to y'all."

"Thank you."

"No, thank you."

"What will you do with all that money, Charlene?"

"Oh, now, I ain't had no time to think about that! But I guess I'll give some to my church, and perhaps buy myself a little house with the cool air machine inside. And I always wanted to go on an air-o-plane!"

The shrieked words of an Irish tinker woman pass through me like a cold blade. Something about 'a blind father who couldn't keep an eye on her'.

'Not a father at all!' I think, as Tony Alliss breathes evenly in front of me, and continues calling out titles of records.

The End.